ACCLAIM FOR

Sacred Voyage is engaging from the start. I was held captive by the twists in the plot...waiting to see what happened next. A great read! —*Diane Spransy, Salt Lake City, Utah*

Sacred Voyage is a masterfully written tale of courage and self-discovery, played out in a land and time where danger and adventure lurks around every corner. I was hooked from page one and couldn't put it down. Definitely a story I will read again and again. —*Dave Dickson, Idaho Falls, Idaho*

What a ride! Just when you think you know where the story is headed something bumps you into another adventure. I can't wait for the next book! —*David Kirk, Temecula, California*

About the Author

Gregg R. Luke was raised in Santa Barbara, California where he spent a good deal of his childhood on the beach. It was there he cultivated a fascination and love for natural sciences and anything related to the ocean. He served a mission in Wisconsin where he developed a love for the simple truths found in the scriptures and a particular interest the stories of the Book of Mormon. He studied biological sciences at the University of California at Santa Barbara, then finished his education at the University of Utah College of Pharmacy. He now practices pharmacy in Logan, Utah. He loves reading, music, and nature. He and his wife Julie Perkins of Roosevelt, Utah have three children and live in Mendon, Utah.

SACRED VOYAGE

Gregg R. Luke

Distributed by Brigham Distributing
435-723-6611

Printed in the United States of America
Grayson Printing, Spanish Fork, Utah
10 9 8 7 6 5 4 3 2 1

Book design by Jeanette Andrews

ISBN: 1-56236-313-1

Sacred Voyage

To Kami —

Best wishes and God
speed thru life.

8-11-04

DEDICATION

I would like to thank all those who helped me with this novel, either by proofreading, offering grammatical suggestions, and/or simply by encouraging me to keep writing. I am especially grateful to the staff at Aspen Books and their faith in me, and to my wife Julie (whom I dedicate this book to) for her invaluable contributions and support. Most of all, I would like to thank my Father in Heaven for the Gospel of Jesus Christ, and it's eternal influence in my life.

*But great are the promises of the Lord unto them
who are upon the isles of the sea;
wherefore as it says isles,
there must needs be more than this,
and they are inhabited also by our brethren.*

*For behold, the Lord God has led away
from time to time from the house of Israel,
according to his will and pleasure.*

2 Nephi 10:21-22

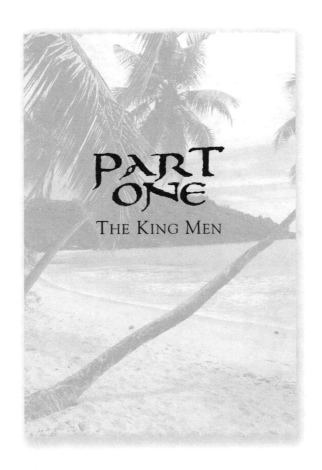

PART ONE

THE KING MEN

ONE

The King men were close behind and gaining on me. Instinctively, I felt that I shouldn't run to any of my usual retreats because they might know where those were, though I doubted they even knew who I was. Still, it was a chance I couldn't take; they seemed to know everything.

That's what the King Men were famous for; you couldn't hide anything from them. And now I was running from them. Running for my life.

I had gone to the city of Moroni to purchase materials for my family's business, a modest boatyard in Mulek on the shores of the Great Gulf, located some two and a half miles south of Moroni. Before reaching the lumberyard, however, I encountered a group of three men harassing an elderly man in a shadow-darkened alley. I knew it was none of my affair, but the thought of three strong rogues badgering a defenseless old man kindled an anger in me I could not ignore. I had no idea what I could do about it, if anything, but I knew it would haunt me for years if I did nothing.

As I started down the alley I heard one of the harassers accuse the old man of not finding a member of the King Men appropriately innocent. The old man, apparently a local judge of some standing, had recently ruled against them. I froze in my tracks when I heard that infamous title: King Men. Rumors concerning the King Men inundated the land. None of them were favorable. Many of the larger cities were thoroughly infested with their kind, and hardly a single conversation was engaged in without mentioning their insidiousness. But for me to actually witness one of

1

their crimes in a city only a few miles from my small village was beyond my worst nightmare. It meant that the King Men were growing in numbers and strength, spreading like a vile plague among my people.

The old man cried out in pain as he was pushed forcefully against the alley wall. Before I had time to consider how to help the old judge, one of the men drew a dagger from a hidden sheath and thrust it into the judge's chest. He fell silently to the ground in a rumpled heap. Even from a distance, I could see a dark stain growing around the haft of the dagger.

As I turned to run, one of the King Men looked up from the lifeless body toward me. That I had stumbled onto this cruel scene purely by accident was of no consequence. Accident or no, I knew the King Men would now seek to silence me the same way they had the old judge. I quickly fled into the narrow streets adjacent to the alley, knowing full well they would be right behind.

I headed back toward Mulek by way of the seashore, an area I knew better than anyone else, I was sure. My childhood had been spent on the shore helping my father, Hezikiah, construct boats and rafts.

I soon reached a loading dock warehouse located on the south end of Moroni's harbor, and hunkered down behind a stack of barrels. I could not see my pursuers, yet I sensed they were close. Carefully, I looked around the dock for any source of help. Other than the usual assortment of dock workers, there was no one I recognized. Asking one of these burly fellows for assistance was out of the question. More likely than not they were in league with the King Men, and even of they weren't, they were very aware that aiding anyone sought by them was tantamount to requesting their own death sentence.

I slipped into the warehouse and moved quickly toward a loading platform near the far end, careful to remain undetected along the way. There, the floor had an open trapdoor to the water below. I eased through the trap, making sure to close it behind me. Clinging to a framework of timber bracing the pillars that supported the dock, I listened to the footfalls on the planks above me. Only a minute or two passed before I heard the angry voices of my pursuers. Realizing I would be discovered the moment they opened the trapdoor, and knowing I could not go back inside the warehouse, I looked to my only route of escape—a fifteen-foot drop to the water below. The tide was low, but the sea was calm so the distance didn't worry me.

The voices of the King Men became clearer as they approached the trapdoor. I had to move quickly.

Hanging from the lowest timber, I dropped into the sea, holding my arms straight over my head to minimize any splashing. Staying a few feet under the surface, I swam toward the end of the dock, then slowly surfaced behind a pillar, keeping only my eyes and nose above the water. Thick flotillas of seaweed bloomed from the pillars of the dock. I quietly removed some and covered my head with it, then I slowly paddled away from the dock, hoping to appear as nothing more than a drifting patch of kelp. Cautiously glancing back, I saw my pursuers looking over the railings of the dock. In the afternoon sunlight I could tell that each man was a Nephite. My own people! I had always thought of our people as honorable and firm in their faith. It soured my stomach to realize these men, probably fellow churchgoers, were involved with the King Men. But as my father had often told me, honor is contingent on action, not words.

I could hear one of the men violently rummaging through the warehouse, turning over casks and bales, and knocking over stacks of cargo. Another man, a large, fierce-looking rogue, began questioning the longshoremen on the dock. I doubted anyone had seen me. At least, I was praying no one had.

Within a few minutes, I was far enough away from the dock that I couldn't hear what was being said. But one of the longshoremen pointed at the pillars under the dock and the King Men immediately lowered a boat from a winch. Moving with the currant, I pulled further away with strong, silent stokes, still being careful to not create a wake. The boat was pointing directly at me and I was sure they had seen me. Yet when the men got in, they began weaving in and out of the pillars, searching the bottom of the dock. I swam a few more yards down the shore before clambering onto the beach. Running swiftly, I headed south, toward Mulek.

Moments later I arrived at a familiar jut of land which extended some sixty feet into the sea. Many used this massive aggregate of lava rock as a favored fishing spot because it was easily accessible and always provided a good catch. However, with the tide being so low, few would be fishing right now.

I knew of a small cave—not much more than a hollow, really—on the south side of the rock which was exposed only at low tide. The entrance was well hidden by sea grass and kelp, but a keen observer could tell it was there; the lack of backwash and spray when a wave struck indicated the absence of solid rock, and when larger waves hit, a deep resonant murmur came from within the hollow. After wading into the waist-deep water, I entered the hollow and paused to let my eyes adjust to the darkness. As my breathing became less ragged I realized I could hear the sound of feet splashing through the surf, and the angry, bitter voices of my pursuers. I hastily moved backward into the hollow and pulled myself up onto a ledge that was just beyond the water's reach. A dozen crabs, frightened by my presence, skittered from the ledge into the water. The hollow was much smaller than I remembered, but I was now in my seventeenth year, and had grown significantly since my last visit.

Soon I heard the King Men through the porous rock directly above me. They were arguing amongst themselves. Someone then jumped into the water in front of the hollow. He was a tall man who had to bend low to peer inside. I couldn't tell who he was because of the sea grass, but his voice sounded familiar. I prayed that he wasn't one of the men I'd seen in the alley in Moroni. Had he seen me enter this hollow? The man dropped to a knee and began feeling around the kelp-covered entrance, but he did not enter. I pulled my knees tighter to my chest, making my large frame as small as possible. Rather suddenly, the man clambered to his feet, bringing in his grasp a surprisingly large crab.

"Nothing here but this," he said, tossing the shellfish to someone up above.

I then recognized the voice. He was Corianton, one of my father's friends and he was our city's chief law enforcement officer. Though an intimidating, powerfully built man, Corianton had a quiet manner that belied a perceptive ability to quickly absorb all pertinent information from his environment. He was honest and completely without guile—or so I had thought.

An ugly confusion clouded my mind. Corianton had not been one of the three men I saw poised over the dead judge, but he was definitely with them now. How could my father's friend be allied with those chasing me? It saddened me to think that he was a member of the King Men. Why was this seemingly forthright man involved with such an evil organization? I wondered if my father knew.

As Corianton began to climb out of the surf, he paused, and then brushed aside enough sea grass to stick his face into the hollow.

"Tide's coming. Don't get stuck," he whispered loudly.

Then he was gone. The bitter, angry voices receded until I was left with only the sound of the surf and my muddled thoughts. Why had Corianton not exposed me to the King Men? Had he known I was in the cave, or had he simply guessed?

He spoke to me, so he must have known.

I waited for what seemed an eternity. The tide was rising quickly and the enterance of the cave was all but sealed off. Still, I was afraid of what would happen if I were caught.

The stories of the atrocities commited by the King Men were not good bedtime tales. Our prophets and judges constantly warned us of their subtle ways, their dark oaths and secret cominations.

Subtlety was the reason for their success. The King Men rarely openly defied the government or the church. They committed their crimes with stealth and much forethought. They enlisted corrupt politicians who used flattering words like: "it's good for the people, both rich and poor," and "where is the evil if everyone benefits?" or "it can't be wrong if everyone is prospering." Few people understood they were actually a sinister malignancy, like some hideous cancer that slowly ate its way into every form of government and business. The true irony was that everyone *knew* the King Men were there, but until they became overtly troublesome, no one seemed to care enough to do anything about it. The apathy of the Nephite people was dumbfounding. Many a night my father had regaled us with the news of which business in Moroni had been taken over, or which judge in capital city of Bountiful had been bribed. He would storm about the house for hours wondering why no one wanted to take up arms and cleanse our people of their filth. He himself had complained to the authorities, and they in turn had relayed the information to higher individuals because they were too afraid to get involved.

The ambient light that had filtered through the sea grass when I first entered the cave was now nonexistent. The tide water had completely sealed the entrance to the hollow and was now up to my chest, but I still had a good pocket of air. I waited until the churning water was to my shoulders, then took a deep breath, and swam out. It was just beyond dusk and not a soul could be seen. The stars were proudly sharing their brightness, but the moon only timidly displayed its presence as a silver crescent in the eastern sky.

A warm breeze dried my clothes as I made my way home through dry creek beds and backstreets, taking care not to be seen. Our house was situated on a gentle rise about a half mile from the shore where our boatyard was located. Mulek was a clean, orderly city surrounded by dense tropical jungle, and veined with numerous ravines, gullies, and gentle streams. It was often joked that Mulek had more bridges than people. But the many water outlets created wonderful estuaries and natural bays that facilitated the shipping-oriented commerce of the city. Several docks and boatyards lined the shores, packed tightly together to better utilize the deeper ravines and lagoons. Our family built mostly small fishing boats and pleasure vessels. I had loved learning the structure and theory of ship design, but as I was still quite young when we began, there was rarely anything useful for me to do. So I would often spend my days combing the beach for anything that caught my eye—which was just about everything. I knew the names and habits of countless shoreline creatures and fish, and I could identify various types of driftwood—no matter how waterlogged they'd become— and even tell what part of the land they'd originated from. As I grew older and larger, my father taught me to read the sky and clouds and wind, and how mathematics related to the stars and navigation. More importantly, he taught me that while muscles and brawn are helpful, there is no substitute for wits and knowledge.

Recently, my father had joined forces with a man named Hagoth, an adventurous man who built vessels big enough to carry large loads of goods and people long distances. My father would not tell me the details of their collaboration, but the project they were working on was located many miles away our small city on the shores of the Western Sea. As he was often gone for long periods of time, the day-to-day work of our boat-yard fell to my older brother, Joshua, and myself. I enjoyed the work and the responsibility that accompanied it. Joshua, however, resented it. He saw the work as nothing more than a troublesome burden and a waste of his precious time.

As I approached our home, I saw my father arguing with two surly characters at our doorstep. I didn't catch the entire conversation, but I did make out that they were inquiring as to my whereabouts. They assured my father that if he didn't cooperate, there would undoubtedly be dire consequences. It was dark, but because these men were small in size, I was certain neither of them had been chasing me earlier. My father, being an unusually strong man, and trusting in me completely, promptly threw the two fellows off our property when they began questioning my character.

As the night was still fairly young, I took it upon myself to follow these two and see where they went. With only a sliver of moon in the sky, I had little trouble avoiding detection as I followed them. They traveled directly from our village to a run-down, seedy section of the city of Bountiful, a distance of about fifteen miles through densely-forested hills. There, they entered a moldering, rank-looking tavern. As I neared the entrance, a heavy hand gripped my shoulder, and spun me around. I looked into the face of a foul-smelling, evil-looking man. He flashed a nearly toothless grin and shook his head slowly.

"You'd best not go in there, boy. That's not a place you're likely to come out of in one piece," he hissed with malodorous breath. "Not if you don't know the signs."

I didn't know exactly what he was talking about, but I knew enough not to come right out and say so. Still, I needed to find out who these men were in league with.

"Really?" I said, firmly grasping his hand and tossing it from my shoulder. "And I suppose *you* know these signs?"

"That I do," he said warily. "But I'll not be telling a fresh-faced boy like you. Not without permission. You see . . . there's an order to the way things are done here." He lowered his voice and added, "A secret order."

I shrugged my shoulders. "Then how can I be sure that you know anything?"

He scowled and stepped closer. He was older and had obviously been a fighter in his earlier years, but I had long since outgrown my youthful stature and stared at him, eye to eye, without flinching.

"You being smart with me, boy?"

"Of course not," I said, not backing down. "I'd never instigate a contest of wits with an unarmed man."

He continued to glare at me but wasn't sure how to respond. I glanced over my shoulder and then continued, "I am young, that's true, but I have many lofty ambitions and many ideas on how to accomplish them." Lowering my voice to a whisper, I added, "What I don't have is influential backing."

The man grunted and flashed his ugly smile. "It's power you're seeking then?" He looked around again and lowered his voice even more. "We've power enough to take this whole land if we wanted."

I chuckled, but showed little amazement. "Oh really?" I asked sarcastically.

He frowned again. "The truth it is, to be sure," he swore. "We've persons—high up and powerful, mind you—in the government, and the army. And not just among the Nephites and Zoramites. Lamanites, too, and Amalekites. There isn't a people who can stand against us."

That was all I needed to hear, but I still had to be sure. "Listen, old man," I yawned. "The wind blows enough around here without you adding to it. Bore someone else with your housewife's stories. I don't believe there is such an organization with so much power."

He puffed up his chest and narrowed his gaze. "Then you've never heard the name 'King Men' before?" he hissed.

Now I was sure, and it chilled me to the core.

I turned away. "It is only a name," I said, and started down the street.

He flung some curses and obscenities in my direction, but I continued walking briskly away. I was sure he didn't know who I was, but I didn't want to give him time to find out either. I considered going to one of Bountiful's magistrates, but I couldn't be sure they weren't involved too. The one thing I was sure of, though, was that if they were after me, and knew who I was, then my family was also in danger.

I returned home quickly. It was well after midnight when I told my father about what I had seen that day. He thanked me, suggested that I don't go back to Moroni or Bountiful for a while, and said that he would talk to the local authorities first thing in the morning. He also cautioned that we all should be more careful, but that we couldn't let them bully us into cowardice, or into withholding the truth.

"Men like these don't give up easily, Gideon," he said sullenly. "They will be back. We can count on that."

As I changed and readied myself for bed, I wondered just what I may have gotten myself—and my family—involved in. I resolved to confine myself to our boatyard, and keep my eyes open for any trouble. A few minutes later, that foreshadowed trouble knocked on our door.

It was Corianton and one of the men who had murdered the judge.

Two

Corianton introduced his companion as Kumran, from Bountiful. He was a good-looking man, a bit taller than myself, and it was easy to imagine people being naturally drawn to his dark eyes and dazzling smile. But there was a false sophistication about him that I did not trust. He carried himself as one who had authority, but how he had gained that authority one could only guess. As I entered the room, Kumran scowled at me maliciously, then he grinned. He nodded slowly, as if saying that he knew what I knew. The scary part was, I think he did.

"It seems Gideon has gotten into some sort of trouble," Corianton said. He turned toward me and asked, "Young man, where were you from about late afternoon until nightfall today?"

I looked at my father who nodded his assent, so I answered. "I was running an errand to Mahonrai's Lumberyard on the north end of Moroni." My answer did not come out as assuredly—or calmly—as I had hoped it would.

Kumran chortled. "That's not all you did. I have two witnesses that say you killed a judge of the court near that same location, and that you ran when they confronted you."

"You're accusing my son of being a murderer?" my father demanded, glaring at Kumran. There was an anger in my father's eyes that I'm sure Kumran did not know how to read. If he had, he would have moved quickly toward the door. "If you were not in the company of my friend Corianton," my father continued, "I would throw you out for such an accusation. Just who are you anyway, and by what authority do you enter my house and insult my son?"

11

Corianton stepped between the two and held up his hands, pleading for a truce. "Now, now, gentlemen," he said, trying to hide a weariness in his voice. "Hezikiah, we did not come here to accuse Gideon of any crime, simply to gather facts that might involve him. A judge was murdered, that's a fact, but we are not placing any blame yet."

My father, never taking his eyes from Kumran, said in a measured voice, "Then you'd better have your friend choose his words more carefully."

Kumran was about to respond, but Corianton held up his hand again, cutting him off. Turning to me, Corianton asked, "Gideon, did anyone see you there? Anyone from the lumberyard or around town who could vouch for your whereabouts?"

"There are always lots of people I run into, but . . . no," I answered remorsefully, "because I never made it to the lumberyard. But I—"

"So no one at Mahonrai's could testify that you were there?" he interrupted.

My shoulders slumped. "No, sir."

"I see. Now . . . you left early this morning, I assume," Corianton continued. "So, exactly when did you get home?"

I again looked to my father, and again he nodded his assent. "Not until late this evening, sir. I got home only a few minutes ago."

"And where were you all that time?" Kumran asked smugly.

"That is none of your business," my father said matter-of-factly. "And now, Corianton, I must ask you and your friend to leave. Normally I would invite you to stay as long as you like" he turned to Kumran and continued, "but tonight you bring an ill spirit into my house that I do not like."

Kumran visibly stiffened at that remark, but said nothing in reply.

Corianton nodded and turned to leave then paused. "Hezikiah, I need to say this: A judge was murdered today a block away from the courthouse in Moroni, near the lumberyard." He sighed heavily. "And some witnesses did say they saw someone who resembled Gideon in the area, perhaps even at the scene of the crime."

My father was about to respond, but Corianton held up his hand, cutting him off.

"Knowing Gideon and yourself as I do," he hurried on, "I'll trust him to your care for now. I'm sorry, but there will probably be more questions tomorrow or the next day. All I ask is that Gideon does not leave Mulek without my knowing. Is that acceptable?"

My father nodded. "As you wish."

Corianton let himself out our door, but Kumran stood defiantly for a moment, scowling at me. When my father stepped up to him, he turned quickly and exited our home.

My father stood for a moment without a word. Then he turned and said, "Son, I know it's late, but let's go over everything you told me earlier one more time . . . and don't leave out any details."

I was surprised when the next day came and went without a single person, good or evil, coming to our house or to the boatyard to question me about what I saw. To keep my mind off of what I had experienced in Moroni, I worked extra hard, stripping the bark from a large trunk of balsa wood. I was making a raft and Balsa was one of the best woods for that project. We worked with many different woods, as the jungle provided an abundance of raw material to experiment with. Several of the hardwoods, such as teak, oak, elm, and ironwood proved to be solid and durable. But balsa, though a softer, more porous wood, was the best material for flat cargo vessels like barges and rafts because of its ability to support heavy loads for long periods of time. No matter how much water balsa absorbed, it consistently provided the greatest buoyancy of any material available.

By noon, I had worked myself into a sweat. I loved exercising my muscles, and found nothing better for clearing my mind than hard, intense work. The day proved beautiful; a light breeze brought the spicy scent of the gulf to shore, and large fluffy clouds offered brief moments of shade as they lazily drifted eastward.

Later that evening my father came by to tell me he had asked around, but found nothing in the way of conclusive information. Curiously, the only people who seemed to know I had been near the dead judge were Kumran and his allies. Everyone knew a local judge had been murdered, but the only fingers that were pointing in my direction were those of the

King Men. My father suggested we continue on with our usual activities and not bring the matter up again for a day or so; that we should wait and see "where the tide took us," as he was fond of saying. He reasoned that Corianton knew how we stood in the matter, and to involve anyone else could cause more harm than good. I asked about the possibility of Corianton being one of the King Men, to which my father simply shook his head and dismissed the idea with a wave of his hand.

Our evening meal was eaten with little conversation. Joshua had not been at the boatyard all day, nor was he home at suppertime. Sitting on our back porch, I tried to interest myself in a book, but found myself staring out at the blackened sea, my thoughts wandering aimlessly with no direction. Later, my mother, Tayani from Gid, said evening prayers with me. My older brother was still nowhere to be found. My mother thought he was probably out with some friends again. We finished our prayers and I went to my bed.

As I crawled onto my cot and pulled a blanket to my chin, I felt an ominous sensation of foreboding that manifest itself as a painful thumping in my chest. Something was about to happen, I was sure. My mother told me she felt the same way, but didn't know what to do about it. My father had gone to gather more information from his friends at the docks. He would not return home until quite late.

My dreams were plagued with haunting sounds and restless shadows. Evil men materialized from dark mists and threatened to carry out heinous plots against my family. As I ran from them, my body moved painfully slow, as if wading through a miasma of thick noxious vapor. I clawed my way forward, trying to flee from the imagined terror, but in my dream-induced paralysis, I wasn't moving at all.

Suddenly I was awake, breathing hard. I immediately sensed a presence. Someone was in my room, someone who didn't belong. Beads of cold sweat traced their way down the sides of my face as I tried to scan the room without moving my head. A wisp of a breath, more felt than heard, told me the intruder was beside me, standing directly above my head. As I tried to sit up, I heard a swooshing sound hiss above me, then felt a searing pain glancing across the top of my brow.

Everything went black.

I didn't even dream.

I don't know how long I was unconscious, but the first thing I could identify was the smell of smoke. It was a thick, acrid smoke; not the stuff from a cooking fire, but from a fire that wasn't supposed to be burning. Then cold water splashed across my face. Someone was shouting at me to get up. I felt myself being shaken and forced my eyes open. A black fog burned my eyes. I turned my head. My father was at my side dipping a rag into a bucket of water. He held it against my forehead. A dull pain throbbed in my skull and coursed down through my spine. When my father removed the moist cloth, the pain grew more intense. I tried to breath deeply to assuage the pain, but only succeeded in choking on the thick smoke.

"You've got to get up!" my father shouted at me. "Come on, Gideon, get up!"

I made an effort to sit up, but the pounding in my skull made me woozy and slowed my efforts. I grabbed the rag from my father and held it against the huge lump just above my hairline.

"The house is on fire, Gideon!" my father yelled. "You've got to get up."

Black smoke was quickly filling my room, roiling along the ceiling like ominous thunder clouds bloated with rain. I rolled onto my side and painfully sat up. Reaching for my father's hand, I eased to my feet. The room spun wildly as I staggered toward the door. Then I was on my knees and my father was tugging at my arm, yelling for me to stand. Something thick ran into my eyes and I could taste the coppery tang of blood on my lips. The noxious smoke was everywhere, clogging my lungs and disorienting my sense of direction. It seared my throat, and a rush of nausea gagged me. I had to pause, gasping for breath, while it passed. My father was ahead of me, beating some flames with a blanket. He was yelling at me to keep coming, so I staggered forward. Then I was outside inhaling huge gulps of fresh air. My head was exploding with every beat of my heart as more waves of nausea rose from my gut. I looked up and saw my father running back toward the house with a bucket of water. Then everything went black again.

⁂

A strong hand gently shook me awake. A coolness was applied to my swollen forehead, and washed my cheeks and chin. I opened my eyes but realized immediately that was a mistake. The glaring morning sky whitewashed everything with a painful brilliance, and I flinched, squinting at its harshness. My eyes slowly focused on my father. His skin was ashen and raw, and he had a vacant, haunted look in his eyes. His hands were burnt and most of his clothing scorched.

I sat up and wrapped my arms around him, holding him tight. It was all I could do to keep from sobbing. I looked toward the pile of cinders and blackened timber that was once our home. All we had worked for was lost. The pain in my head throbbed mercilessly, yet I hurt more for my father than for myself. I was young and had my own road ahead. My father had put heart, might, and soul into the scorched ruins before us. My older brother and my mother would be devastated.

Mother!

"Where are Mother and Joshua?" I asked hoarsely.

My father's gaze slowly turned from the smoldering house. Though he had been tending to my injuries, it was as if he only now noticed my presence. His eyes glazed over and a tear escaped down one cheek. His lips parted, but no sound came out. He looked back at what had once been our home.

I grabbed his shoulders and repeated my question.

"Gone," was his hollow reply.

"Gone where?" I asked with a panic-choked voice.

He didn't respond.

I staggered to my feet, holding out my arms to keep my balance. Surprisingly, I was able to remain steady and even walk without much discomfort. I made my way around the house, gawking at the destruction. I felt a deep sadness for my father and for the rest of my family. At the rear of the house I stopped short. Our stable hand, Samuel, lay face down on the ground. Two arrows protruded from his back and one from his leg. Samuel had been an immensely strong and likable man. It was hard to believe anyone would want to kill him.

Now he was dead. This was the work of an assassin. Whoever killed him did so from behind; probably without warning, without honor. It had all the markings of the King Men.

I checked the stables and found that all our livestock had been butchered. Nothing remained that was of any value. Some of my father's tools were still there, but many of his frames and braces had been destroyed.

I returned to him and held him in my arms. "Father, who did this? Was it the King Men? Was it Corianton?"

"Gone," he said again, softly. "It's all gone."

"Gone, yes, but not all is lost. We can rebuild these things," I said, gesturing toward the carnage and smoldering debris. "There are more important things. We are both alive and strong. Do you know who killed Samuel? Do you know where Mother and Joshua are?"

He looked at me again and his eyes cleared a bit.

I smiled and nodded. "Yes, Father, it's me, Gideon. You saved my life, and I love you. We are safe, but what of Mother and Joshua?"

He absently shook his head.

"We must find them," I said.

He let out a painful sob. "I don't know where they are. Your mother was not in the house when I got here, and Joshua . . . I just don't know." He rubbed his eyes forcefully and his body shuddered with a heavy sigh.

We moved to a pile of lumber that had not been burned and sat down. "I was at Hagoth's shipyard in Moroni when a powerful feeling came over me. The Spirit told me you and Mother were in trouble. I rode my horse as fast as I could and found the house on fire. A good portion of it was already gone. I ran inside and called out, but no one came." He paused as a sob choked his words. "I searched for your mother but could not find her. Then I went to your room and found you with your head gashed open. It was a miracle we got out, the flames and smoke were so thick."

He paused again, looking aimlessly about. "We have neighbors," he said. "Why didn't they come to help? Where was everyone when we needed them?" He buried his face in his hands as his body began to tremble. "I fear . . . I fear your mother may have . . . been trapped... inside."

My heart sank at the thought, but I refused to believe she had died helplessly in an arson's pyre. My mother was very much the epitome of a woman, elegant and tender in every way, but strong-willed, and not one to be ruled by flighty emotion. She had wits and a quick mind that would challenge anyone's intellect. She had been the one to encourage my brother and I to read and study and memorize; to learn from whoever was willing to teach, and to find a lesson in everything we experienced. If something had gone amiss—a lamp unchimneyed or a cook fire not doused—it was through no fault of hers.

I was sure she hadn't started the fire, and that she had done all she could to put it out. And she certainly would not have left me in the house if it had been on fire. She must have been outside before it started. Then I remembered the dark figure at my bedside, and a sickening thought came to my mind: Maybe she had been taken hostage—or worse.

And what of my brother? Where had he been during all of this? He was probably still out in the market place or off with friends. Joshua had scant interest in the building of boats or exploring new lands, and spent little time at home. He had an affinity for flash and sparkle, finery and gold, prestige and position. His idea of success was the accumulation of great material wealth with little or no effort involved. He was tall and strong, and had a handsome, chiseled face with deep-set, pale blue eyes. Making friends with anyone of his own sort was easy for him; he seemed to attract the wealthy and good-looking like a candle attracts moths, or like dung attracts flies, depending on your point of view.

Joshua helped only occasionally with the building of boats. He tried to keep himself buried in the financial end of things. That was fine with me. Even though I was as schooled in finances as he, I enjoyed the process and challenge of creating a fine sailing vessel from an ordinary pile of lumber. And while he passionately disliked sailing, I would jump at the chance to test-sail every new boat we made. I was the first captain many of our vessels had had, and quickly mastered the quirks and temperament of several types of water craft, as well as that of the sea itself.

But our peaceful little world had been turned upside down. Our house and stables were burnt to the ground, one of our workers had been killed, and my mother and brother were missing.

Suddenly a disturbing thought flashed in my mind. I grabbed my father's arm. "Come on, we must get to the boatyard. Whoever did this will not stop here!"

Together we ran to the shore where our boatyard was located. My head pounded fiercely all the way, but I tried not to slow my pace. Gratefully, our boatyard was secure and seemed unharmed. We looked around carefully for signs of sabotage, but found nothing. Father was shaking off his remorse and becoming visibly angry. He began storming about, muttering under his breath. I tried to calm him, saying we should think things through before coming to any conclusions.

We returned home and spent the most of the day salvaging what little we could from the ashes. A few neighbors stopped by to lend a hand but no one knew anything about the arsonist. It was near evening when we returned to the boatyard and met Joshua at the gate. He seemed curiously serene, as if nothing out of the ordinary had happened. I could not believe how nonchalant he acted toward the devastation of our home, until he spoke.

"They've taken mother." It was an announcement, a simple fact of no consequence. He looked at my gashed brow. "How's your head?"

Without warning, my father flew at him and pinned him against a pile of logs. "You knew of this?" he growled.

Joshua was taller than my father, but Father in a rage was enough to make even a giant cower, and my brother did just that, unable to utter a single word. "Where—is—your—mother?" My father spat out each word with explosive force.

Joshua swallowed hard and stammered, "Sh—she's in Bountiful. They've t—taken her—to prove a point." He swallowed again. "But they promised they wouldn't harm her. They swore it."

"Who?" Father asked angrily. "Who is 'they'?"

I stepped up. "It was the King Men, wasn't it?" It was a question in need of no answer. Joshua slowly nodded anyway.

My father turned to me. "Gather your weapons and meet me at the north pier."

"But father, my spear and knife were in the house," I explained.

"You have no need for weapons," Joshua said, regaining some composure. "All they want to do is talk. Mother will be all right."

My father grunted in disgust. "I've heard their words. They are evil men, the whole lot of them. They want their corrupt officers to rule over our people. They want a king instead of the judges appointed by the church. A corrupt king corrupts the people, and that always leads to destruction. They gain power through coercion and fear. They seek for authority and control where it is not earned, and I will have nothing to do with them."

"Authority and power are not things to be earned, they are things to be obtained," Joshua said with new-found conviction. "And the King Men are not all evil. They want to do good things for the people so that none will suffer or go without."

"Joshua, you can't believe that," I said. "It is an obvious lie, because it's an impossibility. They say they can provide for everyone, but by what means? They say they will not tax poor people, but they are doing so already—taxing both rich and poor—by demanding 'protection money.' How can you be so blinded by their flattery?"

"You know nothing of their ways!" he snapped at me. "If you would just talk with them, you would understand." He snorted in disgust, glaring at me and Father. "You are the ones who are blinded! Blinded by the false hopes of an empty religion."

My father's hand shot up. "Enough. We will go get your mother. Then we will counsel amongst ourselves and decide what to do."

"What is to decide?" Joshua persisted. "Can't you see what has already been done? Father, your house is burnt to the ground, and except for this insignificant boatyard, all you have is lost. Even your wife is held captive, and you still deny the power the King Men have? Are you so dense?"

The next thing I saw was my brother lying face down in the dirt, my father astride his back, breathing hard. "Are you so dense, my son? Your mother is in peril. Her life may already have been taken, and you opt to side with the very people who have done this?"

He shook his head, and his words became slow and measured. "If you choose the family of King Men over your own flesh and blood—" he paused to gain some composure, then said softly, "Then that is your choice. But do not expect a second chance. Decisions not pondered and prayed over are the type all men regret."

"Now," he said stepping back and offering his hand to my brother, "do we go get your mother as a family, or are you no longer my son?"

Joshua stood slowly and brushed the dirt from his clothes. A hate was burning in his eyes, a deep, intense loathing that began deep within his soul and seethed its way to clenched fists and cold, blue eyes. For a long while he glared at my father, saying nothing, his jaw muscles flexing as he bit down on poisoned words.

"Come on, Joshua," I said gently. "Let's get Mother, and then we'll discuss this. There is always time for talk. What do you say?"

He said nothing.

He turned and began walking up the road toward Bountiful. My father, also saying nothing, fell in step behind him. I walked in line behind them, nursing my wound and sorrowing over the emotional void that was widening between my father and my brother with every passing moment. I said a silent prayer that Mother was all right and that our family would not dissolve.

But I feared the worst, on both accounts.

ThREE

It was just before midnight by the time we reached Bountiful. Joshua said not a word as we marched into the city and through a labyrinth of dark alleys and backstreets. He lead the way, never stopping to consider our course or to ask anyone where our mother might be held. He knew exactly where to go.

My father and I followed close behind, but neither of us broke the deepening silence. As we made our way deeper into the city, the more concerned my father's expression became. We were now in a section of the city where great stone walls loomed on either side of us, and windows on either side had bars cemented in to prevent unwanted intruders. A cur dog saw us coming, barked once, then whimpered and backed into a dark recess under a gate. An ill wind stirred dead leaves around our feet as we continued deeper into gloomy, unlit passages, dank and smelly. Nervous and apprehensive, my Father was constantly looking to either side and behind us. I could guess why. I knew my father was a cautious man, never trusting anyone too much, yet trusting enough to have many friends. Did he think we were being led into a trap? By his own son? That my brother had accepted the ways of the King Men was obvious; but would he betray his own father? He knew exactly where our mother was held captive, as if he'd known even before she had been taken. What could have possessed Joshua to do such a thing? How long had he been involved?

A hollow feeling of betrayal filled my soul. A fist in the stomach or a stab in the back would have been more welcome to me than these bitter emotions. The very thought of what Joshua was involved in made me shiver as if I were wracked with the feverish tremors of malaria.

I caught a movement to my right and, glancing quickly, I saw a shadow duck behind a building. I looked toward my father, who simply nodded at me. He also knew we were being watched, perhaps even followed. He edged his way toward me and slipped his arm around mine.

"Be alert," he whispered. "If we're attacked, look to your own soul first. We're among the enemy now." He took a deep breath before continuing. "I know I've always said to avoid killing at any cost, that it's a grievous sin. But your mother's life is in danger, and by rescuing her, ours will be too. Kill if you must, but run if you can. There's no shame in having to hide if need be."

I was about to respond when I felt a weight drop into my pocket. Reaching in, I discovered my father's Nubian dagger. It was made of a surprisingly strong steel that held a razor sharp edge better than any steel I'd ever known. It also had a beautifully crafted, jewel-encrusted handle made of ivory. My father had obtained it long ago from a sea captain who claimed he couldn't remember where he had purchased it.

I continued walking as if nothing had transpired between us while my father moved next to Joshua. My nerves were on edge and every little noise or movement sent my senses skittering like a water droplet on a very hot skillet. The throbbing in my head was still present, but paled in comparison to the nervous anguish in my gut. Luckily, the gash on my forehead had stopped bleeding by the time we reached the city; however, I still wore a cloth bandanna to protect it from further injury.

A loud rustling of leaves fluttered behind us. I spun around, but saw no one. Whoever was following us was not very stealthy. It was almost as if they wanted to be heard, so as to scare or intimidate us. I heard my father ask Joshua to hurry along, and we broke into an easy jog.

At first I expected to return to the tavern I had discovered last time I was in this awful city. But soon we found ourselves on the opposite side of town, in what seemed to be a decent environment. No trash or filth littered the streets, no abandoned buildings loomed over us. It appeared to be a civil place where one might expect the most righteous denizens of the area to live. Yet the streets were curiously deserted, and there was a strange foreboding, a sinister feeling that lurked in every dark corner, in every shadow-shrouded doorway, down every vacant alley.

We finally came to a large warehouse in the north sector of the city, made our way down the side of the building through an exceptionally dark alley, and stopped in front of a small, unmarked door. Joshua made as if to knock but my father stayed his hand. An instant later, my father had pushed him into a shadowed corner and pinned him against a wall with his hand over my brother's mouth. I slipped next to them, melding into the same shadow.

"Listen, my son," he whispered forcefully. "You don't know who you're dealing with here. Do you think all will be nice and cordial once we're inside? That these men will simply hand your mother over?" He did not wait for a response. "You are a fool. For all you know, your mother is already dead. These men have been after my boatyard for months now. Did you know that? They want to use it to smuggle Lamanite weapons and other contraband into our lands. But I refuse to give in. These scum think nothing of killing governors, judges, innocent civilians," he paused, choked with emotion, "and even murdering the prophets of God. What makes you think they give a pig's ear about a simple boatwright and his wife?"

Joshua ripped my father's hand from his mouth. "They gave me their word Mother would be safe," he protested.

"*Their* word? You have never once given ear to the words of the prophets, which carry the promise of God." Father hung his head in discouragement. "Nor have you trusted the words of your own father. What makes their word so trustworthy?"

Joshua placed a hand gently on my father's shoulder, but father brushed it off without comment.

"Father, the King Men have power—real power. Not some promise of things to come. They say the church looks down on them because they don't want their followers to see the truth. You've been blinded, Father. The church always promises grand rewards if you 'endure to the end.' But when do we ever receive them? What monetary benefit have you ever obtained from the lofty promises of the prophets?" The ignorant sincerity of Joshua's winning smile turned my stomach. It reminded me of Kumran's malevolent grin.

He continued. "These people aren't bad, Father. Truly. They want everyone to have a good life, not just a few privileged aristocrats. And having a king is how it's done. Letting the government run everything takes the burden off our shoulders, and everyone benefits, no one will be poor, and we'll never have anything to worry about. It's the only way that can happen."

My father shook his head slowly as tears welled in his eyes. "Where did I go wrong that you should be so easily deceived? No one ever has anything just handed to them without there being some sort of payment involved. Hard work breeds success, not lofty dreams. It's as simple the concept as eating to survive. You will never have the slightest idea what kind of payment the King Men will exact from you, Joshua . . . until it is too late."

Joshua opened his mouth again, but my father held up a hand. "Enough. If you haven't learned by now, you never will. You wait here. Gideon and I will get your mother. Untill I signal, do not make a sound. I don't want them expecting our entrance."

Joshua slumped his shoulders and rolled his eyes. He considered my father so misled, so blinded, when in reality it was he who had blinders on. He was blinded by the lure of quick rewards, the heavy feel of gold in the pocket, and the shallow gratification of empty admiration and the flattery of fair-weather friends.

Father motioned for us to crouch down as he made his way around the back of the building. It wasn't long before three men approached the door from the entrance to the alley. Joshua and I remained in the shadows where they would not see us. I wasn't absolutely sure, but one of them looked like one of the heathens who had murdered the judge, and then had come after me. The third was a thin weasel of a man with a bald, sweaty head.

They paused and knocked in a pattern of two sets of rhythmic raps. The door opened and they slipped inside. The doorman stuck his head out and glanced around quickly. He was about to shut the door when something made him stop. He removed a sword from its scabbard and stepped out from the light. His head tilted slightly as he listened for the slightest sound. Then he sniffed the air. Several times he looked directly at us, but being deep in the darkness, we remained unseen. The guard eventually sheathed his sword and went back inside, closing the door behind him.

Time stood still as we waited for my father's signal. Joshua grew increasingly impatient with each passing second. I wasn't even sure what my father's signal would be, but I was sure I'd recognize it for what it was. It was difficult to keep from trembling from nervous anticipation.

Just then the door jerked opened and three men leaped into the street, their swords at the ready. They looked about hastily. One of them carried a torch. We were no longer safe where we crouched. I was sure we'd be spotted. But then the three moved away from us, running further down the alley instead of searching directly by the door. I sighed with relief. Then a hand grabbed my arm. I almost jumped out of my sandals. I didn't scream, but I did gasp loudly.

"Shh, Gideon, it's me," my father whispered from my side.

I smiled a weak I-knew-he-was-there-all-the-time smile, but my dilated eyes and quaking hands betrayed that my heart was lodged high in my throat.

My father placed his lips to my ear. "There are a few small windows in the back. Mother's in there, but she does not look so good. I saw about half a dozen men guarding her, so I know this won't be easy. Are you ready?"

I nodded, my mouth too dry to speak.

Joshua asked why the men had come out searching for us. Father explained that he had broken a window on the far side of the warehouse to lure them out. There was no door on that side, so they came out this way.

"Look, why don't you just let me go in?" Joshua asked.

"Becasue that's what they were expecting."

"But I told you all they want to do is talk." Joshua reasoned.

My father's voice tightened to a hiss. "Your Mother is bound and gagged. Is that the kind of talk you expected?"

Joshua's eyes widened in shock, but he gave no other answer.

"This could get messy," father whispered to us. "Especially if those three come back. Let's see where this tide takes us, but pray it's quick."

We both nodded.

My father stepped to the door and reached for the handle. I stopped him and explained the code of knocks, then I asked him to wait two minutes before knocking. I ran to the back of the warehouse. There was no sign of the search party, but I still moved like a breath of wind in the darkness, creeping silently toward the broken window. Peering cautiously over the edge, I saw Mother tied to a chair in the center of a large room, her mouth gagged with some cloth. Five men were sitting nearby, playing cards and talking softly with each other. Each carried a warrior's sword. No doubt they knew how to use them. I could not see the little bald man. Perhaps he was in an office somewhere. That meant there might be others. My father was right. This could get messy.

A few candles and oil lamps lit the large room, creating multiple shadows in which to move. I eased through the window and became part of a pile of crates. With the Nubian dagger in hand, I waited for my father's entrance. It came almost immediately.

The code of knocks sounded. One of the men groaned and heaved himself to his feet to unlock the door. The others seemed interested only in their card game. The guard pulled the door open and, seeing no one in the frame, leaned his head out. Suddenly he was yanked off his feet and disappeared through the door with only a brief, muffled grunt.

One of the card players looked up. "Who is it, Gisholm? Are they back?"

When there was no response, he went to the door, his sword drawn and at the ready. He jumped outside and was gone only a moment when Joshua stepped through the door and shut it. My father stood up from behind a rope-bound bale, and moved next to Joshua. My father then locked the door securely. How he had entered I don't know. In an instant, the three other guards were on their feet. Joshua held up his hand consolingly. "Please, gentelmen. We've come here to talk, remember?"

The men advanced with swords drawn.

"This is how King Men talk," one of them sneered.

Joshua began to argue but was cut off the man raised his sword at him.

My father threw a barrel at that man and barely managed to duck under the sword of a second man. He ran to the far side of the room—away from mother—while Joshua, obviously confused at this double-cross-dove behind a tall pile of boxes.

I worked my way around and up behind my mother. As I removed the gag and the bands on her wrists, I whispered for her to remain calm and quiet. I began working on the ropes around her feet. Then one of the men saw me and came running. My mother fell to one side a moment before the man brought his sword down with a yell. I was on the other side of the chair and had to roll away as the back of the chair splintered under his powerful blow. His sword stuck momentarily in the seat of the chair. In that instant, I lunged forward, my dagger following the man's arm up to his chest and finding purchase in his flesh. He dropped without a sound. My mother, her feet still bound, dragged herself into a dark corner. Another guard came down from a flight of stairs in time to see the dead guard's body slide off my dagger. He was closer to my mother than to me, but I distracted him with a brazen flourish of my dagger. He smiled a wicked, yellow-toothed grin, and advanced on me. My father had taught me self-defense and somewhat of sword fighting, but as the guard drew near, I began to wonder if maybe this wasn't a foolishly mismatched contest. This man was huge. What if his training had been better than mine? Could I successfully match my speed and agility to his size and strength?

I was about to find out.

The guard thrust and I parried just in time with my short blade. I could feel the strength of his arm, but by the surprised look in his eye, he felt an unexpected amount of strength from mine. As he brought his sword down with both hands, I stepped close and stopped his stroke with my forearms against his wrists. The shock to my frame made my knees buckle and I dropped to the ground. His sword dangled loose as his grip slackened, but he did not lose his weapon. Immediately I struck with my dagger, but hit only a wide leather belt he wore, and did no damage. He backed away and shook the numbness from his hands. The smile was gone from his face. As I jumped to my feet, he came at me again, this time with a little more caution, as I had expected. I intentionally made a sloppy swing with my dagger and he lunged for the opening he expected. Instantly I spun, twisting back, and knocked his blade with enough momentum to evade the razor-sharp point. The move was only partially successful as his weapon sliced part of my shirt, but I was too filled with adrenaline to tell if I was bleeding. I reversed direction and, with my left fist, landed a solid blow to the side of his face. The years of lifting heavy timbers in the boatyard paid off. His body shuddered and his arms slackened to his sides. I twisted on one foot and with the other drove my heel into his abdomen. Air burst from his lungs and he staggered back. I followed him with my dagger and sliced cleanly through his favored arm. His sword fell to the ground as he grabbed at the oozing wound. I switched the dagger to my left hand and with my right, rammed a heavy fist to his jaw. He collapsed to the floor without another sound.

I looked for my mother, but she was nowhere to be seen. I turned to my father. Four men had him backed up against a wall. The new men must have come from the stairway where the fellow I had just beaten had come from. My father was doing well to keep the others off with his sword fighting, but I could see he was tiring fast.

Then his eyes met mine. They were filled with dread.

I stepped forward as he jerked his head toward the door. "She's escaped with Joshua. Go help," he yelled.

I had not seen my mother or Joshua leave, but I trusted my father and moved in that direction. One of his tormentors turned to face me. My father feinted toward the others then thrust his sword through the back of the one facing me. As he did so, another guard stabbed my father's exposed thigh.

He let out a cry of pain, grasping his thigh with his free hand. "Go!" he yelled.

I stood frozen. I was torn between obeying my father's command to help my mother, and helping him. My legs refused to carry me from my father's plight. One man versus three is never good odds, even for someone as skilled as my father. I knew he could best just about anyone in a fair fight, but this was anything but fair. I had to help him. I could not leave.

My father yelled again, "Go, Gideon. Now!"

The look in my father's eyes said it all. I was the only one who could get my mother safely out of this city. He cared more for her than for his own life, and trusted me to help her. An image of my mother rushed to my mind—out in the dark streets, probably being hunted at this very moment by more of the King Men, with only my brother to protect her.

My brother! Was he protecting her or was he taking her to another secret lair filled with King Men? I could not be sure. Perhaps that was my father's true concern.

I looked toward him again. His back was still against the wall, his opponents still on the attack. None of the men dared turn their back on him. My father's eyes pled for me to go. I knew he was right. I could not waste any more time thinking about it. He had a sword and was skilled at its use; therefore, he had a chance. My mother was defenseless and in the hands of a traitorous son. She was probably not even aware of Joshua's affinity for the King Men.

I picked up a fallen sword and ran out of the building into the dark alley. It was desolate and foreboding. Then I heard a woman scream. I ran toward it, through one alley after another, hopelessly lost but determined to continue. I rounded a corner and stumbled over a body. Pausing, I rolled it into the light of a window. It was no one I knew, but a knife protruded from his chest—Joshua's knife. Could he really be helping my mother escape? Or was he simply running away himself?

I continued down the street toward a part of town more populated with night life. In the distance were the shouts and cries of chaotic revelry, while strangers, their faces mostly hidden, darted silently around me.

Racing into an open square, I lost my footing and slid headlong into a fountain. I pulled myself to the rim of the fountain, doused my face with the cool water, and began assessing my wounds. My knees and palms were bleeding, but I hadn't broken any bones or reinjured my head. As I gingerly fingered the gash along my forehead, an arrow careened off the fountain's stone decor, narrowly missing me. I looked up and saw a host of men running towards me, their drawn swords glinting in the torchlight. I ran blindly into the darkness, from one alley to the next, and somehow ended up beyond the outskirts of the city. My head was pounding and I could not concentrate. I wanted to make my way to the seashore, but I couldn't really be sure I was heading the right direction. My instincts were to flee Bountiful and head back to Mulek. But the thought of my father fighting for his life and my mother in the hands of a traitorous son prevented me from continuing with my escape. If I went back to my own city, I felt—no, I knew—I would never again see my parents alive. Yet I also knew that without some rest and a chance to gather my wits, I could very well put my own life in peril. The words of my father echoed in my head: Look to your own soul first. He was right. I realized that until I could get my bearings, I would be of no use to anyone. I needed to get some rest, and I figured any dark recess would do.

I dropped to one knee, bowed my head, and asked God to guide me through these perilous times. I prayed for the protection of my father and mother, for the wisdom to know which path to follow, and for the faith to follow it. As I finished my petition, a warmth burned in my heart and filled me with a reassuring comfort. I did not receive all of the answers I needed, but I knew my first task was to find a safe haven to rest my throbbing wounds and clouded mind.

Hopefully, the following day would take care of itself.

FOUR

Some nights sleep comes to a man without any effort; a complete, blissful rest which thoroughly enlivens the body, cleanses the mind, and refreshes the soul. This night was not one of those.

Dreams mercilessly plagued my slumber—horrid visions of swords, blood, fire, and death; visions of my home, my safe harbor of seventeen years, burning to the ground with no one offering to help us; tormenting images of my mother bound hand and foot, and of my father fighting desperately for his very life. It was as if all our friends had turned against us; as if the world we once thought as safe and forgiving had unleashed a vengeance fiercer than the ten plagues of Moses; as if the Lord himself had turned his back on us.

Curled up in the straw of a sheep stall, I forced my eyes shut and vainly attempted to clear my mind. Without a clear head and rested muscles, my efforts to save my father and mother would be fruitless. Yet my mind would not clear.

My thoughts drifted to the King Men as I tried to figure out why they had suddenly become such a specter in our lives. But not just our lives. They were an evil force creeping its way into every facet of Nephite life. Subtle, smooth, ever-pleasing, the secret order had convinced hundreds to join their pact. It was an unbreakable pact, a blood oath which no one dare sever. Disavowal came only by death, and that was rarely by choice.

But why us? Was my father correct in his assumption that they wanted to take over his business? Did they want to create a contraband inlet?

33

Perhaps it was the lack of total control of the waterfront. With my father still operating, there would always be competition and someone to keep prices at an acceptable level. My father believed in honest work for honest pay. His boats and rafts demanded a solid price. But his patrons never felt cheated, for our crafts rarely failed. Fishermen, merchants, and seafarers were always willing to trade their good money for a reliable vessel of quality workmanship. The King Men had not yet taken over our entire waterfront, but they recognized Mulek as an important center of sea commerce, especially when trading with distant peoples. Our lands had numerous waterways that emptied into the sea, but only a few of these were navigable inland for any great distance. Therefore, even large, thriving cities built directly adjacent to these aquatic highways could profit by sending their wares through a smaller port city. The harbor in Mulek was one of many. It certainly was not the largest, but it was very busy nevertheless. Was that what the King Men were interested in? Was that why they were striving to take over all harbors and warehouses, shipwrights and dry docks?

Again, my gut feeling told me I was on to something. I had little evidence to support my accusation, but it all made sense. Why else would they come after my family? The quality of our boats obviously made for difficult competition with those who had come under their management. It was common knowledge that the shipwrights governed by the King Men charged much higher prices, but delivered a poor quality boat. If the hull leaked or it had a crooked keel, if the sail tore in the first bracing wind or the wood was sawed green and began to warp, no offers for remuneration or repair were ever extended to the buyer. The King Men did not believe in fairness. So there was little anyone could do once they purchased one.

Whatever the reason, I first had to free my family. I was on my own here. Though I had traveled to Bountiful many times before, I knew no one intimately. Perhaps I could ask a member of the government or the church for help. It seemed a logical thought, but I wouldn't know where to begin. What I really needed was a friend, a confidant, someone I could trust, someone to give me just enough information to carry me to the next step in my quest. Such a friend would be difficult to find, and it would take time, precious time I could ill afford. I would simply have to trust the lives of my family to God's hands for a while. And I had to be cautious. By now the seedier part of the city would be alive with a thousand eyes, all looking for me.

Someone was coming. My ears picked up the footfalls of sandals on dry straw. Within moments, they were less than three yards away. My eyes wide, I scanned the area, but didn't move a muscle. *There.* An old man, perhaps in his eighties or older and most likely the owner of this manger, approached the stall and tossed in some vegetable greens. I was crouched in a dark corner, sure he could not see me in the graying light before dawn. A dozen sheep were scattered about, some sleeping, some seated, lazily chewing their cud. They did not seem to mind my presence, and having been motionless for better than four hours, they had all but forgotten I was there. One old ram ambled over to the old shepherd, who scratched its head affectionately.

"You have a visitor, don't you, Riplikish?" he asked, smiling at the ram.

I held my breath. How could he know I was here? The man slowly turned his head as if feeling the air, then made his way along the back fence to the stall near me. "Are you from around here, my son?" he asked without looking in my direction.

I didn't know whether to respond or not. Would he call for help the minute my presence was verified? One simply couldn't tell who was loyal to the King Men and who was not. This old man hardly seemed the type, but I couldn't take any chances. I was sure I could wrestle him down and escape if need be. But what if he was the one who could help me? I had to make a choice right away.

"It's all right," the shepherd continued. "The hour is early and not many are about at this time. You have nothing to fear from me."

Somehow, I believed him. I couldn't share with him too much information about myself, but I had to tell him something.

"I am Gideon," I said softly. "I'm not from around here. There are men in this city who wish me dead. I do not mean to trespass, but I needed a place to hide and rest."

The old man leaned his elbows on the fence rail, but still did not look toward me. "Bad men or good?"

"That depends on one's point of view," I said.

The old shepherd chuckled lightly. "You have a valid point, my son. If you have broken no laws then you are welcome to stay. The sheep don't seem to mind; therefore, neither do I. But I will not harbor a criminal. If you are guilty, I suggest you go now, and we'll be done with this interview."

I stood up to relieve the cramping in my legs, but stayed well within the shadows. "I am guilty of no crime set by our judges and prophets. Of the local authorities, I am not so sure. They seem to follow a different set of laws."

The old man rubbed the whiskers on his jaw. "And make their own up as occasion dictates," he said thoughtfully. "Am I right in guessing you do not agree with the latest developments among our—" he cleared his throat "—civic leaders?"

"I don't know what these developments are, but if they are contrary to the teachings of the prophets or the church, then I do not agree with them," I answered boldly.

The shepherd nodded thoughtfully. He turned around, leaning his back on the fence and folded his arms. "You must be hungry as well as tired."

I made no comment, but my stomach suddenly growled loudly as if responding on its own. He smiled and looked at the ground, nodding slightly. Then he continued, "On the west side of the house you'll find a retaining wall butting firmly against a stone escarpment. There is a tangle of vines hanging down from the soil above. Behind the vines is a small hatch, on the other side of which you'll find a natural limestone cave. It is not very big, but large enough for my wife and me, and a number of provisions. I have been preparing it for some time, and no one knows about it except for my household."

He tilted his head heavenward and sighed deeply. The dull sky was now overcast and threatened rain. "If you choose to leave now, my guess is you'll only have about one hour before sunup. If you would like to rest, you can stay in the cave until tomorrow night, then leave without notice. There is food within and you are welcome to your fill. But I cannot allow you to stay here in my stable, for if you are found, my life too will be in jeopardy. If I do not miss my mark, the men you run from are part of a secret combination which has all but taken over this city. I do not agree with their ways, but I am just one man and cannot do much to thwart their crimes."

I stepped out of the shadows and brushed the straw from my shoulders and arms. "Thank you, my friend," I said humbly. The old shepherd did not turn my way when I offered him my hand. I understood and nodded. "I will not betray your trust, but you must understand you are helping someone who cannot repay you."

"I know," he said softly. "My payment comes from knowing I have helped a believer in the church. One of our great prophets once said that to be in the service of a fellow being is only to be serving your God."

A feeling of warmth coursed through my body. I knew that phrase well from the times my mother would read to me from the scriptures. Both my parents felt a tremendous importance in learning things both academic and spiritual, and I knew the scriptures as I would a dear friend. "King Benjamin was a great man," I said in agreement.

The old shepherd smiled and nodded again. "I thought as much. You have the spirit of one who was raised by goodly parents."

I scoffed lightly. "I have a brother who would give you argument there."

"Freedom of choice is both a blessing and a curse," he said. "I too have sons who have chosen poorly, one of whom who has died because of that choice."

He lapsed into a silent reverie, and I knew it would not be polite to interrogate his thoughts. Instead, I commented, "A few hours of rest and nourishment would be most welcomed."

He pushed away from the fence and stood quietly for a moment. I felt reassured that the Lord was with me after all. Here at last was hope.

"I pray you will be blessed by the Shepherd of us all," I offered sincerely.

"I am," was his reply.

The old man still did not turn around, and again I understood why. The less he knew about me, the safer he was.

"I am," he repeated softly, a tight hoarseness lowering his voice.

The cave was very dark. I left the door ajar until my eyes adjusted, then began looking for a torch and flint. Finding these, I began to explore the old shepherd's hide-out. It was a small enclosure, measuring about twenty by thirty feet, with a ceiling of only five to six feet. Being just over six feet tall, I had to stoop to move about the cave. The old man had indeed been preparing for some time, as the walls were lined with food-stuffs, clothing, and other sundries. I helped myself to some dried beef, a hunk of unleavened bread and an orange. I ate only enough to stop the gnawing in my stomach, then doused my torch and knelt on the floor.

Prayer had always been an important part of my family, and I had grown up knowing that communication with my Father above was one sure way of feeling peace in my heart. I plead with God for the protection of my family, for my brother's eyes to be opened to the error of his path, and for wisdom, that I might help my family escape the dangers that beset us. Almost instantly, the Spirit of the Lord enveloped me with a warm, calming assurance. I still did not know how I was going to help my father and mother, or even where I was to start, but I knew something would work out. The Lord had not turned His back on me.

I finished my prayer, then stretched out on a blanket. Where sleep had forsaken me before, it now welcomed me with a soothing, peaceful cloak that calmed my harrowed soul and eased my weary body. I drifted quickly into a fitful slumber.

A streak of light crossed my face, waking me instantly. I knuckled the sleep from my eyes and squinted at the form in the hatchway. It was an old woman, the shepherd's wife I guessed, and she was motioning for me to follow. I crept hastily from the small cave and followed her into their house. Their home was a modest one, made mostly from stone and stuc-co. It was nestled in a vast grove of trees that flowed off the mountainside like a verdant drift of snow. The exterior was generously covered with gor-geous blossoms of wisteria and other flowering vines. In fact, from a dis-tance, if it weren't for the stable, you couldn't tell there was a house here at all. The interior was also very simple, only the barest necessities of furniture adorned the main room. A kitchen off to one side of the main room produced some magnificent smells, and I was immediately reminded of how hungry I was. The old shepherd was at the table near the center of the room, with a fierce-looking dog sitting by his side. The wolf-like animal growled, curling its lips and showing a fine set of sharp teeth, but the old man hushed it silent.

"Good morning," I said and extended my hand.

The dog growled again, glaring at me with cruel yellow eyes.

"Good morning," the old shepherd replied, but didn't take my hand. He remained as he was, staring straight ahead with a pleasant smile on his face. It was then that I realized he was blind. I quickly withdrew my hand and shoved it into the pocket of my tunic, embarrassed and ashamed by my insulting gesture.

He perceived my discomfort and said, "It is all right. I fool a great many people with my ease of manner. Sometimes even I forget I am blind."

I scratched my head. "But how did you know I was in your stable last night?"

"I do not let my eyes rule my other senses. Where my eyes fail me, my nose and ears more than compensate." He tousled the dog's mane. "And Kateph here makes a pretty good pair of eyes."

I smiled at the dog enjoying his master's touch. He looked back at me and growled again.

"My good wife has gathered some clothing for you, Gideon," the old shepherd said. "There is word about that a young man—looking like you, I would suppose, and wearing what you're wearing—is running from justice."

"I cannot take anymore from you, sir. It would not be right." I said humbly.

He snorted in derision. "Why? Because I am a blind man? Ridiculous. Would you have taken my offer of food and rest if you had known I was blind?"

"No. Probably not."

"And why?"

"Because . . . because you are the one in need," I tried to explain. "I should be the one offering my help to you."

He rubbed at his whiskers again, shaking his head. "I appreciate your kind words, my son, but I am not totally helpless . . . as you may have noticed. Mother and I do all right on our own, and I have many who come to help. Gideon, please don't deny me this. It does my heart good to be able to help you. Remember what I said last night about service?"

"Yes, sir."

"Keep those words close to your heart and you will never go wrong."

I promised him I would. "I don't even know your names, yet I feel as if we're familiar acquaintances."

"My name is Helorum; my wife is Aiya. And she would be offended if you did not first have some breakfast before you left us."

His name sounded familiar, but I could not place it. I sat down to a bowl of fruit and some biscuits with chunks of meat in them. I ate quickly, speaking little, as the old shepherd sat at the other end of the table, scratching his dog's head. I thanked him and his wife again, then went into a side room to slip from my old clothes into the new ones.

"If you need any additional help, Gideon, you will come back here immediately," Helorum said. "You must promise me that."

"I will," I said, again extending my hand to him before I remembered not to.

Helorum smiled. The dog growled.

I wrinkled my face and stuck my tongue out at the dog. Helorum smiled even wider, and I began to wonder if he truly was blind.

I bid them goodbye and cautiously made my way back into the city. I didn't know where I was headed, or what lay before me, but I felt assured that I would soon find out.

FIVE

I remembered my father telling me that sometimes the best place to hide is in plain sight. Since I had nowhere else to go, I decided to put his advice to the test. I arranged my new clothing so as to look my best and roamed the busy streets like an average citizen out for an evening stroll. Though I tried my utmost to appear casual and unconcerned, my eyes were constantly darting to and fro, on the lookout for any sign of trouble.

I decided to walk by the warehouse where I had last seen my parents. This might not have been the wisest place to go, but I had no idea where else to begin. When I got there, I almost didn't recognize the building.

The night before it had been a foreboding place of evil and ne'er-do-wells. In my mind it was a shadowy crypt reserved for nefarious creatures born without souls. I would not have been surprised to see it stained a crimson red with the blood of innocents and dabbled a purulent green with the slime of the underworld. Instead, what I saw was a clean, delightful structure with colorful flags and banners announcing a bazaar filled with an endless variety of wares for sale. There was a multitude of little stalls lining the street in front of the warehouse, selling all manner of clothing, apparel, baked goods, cutlery, jewelry and knickknacks. The area was thronged with evening shoppers: several small groups of young women chattering like an excited gaggle of youthful geese, bedraggled mothers trying to keep a leash on unruly children, young men in small groups trying to win the attention of the young women while at the same time appearing nonchalant, and men of varying importance haggling for the open-market trade. All were wandering about, their coin purses at the ready. I couldn't help but smile in amusement, then frown in confusion. There was not one sign of anything evil here. Had I come to the right place? I was certain I had.

I decided to meander among the patrons, pretending to be interested in the goods offered, while slowly working my way toward the warehouse. I paused at a jewelry booth and looked around.

There! I knew that man. He was the little bald man who had entered the warehouse last night. I didn't know where he had gone to during the fight, but he was here now and acting rather curious—intensely inquisitive and nervous. His bald pate was glistening with a profuse amount of sweat, even though it was late in the day and the afternoon heat had long since dissipated. His rodent-like eyes darted here and there as he moved down the street. Then he looked toward me. I quickly turned toward the jeweler's booth, praying he hadn't recognized me. Before me was a beautiful array of fine craftsmanship. One bracelet in particular caught my eye. The bracelet was made of an extremely lustrous metal that reflected an iridescent bluish-green in the sunlight. At the crown of the bracelet sat a large, translucent stone which appeared to glow with a hypnotic marbling of muted pastel colors—blues and pinks, yellows and greens.

"It's an opal," a soft, sweet voice announced.

I looked up into the most alluring green eyes I had ever seen. I was instantly swept into another world, mesmerized by an impish grin and playful dimples.

"Would you like to hold it?"

I blinked hard, believing that my eyes were deceiving me. But they weren't. The breathtaking young woman who stood before me was as real as I was—the same flesh, the same blood as anyone else on this planet— yet she had an other-worldly presence about her. Her poise, her charm, her hypnotic gaze had me totally tongue-tied. She had thick, lustrous mahogany-red hair cascading in gentle waves behind her ears and to her shoulders. Her face was that of an angel, perfectly oval, yet with a delicately defined jawline and prominent cheekbones. But those eyes. They were greener than any I had ever seen before. A limpid-green, not pale or dull, and yet nowhere near dark or severe. There was a depth to them that seemed to go on forever. They reminded me of the water in some of the lagoons I had seen on many coastal voyages. In fact, I could not remember seeing that color anywhere else, except in those shallow, tranquil pools. And I found myself drowning with pleasure in her eyes.

I smiled and opened my mouth to speak, but nothing came out. Not only could I not bring myself to speak, I simply could not think of anything to say. I numbly held out my hand and made a feeble grunting sound. She immediately gasped and covered her mouth with her hand.

"Oh, I am so sorry," she cried softly. "I didn't know you were a mute."

I shook my head, but still could not force words past my lips. I almost laughed, and smiled even broader, but she seemed to acknowledge that as my telling her she'd hit the nail on the head. The funny thing was, I *had* at that moment gone totally mute; her beauty had so totally dumbfounded me.

She smiled ever so graciously and picked up the bracelet, putting it into my hand. Then she pushed my hand gently toward my face, encouraging me to examine more closely the magnificent piece of jewelry. That only made things worse. The touch of her hand was intoxicating. Her skin was softer than anything I had ever felt, and the gentleness with which her fingers touched the back of my hand had me floating at least ten feet off the ground. I glanced at the bracelet, then to my feet to be sure there were still on the cobblestones, then back into her eyes.

"It's a little expensive," she said hesitantly, "but it certainly is one of the most beautiful pieces we carry."

She ducked her head a little and tucked an errant strand of hair behind an ear. She waited patiently for a response from me, but when I offered none she looked out from under delicately arched eyebrows.

"Are you buying a gift for a special someone . . . a lady friend perhaps?" she asked timidly. Then, more boldly, "I'm sure she'll love it."

I shook my head again, this time with a stupid grin plastered across my face that could well have announced that I had happily won the title of Village Idiot of the Month. I had always prided myself on being able to converse on just about any subject, with any person. But here, in the presence of this apparition of loveliness, I was at a total loss for words. And what was worse, I didn't care in the least that I was.

Her angelic voice sounded in my ears again, "If you'd like to see something less expensive, I could show you another lovely piece."

I nodded my head, handing back the expensive bracelet to accept another bauble of jewelry, or anything else she wanted to hand me. There weren't many pieces to choose from, but each seemed to be of excellent craftsmanship. She turned around to retrieve a simple malachite ring with a single, small blue stone embedded in it. It's beauty came from its simplicity and dark hues, as the steely-gray tint of the malachite perfectly accented the intensely deep blue stone.

"This one is very nice," she began, "and it will remind whoever wears it of your eyes—" She cut the last part of the sentence off quickly, embarrassed by her own audacity. I have never been what most people consider extremely good-looking. Not bad by any means, but I would never win more than a consolation prize in a looks contest. Joshua had the really good looks. No one had ever gave me a second glance, especially an attractive young woman like this. But my mother always claimed that my eyes were the most intensely blue she'd ever seen, so I guess that was my strong suit. And this gorgeous creature in front of me, talking to me, had just commented on them.

I looked to my feet again to see if they were still on the ground.

"I didn't mean to be so forward, but you do have the most honest blue eyes I've ever seen," she said with head ducked and cheeks coloring delightfully.

I bowed slightly, not knowing what else to do. I tried the ring on my index finger but it was too small, so I slid it onto my little finger. It was tight but seemed to go on all right. This elegant piece of jewelry, no doubt, was meant for a woman. I admired it for a while, letting the sun dance from the many facets cut in the stone.

"It's a sapphire," she said. "I know they're fairly common—that's why this one doesn't cost a lot—but the design of the ring and stone is what I find most appealing. I like things that are simple; there's a trustworthy, enduring beauty about them."

I nodded and slid the ring off. Her shoulders noticeably drooped as I handed the ring back, but when she reached for it, I took her hand and slid it onto her finger. She flinched in surprise but didn't remove it from her hand. I was about to say something when her gaze shifted from the ring to my eyes, and my tongue lost its mobility again.

"You're very perceptive. This ring is designed for . . . a woman," she stammered, trying to muster some composure.

I grinned and nodded.

"Are you from here? From Bountiful, I mean?"

I shook my head. My inability to speak embarrassed me, but only until I looked into those translucent green eyes again. She smiled a soft, honest smile that displayed her beautiful white teeth.

"Bountiful is a big city, as you may already know. If you don't have any friends here it's easy to get lost." She cast a quick glance up and down the street. "It's also easy to get swindled."

I frowned a bit and looked around quickly. I had forgotten I was in the midst of a busy market place, just another body in the maelstrom of humanity, and that danger was lurking nearby. The bald man was no longer next to the warehouse. In fact, I couldn't see where he was, and that worried me . . . until she spoke again.

Her head was ducked slightly as she timidly said, "If it's not too presumptuous, I would be happy to show you around town after I close up shop."

The Village Idiot grin spread instantly across my face. I opened my mouth and—

"You're wasting your time with this one," said a high-pitched, nasally voice from behind me. I turned to face its owner, the bald man from the warehouse. Up close, the man resembled a weasel even more than before. But the wiry, distasteful looks were not the only unpleasant aspect of the man. He exuded disdain, corruption, and evil. My feet returned to the ground with a thud. The man sneered at the young woman and then he turned me around by my arm while running his eyes over my apparel, smirking with pleasure.

"Judging by your excellent clothing," the man went on, "you strike me as young man who seeks only the finest wares available." He spun me around again. "A man of impeccable tastes, I can tell. You seek only the most precious, to be sure. And no mistake, I know just where you can find such."

I really hadn't noticed the clothing Helorum and Aiya had given me, but after a quick inspection, I discovered they were very fine indeed. I was dressed like the son of a wealthy politician or even royalty. Where had a lowly, blind shepherd acquired such finery? The bald man took my arm and began to lead me away from the jeweler's booth. Did he know who I was, and was only being obsequious as a ruse? I turned back to the girl who, with shoulders sagging and a forlorn pout on her face, was removing the ring from her finger and putting it back on the display table. She never once looked up at me.

As the bald man led me toward the warehouse, my mind was racing. If he did recognize me, I had to do something before it was too late. When we reached the door, I shook my arm from his grip and found my tongue at last.

"I liked what I saw back there," I said, trying to sound annoyed.

The man gave a sly glimpse over his shoulder. "Oh really? Was it the cheap trinkets or the cheap girl?"

The way he said 'cheap girl' angered me, and I felt my muscles tighten with rage. I knew precisely what he envisioned when he looked at her, and I wanted to beat him until he apologized for the indignity he heaped upon her with every glance from his little beady eyes.

"I don't even know who she is," I managed say without emotion.

He glanced her way again and huffed. "Just some no-account daughter selling the goods her father produces."

"And where is her father?" I asked.

He shrugged his narrow shoulders. "Old Ashod? He's probably still sleeping in his house, or he's down at the tavern drowning his miseries."

The weasel reached for the door, but I grabbed his hand. He tried to pull away, but my grip and arm strength was sufficiently more than he could overpower.

"What sorrow could a man have with a daughter like her?"

A sinister grin crept across the man's face, and it surprised me that I didn't see a row of pointy yellow teeth in that smile. "His wife died some time ago. Now he does very little work because of his sorrow. The girl does what she can to help, but he's rarely seen."

I looked toward the booth, but the young woman had disappeared into the tent behind the stall. "How did the mother die?" I asked, barely above a whisper.

The evil grin widened slightly. "It was ruled an accident."

Instantly I was furious. I knew just what this vile little animal was saying, but I had to hear it for myself. Undoubtedly it had something to do with the King Men and their coffers of protection money. They loved to prey on innocent, helpless families. No doubt this man Ashod had refused to pay— or simply couldn't pay—and the King Men had resorted to coercive means to get their way. My grip tightened on his puny arm, causing him to grimace.

"What accident?" I hissed.

"She fell off a balcony from some building downtown," he whined.

"Fell?"

"That's what the authorities ruled, yes. Now the father wastes his time away doing nothing." He scoffed arrogantly, "He's just another bum scraping by on his daughter's efforts. In my opinion, he never had any true wealth to begin with."

I put my face right next to his and growled, "And in my opinion, you're no better than the vermin that eat the crumbs from the table of a man like that."

He jerked his arm free and growled right back. "You'd better watch your tongue, my young friend, or your family may suffer a similar fate."

"Your threats are useless, little man. You do not know my family, and we do not fear you or anyone else for that matter," I stated.

The ugly grin reappeared on his rat face. He noticed the wound at my hairline and an eerie recognition filled his eyes. Did he know?

"Fear comes in many forms," he sneered. "Does the name Kishkumen mean anything to you?"

"No." It was a lie.

The name Kishkumen was one I was all too familiar with. Kishkumen was a man who had started low in the political ranks of judges. He was a large, handsome man with great oratory skills and the ability to make anything sound right and good. He had become very popular among the people and had gained much influence in the city of Bountiful. Rumor had it that he sought the chief judgment seat of Pahoran, but because he was not aligned with the church, he would never be appointed to such an important office. Instead, he had begun a secret order with his friend Gadianton, through which they had slowly gained power through coercion, threats, and violence. Many of the King Men had allied themselves with them, and it was difficult to tell one faction from the other. But nothing could be done to halt their growth. So secret were their combinations and so intimidating was their presence that no righteous branch of government was able to thwart their evil designs. In fact, neither Gadianton nor Kishkumen had ever been proven guilty of countless crimes, though everyone *knew* they were the guilty ones.

The scrawny man read the angst in my eyes, and grinned with satisfaction. I shrugged my shoulders and tried to smile back with nonchalance.

"It is only a name," I said, figuring that this man was willing to talk, and that he still didn't know who I was. "If you are as powerful as you say, why don't you just take over Ashod's business?"

He rolled his beady little eyes. "Do you think we need a measly little jewelry stand like his to survive? Don't be so naive. Ashod is well known in this sector of town. He made a . . . good example. That is all."

My anger was back, but I held it in. "So you destroy families just for show?"

"Not for show. For power."

I nodded slowly. His eyes twinkled when he saw that I understood his point of view. It excited him that I might be another potential member of his group of robbers and malcontents. I decided to play along with this tactic to see where it would take me.

"Power, influence, and authority . . . without ever having to earn it," I mused out loud.

"Precisely, my young friend." He practically oozed. He placed a hand on my shoulder and moved closer so as not to be overheard. "You impress me as a gentleman of means in this city. Perhaps from a family of some importance? Am I right?"

"We are known in some circles," I offered, "but it is mostly my father's affair. I am my own man, and get bored with his constant involvement with the church and civic doings."

Rat Face smiled as if he had just found a lost wallet bulging with money. "And you are not happy with a life of sacrificing everything for others, with nothing to show for gain on your part, correct? Tell me, my friend, is it power and influence of your own you seek?"

I looked back to the jewelry stall. She was back, trying to get passers-by to look at, and hopefully purchase, one of her father's creations.

"I'd like some influence with her," I sighed. That was not a lie.

"Ah, she is a wonder to gaze at, I agree." *Gaze at or lust after? You pig.*

"What is her name?" I asked.

"Ashod's daughter is called Elsha, I believe. But under that fawn's exterior she is a lioness with sharp teeth and claws. I would not get my desires too high with her. Many a worthy suitor has called on her, from many a wealthy family, with no success whatsoever."

"So, she is still . . . available?"

"Yes, as far as I know." I saw an ugly look come to his beady eyes. "If the right influence were used over her she might easily be yours," he thought out loud.

"The right influence?"

"Yes. She'd do anything to save her father . . . "

Again, my blood boiled at the thought of coercing her into any kind of relationship, especially the kind he was inferring. Why was I so smitten by her? It was more than her outward beauty. There was a righteous spirit in her eyes, and a gentleness in her demeanor. She truly cared when she assumed I was mute. I knew she was . . . '*good.*' That was the best way to describe what I felt. I simply *knew* she was good. And the way this gutter rat looked at her and talked about her filled me with a protective fury. She was my responsibility to watch over. She didn't even know my name and I had barely learned hers, but I was going to protect her, especially from filth like this vile, sweaty, little man.

My hand shot out to his throat and clenched it. "If you touch either of them again—Elsha or her father—I will personally seek you out and pluck your head from your scrawny little neck. Do you understand me?"

He croaked out a feeble yes.

"I don't want to see you near them ever again. I don't care who your powerful friends are. If Ashod's family suffers in any way, I'll come looking for you."

I pushed him against the warehouse door, releasing my grasp, but I stood my ground. He gasped for breath, scowling at me with scathing eyes. If it was possible to set someone on fire with just a stare, I would have been instantly turned to cinder. Instead, the little man turned abruptly and opened the door to the warehouse.

"Ashod is no longer of use to us; he has nothing to fear," he hissed over his shoulder. "But you have."

He quickly entered and slammed the door without uttering another word.

My mind was whirling with what had just transpired. What had I done? Were Ashod and Elsha truly out of danger or had I just placed them back on the 'example' list? And what greater danger had I just placed my own family in?

SIX

I stared at Elsha for a long while. Her presence was a paradox of uncommon radiance, she being such a pure, resplendent lily in the middle of a quagmire of commoners. The irony was that many considered her the commoner. They obviously looked at her through different eyes than mine.

An occasional passerby would stop to examine a trinket or two, but no one purchased anything. I wanted more than anything to go back and start over with her, to show her—no, tell her—I could speak, and express my desire to get to know her better. But my emotions were frightfully confused. If I went back now, I could put her in greater danger with the weasel-eyed bald man. I had to assume he had numerous cronies about, watching either myself or Ashod's family, or both. Of course, I could also be assuming too much about her emotions toward me. She probably didn't even have an interest in me beyond the selling of merchandise. So why bother?

Why? I asked myself. *Because she has effortlessly captured your heart with nothing more than a glance and a smile and a few kind words.*

I have always thought love developed through lots of work, constant sincere input, and an altruism expressed by both parties over years of time. I'd never really felt like I've been in love before. I'd had many friendships in my youth with girls I cared about and felt affection for, but never love. Never the deep piercing desire to constantly be near the one your heart longs for. So I'd simply assumed love took a long while to mature. But I had only spent a moment of time with Elsha. I shook my head, trying to clear my love-struck thoughts. My first concern was to my parents. It had to be.

I circled the warehouse as if I was just strolling along without a care in the world. The window in back was still broken, the glass scattered randomly below the sill. Glass, while a common enough substance, was not always easily procured. Many of the grand buildings and churches in Zarahemla used glass in countless forms, with various colors and sizes, textures and hues implemented in the most imaginative ways. It was so common in larger cities that even modest shops and smaller homes had a window or two. Here in Bountiful, however, glass was reserved for store fronts, churches, or wealthy homes. Those who had money for such extravagances used it extensively. Apparently, the King Men fit that category.

As I wandered past the broken window, I glanced quickly inside, but because of the darkness inside and the brightness outside, I could not see in. I reviewed the previous night again in my mind. Had my father died and entered the Spirit World from in there? If not, where was he now? I felt he wasn't dead, but I also felt sure the answers to these questions could not be found on my own. Try as I might, my thoughts were jumbled in a unsolvable puzzle of facts and emotions. I needed help, and Helorum was the only friend I could think to turn to.

The old shepherd was sitting on the large hillock behind his home. The back of the hillock sloped gently to a creek bed choked with trees, while the front dropped steeply toward his house. The hill provided a view of the countryside all around, which was lush and green this time of year. The cave under this hill must have been formed when the earth underwent one of its many geologic changes. Caves and hollows of this sort were common throughout the mountainous landscape of this region. In fact, the terrain in general varied greatly between the western and eastern coasts of Bountiful.

Here on the east coast, the land was mildly undulant with few truly tall peaks, yet it had plenty of lofty hills and deep ravines. An inexhaustible supply of timber for building stretched from shore to shore, wooded with countless varieties of trees and lush tropical vegetation. The western coastline had incredibly high mountain peaks with eternal caps of snow, especially toward the south. Curiously, some of the tallest mountains were only a few miles from the western shoreline. Huge balsa, teak, and ironwood forests blanketed the landscape from the water's edge and up the mountainside to several thousand feet above sea level. Occasionally, uniform plateaus and valleys were found nestled between these mountains. They provided abundant pasture for grazing and farming. Because of the regular rains we received off the ocean, the mountainsides east and west of the continental divide were laced with rivers large and small, making their way inexorably toward the sea.

Helorum appeared to be staring off toward the mountainous western horizon as I approached quietly from behind him. I stood silently, taking a moment to enjoy the tranquil beauty of the setting sun. A warm, gentle breeze played with his gray ponytail and tickled the grass around him.

"Come sit down, Gideon," he said without turning around.

It didn't surprise me that he knew I was there. This man's power of discernment was beyond any I had ever known. It might have been my footfalls on the ground, or my body's unique scent drifting to his nostrils, or the sound of my legs brushing against my tunic that betrayed my presence. I shrugged. Perhaps it was simply a one-on-one communication with the Spirit that allowed him to be privy to everything around him. Whatever his source of information, I had a profound respect and trust for this man who had befriended me only a day ago.

I sat next to him and gazed out toward the horizon. Clearing my throat, I said, "I was trying to figure out what you were staring at, but then I remembered an important physical trait you seem to forget you lack."

He laughed openly and deeply. "I see more than you think, son of Hezikiah."

I flinched, and he laughed again. "Do not think because I am blind that I am simply a pitiful recluse condemned to sit in dark rooms, bemoaning my poor condition while having my meals spoon-fed to me." He reached out and felt for my knee, patting it firmly. "I enjoy a sunset as much as you do, my young friend."

The shock was still in my voice when I asked, "How did you know my father's name?"

"I have a few faithful servants who run errands for me and get me things I require from time to time. Information, among other things."

"Information on who is hiding from the authorities, for example," I said. It was not a question.

He nodded and stroked his bristly whiskers. "You come from a good family, Gideon. Your father is well respected and your mother is known as a compassionate woman of virtue."

"Thank you," I said. "Your words are kind, but I fear for my family. I do not know where they are. I've spent all day searching for clues about them, but have found nothing. My parents were in the hands of evil men the last time I saw them, and I fear—" My voice choked with emotion and I paused to quell the sob that rose in my throat. "I fear they may not be alive."

Helorum nodded thoughtfully. "I may have a way to help you there," he mused. "But you'll have to lay low for a few days. You'll just have to trust me."

I sighed heavily. "I don't mean to be impudent, but I may not have a few days."

He drew a slow, deep breath through his nostrils and held it a moment before exhaling through pursed lips. "I understand, and your concern is justified. But I feel we cannot rush matters; there is time yet to figure things out. Sometimes we must trust in the Lord's time."

I felt an overwhelming peace come over me as I listened to his words. I'm not sure how, but I knew he was right. My mother had taught Joshua and me about the burning of the Spirit; that when the Spirit of God communicates with you, it is often through a warm feeling deep in the soul, a burning in your heart. And this manifestation could come at any time. It didn't matter if you were praying. Anytime a truth was mentioned, a truth that had great importance to your happiness or well-being, you would feel this burning, this warmth. Curiously, my father had explained it another way. He had said he felt the burning only rarely, but that his answers came as a clear, perfect comprehension of things. He said it was a comforting 'peace' spoken directly to his heart, a calming feeling that everything was right and true. It simply made sense, and there was no doubt it was true.

I knew Helorum was indeed telling the truth. Maybe it was the *way* he said it more than *what* he said. But when he said that there was time, I simply knew there was.

"What should I do?" I asked.

He looked up at the sky with eyes that saw more than mine. "How much time is there before sunset?"

I watched the lowering sun slowly sink toward the hills in the distance, eventually to settle into the ocean on the far side of the mountains. "I would say at most, one hour," I guessed.

He nodded. "Very well. Have you tried praying yet?"

"Yes, of course," I said, "but I don't really think I'm getting any answers."

"Do you know what to look for as an answer?"

I told him all that I had learned from my parents on the subject. He confirmed the truthfulness of it and asked *how* I prayed.

"I ask Heavenly Father to help me help my family," I said earnestly. "Whether he listens to me or not is the real question."

He placed a hand on my knee and said, "Gideon, know this: Our Father hears all prayers, and answers them too. Whether or not we are in tune with the Spirit enough to hear those answers is the real question."

He was right. I'd always felt I had a good rapport with the Spirit, but then I'd never had to call on the Lord for something this important before. I wished I had the faith of Nephi, who asked the Lord where to find meat for his starving family, and the Lord showed him; who asked the Lord where to find ore to make tools to build a ship, and the Lord showed him; who asked the Lord to save his family from a perilous maelstrom, and the Lord did so. I was asking the Lord for help to save my family, but as of yet had not received a definitive answer. Was I asking for an inappropriate blessing? Was I asking with the wrong words? Or was it simply a lack of faith on my part?

As if discerning my thoughts, Helorum said, "Your faith is sufficient to receive an answer, Gideon. Your faith may not be strong enough to move a mountain, as the Brother of Jared moved Mount Zerin, but it is strong enough to converse with God."

"Then can you tell me what I must do to receive an answer?"

He nodded again. "Remember, answers are not always a direct response to a specific question. Perhaps it would be best if you were to ponder for a while."

"Ponder?"

"Yes. Do you not know what that means?"

"Sure I do. It means to meditate, to mull something over in your mind. But what do you want me to ponder on?"

He chuckled softly. "I thought you would ask. You see, you're concentrating too much on a specific, undeniable answer to the problems you're facing. That's not wrong in itself, but you need to free your mind and allow the Spirit to take over. That is what is known as 'being led by the Spirit'."

I nodded but said nothing as I mentally chewed on the concept.

He continued, "Tell me, Gideon, what is before you—right now, at this very moment?"

What is before me? Did he mean what were we looking at? I was looking at the setting sun. I didn't think he was able to look at anything. But I knew that was not what he wanted me to say. Then the thought occurred to me that perhaps he had never seen a sunset before. Did he want me to describe the details of everything within my sight, or a general picture of our surroundings?

I rubbed the back of my neck and said, "I'm sorry. I'm afraid I don't know what you mean."

He smiled patiently. "Just tell me what lies before you, as you know things right now."

"Well, the sun is just above the horizon. There are a few clouds in the sky and a few birds flying in the distance."

"I see. Is that all?"

"No. There is a low hill in the distance and a road cutting through the jungle, heading toward the mountains."

Helorum shook his head. "You are only looking with your eyes," he said.

Well, of course, I thought. But instead I asked, "How should I be looking?"

"I did not ask you what you saw, I asked what lies before you."

Now I was really confused. Here was perhaps the only friend I had in Bountiful and I certainly didn't want to offend him by telling him his questions were ridiculous. But I couldn't make any sense of what he was asking.

Again, he sensed my discomfort. "Gideon, I want you to know that I am blessed by my blindness. I used to see as well as you in a physical sense. But, like you, I trusted too much in my vision and not enough to my other senses, including the Spirit."

"Oh, I think I understand," I said cautiously. "There are sounds . . . some birds, the wind, someone chopping wood in the distance. There is also the smell of wet vegetation . . . of someone frying bananas . . . and . . . and the saltiness of the ocean."

He tilted his head to one side and asked, "What else?"

I strained to detect any other essence, any other informative clue manifesting itself around me, but sensed nothing.

"I guess I don't know what to say. What is it you're looking for?"

He sighed heavily. "Sit here for a while and sense everything, only sense it as you never have before. And then, ponder everything you feel, everything you sense. Open your mind and ask yourself why things are the way they are. Then you'll come to know what lies before you."

He struggled to his feet. I went to help him but he waved me away. This man had no need for eyes, he saw everything without them. I was thoroughly confused at what he wanted me to do, but he seemed to see that too.

He stretched and groaned fitfully, then rested his hands on his hips.

"Don't think so hard, Gideon. It hurts the brain."

"That, I understand," I said with a chuckle.

He began his trek down the hill, then paused. "I'll give you a hint," he said, turning around to face me. "Spiritual things are discerned with a spiritual mind. When I asked what lies before you, I did not necessarily mean a description of the physical world you can see. Remember, the scriptures teach us that all things were created spiritually before they were created physically. So . . . try to absorb things spiritually. Do you know how?"

I shook my head but didn't respond. It didn't matter.

"Just sit there and listen to the sun go down," he suggested. "Taste the flavor of the air. Feel the spinning of the earth. Smell the fragrance of the clouds on the eastern horizon. Ponder what you sense and why. Then come down and have some supper with us."

And I thought I was confused before!

The sun had long since set, but still I hadn't been able to do any of the things Helorum had asked of me. Feel the spinning of the earth? I had been in a few earthquakes before and felt as if I were spinning around, but to feel the earth spin through the heavens, was that possible? I had often smelled rain before it came, but I don't know if that was the same as smelling the fragrance of the clouds, whether to the east or west, north or south. Taste the flavor of the air? I could sometimes detect scents on the wind, but I don't think I could really taste anything. And how does one listen to the sun go down? Was I supposed to hear it sizzle and pop as it touched the tops of the trees on the rim of the horizon? Exactly what was I listening for?

I walked down the hill, my head pounding with confusion. This old shepherd knew so much about me. How? Why? I knew he was right about trusting in the Lord's time, but the more I sat around trying to perform his sensory magic tricks, the more my troubled mind reverted back to images of my father with a bloodied sword in his hand, fighting off three strong men, and my mother, bound helplessly hand and foot.

I had to help them—and soon.

Helorum was sitting outside with his dog. Not surprisingly, the animal growled when it heard me approach. When I came into the lamp light, it recognized me, and growled again.

"Hush now, Kateph. It is only our friend, Gideon." Helorum tousled the dog's coat and waited until I sat across from him. "Did you come to a spiritual understanding, my son?"

I sighed heavily, "I'm afraid I didn't. Perhaps I am not as spiritually minded as you hoped I was."

"Oh Gideon," the old shepherd said with a haunting reverence in his voice. "If you only knew. But then . . . you will. Soon enough. Trust in the Spirit."

"But Helorum, I tried. I was up on that hill for hours, and I still don't know what you're talking about. I think I'd have better luck conversing with your dog."

Kateph bore his teeth and growled at me again. Even the dog seemed to possess Helorum's powers of discernment.

The shepherd rubbed the dog's ears. "For hours, you say? I knew of a man named Enos who prayed all day and all night before he received an answer."

Was I supposed to be praying or pondering? I wanted to argue that point, but instead I asked, "Does it always take so long to get an answer?"

He leaned forward, placing his elbows on his knees, and rubbed his hands together. "Even I have a few prayers that have never been answered. I have a wayward son, not unlike your brother, whom I pray for day and night."

I saw an emotional pain cloud his sightless eyes. I felt sorry for the old man and his hardships. But there was a lesson he was trying to teach me, and I was only beginning to understand it. Almost instantly, Helorum's mood changed from melancholy to merriment.

"My good wife has prepared some food for you. Come, eat and get some rest. I have a feeling tomorrow will be a busy day for both of us."

"Both of us?"

"Yes," was all he said.

As we entered his house, Helorum led the way to a large room in the back, and we sat at a sturdy table made of beautifully marbled burl wood. The walls of this impressive chamber were lined with books, scrolls, and manuscripts. It was Helorum's own personal library, a veritable treasure-trove of literature. Why would a blind man have so much reading material? I wondered if he had read them, but didn't know how to ask without being offensive. Then it came to me.

59

"You've acquired quite a lot of reference material," I said, as Aiya placed a plate of fried meat, leeks, breadfruit pudding, and papaya slices in front of me. "How long have you been collecting them?"

"A long time. But these are only some of the writings I've gathered during my many years. Most I've purchased. Some are gifts. I've even written a few of them, too," he said, helping himself to a piece of papaya. "Before I was blinded, of course."

I wanted to ask how he lost his sight, but thought it improper to pry into such a personal issue. Instead, I asked, "What do they all contain?"

"Our history and the history of the old world. Holy words, mostly. I received a lot of them from Helaman, the son of the prophet Helaman. He's made several copies of the brass plates and other records, and gave me my own set. They're now being kept by Shiblon in Bountiful."

"I've heard the names, but never met any of them," I said, glancing over the impressive collection. "Are they all considered scripture?"

"No, not all. Some are texts on medicine, some on architecture and horticulture. I like to keep an open mind, you see. The glory of God is knowledge—intelligence, if you will—and not just about spiritual matters, either. Learning is the basis of civilization. The more a man knows, the closer to God he can become. It's when men think they know *more* than God that they begin to falter. That's why we have so much scripture; to remind us who we are and where we're going. Most of these volumes are transcripts of scriptures from our forefathers and prophets, and personal revelations I've received."

I swallowed hard on a lump of breadfruit not thoroughly mashed into the pudding. "Are you a prophet?" I asked softly, somewhat shocked.

He chuckled. "Heavens, no. I am merely a servant of God, like you. However, we are all entitled to our own revelations now and then. They are strictly for our own benefit, though, and are never for church instruction. That's the prophet's job."

Our own revelations. Maybe that was what Helorum was trying to get me to see on the hill. What lies before me . . . in my future.

The dog continued to glare at me with threatening, yellow eyes and with a ready snarl on his lips. A thought came to me, and I took a small piece of meat and nudged it toward him. The dog took it—without growling at me this time. Progress.

"You're learning how to make friends with your enemies. That is a revelation of your own right there," Helorum said lightly.

I laughed. "Surely your revelations are more significant than making friends of overprotective animals with a piece of meat."

He grew somber very quickly. "Oh yes," he breathed softly.

"Tell me then," I chuckled, trying to keep the mood light, "what are your most recent revelations about?"

He leaned forward, his palms flat on the table's surface. "You, mostly."

SEVEN

If I thought sleeping last night was difficult, this night was completely impossible. The cot in the cave offered comfortable enough bedding, and the night was reasonably cool, but my mind would not slow down. Horrible images and vexing questions denied me any peaceful slumber.

Helorum had not expounded on his revelations about me, though I had pelted him with questions. At one point I became so fervent with my interrogation that Kateph took it as a threat to his master, and growled with raised hackles and froth-speckled lips. This time I couldn't blame him. But Helorum held fast and said I wasn't ready for the information he had about me. I was somewhat affronted by this, assuming that I should be privy to anything that concerned my family or my future. But he replied again that I needed to trust in the Lord's time. Still, why would a man I had just met, someone I had never even heard of before and who had just met me, be having revelations about me?

The old shepherd said I should be more concerned about my family, and that the information regarding myself would come to me at a later date. He was right, of course. My parents and brother were desperately in need of my help, and I was anxious to get moving. Helorum said he had some connections with informed people in Bountiful and would inquire after my family. He had to do so cautiously because any overt curiosity would not only lead the King Men back to me, but also to his wife and home. That kind of attention, he said, he could do without.

I was to remain out of sight in case anyone did come snooping around. I wanted to wander around Bountiful again to see what I might stumble on to, but Helorum recommended against it. The less I was out stirring things up, the more information he'd be able to gather without creating too much attention.

So I went to bed, with no hope of getting any rest.

The next few days I spent with Helorum and Aiya were slow and difficult, yet enlightening. I busied myself with reading everything I could lay my hands on, then discussing what I read with Helorum. I have always had a quick mind, one that absorbs information like parched ground absorbs rain. I soon found that Helorum had the same thirst for knowledge, and was a man of infinite acumen. One discipline that intrigued me in particular was medicine. I learned many useful things I had not known before, like true healing was in no way magical or occult, and was often nothing more than common sense. I have known many healers in my days, but never conversed with them at length. Most were simply egotistical soothsayers able to perform awe-provoking wizardry and illusions. They were rarely men of science who could explain the origin and cure for our local ailments. Some went to great lengths to make a good show of their efforts in behalf of a sick person, even to the point of disemboweling hapless chickens or snakes and using the spent blood to paint elaborate designs on their own faces and torsos and those of their patients; or cutting themselves and their patients with sacred knives, allowing their magically powerful blood to mix with the toxic, demonized blood of the sick, while calling upon some unseen force in a disturbing, mutant language no one could understand except the healers themselves. It had always struck me as curious that the richer the client was, the greater the show—and the accompanying charge—necessary to cure the patient.

There were a few solitary individuals, however, who took the healing art seriously, and who practiced medicine with more scientific backing than flamboyance. One man in particular lived in Zeezorum, a city some 150 miles west of Bountiful, about 20 miles southwest of Zarahemla. His name was Jahrim, and he was known throughout the land as a Master Healer. Some said he had even learned how to perform surgery on the brain by creating a small, thumb-sized hole in the skull, performing the operation, and then fitting the bone back in place, as one would a cork in a bottle. The stories concerning him and how he became a healer were legend.

Somehow, Helorum had obtained a book written by Jahrim on herbs used for treating common ailments. It was from this book that I learned about using the ginger root to treat motion sickness. Many people I had met in the past were discouraged by the queasiness they'd experience every time they set foot on a boat or raft. I've always known it as 'sea sickness' or 'land-lover's disease,' but this healer referred to it as 'motion sickness.' He said that eating some ginger a few minutes before the sickness manifested itself often prevented it from ever occurring. He also mentioned a plant called Nightshade, which produced a substance that, when rubbed into the skin just behind the ear, would have a more powerful and longer lasting effect on motion sickness. However, too much of the substance could kill a man. As with all medications, proper manufacture and administration was essential. I had plenty of the ginger, but I had no idea where to obtain the other plant. Ever since receiving the blow to my head, I had been experiencing a spells of nausea. *Would taking ginger help?* I mentioned this to Aiya, and she straightway made me some delightfully tangy ginger tea. Within an hour my nausea was gone. *Amazing.* Medicine will always seem a miracle to me.

I found that as long as I kept my mind immersed in studying this and other manuscripts from the old shepherd's library, the time passed quickly. But the minute I tried relaxing or pondering, as Helorum suggested, my thoughts would once again race back to the plight of my family. After three days, my anxiety became overpowering, and I begged Helorum for advice.

"Why not go to Lehi?" the shepherd suggested.

Lehi was a smaller city right on the eastern coastline, just a mile or two north of Mulek. The city was more familiar to me than Bountiful, and I had more friends there. But Lehi shared a common border with the city of Moroni, where I had witnessed the murder of a judge. If information and gossip spread like it usually did, I was probably considered a dangerous fugitive there. I did not think it a safe idea.

"It will be all right," Helorum said. "The men who were chasing you were most likely from Bountiful, not Lehi, and probably not from Moroni either. And I doubt any of your friends were involved in the incident."

"How can you be sure of that?" I asked. "Corianton—he's a law officer in Moroni—he knows about the accusation against me. He came to my house with a man named Kumran the night it happened. He didn't arrest me, but said he'd be back to question me. He told me not to leave, but I did anyway to find my mother. They both think I killed that judge."

The old shepherd nodded thoughtfully, a strange sadness in his face. "I know about Kumran," he said heavily. Then, "I know Corianton, too. He is a good man. I doubt he would pass judgment without all the facts. He's a cousin to Hagoth, if I'm not mistaken."

"Really? My father works with Hagoth sometimes. They are both shipwrights. But I didn't know Corianton was related to Hagoth."

"Only distantly," he said absently, as if not even hearing his own words.

Helorum brushed his whiskers again, then turned his face heavenward. "What do we do?" he whispered, barely making a sound.

Almost instantly the sadness washed from his face and, as his lips parted slightly, a timid smile crinkled the skin around his sightless eyes. He was thinking of something—pondering for all I knew. I waited patiently for his thoughts to congeal into something he could share. I knew better than to disturb his reverie, but why had he become strangely cheerful? It was almost as if some kind of preternatural light were softly glowing from beneath his skin. The strangest thing was what I felt from him. There was a gentle but overwhelmingly powerful contentment emanating from his countenance. I watched him, transfixed.

Aiya brought in a thick, frothy drink made of coconut milk with whipped bananas and shredded coconut meat. I thanked her. It was delicious. She set a cup in front of her husband, but he acted as if no one else was in the room. I cast a glance at Aiya and shrugged my shoulders. She knelt beside me.

"He's talking with God," she whispered reverently. "You might want to read for a while. When he gets like this he could be lost to us for hours."

She winked at me and patted my shoulder while sliding a plate of small cakes toward me. "Help yourself to another snack." I felt like a little six-year-old boy the way she was fawning over me, but I didn't really mind. Her cooking was excellent.

I got up and perused the litany of manuscripts in the next room. Some were in languages I didn't recognize, but most were in Hebrew and Egyptian, or dialect of those tongues. My knowledge of languages was fairly extensive because of my work around the harbors and shipyards. The variety of souls who passed through our village brought with them languages, customs, and cultures that, while having similar roots with ours, displayed a fascinating tendency toward evolution. I had become familiar with the languages of the Amalikites, Mulekites, Ammorites, Zoramites, and Lamanites, in addition to my Nephite tongue. Most merchants recorded their transactions in languages that utilized concise, abbreviated characters, so as to lessen documentation and conserve writing material, Reformed Egyptian being the most common. I even knew a smattering of an ancient language known as Jaredite.

The Jaredites were great shipbuilders in their own right, having sailed from the old world to this promised land many years before Lehi and his family fled Jerusalem. Jared, the leader of his people, and his brother Mahonri, a prophet and a man of amazing faith, had constructed ships that were sealed from the elements both top and bottom, like a seed pod. It was the equivalent of two hulls placed deck to deck, so that one could not tell the top from the bottom. I had never seen one of their ships, but their construct was well known among the shipwrights who spoke of the bizarre design. No one ever berated the craft, because the design was said to have come directly from God. And the scriptures said they worked so well during the long voyage that not one soul, animal cargo included, was lost. My father, having seen a old parchment drawing that detailed the boat's construction, said it reminded him of a shark's egg sack, or a sea turtle without head and leg holes. Ships of today were traditionally much bulkier, not streamlined like the Jaredite barges. My father tried to incorporate the best design features from both traditions in his boats, which proved to create a very seaworthy craft.

Suddenly, I realized Helorum was staring at me, or at least looking in my direction. I shelved the scroll I was looking at and sat down next to him.

"You are to go to the city of Moroni to meet with Hagoth," he said without fanfare.

"You had another revelation about me?" I asked.

He nodded.

"What should I say to Hagoth when I get there?"

"He will tell you. Hagoth is a remarkable man; he is as inquisitive as a house cat. His curiosity is always driving him to explore and discover on his own, and yet he possesses a wonderfully obedient rapport with the Spirit of the Lord."

"I know what you mean. I've met Hagoth a few times and—"

Helorum was scribbling something on a piece of foolscap, apparently ignoring me. How a blind man could write baffled me, but I had come to expect the unexpected from this old shepherd. I sighed and picked up another small cake. I was about to bite into it when I glanced toward Kateph out of the corner of my eye. He had a pitiful look of one being neglected on his face, as he eyeballed the cake in my hand. I looked at the cake, then back to him as he licked his chops and shifted his forepaws in eager anticipation. I couldn't imagine a dog would like one of these cakes; they were a solid pastry made with a sweet, spongy batter, macadamia nuts, and slivers of orange rind for added zest. I broke the cake in half and edged a section toward him. The animal snatched it up almost before my fingers let go.

"Try not to spoil my dog," Helorum said while continuing to write. I guess he was paying attention after all.

"You were saying you know Hagoth quite well then?" the shepherd asked as he rolled the parchment and tied it closed with a bit of twine.

"No, not intimately well," I said. "I occasionally accompanied my father to Hagoth's shipyard in Moroni, but I'm left out of most of their dealings. I wouldn't say we're close friends, but I know he'll know who I am."

Helorum chuckled lightly. "He may very well know more about you than you think, young Gideon."

I opened my mouth to ask his meaning, but he raised a hand indicating the topic was closed. He handed me the scroll and said, "Take this to Hagoth for me, will you?"

I said I would and helped myself to another cake. Aiya was a *terrific* cook.

As I was leaving their home, Helorum put a gentle hand on my shoulder. "Gideon, I know there is so much you want to know about me, and what it is that I know about you, but you must understand that the time is not right for you to know all things."

"I don't like it, but I do understand," I assured him. "It's much the same as when Nephi of old said he'd seen many things from the Lord, but he was not allowed to write them because we were not ready for them, or that it was given to another to teach us those things."

Helorum's smile was one of pure joy, and I thought I could actually detect a twinkle of life in his blind eyes.

I continued, "I would like to know precisely what I'm supposed to do, how I'm going to help my family, what Hagoth has to do with everything, and especially what your revelations say about me. But if you say it will come in due time, then I'll try to be patient. My mother used to say, 'Sometimes you just have to make it through the day the best way you can, with no thought for the morrow, no matter what obstacles cross your path.'" I shrugged. "I've always figured that success in life is not necessarily determined by the destination we reach, but in how we handled the journey."

The old shepherd nodded. "Remember to ponder that journey too. For yours, Gideon, will be a great one. But you must hurry. I fear your time is short. Make sure you go straight to Hagoth without delay. You must promise me."

I promised.

To my surprise, tears sprang to his eyes as he took me by both shoulders. "Go with God, Gideon, my young friend."

I clasped his shoulders firmly. "Go with God."

Toward the edge of town I paused to look in the satchel Aiya had given me. It contained some more of her wonderful cakes, some dried meat, a couple of bananas, and the foolscap scroll Helorum had written on. I removed the scroll and turned it over in my fingers.

What was written on it? Was it about this great journey he said I'd be going on? Did it have anything to do with me finding my parents?

The scroll was held in place by a simple band of twine. I could easily remove the twine and read the inscription, then return it to its original form. No one would ever know it had been opened. But that wouldn't be right. The old shepherd had entrusted me to take it to Hagoth, and that was what I intended to do. My father had taught me that a man's true character was the one he exhibited when no one was around to see it. That was the foundation of honor, of trust. And those were characteristics for which I wanted to be remembered.

Yet the words on the scroll were important, vital, life-saving. I simply *knew* it. Helorum's parting words kept repeating in my mind: I fear your time is short, I fear your time is short. Only eight days ago he had said we had time to spare . . . hadn't he? Now there was an anxiety in his voice that scared me. Could it mean my father and mother were in even more peril than I had originally thought? I turned the scroll in my hands again, feeling a need, an urgency to read what was inside. My future—be it good or bad—was here in my hands and I was not allowed to see it . . . yet.

I sighed and stuffed the scroll back in the satchel. The sooner I got it to Hagoth, the sooner I'd find out. I knelt to lace my sandals, figuring that if I went at a steady trot I'd make it to the city of Moroni well before nightfall.

"Hello again," a sweet, pleasant voice spoke.

My heart skipped a beat as I looked up into Elsha's arresting green eyes. She was carrying a pouch of her own, probably filled with her father's beautiful creations. I tried desperately to think of ways to explain to her that I was not mute. But each one sounded dumber than the last because they all had to do with the fact I was completely smitten by her. I simply *could not* tell her that. Not now anyway. For all I knew she was just being kind to me out of pity. I resented the pity, but basked in the kindness.

"I was just on my way to our shop," she said happily, "when I saw you standing here. It occurred to me that I haven't introduced myself." She frowned slightly, looking at my traveling attire and satchel. "It looks like you're leaving."

I held my hands open and nodded.

"Oh. Will you be coming back?"

I was about to answer when a man appeared from nowhere, violently knocking Elsha down as he grabbed her pouch and fled. Acting instinctively, I dropped my satchel and was ran after the man. He was a good runner, but I was younger and much faster. I soon overtook him and, grasping him by the collar, I yanked him off his feet and slammed him down on the ground.

He had a bewildered look of confusion on his face because he had not heard me come up from behind and suddenly he was lying on his back in the dirt, with the wind knocked out of him.

I yanked Elsha's pouch from his hand. "You picked the wrong day to steal, my friend. And the wrong girl to steal from."

The man sat up and brushed the dust from his breeches. He cursed and glared at me with a surprising amount of malice for one sitting defenseless in the dirt. I was considerably larger than he, and I thought it obvious he would lose a physical contest against me, but he stood and squared up to me.

"You stupid little upstart," he spat. *Little?* "Just look at what you've done to my clothes! They're ruined. You'll pay for these, I swear it."

"I'll pay for nothing, no matter how much you swear," I said without emotion. "Be glad I don't drag you back to that young lady and make you apologize while licking the dirt from her feet. I have half a mind to haul you swearing all the way to a magistrate and tell him of your crime."

He laughed with evil mirth. "You have no power over me."

I stepped up next to him and glared down from a five-inch advantage. "Oh?"

"Ha! You don't scare me with your size," he said with a slight quiver in his voice. "I have every right to steal from that girl. She owes us money."

"Really? And who is 'us'?"

Evil oozed from his countenance like slime squished from moldering fruit. "Those who have power over everything here, including your magistrate friends."

I scoffed. "I don't care what power you may think you have, mister, but I don't know any government that condones stealing from good citizens. The scriptures clearly say, 'Thou shalt not steal.'"

He placed his fists on his hips and laughed arrogantly; a red glare of superiority burning in his eyes. It sent a shiver down my spine like the numbing fire from a shard of ice.

"So . . . you're a church-goer," he mocked. "Well your church is about to fall, you pious imbecile. So go and tell whomever you want about my supposed crime. It'll get you nowhere. And I'll still get my money in the end."

He turned and stormed away, brushing more dirt from his clothes and cursing spitefully. I watched him walk away for a minute, willing the anger in me to dissipate. Only once did he turn around to glare at me and cast some noxious curses my way. I smiled and waved, then went back to Elsha. To my surprise she was also glaring at me.

"Did I see you *talking* to that man?" she demanded.

No "*thank you for saving my father's livelihood.*" No "*thank you for your brave gallantry.*" No "*thank you for rescuing me from that evil man.*"

Just accusation and venom.

I gawked at her sudden change of demeanor before I remembered that, until a few moments ago, she still believed I was mute.

I hung my head slightly and said, "Yes."

She drew in a raspy breath of air through clenched teeth. Her beautiful limpid eyes no longer welcomed me to fall into them, but seared me with a sharp, icy-green glare, like that of a jungle cat or poisonous snake about to attack. Yet, no matter how mad she was, I still felt myself bewitched by her presence.

"I don't know what to say. I didn't mean to . . ."

"No! Don't even try to explain why you wanted to make me look like a complete fool," she snapped. She grabbed the pouch from my hand and thrust my satchel toward me. "Here. Thank you for helping. Good-bye."

She pushed past me and marched quickly toward town. I stood there, dumbfounded at her response. Suddenly I was the bad guy, when I had fully expected to come back a hero. *What had I done wrong?* I had never said I was a mute—now there's a play on words. I watched her disappear into the city.

It's downright painful when your heart longs to say you're sorry, yet your mind convinces you there's no need to say it. I hadn't intentionally tried to deceive her. In fact, I'd never even had a chance to do anything, good or bad, toward her. Why was she treating me like I had publicly humiliated her? It didn't make sense. If I had exposed some vile secret to hundreds at a church meeting—like she secretly dressed baby goats in doll's clothing, or that she drooled on her pillow at night and snored like a warthog—I'm sure I would have received less venom from her reproach than I had just now.

A breeze blew the satchel against my leg and I shook my head, wrenching myself from the conundrum of womankind. *Perhaps it was for the best.* I needed to get to Moroni to see Hagoth as soon as possible, and didn't have time to pursue Elsha for whatever reason. Whatever Helorum had received from the Lord, it was vital to my family. It could even mean life or death. It was my future, and I doubted very much it had anything to do with Elsha.

I hiked the satchel over my shoulder and began a slow trot toward my future.

eight

hen one thinks of a true sailor—someone unafraid of the mysteries of the deep, with an insatiable appetite for adventure, who is willing to risk his life to journey into parts unknown, and is never happy without the roll of a deck under his feet and the salty spray of the sea in his face—one usually congers up images of a broad-shouldered, handsome, powerful man who causes other men to cower in his presence, young men to envy his life, and women of all ages to swoon at the very thought of him.

Hagoth was not that man. Though a true sailor and adventurer in the most accurate definitions of the words, he was definitely not the rugged, burly, brute of a man you'd expect in a seasoned explorer. Instead, Hagoth was a lean, wiry, energetic man of medium height, who in every way exemplified the characteristics of a cat. It was easy to see why most of his friends referred to him as 'exceedingly curious.' He exuded a boyish love for life which seemed an extreme contrast with his chiseled, wind-tanned face and steely dark eyes, in which the pupils were all but lost in the obsidian blackness of the iris. He gathered his shoulder-length hair— thick, straight and raven-colored—into a neat tail with some reddish twine. Hagoth's attempt at a mustache, which came just short of what a fourteen year old might grow, only added to his boyish appearance. Though a man of infinite patience and few words, Hagoth's incessant movements and seemingly random concentration made one tire just watching him. And yet, I loved to watch him.

The man had a purpose about him, a desire to glean as much as possible from each and every day. He could converse on any number of subjects, though he rarely ran on with the verbal diarrhea that many would-be know-it-alls do. Hagoth's sentences were usually concise, to the point, and always accurate. To get involved in a debate with him was to lose an argument before it even began. The man was brilliant, but never condescending. That's probably why he had so many good friends.

Hagoth was calling out instructions to a group of workers aligning hull beams perpendicular to a braced keel as I approached him. He glanced my way and nodded curtly before continuing to orchestrate the movements of those before him. It was fascinating to see this master at work, yelling out instructions while holding a splinter of pine between clenched teeth. It was also somewhat comical to see his flailing arms beat the air as if he were conducting a run-away choral number while warding off a swarm of killer bees at the same time.

The ships of his construct were much larger than the ones my father and I built, and, though there were many similarities in the design, there were also noticeable differences. One major difference was that Hagoth's ships didn't utilize a very deep keel, only a thick, flat rib a few inches tall that ran the length of the vessel from bow to stern. His reasoning was that a sailing ship should be driven by the wind, and that a large keel dragging through the water slowed the ship and made it susceptible to the vagaries of ocean currents. My father reasoned that the power of the wind striking a sail created a force which traveled down the mast to the keel, which in turn caused a pressure against the swell of the water, and directed the movement of the vessel, thus producing a more maneuverable craft.

I reflected back on the many friendly arguments my father and Hagoth had had over this one subject. Neither man would say the other was totally wrong, but neither would waver an iota from their convictions. The interesting thing was, both arguments seemed to prove true in the design of their respective sailing vessels.

Hagoth stepped back a few feet to survey the line of the keel. It was perfectly true—not a bow or a yaw in any portion of it.

"Your keel is too shallow," I said authoritatively.

He snapped around with a mock fury in his steely eyes. He stepped up to me and looked me up and down.

"You've been spending too much time with Hezikiah in Mulek, young man," he said, chewing on the splinter of pine.

"Ever since I was born," I replied.

His eyes narrowed as he looked me over again more slowly. He grunted and nodded. "You have your father's strong jaw and brow, Gideon. I didn't recognize you—you look different somehow. And I don't think it's the new clothes."

I had forgotten about the fine apparel I received from Helorum and Aiya. It really did make me look quite the young socialite. I explained that they were a gift from Helorum in Bountiful.

"So that's were you've been hiding," he stated. It wasn't a question. "You know you're a wanted man, do you not?"

"I do. But I am innocent."

"I know. When I heard the accusation, and that it was the younger son of Hezikiah, I knew it was a lie."

I thanked him, then asked if he could spare a moment to talk about some things.

"You know where my office is. Go wait there and I'll be along shortly."

Hagoth's office was scattered with the trappings of genius. Charts, graphs, and drawings were randomly tacked to the walls, and small ship models, wood samples, and sail cloth remnants were strewn about in haphazard disarray. Yet each piece would have been out of place anywhere else in the room. All items were expressly intended for the design and construction of sailing craft. This was a thinking man's space, a space which perfectly described Hagoth.

One particular drawing caught my eye. My father's handwriting spotted it like so much graffiti. The design was a large version of what my father called a catamaran, a two-hulled vessel connected by a central platform. We had built several such pleasure craft, only on a smaller scale. They were inexpensive and fast little boats. But this one was huge, apparently intended to carry more than just passengers—large enough, in fact, to support a sizable cabin on the platform. It had the look of something unstable, bulky, and unseaworthy. But I knew it would be just the opposite. I trusted my father's engineering better than any other shipwright I knew. He obviously had something in mind for this craft, some task for which no other sailboat would work.

The two hulls were patterned after the Jaredite barges in that they were sealed top and bottom, much like a shark's egg sack, only these stood on the narrow edge, like a narrow pea pod resting on its seam. The hulls were essentially hollow with small hatches on top, which my father had labeled as storage areas. They were large, each about 100 feet long, six feet tall, and about three feet wide, and were tapered to an edge front and back. A person would not want to travel inside either of them, as in a traditional boat, because of the lack of comfortable space. Their main purpose was buoyancy. An unusual keel measuring only three feet wide and a few inches thick extended almost five feet down from each hull to keep the vessel from drifting sideways. The connecting platform spanned an area of about thirty feet by fifty feet. The cabin looked large; roomy enough for about twelve souls to sleep in, with ample storage for food and other provisions. A large central mast extended through the cabin into the air and down to another keel running the length of the cabin. A rudder at the back of the craft provided steerage and an adjustable cross member on the mast allowed for maximum wind capture.

I was enthralled by the proposed vessel, and imagined what it would be like to sail her, to test her against nature's elements and the whims of the sea. Why had my father had never mentioned this ship? Why was he using Hagoth's shipyard to develop it? Perhaps it had something to do with the project he and Hagoth were involved in on the west coast, near the city of Tonalai.

"It'll never make it past the reefs," Hagoth said from the doorway behind me. I hadn't heard him enter the room, and the sharpness of his voice startled me. "It's only good as a smooth-water vessel; won't be any good in the open sea."

I shrugged. "Reefs won't be a problem. The hollow hulls and shallowness of its draft will allow it to go over reefs that normal boats would founder on. And the twin hull design provides a smoother ride in rough seas, that's been proven time and again."

Hagoth's eyes narrowed as he stared at me intently. He crossed the room and concentrated on the drawing for a moment, running a finger over various parts as if to amplify his focus.

"The keels will drag; they're too deep."

I looked at my father's sketch again. "I think you may be right. There's got to be some way to raise the keel if necessary, for shallow water and reefs."

Hagoth said nothing for a while, lost in concentration. Then, "Can't be done. The center keel maybe, but the hulls will leak if they have a retractable keel."

He was right. I could think of no way to make an adjustable keel without compromising the water-tight integrity of the hull.

"Don't need three keels anyway," he went on, heading toward a desk across the room. "Don't *need* any if the hull design is good enough."

I chuckled. "I'm not getting into that argument. My father warned me about your thoughts on keels."

He nodded curtly and folded his arms. "All right, then. What can I do for you, Gideon?"

I removed the scroll from my satchel and handed it to him. "I'm supposed to give you this."

He read it standing. He then played with his sparse mustache while boring through me with those steely eyes. He read the scroll a second time, then sat down heavily.

"You read this?" he asked, indicating Helorum's writing.

"No, sir."

Hagoth ran his palms over his hair and blew air through pursed lips. "Where is Hezikiah right now?"

I explained the events of the past few days with as much detail as I could remember. He asked me to lift my headband to examine the scar on my forehead. It was still red and bruised, but the swelling had gone down.

79

He then began pacing around the small room with hands clasped behind his back. A deep concentration furrowed his brow and caused his eyes to dart to-and-fro in vacant exploration.

I cleared my throat, growing impatient as he pondered his next move. "Helorum said he'd do what he could to find out where my family is, but I don't know how I'm supposed to help. I feel so useless."

He stopped in mid-stride and fixed his eyes on mine. "You have a great responsibility, Gideon, a calling, if you will, the magnitude of which you may not realize for some time."

"What calling!" I snapped, not really asking a question. Now I was out of patience. "Please tell me exactly what this great responsibility is. I'm tired of being told I've got something important accomplish, and yet no one will tell me just what to do."

His eyes softened as he placed a hand on my shoulder. "I'm afraid it is something you need to find for yourself. Helorum can tell you, but then you would only be following orders, without understanding the importance of why you're doing it."

I closed my eyes, while rubbing my temples. "How can I understand the why when I don't even know the what, where, or when?"

A short burst of laughter escaped Hagoth's lips. "A valid question. Perhaps I should tell you first what your father and I have been working on the past year, and why. Then perhaps you'll understand."

I nodded and sat on any empty stool. "That's a start."

He pulled a chair out in front of me and sat staring at the floor while running his palms over his long hair. I could almost see gears working in his head as he struggled to find an appropriate beginning to his narrative. Several times he took a deep breath as if to start, then slowly exhaled through his nostrils. At last he sat back and folded his arms across his chest.

"Your father and I have been friends for a long time, since before you were born. We used to make rafts together and drift down the coast for days." He paused as a gleam of nostalgia passed over his face.

"The Intrepid Voyagers," I said, mentioning the nickname my father had told me about.

Hagoth smiled. "Intrepid Idiots would have been a better name. We were always getting lost, and in trouble with our parents. Many times we drifted into Lamanite territory and had to sneak back across the border."

"One time it almost started a war, if I'm not mistaken," I chuckled.

Hagoth's face fairly split in half with an even, toothy smile. "Yes, that it did." Then he sobered quickly as he tried again to share his thoughts.

"Those were better times, Gideon, and enlightening. Your father may not have told you this, but we actually had several encounters with Lamanites over the years. Guess what we found out?" he asked, a boyish eagerness in his voice.

I shrugged my shoulders, letting his random prattle empty his mind. I had never heard this many consecutive words from Hagoth in my life. I doubted if anyone had.

"Even though we were constantly at war with the Lamanites, we found that many of the Lamanite converts—and even some who were not converted—were good people. God-fearing and down-right neighborly. Better than many Nephites, in fact. But we still had to protect our lands from those who weren't so friendly, and there were plenty of them."

We were constantly hearing of Lamanite invasions and skirmishes. The border was never a safe place to be. That's why Pahoran, chief judge and governor of Zarahemla and the surrounding lands, set up governorships throughout the land. It was a good plan. Some used their power to benefit the Nephite people, but some used it to benefit their own greed. A man named Pachus was one of the latter. "Have you heard his name before?"

"Yes, but isn't he dead now?"

Hagoth nodded, a fiery glint shining from his eyes. "And good riddance, say I. He tried to take over the judgment seat in Zarahemla, and even drove Pahoran out for a time. But Captain Moroni and some of his men joined up with Pahoran and killed Pachus, right there in Judgment Hall. Oh, how I wish I could have been there. I'm not a violent man by nature, you know. But when he destroyed the sovereignty of the Freemen and their God-given rights, and tried to establish his own form of government . . . well, it still causes a temper to rise in me just thinking about it. Luckily, most of Pachus' men were taken captive and judged, and those who would not covenant to change were slain—which was just about all of them."

"What form of government did he try to establish?" I questioned.

Hagoth leaned forward and again seemed to stare through me with his eyes of obsidian. "A King's monarchy. Those who agreed with it were known as 'King Men'."

The history sounded familiar, but I was a little confused, and asked, "If they were all supposedly slain, then why are so many still around?"

"Because of secret combinations," he breathed ominously.

I took on Hagoth's hushed, apprehensive tone and whispered, "What secret combinations?"

"The blood oaths, the life pacts, the vows of allegiance to that evil family, actual covenants with Satan; all of these things are done to get gain among men, but it is a bond that once made, cannot be broken. Not all the King Men were wiped out. Those in Zarahemla were, but in Bountiful and other cities they still grow strong."

The conversations I'd had with the weasel-eyed bald man and the sentry at the tavern entrance suddenly came to mind. Hagoth was right.

"They have a new leader now," I said, thinking out loud.

Hagoth sat up, his focusing his attention on me.

I continued, "I think his name is Kishkumen. And there's another, too. A man named Gadianton, I believe."

Hagoth was on his feet, pacing the room again. His hands were clasped tightly behind his back so as not to damage anything by allowing his arms to flail recklessly with pent-up rage.

The more I thought about it, the easier every loose piece of the puzzle came together. Yet I was still confused about one thing: "This is all just politics. Other than the obvious, how does this affect my father and you?"

He shuffled to a stop and stared blankly at the floor.

"Because they need your father to join them. And . . . because I work for them," I heard him softly confess.

If I had not been sitting down, my legs would have surely buckled and dropped me to the ground. Hagoth—a loyal churchgoer, a successful and respected business man, a friend to prophets and judges—a member of the King Men? It couldn't be. It simply could not be, and yet he had just admitted as much. My jaw hung open as I stared at this humbled man. The awe, the confidence, the unshakable respect I had for him had just vanished. I tried to conceive any possible way to explain what he had just uttered, but I couldn't.

Then another thought exploded into my mind: If he worked so closely with my father, did that mean my father was involved, too? No. It couldn't be. I had seen my father throw these people from our property. Was it a ruse? No. Again, no. The King Men were the ones who had set fire to our house. They were the ones who had kidnapped my mother and were holding her hostage. They were the ones who had tried to kill me.

I looked to Hagoth, who now seemed a mere shell of a man. I pitied him, for I somehow knew he would not voluntarily be involved. He must have been coerced into joining them, somehow forced or threatened into a pact of some kind.

This time it was I who stood and put a comforting hand on his shoulder. "Are you a King Man?" I asked softly, with caring and without the least bit of condemnation.

He spun and glared at me. "Absolutely not!" he fairly screeched. "I said I only worked for them. There's no way come heaven or hell I would ever join them."

"Then . . .?"

He softened a bit and led me back to our chairs. He again ran his palms over his long hair and took a moment to organize his thoughts.

"As I said, this all began a long time ago. When I started building ships, I had no money, no capital, nothing with which to buy materials or anything—just a drive in my heart, an idea in my head, and a love of the unknown. I was offered a few small commissions, but nothing substantial until the King Men came along. Only they didn't call themselves that. At first I had no idea who I was working for, but as time went on I began to see signs and gather clues that caused me to question my relationship with them. Then Hezikiah, your father, took me aside one day and pointed out everything I had been overlooking for one reason or another. It was plain and simple. I was one of their cronies, their cohorts. I was on their payroll, and I couldn't think of any way to get out. Oh, they have asked me several times to take the oaths and pacts, trying to use their secret combinations to bind me to them, but I have refused. Because I produced such good work, they never pressed the issue. But it's getting worse, and the pressure is increasing, just as your father said it would."

"I understand," I assured him, "I truly do. But I still don't see how this involves some secret project my father is working on."

He smiled wanly. "Don't you? If I simply stop, they'll kill me and my family. The only way I can get out is to sail away. Just vanish, and never be heard from again."

I scratched my head. "But, won't they know what you're up to? They seem to know everything."

The smile grew. "Ah, but there's the trick . . . and the part you must keep secret. I'm doing this right under their noses, and with their money. They know I have a big project going on somewhere to the west. They may even have spies watching what I'm doing, but that's all right. I plan on sailing north with the coastal currents to the land beyond Desolation. It is a good land, a bounteous place with abundant resources, or so I'm told by those who have been there."

I shook my head as my brow knotted from a lack of understanding. He patted my knee.

"The King Men want a new source of gold, silver, bronze, timber, and what-have-you. I've told them about this wondrous place beyond the Land of Desolation, and that I'm building a large ship to go there. I've told them that I'm planning on taking a few men to help with gathering the plunder from the new land. But in reality, I'll take a bunch of people—those loyal to the church—and drop them off at an uncharted location way up north. There are many who want to escape the evil influences that are creeping into our lands, your father included, and my ship is the perfect way to do it."

"But why do it 250 miles away on the west coast?"

"Isolation mostly. It's not as populated there and will be easier to mask my true intentions. Remember, you can easily track someone on foot, but it's a lot more difficult in a ship, especially over unfamiliar waters. You'd need a good man who's familiar with the temperaments of the sea, and from what I've seen, the King Men don't have anyone like that. Your father is involved because he is one of the best sailors I know. Besides, I owe him for waking me up to the predicament I was in. That's why he's been included in this scheme from the onset."

"First you drop one group off . . . then you'll be coming back?" I asked, still not fully understanding.

"As I said, it is difficult to track someone at sea, but not impossible. The way to do it is to look for clues on land every few days. Unless your ship is large enough to carry unlimited stores, you have to come ashore every so often for water and food for yourselves and whatever livestock you're carrying."

"But why come back at all?" I pushed.

"I want to bring out as many people as possible before the King Men grow into something worse, and take over the entire nation. I believe they can, Gideon, and so does your father. So I'll come back and take another ship-load of believers away, but not to the same place as before. I'm not sure where, but it will be far away, perhaps far to the north where great whales are said to migrate. Or I will simply head due west and see where the wind takes me."

All this information was overwhelming. How could such a huge operation be kept secret, especially from those evil souls who seemed to know everything about everyone? Hagoth provided the answer.

"The beauty of the whole thing is that the King Men know what I'm doing and are helping me do it. I don't have to hide a thing from them as I prepare to sail off into the sunset. Only, they expect me to keep coming back."

I couldn't help but admire the audacity and sheer temerity of the plan. It was so simple, it had to work. The difficult part would be keeping all the other passengers silent about the escape before the ships were built. I shared this with Hagoth, who already had an answer for it.

"Your father came up with this part. They won't know how far we're going until the moment we set sail. They all understand we're going off to settle new lands, so the rest of our plan shouldn't really matter to them. Some groups are talking about leaving on an exodus up north by land, and I'm helping with those preparations, too. As you know, I've been involved with numerous explorations of the northern country and its terrain. Everyone is preparing for that, to travel north by some familiar land route. If I'm not mistaken, Corianton is planning on leading them. Hopefully, they'll make their escape before the King Men realize what is happening. In the meantime, I'll load hundreds of people into my ship and sail off."

"Why not ask them all to come in your ship?"

"Some want to travel by land because they are afraid of the deep. But we won't tell anyone how far we're going until after we cast off."

The weak spots in his plan kept coming to mind, but Hagoth always had an answer for my questions.

"Will that really work twice?" I asked.

"I think so, but only twice. Kishkumen and his men are not stupid. They might catch on the first time, but I think if I bring back gold and such from the first trip, I'll be able to do it once more."

"What if you don't find any gold?"

He laughed. "I will, and plenty. It's already hidden in the hull of the first ship in Tonalai. I'll come back a rich man, guaranteed."

I couldn't help but catch his enthusiasm and fervor for this adventure. But one question still plagued me.

"What if a few loyal King Men get on board and you don't know it until you're out to sea?"

He shrugged. "Chances are that they'll be greatly out numbered. If they don't change their loyalties, I guess we'll have to make our own judgments against them at that time. But I hope it won't come to that."

I looked at the drawing of my father's catamaran. "Are you using my father's design for this ship?"

He scoffed. "Of course not. Your father builds respectable pleasure craft, but nothing of the size we'll need for this venture."

"Then why was he working on this?" I said, tapping my father's drawing.

"Your father planned on following us, then continuing on somewhere beyond where we land. At least that's what I thought until you brought me this," he said, picking up Helorum's scroll. "I also thought we had a little more time, but now I see that's not the case."

Time was definitely an issue. My head hung as I considered that I still did not know where my family was, or even if they were still alive. I had to find them soon, because the way Hagoth was now talking, his first ship was going to leave any day.

"It is," he said when I questioned him. "In fact, probably within two weeks."

That didn't leave much time.

My eyes drifted to the old shepherd's scroll in Hagoth's hand. "Can you tell me what Helorum has to say about my family's part in all this?"

The familiar intensity return to his face in an instant. "Your father and mother . . . and your brother, if it's not too late, will be going with me . . . in my ship."

I looked up from under raised eyebrows. "And what about me?"

He cleared his throat, handing me the scroll. "Apparently, you won't be coming with us."

NINE

I accepted the scroll with shaky hands. I was equally excited and apprehensive. I wanted to read it, yet I was afraid to read it. Was this simply a feeling Helorum had had about me, or was it a prophecy I could not avoid? Was this truly my destiny, unchangeably etched in stone?

No, I told myself, *it couldn't be*. That wasn't the way life worked. At least that's what I had always been taught. If my life were completely decided for me from birth to death, with no option for change, then that would eliminate any chance for choice. It would negate agency. My future may well have a mission, but it was not pre-destined, without option. Predestination was a doctrine taught by some opponents to the church, but the concept never made much sense to me. If my life were already determined, then why live it? A person's calling in life was realized when he or she had enough faith and works to obtain it. Even the ancient Israelites had many prophecies concerning their personal callings in life—some were actual promises from God—but because they lacked the faith to follow the commandments that would produce the promised blessings, their rewards for fulfilling their missions were delayed, several times.

This scroll contained something about my future. Helorum himself claimed that he was not a prophet, and yet this revelation was about me. *Why would an old shepherd be receiving enlightenment about my future?*

"You'll be needing time to yourself," Hagoth said as he left the room. "I'll be outside if you need me."

When he closed the door, it felt as if all of the air in the room had been sucked out with him. It was difficult to breath and the foolscap scroll in my hand felt like it weighed 100 pounds. I immediately longed for the company of family or friend. Up until this point I had not been aware of how lonely I felt.

Sitting down, I unrolled the long sheaf of parchment. It was written in Nephite, so no translation was necessary. The scrawl was neat, much more so than I would have expected from a blind scribe, and was divided into two sections. The first was a collection of quotes from scripture and historical accounts from our forefathers; well, more like a random smattering of verses than a structured list of doctrine. I stopped reading after the first few verses, trying to figure out what these had to do with me. They all talked about the ancient Israelites, the people my people were descended from, and more specifically about the direct descendants of Nephi. The other nine tribes of Israel were mentioned, but none specifically by name. What was mentioned time and again was that a few of these descendants would someday inhabit the isles of the sea. The verses all sounded familiar, like passages I had read from the small plates of Nephi.

Helorum knew these verses well, because they seemed to be written almost word for word from the scriptures. In particular, he referenced the prophet Zenos. According to Zenos, the three days of darkness that would accompany the Savior's death were given as a sign not only to his crucifiers, but also to those who inhabited other lands, especially to "those who should inhabit the isles of the sea." I had heard that that sign would come to the Nephite people on this continent, but I had never considered it being shown to anyone else. It made sense that those other people would want to know when that great and terrible event took place. Another verse from that same prophecy of Zenos caught my attention. It read:

"And the rocks of the earth must rend; and because of the groanings of the earth, many of the kings of the isles of the sea shall be wrought upon by the Spirit of God, to exclaim: The God of Nature suffers."

Who were these island kings Zenos spoke of, and why would they refer to Heavenly Father as the God of Nature? More importantly, what did they—or any of this—have to do with me?

I was very familiar with the words of Zenos and Zenoch, two prophets who lived in Jerusalem more than 500 years ago. They had preached and prophesied many great things. Their revelations talked mostly about the life and mission of the promised Messiah, the Son of God who would come to earth to redeem mankind from their fallen state. Their's were powerful words, filled with references to the signs and wonders concerning the life of the Savior, whose name, it was written, would be Jesus. Most of their writings were contained in the plates of brass that Lehi had brought with him from Jerusalem. Nephi had included many quotes from Zenos and Zenoch in his writings because of their spiritual importance, but their complete writings were found only in the brass plates. To my knowledge, only a precious few copies of these were still in existence. Helorum had mentioned that he had tried on several occasions to get himself a copy, but never succeeded. He had once had the opportunity to personally handle and read the originals obtained from the treasury of Laban, and had gleaned many spiritual things from that experience. I assumed that was before he had become blind.

My family had a copy of the small plates of Nephi, and some chapters from the brass plates, but not much more than that. Our church leaders provided much of our knowledge about the scriptures, and were always willing to let us borrow their copies for our personal study. That was why these quotes Helorum had inscribed had such a familiar sound to them. But their importance in regard to my mission in life still eluded me.

Most of the other verses declared the Lord's knowledge of the inhabitants of the isles of the sea, and that he would remember them when the gathering of Israel took place.

That made sense. Why would he give his gospel to one people and not to another? Israel was his chosen people, but I had been taught that anyone who believed could be adopted into that great lineage. So unless these islanders were not worthy, or had dwindled to a state of complete unbelief, they too should be privy to the revelations and blessings of the Lord.

I read on, covering the remainder of the verses quoted. Then, as I read the last verse, I literally flinched as if I had been struck by a bolt of lightening. Illumination brightened my mind like a blinding flash of light, and gave me the first glimpse of understanding about the inhabitants of these islands. And about me.

But great are the promises of the Lord unto them who are upon the isles of the sea; wherefore as it says isles, there must needs be more than this, and they are inhabited also by our brethren. For behold, the Lord God has led away from time to time from the house of Israel, according to his will and pleasure.

God leads his people . . . my brethren . . . away, from time to time . . . Nephites . . . to the isles of the sea . . . and blesses them according to his pleasure.

Did Helorum think I was going to be one of these people to be led away? That I was to be one of the remnants of the house of Israel spoken of in these scriptures?

I shook my head, trying to clear my thoughts. It was impossible to catch hold of the ideas as they whipped frantically around in my mind. I placed the scroll to one side and paced the room, trying to bring order to my confusion. I chanced another look at my father's drawing. The catamaran was large but not so much so that three or four men couldn't handle her. According to Hagoth, my father was building it to follow him and his large ship to a new land, presumably to the land north of Tonalai and the Land of Desolation. Hopefully to a land where no civilization had yet been established. To a place where faithful sons and daughters of God could start afresh. But that plan didn't fit the scriptures Helorum had quoted. The lands to the north couldn't really be considered the isles of the sea; they were still part of the mainland. True, those people migrating there would be recognized as a remnant of Israel, but there was no way that land could be misconstrued as an island.

So how did these inferred islands become populated?

A breeze wafted through an open window, fluttering the diagram. My father's catamaran was large enough to easily carry four or five families. My mind cleared slightly as I pictured what travel would be like on this boat. The thought of sailing her into the great deep of the western ocean excited me more than anything I could ever remember. I closed my eyes and imagined my hands on the rudder, the wind whipping through my hair as I guided the craft over mountainous waves, my father making fast the lashings on the sail and—

My father!

According to Hagoth, my father would be on his ship, not on this catamaran. By saying I wasn't going to be on his ship, did Hagoth mean I was simply following behind him, like my father had originally planned? That had to be it. And yet, something deep within me said otherwise. Clearly, I would not be on the same vessel, but the way Hagoth had phrased his words, he definitely said that I would not be going in the same direction, along the same course as his ship. Then the scripture I left off with came to mind again. If Hagoth was not the one going directly to these isles of the sea, then . . .

I was.

Alone.

Uneasy, I returned to the chair and sat down heavily. I had to will my hands to pick up the scroll again. I didn't want to see what the rest of Helorum's prophecy revealed about my future, yet I knew it was something I could not avoid for long.

It was almost as if I had no choice in the matter. For a moment I considered jumping out the window and running far away. Then I thought of the story of Jonah trying to hide from the Lord when he was commanded to call to repentance the city of Nineveh. He got in a boat, was thrown overboard and swallowed by a large fish. Though I had never seen a whale, descriptions of their size was along the lines of the Jonah story. I certainly did not want a fate similar to his, but I was still reluctant to read the words that would tell me I would never see my family again. I knew I was at the age when most young men got married and left their parent's dwellings to begin their own families, but I had always assumed my parents would at least live close by. So far, Helorum's words implied a separation of incalculable distances.

The parchment scroll shivered in my grasp as I began to read the second part. Again, it sounded a lot like scripture. Helorum talked about the revelations of Nephi and Jacob and others who had prophesied concerning the complete destruction of the Nephite people. And yet, it was also prophesied that the posterity of Nephi played an important, irreplaceable role in preparing the world for the second coming of the Lord.

How could these two prophecies coexist? I wondered.

It came to me almost before I finished the question. The destruction foretold would occur specifically on the mainland. It saddened me to think of our great nation being obliterated from this choice continent, this promised land.

The reason for the destruction had to be disobedience to the commandments of God. Pride, envy, lasciviousness, hatred, and greed would all eventually lead to the overt disregard and eventual denial of God and his laws. That had always led to downfall and destruction. It had happened so many times in the scriptures that I had been amazed. Didn't people ever learn?

I sighed heavily over the sinful nature of my people. Then a spark of hope glowed in the darkness of my despondency. There were always a few who held true to the word of God. Hagoth had mentioned a number of people who were traveling north by land to escape what was happening around Bountiful, and Hagoth himself was guiding a shipload of believers to a new land, so they can worship without embarrassment or fear. Perhaps I was not as alone as I thought.

I read on.

In the scroll, Helorum asked Hagoth to personally assist me in quickly preparing a boat capable of crossing vast distances of water with little effort on the sailor's part. He stated that I would be one of a few who would escape the evils spreading throughout this land, and that I would play a vital role in saving the lives of others as I made my journey. Then the next paragraph fairly leapt from the scroll.

Gideon has been blessed of goodly parents, and is highly favored of God. His posterity will be instrumental in the events leading to the Savior's return if he remains faithful to the commandments. The children of Nephi will live on through his seed and shall be a key factor in the fulfilling of prophecy. He will be a leader among men, the founder of a great nation of people close to the Spirit of God. Though his journey will be difficult and wrought with hardship, Gideon, son of Hezikiah, will be blessed beyond his ability to receive if he remains true. Though he will leave many loved ones behind, he will be guided by the power of God, for his voyage to the west shall be blessed and sacred.

94

I could hardly breathe. I stared at the wall in front of me for a long time, not moving, not focusing on anything in particular. I simply went blank. The words themselves were important, because they concurred with my assumptions regarding the previous scriptures. But more than that, the spirit of what was written spoke to my soul communicating on a plane that lacked expressive coherence, yet made perfect sense. I was in awe.

I felt blessed. I felt humbled. I felt . . . confused.

Why me? What had I done to be placed in this position of tremendous responsibility? I had been a fairly decent person all my life, but I certainly hadn't lived in a way that would single me out as a rose among thorns. To my mind, I was definitely more a bystander than a hero, more a lowly sheep than a shepherd.

The rest of the parchment said little about me specifically. It mentioned Hagoth's role in all this and that he would also be blessed for helping me and for providing a means for some of Nephi's posterity—including my father and mother—to escape the final destruction. The more I thought about what this revelation said, the more I understood why Hagoth had said that he didn't think I was going with him.

Again, I asked, *Why me?*

Hagoth entered the room. He walked directly over to me and placed a firm hand on my shoulder. He looked deeply into my eyes without emotion or pretense. He knew what I was going through, because he was undoubtedly experiencing many of the same feelings. There was an understanding between us that words would have demeaned. I nodded slowly to him as I rolled the parchment and placed it in my satchel.

"Where do we begin?" I asked, my voice sounding much more choked with emotion than I expected.

"We already have," Hagoth answered as he tapped my father's drawing with a work-worn finger.

I looked at him in surprise. "You mean, it's already built?"

"Not completely, but the materials are all collected and ready to be assembled."

"Where?"

"In the jungle, near Tonalai."

"But . . . won't the King Men know about it?" I asked, hoping my father's secret project would not already have been fouled.

Hagoth chuckled. "I doubt it. Besides, right now it looks like anything but a boat." And then he added with a smirk, "At least not one I would put *my* name on."

I felt overwhelmed. "If my father and mother are going with you, how am I supposed to finish it?"

"Gideon, my young friend, you underestimate yourself. How long have you worked by your father's side learning his trade? Who knows better the design and theory and construct of his ships than you?"

I shook my head. "But it's too much. I doubt I can do it by myself."

Hagoth placed his fists on his hips and gave me a stern look. "Are you saying that you doubt the Lord is able to help you succeed?"

"No." My shoulders slumped. "And yes."

"Gideon, remember the old saying: 'With God, all things are possible.'"

I looked up toward the ceiling. "Lately, I've been feeling like God has been anywhere but with me."

He nodded. "Yes. I can see how you'd think that. And I don't have an answer as to why you're going through all this. But I do know you have a great responsibility to try your hardest to accomplish these things Helorum has written."

He walked over to the window and leaned heavily on the sill, looking out at nothing in particular. He then turned to me and folded his arms.

"I am going to help you, as Helorum requested in the scroll. I promise I will do all I can without jeopardizing what I am trying to accomplish. You are still a wanted man in this region and we must be cautious." He thought silently for a moment, his eyes darting about as if reading words randomly scattered about the room.

"What should I do?" I asked timidly.

He looked at me sternly as if I had interrupted an important conversation with himself. I probably had.

"You should go immediately to Tonalai and finish the catamaran. I will write a letter for you instructing my workers there to aid you when they're needed."

"But what about my family? I don't even know where they are or if they're still alive. I've got to find them first."

He considered my words for a moment then nodded curtly. "I'll see what I can find out and send word to Helorum. Gather what things you think you'll need, but stay low." He glanced out the window again. "It's getting dark. Best be on your way."

I folded the catamaran drawing and put it in my satchel with the scroll as Hagoth wrote me his letter.

As I was leaving, Hagoth stopped me and said, "Gideon, I don't want this to sound mean-spirited, but don't spend too much time looking for your parents. If they are meant to come with me as it said in the revelation, then it will be so. Your future flows with a different tide."

I thanked him, but knew I simply couldn't let my family's plight go ignored.

"I will find them," I assured him. "And I will help them escape to the new land the revelation talked about. Whether I go with them or not will be decided at a later date. I know it is foolhardy going after them, but it is something I must do. I have never shied from something just because it might be difficult. You know that."

"Going after your parents may be closer to impossible than difficult," Hagoth said evenly.

I nodded. "I understand that," I said. "So, I'll take it one step at a time. The difficult I'll do right now; the impossible . . . may take a little while."

Ten

The sun had set long ago. I stared, not seeing the bold face of a near-ly full moon work its way through the star-studded sky. Sporadic clouds masked the twinkling night-lights, their nebulous blackness intermittent-ly obliterating the magnificent firmament that for centuries had guided navigators and wanderers alike toward their destinations.

My own future was slowly unfolding before my eyes, though the final destination remained a mystery. So much had happened in the past few days, more than either my mind or emotions could comfortably handle. I sighed and looked again at my satchel. What was written on Helorum's scroll had a certain spirit about it; I knew it was true. What it said made perfect sense. But that it inexorably involved me—and my offspring—did not. More importantly, it renewed my urgent desire to locate my family and leave immediately for Tonalai.

I decided to visited our family boatyard under the cover of night to glean what I might from those I could trust. Everything seemed to be in order, but there was something different about it. There were piles of fresh cut-lumber and other materials that we had not purchased before our house was set on fire. I reasoned that one of our workers had ordered these materials to keep things running while we were away. And yet, the news of my run-in with the law and our house burning to the ground would cer-tainly have raised some questions among our workers, let alone among our friends. Nothing looked out of place or awry. It was all as it should be. I had expected at least a little chaos, but our business seemed busier than ever. That was good, but it was not right.

I crept silently toward the office. A guard was posted outside the door. He was no one I recognized, so I thought it best not to approach him. Searching for clues of any kind, I made my way toward the dry dock area where I knew I'd find Ham.

Ham was an old sea salt who had a shanty on our small pier. He was a hermit by nature and had spent his life among the denizens of the shoreline. My father had befriended this likable old man before I was born, and I had grown up knowing Ham as an uncle of sorts, a coworker sometimes, and a friend and confidant always. Despite my knowing Ham from birth, I didn't know much about the man's past. Ham was an introvert of the most stringent magnitude, who had maintained strange habits to ensure his privacy. Most people left him alone, fearing he was possessed by an evil spirit or that he had a pox hexed upon him by some prophet or soothsayer. I, thankfully, knew him better than that. Ham was a very nice person who minded his own business but who was always ready to help when needed. As he had never asked for anything from my father, I didn't know exactly how he had come to live in the shanty on our pier. I had asked my father several times, and each time his answer had been that he didn't know either; but since he liked the old man, he would let him stay awhile. I asked Ham once, and he replied that he woke up one morning and his shanty was somehow nailed to our pier. Then he'd smile a mischievous, toothless smile, place a gnarled, bony finger to his temple, and wink at me, meaning that that was all I needed to know. I took it as that was all was ever going to find out. But it was enough.

There were a few small huts on the pier in addition to his shanty, and one large warehouse adjacent to the dry-dock. A new hull was braced between the winch stanchions on the dry-dock, one that we had not placed there. In fact, it was not a hull design we used in our boat making. This one looked more like something Hagoth would make, only smaller. I studied it for a while, then moved like a shadow past the warehouse, staying behind some large boxes until I was close enough to see a faint amber glow from a candle just inside Ham's window. I eased my way to the window and crouched under it. I listened for any conversation that would indicate there was more than one person in the shanty, which was rare. But all that I'd seen thus far had made me edgy, and the need to consider every possible trap was foremost on my mind. I listened intently for a long while as a slight breeze drifted in from the sea carrying with it the familiar fragrances of brine and rain.

Then I heard a noise—the creak of old timber under foot. It was faint, and I had trouble pinpointing a bearing on it because it was gone as soon as I heard it. A moment later it sounded again, from directly within the shanty near the window I was crouched under. I looked up to see a bucket of chum-water and fish guts being dumped on me, and tried to avoid the deluge but was not quick enough. The water was disgusting, sticky, and foul-smelling, and a portion of it regrettably splashed into my gawking mouth. I choked on the repulsive stuff as an errant fish head went down the nape of my neck and lodged itself between my shoulder blades. I couldn't help but let out a cry of disgust as I rolled away from the draining bucket. Then a face appeared at the window, studying me. It was Ham.

"Is that you, Gideon?" he whispered into the night.

I sat up and forcefully wiped my face with my sleeve. I tried to spit the brackish chum-water from my mouth as I coughed out, "Yeah. *Hack!* Thanks for the warm welcome."

He chuckled pleasantly. "Hey, you were the one who came creeping up in the middle of the night. How was I to know who you were?"

I spat again, the foul taste growing more bitter on my lips. "How about asking, 'Who's out there?' for a start."

"And what if it was an enemy?" he retorted. "That would ruin my element of surprise."

"Your best defense against an enemy is a bucket of fish guts?" I asked, trying to hide the honest amusement in my voice.

"It worked against *you*, didn't it?"

I chuckled and said sure, I guessed he was right. I began to get up when he stopped me with the raising of his hand.

"You sure you weren't followed, Gideon?" he asked in an urgent whisper.

"I don't think I was. If so, I doubt they knew who they were following. I just came from Moroni, and no one knew I was there either."

Gregg R. Luke

"Good. Come on in after you dip into the lagoon."

"What? You want me to go swimming at this hour?" I asked without mirth.

"The way you smell now? You bet I do," he said, lowering a blind on the window.

I sniffed my bile-soaked sleeve and winced at the pungent aroma. He was right. I placed my satchel against a box and climbed down a ladder to a small loading platform. It bobbed lightly on two large balsa wood logs. The buoyancy of balsa always amazed me, especially logs like these that had been supporting this platform ever since I could remember. No matter how water-logged they became, they still retained their tenacious buoyancy. I slid myself gently into the sea and swam quietly around for a minute or two, ducking my head underwater and scrubbing the scales and fish entrails from my hair.

The clarity of the water in the estuaries and lagoons by the shores of Mulek was incredible. Some days, when we hadn't had a storm in weeks, I could see almost as well underwater as out of water. I had long ago grown accustom to opening my eyes underwater, and could discern between a rock and a coral and a stone fish some fifty feet away. Our seas were filled with a breathtaking array of animal life, all of which I could name by heart. Curiously, some of the most beautiful creatures were also the most deadly, including the stone fish. Many a careless beachcomber, wading in the cool of a lagoon, had haplessly stepped on what he had taken to be an algae-covered rock, only to have his foot impaled by a poisonous dorsal spine. The venom would immediately numb the leg, rendering it useless, and if not treated quickly, would nearly always cause the leg to go gangrenous. At worst, it could kill the person. Sea snakes were also a potentially deadly problem, but only when they were aggravated or handled too much. Perhaps the most stunning animal of all was the dragon fish or lion fish, or, as some called it, the turkey fish. It had two large, elegant pectoral fins and a grand dorsal fin, each of which blossomed out in a serrated array of feathered spines, making it look more like a spray of plumage rather than fish fins. The beguiling tranquillity and grace of these fins sometimes enticed many an unwary swimmer to touch and fondle the frilly, slow-moving fish. But again, the person who tried this was often injected with poison by the dorsal spines, which caused a painful swelling and eventual numbing that sometimes never went away.

I loved the variety of colors found in our shallow lagoons. Perhaps my favorite marine dwellers were the brilliantly-hued anemones and corals. They ranged in colors from crimson reds and dazzling yellows to phosphorescent greens and glowing blues, painting the rocks and formations with entrancing collages worthy of any art gallery in Zarahemla. I never tired of gazing at them. At night, the colors all melded into a subdued spectrum of blues, grays, and blacks, with an occasional flash of yellow refracted from an out-of-water source.

I crawled back onto the platform and stripped my clothing off down to a loin piece. After washing my clothes again in the lagoon, I carried the bundle up to Ham's shanty. Before entering, I scanned the pier for any sign of movement. There was none.

Ham had a small fire glowing in a stone enclosure that vented through a bamboo chimney on the seaside of the shanty. He had positioned some wooden racks in front of the fire.

"Dry your breeches there," he said, indicating the racks.

I laid my clothes out in the best possible way to dry them quickly. He then tossed me a towel to dry myself with. He also laid out a few hard biscuits and some dried fish for me if I was hungry. I was starving.

"What's going on around here?" I asked after seating myself and swallowing a mouthful of biscuit.

He hung his head and rubbed his bushy eyebrows. "Bad things, Gideon. Bad things done by bad men."

His pale brown eyes had a profound sadness in them I had never seen before. I searched for meaning in those eyes as I brushed my hair back, but found none. I retied my headband securely, then rotated my clothes in front of the fire.

"Who's running this place? Are you?"

"Heavens no," he exclaimed. "I wouldn't be caught dead helping the likes of these people. They have no sense of pride, no integrity or honor. I despise them and what they've done. I've heard rumors, too. Are you and your family all right?"

I copied his slouched pose and exhaled heavily. "I don't know. I'm doing all right, I guess, but the longer I hear nothing about my parents, the more worried I am that I may never see them again. What, exactly, have you heard about us?"

"Your house was burned and you've been hiding from the law," he said, "and I don't want to know where," he added quickly. "At some point, I assume you got separated from your folks, because you're still free." He paused in a reflective moment of thought. "You probably don't know about your parents then, do you?"

I sat up. "Know what?"

"That your father and mother are being held in a fortress near Nephihah."

I was on my feet. "In Nephihah? Are they all right?"

He shrugged. "Not in Nephihah, Gideon, near. As far as I know they're all right; they're both still alive. How they're faring in the hands of the King Men and Lamanites, I can only guess."

"So can I. Which fortress are they in?"

"It's one Moroni started to build to keep the Lamanites out of the land of Bountiful a few years back, in a village called Limhi. It was only partially constructed before he was called to help Pahoran in Zarahemla. The Lamanites took it over and added quite a bit to it before the Nephite army came and drove them out of Nephihah. But Limhi is right on the border and the fortress itself was never retaken. I guess the army figured it wasn't worth it, so it's now considered Lamanite territory."

I rotated my clothes again, then paced the room. "How do you know all this?"

He smiled. "I may be an old coot that nobody pays attention to, but I still have good hearing. You'd be surprised how much information gets thrown around here as the longshoremen try to one-up each other's stories of bravado."

"What longshoremen?"

"King Men, mostly."

"What about our regulars? Aren't they still working?"

Ham snorted. "The minute news was out that your father had been burned out, they scattered. Ain't nobody left from the old crew but me."

I felt so empty inside. Everything I knew and loved had vanished in a matter of days. It had all happened so quickly, so violently. *Why?* That was the question foremost on my mind. Why had it happen? Why hadn't anyone done anything to stop it?

"Hasn't the law done anything?" I asked.

Ham stretched his arms over his head. "Oh, Corianton has been by a time or two and asked a bunch of foolish questions, but he got nothing out of me, 'cause I had nothing to give."

My shoulders sagged. "He probably still thinks I killed that judge. That's why I'm a criminal," I commented softly.

Ham leaned forward again. "Is it true then?"

"What? That I killed a judge? Of course not," I snapped, a little too forcefully.

Ham did not flinch. He stared at me a while before continuing.

"You know, you're wrong about Corianton," he finally said. "He may be a wily lawman, but he's nobody's fool. You're still wanted, that's a truth, but I don't think you're on his list of possible suspects."

"Then why did he come to question me that first night?"

"He questions everybody. That's his job."

"Does he know my parents are at Limhi?"

"Probably. Not much he can do, though. That's not his jurisdiction."

I dropped into a chair and put my face in my hands. Finally, I had some viable information, but no way to get any help with it. I could go to Zarahemla and ask one of the army generals for help, but that great city was 150 miles in the wrong direction. For all I knew, my father had already been through a mock trial with a rigged jury and a bloodthirsty judge, and was now preaching to the spirits on the other side of the veil. Ham had little to recommend as to my next course of action. He was planning on leaving with Hagoth in one of his ships within the week. Figuring no one would miss him, he wasn't worried about his escape.

Anonymity was what he enjoyed most about being a hermit. The only thing left for me to do seemed obvious. I had to go to Limhi. And I had to go alone.

"One more thing," Ham said with a knot furrowing his brow. "If you're going there you'll need to know their signs."

"What signs?" I asked.

"Their secret combinations and signs. It's a code of sorts, a system of passwords that'll prove you're one of them. If you don't know 'em, your word will be worth nothing more than fish bait."

"How is it you know them?" I asked with one eyebrow raised in question.

He chuckled. "I told you, this old coot doesn't miss a thing on these docks."

Ham then proceeded to teach me as much as he knew concerning the secret signs and combinations of the King Men. I committed as many of these to memory as I could, then got dressed.

After donning my clothes and thanking Ham, I slipped into the transient shadows of the night and drifted with them like a ship drifts with the tide. Moving naturally with the surroundings was the best way to remain unseen. This was a dangerous place for me, and I had to get away before it was too late.

As I neared the warehouse, I heard a voice that sounded somewhat familiar. I paused to listen but could not make out any details of the conversation being held inside. I crept to a side window. Just as I was about to peer over the sill, the front door opened. The voice was clearer now, and I was sure I had heard it before, but I didn't know who it belonged to. It wasn't so much the timbre of the man's voice as it was the way he said things. He spoke with abounding confidence, almost to the point of being cocky, and yet with undertones of something sinister. He was arguing with another man about wasted time, about trouble with a few men who were not being pressured enough . . . or something close to that. Names were mentioned, but none I recognized. I pressed myself to the planks of the dock and slid behind some crates, inching my way forward on fingers, belly, and toes, toward the front corner of the building, twisting from side to side like a legless reptile slithering toward the safety of a hole under a rock.

The light from the open door lit the handsome face with the familiar voice. The man was well dressed and carried himself like one who had authority. At first I couldn't place him. Then, as a wicked smile spread across his face, the recognition jolted me like unnerving shock from a river eel. I recoiled from the memory as a burning hatred and paralyzing fear simultaneously coursed through my frame. I had seen this man twice before: once at my father's house, accompanied by Corianton, and once in a dark alley in Moroni with a dead judge at his feet. It was Kumran.

I was about to retreat into the shadows when I felt the pressure of something moving along my back. At first I thought it was a shiver of revulsion from seeing Kumran again, but the pattern of tiny footfalls making their way toward my shoulders told me otherwise. Because I could not turn around in the cramped quarters I was wedged into, I partially twisted my head to try and see what it was. In the subdued light behind the crates I saw only a furry, black form prancing lightly on dainty clawed feet, inching its way toward my face.

As I frowned, it paused and stared at me with beady red eyes that glowed in the darkness with that bizarre, reflective eye-shine seen only in animals. It chirped out a faint squeak as it sat up on its haunches and sniffed the air. It was a large wharf rat, the kind that usually tried to avoid humans, but when cornered could inflict a painful, infectious bite. I tried to twist my back to throw the vermin off to one side, but its clawed feet had a good purchase on my tunic. I retreated back into the shadows so as not to be seen by Kumran, but only moved an inch or so before the rodent resumed his trek toward my head.

Its moist feet and needle-sharp claws touch the back of my neck, and I felt the coldness of its nose as it sniffed through the base of my hair. I tried reaching back to shove it to one side, but only angered it, causing it to squeak and chirp loudly as it dug its claws deeper into my flesh. Suddenly the rat jumped on top of my head and started sniffing and rummaging through my hair, as if looking for some morsel that may have been left there after my last food-fight. I realized it was probably smelling the remnants of Ham's surprise attack with his bucket of chum-water and fish guts. I made a quick swipe with my hand and knocked the disgusting rodent from my head into the open space in front of me. It landed hard and rolled a few feet, screeching and chirping loudly at me before scurrying quickly under the warehouse.

Kumran glared in my direction. The rat had appeared too suddenly. He sensed something wasn't right. I could swear he was looking directly at me, though I was well concealed in the darkness of a shadow. Or was I?

"Wait a minute," Kumran said to whoever was just inside the doorway.

He unsheathed a long dagger, probably the same one he used to kill the judge, and started moving cautiously toward me.

ELEVEN

I didn't move a muscle. I couldn't. I was frozen with fear. Kumran cautiously stepped to within a few feet of me, his dagger in hand. He stopped and squinted into the blackness where I was hiding. I knew he couldn't see me because he hadn't come directly at me. Then I saw something in his eyes, something in the way he searched the shadows where I lay, a hesitancy that gave him pause. A fear. I suddenly realized this man feared the unknown. What he couldn't understand, what he couldn't touch, see, hear, or feel, were things that instilled in him apprehension and anxiety. Perhaps that was why men of his sort could not accept the teachings of our prophets; perhaps it was simply a lack of faith.

Kumran advanced another step. "Who goes there?" he called out.

My heart pounded so loudly I was sure it could be heard by anyone within a mile of me. I held my mouth open to silence the coarseness of my breathing. I squinted my eyes to diminish the possibility of light shinning off their glossy surface. And I prayed that I would remain undetected by this evil man.

Kumran stood for a moment longer before straightening and relaxing his stance.

"What is it?" the man inside the doorway asked.

"Don't know," Kumran answered softly, cautiously. "Thought I heard something."

Just then a mangy, orange-striped cat stepped out from behind the crate I was lying next to. I don't know how the cat got there, but at this moment I didn't care. I only hoped it would not approach me and betray my position. It blinked at the light from the doorway and gave a half purr-half meow as it kneaded the pier with its front paws.

Kumran blew a heavy breath of air past his lips and sheathed his dagger.

"Stupid cat," he hissed.

He then squatted and coaxed the cat toward him with cooing, soft words. The cat obliged and went to the hands that promised a pet, a scratch, or a rub, and maybe even a scrap of food. Kumran picked up the cat and made to grace it with pet kisses.

"You stupid ugly cat," Kumran mewed lovingly through pursed lips. "I'm going to teach you for scaring me like that."

The cat, I'm sure, expected to be inundated with affectations of kindness. What the trusting animal didn't expect was to be hurled into the night sky, over the railing of the pier, and into the sea below. Kumran began this launch with a gleeful smile, but as he heaved the cat over the railing, it delivered a final blow in by swiping a claw-laden paw across Kumran's upper lip. Kumran swore in painful shock as the cat's claws sliced a large gash through his lip. The cat hissed-screeched in horrified anger as it flew, legs splayed, hackles raised, over the side of the pier.

I was still very frightened but could not help but smile, thanking the cat for dealing with Kumran in a way I could not, and praying it could swim. The cat most likely had been following the wharf rat that had alerted Kumran to my presence. That mangy, flea-bitten, *beautiful* animal had also unwittingly been the source of my salvation.

Kumran withdrew a blood-covered hand from his lip and cursed again. The cat had done more than simply scratch him; Kumran apparently could not stanch the bleeding as he repeatedly dabbed his fingers to the laceration. I caught a glimpse of the nasty gash as he turned toward the door and asked for a piece of cloth. It would leave a scar. The man inside the warehouse handed him a moistened cloth remnant, then closed the door.

Kumran walked away cursing under his breath while holding the cloth against his swelling lip. He went to a new stable next to the wharf entrance and untethered a horse that had been hitched to a wagon. I slithered out of my hiding place, and crept up quickly behind the wagon.

To follow Kumran would be next to impossible as the horse would eventually outdistance me, but I had to know where he was going. I was sure this man had everything to do with my parent's imprisonment, and was probably on his way to them right now. He was undoubtedly a key leader in the hierarchy of the King Men, perhaps even second only to Gadianton or Kishkumen.

The wagon was filled with boxes, hardware and other goods, and was covered with a tarpaulin. The tarp was lashed to hooks on the sides of the wagon, but the back was loose and invitingly dark. As Kumran clucked the horse into motion, I made a desperate dive onto the tailgate and rolled under the tarp. I held my breath, hoping he did not notice the sudden change in weight of the wagon. Evidently, he was more concerned about nursing his sliced lip and paid little attention to anything else but his own misery. I had the scroll, catamaran diagram, and map of Tonalai folded tightly in the satchel, and tucked firmly inside my tunic. I patted them to make sure they were still with me.

The first thing I noticed was that we were heading north toward Bountiful instead of south toward Nephihah. I thought for sure we'd be heading to the King Men fortress, but then I remembered Corianton saying Kumran was from Bountiful. I was about to roll out of the wagon, but then thought it a good idea to visit Helorum one more time to glean whatever information he had gathered about my parents. To go blindly running down to Limhi would be suicide. There was no way I could save my parents by myself. I needed help, and quickly. My father had always said most battles were won with brains, not brawn. Right now, I could think of nothing that would work. Helorum was my best hope.

The moon had set, but it was still a few hours away from the first graying light of morning. I felt surprisingly secure in the wagon box as we traveled along the graveled road. I laid my head on a sack of meal and suddenly realized how very tired I was. When you're running for your life while searching for loved ones at the same time, and trying to make sense of a world turned upside-down, adrenaline will carry you only so far before total fatigue sets in. That's what had happened in Helorum's sheep pen many nights ago, and that's what overcame me now. It was a dangerous thing to do—stupid and careless, but something I could not fight. I had to close my eyes and rest, if only for a moment.

I awoke suddenly, a sticky sweat dripping from my soaked headband. The tarp I was under was still secured to the wagon box, but the loose back allowed me to lift it slightly and catch a glimpse of the activity around me. It was well into the morning hours and there were many men bustling about in a stockyard where the wagon was parked. It was very warm under the heavy tarp and I was already soaked with perspiration. The thick air and hazy sun boded for an oppressively humid day. I waited for a break in the activity near the wagon, then rolled out, taking with me the sack of meal that had acted as my pillow. I shucked the sack onto my shoulder and began walking toward the entrance of the stockyard. I was disoriented and woozy from my sudden awakening, but knew enough to try to blend with the many men around me. I drew a few deep breaths through my nostrils to clear the fog in my head.

Just then, a gruff voice called out, "Hey you! Boy! Wait a minute."

I knew he meant me so I stopped. I peered over the sack on my shoulder. A large man carrying a sheaf of paper was walking toward me. It was probably the stockyard foreman, I reasoned. I considered dropping the sack and running for the entrance, but the distance was still too far for a sure getaway, and I wasn't convinced my legs were awake enough to carry me very fast. The large man came closer while concentrating on his papers. I cursed myself for falling asleep in the wagon, for not being more careful. When the man was a few yards from me, another man stepped between us. It was Kumran.

The King Man's back was to me as he began talking with the foreman. The large foreman looked over Kumran's shoulder toward me and called out, "Take that sack over to the granary."

I nodded and turned toward a group of buildings to my left.

"Not there, you idiot," the foreman yelled. "Over here," he said, pointing to the buildings behind where he and Kumran were standing.

That meant I had to walk right past the two of them. I shifted the sack of meal to my other shoulder and set a brisk pace toward them. The sack did little to hide my face from Kumran, but I hoped the nonchalance of passing within inches of him would not raise suspicion as to my identity. I marched right past the two men who were now in a heated discussion about the something happening in Zarahemla. Just as I passed them, the foreman called out again, "Hey, kid. When you're done with that, go help with the wagons headed for Limhi."

I raised a hand to acknowledge his command and continued on my way toward the granary. I could feel Kumran's eyes on my back as I followed some other men who were carrying sacks similar to mine into a large barn. I wondered if he was curious about my clothing. It was definitely better than what most of the other stockmen were wearing, but I was sure its newness would have worn off some, considering what I had been through since I first put them on.

The cavernous barn smelled pleasantly of milled grain, sacks of oats, and bales of wheat awaiting the thresher. I hefted my load onto a palate where the others were unloading theirs and turned to look out the doorway. Kumran and the foreman were heading toward me at a vigorous pace. I made my way to the back of the barn and up some stairs to a loading chamber, and slipped through the chamber door just as Kumran and the foreman entered the barn. They were searching for me, I was certain. Had Kumran recognized me? I wasn't going to wait around to find out.

The rear of the chamber was an open loft that overlooked the back of the barn. To the far side was a steep loading chute that went through a small hole in the wall to the outside. It was big enough for an average-sized bale of straw or bag of oats, so I figured I could fit through it too. The scary part was that most chutes like this ended just outside the wall, and the impending drop was two stories high. To survive such a drop without breaking a leg seemed unlikely.

I carefully peeked out the chamber door and saw Kumran talking to a stockman. I could not see the foreman. He had gone looking elsewhere. The worker turned and pointed up to the room I was in, and Kumran walked quickly toward the stairs. I scanned the chamber again. I could jump from the loft onto the bales below, but the stockmen were likely to see me. I had no choice. I slid a large bale in front of the door, then said a quick prayer as I jumped onto the loading chute. The surface was smooth and the silkiness my clothes made for nearly frictionless contact. I flew down the chute, through the opening in the wall. As I suspected, the chute ended abruptly and I found myself in midair, flapping my arms like some baby bird trying desperately to learn the art of flying much too late. Fortunately, there was a wagon filled with straw below. I hit the straw flat on my back with enough force to knock the wind from me, but broke no bones.

I didn't wait to catch my breath. Instead, I rolled off the wagon, landing shakily on my feet, then headed for the jungle behind the barn. There was a vague animal trail riddled with vines, rocks, and ditches, things that slowed a man's progress, but I bounded along at top speed regardless of these obstacles. I didn't even look back to see if I was being pursued. I was sure the wagon would be searched, but I doubted that they would follow me into the jungle. Still, I ran until my legs gave out from under me, and then collapsed behind a spray of large ferns.

My breathing was coarse and labored. It occurred to me that I didn't even know where I was. I had to assume that I was near Bountiful, because the wagon had been headed in that direction before I fell asleep. It took a moment to catch my breath, then I began a slow lope along the trail. Soon I came to what I was looking for—a large tree with plenty of vines and branches for climbing. My mother used to joke about my ancestry, saying I must be part monkey because of my ability to scale any tree with ease. In no time I was in the top branches looking over the canopy of jungle foliage surrounding me. I could see the depression where the stockyard was some miles behind me, and the nearby shoreline. More importantly, I could see the city of Bountiful not a few hundred yards in the opposite direction. Though it was still very dangerous, I knew that was where I had to go.

Rather than trying to skulk through vacant alleys and paths along waterways, I decided to hide in plain sight. Meandering through the crowds along Bountiful's main street, I walked a steady but carefree pace toward the opposite end of town. I had the creepy sensation of many eyes being upon me, and the unmistakable feeling that I was being followed, but I acted as if nothing was wrong about my being there. I paused to buy a large orange with a one of the few coins in my pocket, and then stopped to examine some tapestries hanging from a weaver's booth in a bazaar. Then I continued on, recognizing the fountain I had slid into when searching for my mother.

I passed the King Men warehouse where my mother had been held. All seemed normal in the small marketplace in front of the building, except that Ashod's jewelry stand was no longer there. I asked an old merchant where he now sold his wares. The merchant had an apprehensive, nervous look in his eyes as he shook his head and said that he didn't know. I understood what he was really saying, and thought it best not to involve the old man in my problems. Without a doubt, Kumran's lackeys were close by, and I didn't want to draw undue attention to myself, or anyone who might suffer because of my inquisitiveness. I was positive that was what had happened with Elsha. I winked at the old merchant and said I understood. A wan smile of relief passed quickly across his face.

What had happened to Ashod and his lovely daughter? The two times I had met Elsha, I had come between her and some subversive act of the King Men. That I had unintentionally caused her more trouble, I was certain, and I felt awful because of it. Their lives were again in jeopardy, and I was the reason behind their misery. I felt obligated to help them too. Perhaps, if I could convince them to come with my family after I rescued them from the fortress in Limhi?

No, that would not be likely. Judging by our last encounter, I was sure Elsha hated me. To talk her into traveling anywhere with me would prove futile. The best recourse would be to tell them of Hagoth's plans, and at least point them toward Tonalai on the west coast. But first I had to find them. They were no longer at the bazaar, and no one there could tell me where they were at least, not without endangering their own lives. I had only one course of action.

Helorum was not at home, but Aiya invited me in and immediately placed a bowl of onion soup in front of me. I didn't object. In fact, I drained two more bowls before noticing Kateph was not there either.

"My husband took the dog with him," Aiya said.

"I thought he'd leave him here to protect you," I reasoned.

"Normally, he does. But he was heading toward the center of the city, and not many people there are interested in helping an old blind man." She frowned and added, "Many would try to take advantage of him."

I agreed and thanked her again for the soup. She said Helorum would be back soon if I'd like to stay, but the thought of simply sitting around waiting made me uncomfortable. I thought it would be best if I went looking for him, or at least tried to find out what had happened to Ashod and Elsha.

Aiya handed me an apple as I made my way to their front door. I opened the door and stood staring at a man's chest. Now, I may be only thought of as a young man, but I am still considered fairly tall for my age. Yet here was a man at Helorum's doorstep whose chest was at my eye level. If he proposed to enter, he would not be able to do so without a great deal of bending. I looked up into the face of this giant with an awe he probably encountered every day. Not only was he tall, at least seven feet by my estimation, but he was powerfully built, with a broad chest and thick, muscular arms. He must have weighed two and a half times what I did. And very little of that appeared to be fat. He looked down at me with a vengeful smirk that very well could have meant I was about to become his lunch.

Then I heard him growl exactly like a dog. Panic, shock, awe-struck horror, whatever it was, it held me motionless. I could only gawk at this behemoth of a man. the growl again, but this time it sounded like it came from *behind* him, not *from* him.

"Hush now, Kateph," Helorum's voice commanded.

Suddenly, an enormous fist clenched the front of my clothing, lifting me off my feet, and yanking me outside. I instinctively grabbed his wrist to break free and prevent myself from being tossed aside, but that was like trying to stop the ocean's tide with a bamboo cup.

"Wait, please," I gasped, knowing with certainty my last seconds on earth were coming quickly to an end.

"Just a moment, Noah," Helorum's voice said. Then the old shepherd stepped out from behind the giant with Kateph on a tether. "Gideon?"

"Yes, it's me," I said, a nervous panic cracking my voice like I had just reached puberty yesterday.

"Oh, Gideon, I'm glad you're here," Helorum said, placing a hand on the giant's massive arm. As if by magic, the blind man's gentle touch unlocked the grip the huge man had on my clothes, and I almost dropped to my knees.

"Come on inside," he said, leading the way.

I looked at the giant and smiled weakly. The big man grinned again, not the malicious smirk from before, but an honest, you're-now-my-good-friend smile that I was more than happy to accept. I gestured for him to enter before me, and he did the same for me. I wasn't about to argue.

Helorum held out his hand for me to shake. Kateph growled at me. It was good to be back.

"Hello, Noah," Aiya said as she went into the kitchen. If she was planning on feeding this gargantuan, she'd have to empty three-fourths of her pantry, and then some.

This giant, Noah, could not even stand upright inside Helorum's home. He came over to the table, but did not try to take one of the chairs. It was doubtful a common chair could support him anyway. Instead, he opted to sit cross-legged on the floor. It didn't matter. Even on the floor, he could see comfortably over the table top.

"Noah, this is Gideon, the young man I was telling you about," Helorum said.

The giant nodded and held out his hand. I would like to say I shook it, but that would not begin to describe the way my hand was swallowed by his enormous fist. That he shook my whole arm was closer to the truth.

"Happy to meet you," I said. He simply nodded again.

Aiya did bring out some poppy seed loaves, and, to my surprise, Noah took the smallest of the bunch.

"Noah, here, has been a friend of mine for some time. He lives outside the city by himself . . . for obvious reasons."

"I can't see why," I said, smiling at the big man. "I'd think he'd be rather popular wherever he went, whether people liked him or not."

"That's just the point," Helorum explained. "He doesn't like being the center of attention just because he's big. It's as much a handicap to him as it can be a blessing."

"Really?" was all I could think to say.

Helorum took a bite of his poppy seed loaf before continuing. "Gideon has been learning how to ponder," he said to Noah. "Any luck yet, Gideon?"

Not this again! I shook my head. "No. I'm not much good at it," I admitted. "I think I need more help."

Helorum sat back and smiled. Then he laughed. Noah laughed too, and I joined in, until Helorum spoke.

"Look at us," he chuckled. "An old blind shepherd, a man of mind-boggling proportions who chooses not to speak, and a fully functional, healthy young man. And yet which one of us needs the most help?"

I suddenly felt humiliated and belittled. Helorum sensed that and said, "Of course, I should also ask, 'Which one of us has the biggest responsibility ahead of him?'"

I smiled awkwardly, and said that it was all right.

"I'm sorry if I offended you, Gideon," he continued. "You have a calling greater than my lineage or Noah's size. By needing help, I meant that you have not come to a complete understanding of your responsibilities."

I removed the scroll from the satchel inside my tunic, and gently flattened it on the table with my palm. "I understand what you wrote on this scroll, and am humbled by it. I just don't think I have enough faith to make it happen. There's so much left unsaid."

"Oh, Gideon," Helorum sighed solemnly, "be patient. Many things are left unsaid because they are for us to decide. If the Lord spelled everything out point by point, then our freedom to choose would be taken away. That is why we ponder, in order to use our agency to determine the course we must take, be it good or bad. And as far as not understanding everything, I will tell you this: your lack of understanding is not from a lack of faith. Just the opposite.

"A great man once said, 'Understanding is the reward of faith. Therefore, seek not to understand that you may believe, but believe that you may understand.'"

Noah looked at me with an earnestness in his eyes as he nodded slowly. I felt a sincere love from both men as I pondered what Helorum had just taught. It did make sense, and the more I thought on it, the clearer it became.

I had to believe first, then I'd understand. All this time I had been trying to figure out what Helorum's revelation meant so I could have faith to act on it. But I was supposed treat it the same way I treated the scriptures: I believed in them without question *first*, then through faith followed their teachings. It was so simple.

Strange tears filled my eyes as I felt a warmth course through me. "I think I finally understand," I said softly as the warmth grew stronger.

Helorum leaned over and grabbed my wrist. "I knew you would."

Noah put a beefy hand gently on my shoulder and gave me a light squeeze. He too had a warm mist in his eyes, and the most kindhearted smile I had ever seen.

A moment passed in silence. I didn't want it to end. Then Helorum folded his arms and cleared his throat.

"Have you found out anything about your parents?" he asked.

"Yes. They're being held in a fortress in Limhi."

Noah's head snapped up and his eyes fixed on mine.

"I assume they're alive," I continued, "but I don't know if I can get them out by myself. Can you help?"

"Oh dear," Helorum said with some gravity. "We were planning on beginning our journey in just three days."

"Journey? To where?"

"I don't know," the old shepherd said with unashamed ignorance. "We are heading to the north with a large group of fellow saints in Christ. Noah is going too, and has agreed to help my wife and I. I don't think we can be of much help to you."

I panicked. "But what about your prophecy concerning me? Hagoth was little help, and I'm still very much on my own. I can't leave without my parents, and I have nowhere else to turn."

Helorum sighed and ran his palms over his gray hair. "I'm sorry, Gideon. I don't have a solid answer right now. Do you have any suggestions, Noah?"

The giant shrugged his massive shoulders with a air of true concern, but shook his head.

"Let's sleep on it tonight," Helorum said with a strange happiness. "I feel confident we shall have an answer in the morning."

Sleep? That was the last thing on my mind.

TWELVE

The morning air was crisp and free from the oppressive humidity that thickened yesterday afternoon. The sun had just appeared from its resting place in the eastern sea and was already melting away the few clouds that hung in the bluing sky. To my surprise, I had slept well. It must have been the lack of sleep I'd suffered from over the past few days. Whatever the reason, I was up and eager to get things done long before the rest of the city would even considered prying themselves from the captivating serenity of their beds.

I thought it would be refreshing to go for a walk while the early hour still provided some solitude. I quietly exited the rear door of Helorum's home and stood for a moment inhaling the fragrance of the prolific wisteria that canopied his porch.

A movement to my left caught my eye. Perhaps a flash of clothing or a wisp of hair? I couldn't be sure, but something had moved quickly by the sheep stall Helorum kept behind his house. I crouched behind a feathery palm and looked around. Nothing. I heard a few of the sheep stir a bit as if awakened before their usual time. Cautiously making my way to the stall, I peered inside. The old ram wobbled to his feet and came to me with his stubby tail wagging.

"Good morning, Riplikish," I said softly. "I didn't mean to wake you."

I scratched the ram's ears and continued looking around. I sensed someone was near, but I couldn't tell if they were friend or foe. They were probably hiding among the sheep. The scene reminded me of the night I had hidden myself in this very stall. I smiled as I recalled Helorum's kind-ness toward me, and decided I couldn't go wrong by following his example.

"So, Riplikish," I said a little louder to the ram. "You have a visitor, don't you?"

A movement stirred in the shadows of the stall. I nodded to myself. There was someone there.

I continued to look at the ram as I said, "It's all right, whoever you are, my friend. This old ram won't hurt you, and there is nothing to fear from me, unless you mean harm to Helorum or his wife."

There was no response. I turned my back to the stall and leaned on the fence, taking in more of the wonderful morning. Even though the rev-elations in Helorum's scroll still made me anxious to get to Limhi, I was strangely calm and happy at the moment. With my back turned, the ram bleated softly and then returned to his place in the straw. I stretched and folded my arms.

"Are you from around here?" I asked the stranger in the shadows of the stall.

After a moment, a soft female voice answered, "Yes."

"Are you in need of help, or are you in some kind of trouble?"

"Yes," the voice said again. It was a gentle voice, with a familiar timbre.

I continued staring at the morning sky with my back to the stall, so as not to intimidate or frighten whoever was inside. Just then Kateph came trotting outside and over to me. I was very surprised, even shocked that he didn't growl at me. He came right to my feet and stood beside me, peering into the sheep stall. His hackles raised slightly as he scented the stranger in the shadows. His lips curled back and a low grumble resonat-ed from his chest. I took a chance and reached down to tousle his mane.

"Hush, Kateph," I said lightly. "She is a friend and needs our help. Don't you be frightening her with your growls and bad manners."

The dog whimpered a bit and licked his muzzle impatiently as he stared into the stall. He then looked up at me and suddenly flinched as surprised recognition filled his yellow eyes. He took several quick steps backward and commenced growling at me. I couldn't help but laugh.

"Fooled you, didn't I?" I said to the confused animal. "Now go inside and leave us alone like a good cur, will you?"

The dog cuffed and stood his ground for a moment, not sure what to do. He actually seemed to have an embarrassed look on his face as he finally conceded to his error of proffered friendship. He whimpered again, then let out a feeble bark and returned to the house with his tail between his legs.

I was still chuckling to myself when the voice thanked me from directly behind me, causing me to jump.

"Oh, I'm sorry," she said quickly. "I didn't mean to scare you."

It was Elsha! My back was still to her, so she probably didn't know who I was. *Of course she doesn't, or she wouldn't be talking to me!*

I quickly regained my composure and shrugged my shoulders. "It's all right," I said without turning around. "How may I help you?"

"I'm not sure you can. I'm very sorry for intruding on you, but isn't this Helorum's home, or am I mistaken?"

"You are not mistaken. This *is* the home of Helorum and Aiya. I'm just a guest of theirs. Did you need to speak with Helorum? I could introduce you."

She placed a gentle hand on my shoulder, and I fairly melted. "Oh, would you be so kind? I'm afraid his dog won't let me near the house."

"I will on one condition," I offered.

Her hand left my shoulder. She hesitated for a few seconds before speaking. "What condition?" she asked cautiously.

"You must promise not to be angry at me . . . for whatever reason."

"Why should I be angry with you?" she asked from behind me. "I don't even know you."

I folded my arms resolutely. "That's the condition. That's all I ask. Take it, and I promise I'll do everything in my power to help you with anything you need. Leave it, and you're on your own with Helorum's wolf-dog."

He wasn't really a wolf-dog, but I thought the sound of it might encourage Elsha to accept my mandate. Kateph did look fierce, but I had learned by experience he was all bark and no bite.

She playfully poked a finger between my shoulder blades. "Be careful what you promise, kind sir," she said lightly. "The help I need may not be something you want to volunteer for."

If she only knew! Just the sound of her voice and the fact that she was freely conversing with me had me so elated I was sure I was still in bed dreaming. But despite the levity in her voice, there was an underlying worry in it, a tone which belied anxiety and dread, and I knew she was not simply here for a cordial visit. There was something wrong, and I felt willing—no, compelled, obligated to help—even if it meant delaying the search for my parents.

"Be that as it may," I continued, "my father raised me to be a man of honor, and if I say I am willing to help you, it is not meant as a flippant or trite remark. Nor is it condescending. I feel a gentleman should always help anyone in distress, especially a beautiful young woman."

What was I saying? It was too late, I had already said it. I felt my face flushing with embarrassment, and was very glad my back was still to Elsha.

A moment passed before she spoke. "Thank you. I feel I can trust you . . ." She drew out the last word as if asking me to fill in the rest.

"Gideon," I said.

"I feel I can trust you, Gideon. But I'm still somewhat confused as to why I would ever be mad at you. You seem quite the gentleman."

"That is an answer you'll know soon enough. Do you agree to my condition?"

She reached around to offered her hand to one side of me and said, "I agree."

I took her hand and repeated, "And you promise not to be angry with me?"

"Yes, of course."

Holding her hand, I turned around and smiled sheepishly. Her arresting limpid green eyes did not indicate that she recognized me. Maybe it was because I was no longer wearing a headband and was wearing differ-ent clothes, or maybe it was because it was still fairly dark in the stall. Perhaps it was because I had conversed with her so openly that the Gideon she knew from the market place was the last person she expected me to be. Whatever the reason, Elsha smiled ever so prettily, causing my knees to weaken and my heart to thump loudly against my chest. And those eyes! They were doing it again. The mysterious warmth that radi-ated from them was more enchanting than a sorcerer's talisman. I took in her disheveled hair, her rumpled clothing, and smudged face with eager relish, and it didn't even register that her less-than-ideal appearance was probably a source of embarrassment to her. Even in her bedraggled state, Elsha was beautiful.

We stood there silently holding hands as we looked into each other eyes. I could not bring myself to lead her to Helorum's house because it would mean letting go of her hand. I could have stood there staring at her perfect face and hypnotic eyes for the rest of eternity. That she felt the same about me I highly doubted.

Finally, she softly cleared her throat and looked at my hand grasping hers. I snapped out of my dreamlike trance and released my grip.

"Sorry," I said awkwardly. "I didn't mean to . . . well . . . let's go find Helorum."

She stepped through the railing and we walked out into the sunlight.

She gasped, recognizing me instantly, and the look in her eyes snapped from warming to chilling. She froze in her tracks and put her clenched fists on her hips. She opened her mouth to speak, probably to hurl some acrid curse at me, but I spoke first.

"You promised, Elsha. You said you wouldn't be mad at me."

She stewed in her silence as she continued to glare at me. Then, rather calmly, she said, "Do you always make a habit of deceiving young women?"

Her question struck me like a fist to the stomach. I flinched, visibly offended.

She continued before I could answer. "First you lead me to believe you're mute, twice I might add, then you trick me into a promise I have every right to break. Why should I feel anything else but anger toward you?"

125

"Elsha, believe me, none of that was intentional," I stammered.

"Oh, really," she snapped, not as a question.

I sighed heavily, put my hands in my pockets, and stared at my feet.

"Honestly, I wish there was some way to start over," I said. "I swear I didn't mean to deceive you or lead you to believe anything that's not true. And I am truly sorry if I have offended you, Elsha. It's the last thing I'd ever want to do."

She stuck a finger forcefully in my chest. "And that's another thing. How do you know my name? Have you been spying on me? Checking up on me?"

I looked into her translucent green eyes, which had thankfully softened some. "No, not really. That man who pulled me away from your father's booth, the bald one with beady eyes, he told me. He also told me about your mother. Again, I am very sorry."

She looked vacantly to one side as she remembered the events of that day. A profound sadness veiled her countenance as tears brimmed on her dark lashes. I wanted more than anything to reach out to her, to hold her and comfort her. But I knew that action would have been misconstrued as something else at that moment. I simply lowered my eyes and waited for her response. She shook her head quickly and wiped the tears away. Then she turned back to me, and looked me over from head to toe.

"You're not . . . one of *them* . . . are you?" she asked, a careful challenge in her voice.

"Absolutely not," I almost shouted, with fists clenched. "Those men are responsible for the loss of my parents too. I would no sooner join them than—"

She reached out and grabbed my sleeve tenderly.

"Your parents weren't . . . killed, were they?" she asked with the most sincere, heartfelt compassion in her voice.

At first I thought she was mocking me, but the look in her eyes told me otherwise.

I shook my head. "They're being held captive. That's all I know. I came to Helorum to get help, same as you, only . . . I've come here before, this is my second or third time, and I still don't have much to go on."

She stood her ground, sizing me up. I shrugged my shoulders and forced my hands deep into my pockets again. I tried to look sincere, but had a bad feeling that I looked more pathetic than anything else. Finally, Elsha's eyes softened as she turned up her hands.

"I guess I believe you, Gideon," she conceded. "And I am sorry about your parents. But I still don't like the way you deceived me earlier."

"But *you* said I was mute, not me."

"I'm not talking about that," she said moving past me. "You tricked me into promising not to be mad at you, even though I'd truly like to be."

There was a hopeful playfulness in her voice, but I decided not to press my luck by speaking. I lowered my eyes, nodded my agreement, and let her pass. Things were looking up, if only slightly, and I knew my inexperience in communicating with women would shatter our fragile relationship the second I opened my mouth. Whatever I said, no matter how sincere my delivery, it would not come out right.

Kateph had disappeared. As Elsha and I entered the house, we smelled Aiya cooking something wonderful in the kitchen. The shepherd's wife looked into the main room and smiled at the two of us, but then returned to her cooking with nothing more than a brief nod.

I leaned over to Elsha. "Have you met Aiya before?"

She shook her head.

We sat silently at the table for a few awkward moments. Then Elsha softly asked what had happened to my parents. I told her about everything that had transpired in the past couple of weeks, though I didn't go into much detail about Helorum's revelation about me, thinking it might come across as too egocentric.

The more she understood all that I had lost, and how desperately alone I was, the more her demeanor softened into the angel with which I had fallen in love. Then I mentioned how I had come to Helorum to ask for his help in going to look for my parents near Nephihah.

"But that's where *my* father is," she gasped.

"In Nephihah?"

"Yes. There's a prison there where he's being held captive by the Gadiantons."

127

"The who?"

"The Gadianton Robbers. Surely you've heard of them before, espe-cially if they are the ones who took your mother and father."

"But I thought they were called King Men," I explained.

"Well, maybe a few still are. But since Gadianton took over, people are calling them Gadianton Robbers instead. The King Men are thought to be all wiped out, but I believe that that is just part of the Gadianton's ruse."

"That is what I have heard, too," Helorum said as he entered the room.

I rose to my feet. "I'm sorry if we awakened you, Helorum," I said quickly.

"No, no, Gideon. It was Aiya's cooking that woke me. Please, sit down."

I did and smiled at Elsha. She actually smiled back with a spark of hope in her eyes, which made me smile even more. Aiya then brought in a large plate loaded with rice fried in some sort of sweet-smelling sauce and riddled with shrimp and cashews, and what looked like sliced water chestnuts. Elsha's eyes lit up when she saw the food, and it occurred to me that, as she was on the run, she probably hadn't eaten in a while.

I softly cleared my throat. "Helorum and Aiya, I'd like for you to meet Elsha, daughter of Ashod, an exceptionally gifted jeweler from Bountiful."

Elsha looked at me queerly as if to ask how I knew so much. She then extended her hand to the old shepherd and smiled.

"I am happy to meet you, sir."

"I thought I heard someone with you, Gideon," Helorum said, not taking her hand. Elsha awkwardly withdrew her proffered hand and slipped it under the table. She turned and asked me with her eyes why I had not mentioned his blindness.

"She's a vision," Aiya said with honest praise. Then to Elsha, "If you are a friend of Gideon's, you're always welcome here, my dear."

"Thank you," Elsha said timidly.

Helorum asked for a moment of silence while he blessed the food, then served out generous portions to both Elsha and myself. Elsha dove right in, then softly asked why Aiya had prepared so much to eat.

"You'll see," I whispered back. "His name is Noah."

"Noah is not here right now," Helorum said through a mouthful of rice. He swallowed and continued speaking. "He left late last night to find out if the other saints are ready to leave. Rumor has it the Gadiantons might try to stop us, and we want to go as quickly as possible to avoid bloodshed."

"Bloodshed? But what about the Nephite army?" Elsha asked.

Helorum nodded. "There might be a few soldiers who could help, but most are away fighting the Lamanites. The trouble is, the Gadiantons are considered a domestic problem, not a national threat, so it falls to the local government to solve."

"A lot of good that does. Isn't the local government pretty much run by the King Men—or the Gadiantons?" I asked, still not used to the name change.

"Yes, that's true," Helorum answered, taking another spoonful of rice.

"Then . . . who regulates the government?" I pondered out loud.

"The church is supposed to," Elsha answered. "The reign of church judges was set up to see that God's laws were being upheld through the government's laws. There is supposed to be a church court system, which goes all the way to the prophet if need be, through which any issue not settled at the government level can be resolved. That way, no matter who is in power, the highest authority is still God. The problem is, many of our current leaders have managed to separate the church from the affairs of state, and have usurped power from church control by appointing their own tainted judges who never call on the prophets for help with moral decisions. That is how evil leaders like Kishkumen and Gadianton have gained so much power. They are protected by the government because the church never has the chance to get involved with state appointments or any lawmaking decisions. Basically, the government has removed the need for God in our lives. That's why we are falling into corruption. The same thing happened in King Noah's days. Why people can't see something so obvious I'll never understand."

Helorum leaned forward and stared at Elsha with his sightless eyes. "You have an amazing spirit about you, young lady. Such depth of wisdom and strength of conviction is refreshing in a youth. I feel there is more to you than meets the eye."

Elsha humbly thanked him. Then Helorum turned to me and said, "You have an unusually wise and intelligent girlfriend, Gideon. You are a very fortunate young man."

Elsha glowered at me, as if I had put the 'girlfriend' idea into his head.

"She is very intelligent," I quickly said, "but she is not really my girlfriend."

Helorum sat back, a look of confused mirth on his face. "Why not?"

I blushed as I fumbled for an answer. The truth is, I didn't want to come up with a reason, because I enjoyed the idea immensely. But I knew if I didn't say something, Elsha would never forgive me. She undoubtedly loathed the idea.

"It's a long story," I finally said. "Besides, she came here to ask your help with something."

"Oh?" the shepherd said. "And what would that be?"

Elsha was suddenly near tears, and her angst choked her voice. "My father always told me you were a private man, but one with great influence in the church. And . . . I didn't know where else to go. I am sorry if I have assumed too much by bothering you."

Helorum reached over and patted her hand. "You are here, and it is no bother. Now, how can I help?"

She was wracked with a momentary sob before she gained enough composure to speak. "My mother was killed by the Gadiantons."

"Yes, I know," the old shepherd said tenderly.

She nodded and wiped away her tears. "I thought you might. But now my father is being held captive in Nephihah. I don't even know if he is still alive. I don't know where to turn. I don't know what to do."

Elsha buried her face in her hands and shuddered. Her battle to control her emotions was more than I could bear to watch. My heart went out to her. I wanted so much to console her, to reach over and put a caring arm around her. My own eyes burned with tears as my problems simply vanished. I wholly, truly sympathized with this beautiful young woman beside me. Then I noticed Helorum was again looking at me with a sly smirk on his lips. For the life of me, I could not tell what this old man could find amusing at this moment.

Elsha continued to cry into her hands, unable to bring her emotions under control. My heart literally ached watching her plead for help, begging for an answer that would show her she was not alone. Yet Helorum just sat there saying nothing, and Aiya was nowhere to be seen. Without thinking, I scooted closer to Elsha and gently put my arm around her.

"It'll be all right, Elsha," I said softly. "You're with friends now."

To my great surprise and total elation, Elsha leaned into me and put her head against my shoulder. Her sobbing stopped, but she was still trembling with spent emotion. I gave her shoulder a light, caring squeeze and said, "Please don't worry. We promise we'll help all we can."

Helorum still had the smirk on his face as I waited for him to say something. Finally, I got frustrated and said, "Helorum, Elsha is in need of our help."

"Oh, she'll get plenty of good help, never fear," the old shepherd said, returning to his plate of food.

Assuming Elsha might not fully understand Helorum's cryptic words, I said, "That's good news." Then, squeezing her shoulder again, I said, "Elsha, if Helorum says he'll help, then rest assured he'll do everything he—"

"Hold on, Gideon," Helorum interrupted. "I said nothing about *me* helping her. I simply do not have time. Aiya and I will be leaving with the saints tomorrow. I have promised to accompany them, and have many obligations toward them."

Elsha lifted her head from my shoulder with a panic-stricken look. I had been certain Helorum would help. He had all but said it. But now he contradicted himself by saying she was on her own.

"But you said you'd help her," I stammered.

"No, *you* said I would," Helorum corrected. "I said she'd have help. Good help. Even though I'd like to, I personally can't take the time. I'm very sorry."

"But if you can't help me, then who will?" Elsha asked in a hoarse voice.

The shepherd pointed at me. "He will."

Elsha's head jerked around to face me. She was not smiling. I opened my mouth to protest, but Helorum held up his hand, cutting me off.

"Are you not going that way yourself, Gideon?" Helorum asked.

"Well yes, but my parents are in Limhi, not Nephihah."

"And how far is Limhi from Nephihah?"

I shrugged my shoulders. "About three or four miles I guess."

"Then you will get Elsha's father first, then you can find your own parents," the shepherd said matter-of-factly.

I gawked at him and noticed Elsha was doing the same. "But Helorum, I am not a one-man army. How am I supposed to pull off these miraculous rescues alone?"

He sighed and leaned back in his chair. "Gideon, you must have more faith. What do you suppose young King David thought when he went up against Goliath?"

"Probably the same thing I thought when I met your friend Noah," I said with half a chuckle.

Helorum nodded. "But did he shy from his responsibility?"

"No."

"Why am I suddenly Gideon's responsibility?" Elsha asked, a little perturbed. "What if I want to find someone else to help?"

"Because Gideon is your responsibility as well," Helorum responded.

Elsha and I looked at each other with bewilderment, neither of us knowing what to say. What exactly was Helorum talking about?

Helorum cleared his throat and paused to organize his words so they would come out right. He then smiled and said, "It often amazes me how I can see things more clearly than those with perfect eyesight." Then, more solemnly, "Alone, you each have a strength sufficient for your needs. But together your strengths become something very powerful. And I'm not simply talking about physical strength."

"What then?" I asked.

"Intelligence, wisdom, cunning. And the Spirit of God. Remember, Gideon, with God all—"

"All things are possible," Elsha finished the sentence.

Helorum nodded again. "Now, you are welcome to gather whatever you need from my supplies. But I suggest you do so quickly. Time is short, and I have much to do myself."

I looked at Elsha, not knowing where to start. She continued to stare at Helorum, disbelief in her eyes. Then she leaned forward and bowed her head as if in prayer. I got up and went into the library. My mind was in such a state that I wasn't sure if I had heard everything correctly. Somehow, it all made sense, but the structure and logic behind it eluded me. Then Elsha was beside me.

"We'd better hurry," she said resolutely.

"But Elsha, I'm not sure I understand how we're supposed to—"

"Gideon, listen. I don't understand how we're supposed to do this either. But my father always taught me to trust in our church leaders because they have been given a special spirit of discernment on behalf of the saints. If Helorum says it will work out, then it will. No argument. If we doubt, then we'll fail. So let's go and just do it."

If I'd had warm feelings for this young woman before, they were now a hundredfold greater. I thought I had faith, but the courage and unabashed trust Elsha displayed made me ashamed to call myself a member of the church. She was right. It was as simple as that. We had just been told by a man who had perfect communication with God that we were to go rescue our parents. How, did not matter . . . much. Blind faith can lead to disaster, so the Lord expects us to use our own wisdom, strength, and common sense to do much of what He asks of us. But if He said "Go," then go we would.

I only wished I had come to that conclusion before Elsha had.

ThirTeen

"May I ask one favor, Helorum?" Elsha voiced timidly.

"Of course," the old shepherd answered.

"My father said you were the patriarch in this city and thus had a unique communication with God. He suggested I should contact you at some time to receive a special blessing from you. In light of our circumstances, I think now is as good a time as any. Would you please give me a blessing before we go?"

Helorum smiled and nodded. "I would be honored." He then turned to me. "How about you, Gideon?"

"I'm sure it would help," I said.

Helorum pulled out a chair and asked Elsha to sit in front of him. He placed his hands on her head and pronounced a blessing of health, peace of mind, and freedom from harm. Curiously, he said nothing about rescuing Ashod, her father. Then he said something that shocked me to the extent that I thought at first he must have been joking.

Helorum told Elsha that the Lord had a special calling for her, and that many generations would call her name blessed because she chose to risk her life on the open sea to preserve her Nephite lineage. It was almost the same words as in my revelation.

I couldn't help but look up in the middle of the prayer and stare at this patriarch of God who was blessing Elsha. Had I heard him correctly? If so, did that mean . . . ?

No, I was imagining things again. Wishful thinking. It probably meant she was going to sail away with Hagoth and his group.

When Helorum finished, he bade me sit in front of him and gave me a blessing with some of the same words in it that were in my revelation. He also said that I would be an instrument in God's hands in fulfilling a great prophecy that would have an impact on all the world. Helorum also blessed me that I would be successful in my quest, but reminded me to constantly remember what the Lord had in mind for me, and that I was not to counsel the Lord but to take counsel from Him. I was promised that I would be guided in all things if I took the time to ponder and to pray. I'm sure Elsha was curious, maybe even impressed by the tenor of the blessing, but she gave no indication of that when the old patriarch finished.

Aiya then took Elsha to the cave behind their home to prepare some things for our journey. Helorum and I sat down in his library to discuss my plans for rescuing my parents and Ashod. But all I could think about was the blessings we had just received.

"How come you never told me you were a patriarch?" I asked.

Helorum shrugged. "There are many things about me you do not know. Besides, a calling from the Lord is not something you flaunt with worldly pride. Anyway, I thought you knew, because you didn't question the first blessing I gave you."

"Blessing? I thought it was a revelation."

"That's what a blessing from a patriarch is—a one-time revelation to a single individual containing admonitions and promises regarding their future."

I scratched my head, determined not to get confused. "If it's a one-time thing, what about the blessing you just gave me?"

An embarrassed look spread across his face and he softly said, "I was thinking of it more as . . . a father's blessing."

I winced, then softened. A tight constriction suddenly gripped my throat. Did Helorum really care for me that much? I couldn't think of what to say, and even if I could, I wouldn't have been able to speak. I somehow managed to thank him as I wiped at my burning eyes. Helorum also had tears running from his sightless eyes as the two of us sat in awkward silence for a few moments. I loved my father dearly and no one would ever take his place in my heart, but I had grown so close to this old man who had given me fatherly counsel and love over the past few weeks. I found myself swelling with pleasure, and not a little pride, at the thought of him as my father.

That is what patriarch means—a father. But this was more than simply a church calling, much more. I thought how my father would like to meet Helorum when this was all over. The two of them would become fast friends, of that I was certain. But it also occurred to me that, in light of my blessing and revelation, they may never get the chance to meet.

I looked at Helorum with a heartfelt warmth burning within me. This man had done so much for me, a stranger who stumbled into his sheep stall trying to escape from evil men. He owed me nothing, yet had given me so much. I owed him everything, yet had nothing to offer him. It saddened me to think on it.

As if reading my thoughts, Helorum said, "Do not worry about repaying me for anything I may have shared with you, Gideon. It has been a privilege and a blessing I have been looking forward to for a long time."

Emotion again clenched my throat, making it difficult to speak. "Why me? I have done nothing for you."

Helorum smiled. "Oh, but you have. You have fulfilled a prophecy in my own patriarchal blessing, one even I was beginning to doubt would come to pass."

"What? How could I—"

Helorum held up a consoling hand. "Do not dwell on it, Gideon. It is not important for you to know the details. Suffice it to say I have been blessed by your presence, and I thank you from the depths of my soul."

But I couldn't simply leave it hanging there. What was this man of God really saying? How could I have such an extraordinary impact on his incredible life? I was just an ordinary man; a boatwright, like my father. Nothing more.

"Helorum, please," I said softly. "You have done so much for me, and I feel I've done nothing for you. Please, at least let me know how I have helped you, if only for my own peace of mind."

Helorum rubbed his whiskers thoughtfully. Then he leaned back and laced his fingers behind his head. He looked heavenward and sighed deeply.

"You are familiar with the teachings of King Benjamin," he began, "of that I am confident. But do you know much of the king's family?"

I shrugged my shoulders. "He had a few sons, three I think, and one or two daughters."

The old shepherd smiled. "And what became of his sons, do you know?"

"His eldest, Mosiah, became a great king, like he was."

He sighed again, a look of sorrow crossing his brow. "That is correct. But what about the other two? Did they follow after Mosiah and help in his administrations?"

"I don't know."

Helorum suddenly pounded a fist against the table as his voice raised painfully in a tremulous sob. A look of shame distorted his face, and he appeared to be suffering from an emotional burden that was more than a man could bear. He didn't look directly at me, but stared blankly at the table top, as if I was no longer in the room and he was pouring out his soul to a spiritual confessor.

"They did not!" Helorum cried wearily. "They were wrapped up in jealous envy, and were blinded to the spiritual guidance of their father. King Benjamin conferred everything on his son Mosiah. Everything—the kingship and all the political rights and privileges of the kingdom, the sacred Nephite records, the plates of brass, the sword of Laban, the compass they called Liahona—everything. And how do you think the other two sons felt about that? Did they see the wisdom in it? Did they see that it was the will of the Lord and not simply the wishes of an old, doting father? They did not. They foolishly rebelled and left the church, and caused many others to stray from the truth, to reject the very word of God."

I watched as this wonderful old man shuddered with pent-up emotion, wracked by someone else's ancient misdeed that to this day plagued his soul and made him miserable. I didn't answer his questions, as they were rhetorical. He was simply venting his anger toward these young men, but I didn't understand why he was doing so.

"It was such a waste, such a foolish waste of young life," Helorum said, continuing to talk to himself. "And to drag so many other souls with them, not only by their bad example but by their hateful, jealous words."

He paused and sighed deeply, painfully. Then, "One of the young men finally saw the error of his ways and came back to the church. Thank the Lord for that lad's penitent soul."

"And the other?"

"It took an act of God to convince the other to repent."

He shook his head slowly and wiped remorseful tears from his eyes.

"So they both eventually came back into the church?" I asked gently, confused by his display of bitterness and sorrow.

He nodded. "Eventually. But not without payment. Not without penance."

"What penance?"

He looked up at me with an expression that once more made me wonder if he truly was without sight.

"An act of God, Gideon. That's what it took, in spite of all the admonitions of King Benjamin, his father, to study the scriptures and remain faithful to the church. Can you guess what God's punishment was?"

I shook my head. "Except for Mosiah, I don't even know what the names of the other son's were."

The old shepherd smiled an awkward, almost embarrassed grin. "King Benjamin's three sons were named Mosiah, Helaman, . . . and Helorum."

This old man, this patriarch and man of God, this dear friend was the once rebellious son of King Benjamin. I shook my head to wipe the confusing thought from my mind. I could not imagine Helorum as an enemy to the church, yet he had just confessed as much. The origin of his blindness suddenly became clear to me.

"You were struck blind by God?" I breathed.

"Yes," he answered humbly. "But in becoming blind, my eyes were opened. I knew that I had offended the Lord. I knew that I had wronged the church, and I was deeply ashamed that I had disgraced my father's name. I thank God for Mosiah and his faithfulness. I thank God for the darkness that allowed me to see the light. I thank God for the sacrifice of His son Jesus, which allowed a sinner like me to be forgiven of the error of his ways."

"But if you repented and were forgiven, why are you still blind?" I asked.

"Because I needed to be," Helorum said plainly. "Blindness allowed me to see. I am afraid that if I had been returned to my whole state, especially back then, I would have eventually been led down the path of darkness again by jealousy and covetousness. I needed something to remind me of how fragile and helpless the soul is to the incessant buffeting of Satan. So, when I heard the voice of the Lord saying my sins were forgiven, I knew that I needed to remain in my weakened state as a reminder to always be obedient to the will of God.

"Do you understand what I am saying, my young friend? I am grateful, truly grateful, and have never once regretted my curse. In fact, thinking back, it was almost as if I had asked for my blindness to remain."

"Why? Wasn't the experience alone enough to convince you?"

"No, Gideon, it wasn't. You must remember, I was an impressionable lad of fifteen then. I was the son of a king that everyone loved. I was coming into manhood and had a lot to prove to the world. I was very egocentric and had plans for my upcoming greatness. I was going to be revered throughout history. You can't fulfill those kind of dreams if your father places all the authority and glories on your older brother . . . or so I thought."

I was speechless. I did not condemn this humbled man, but rather grew in admiration and love for him. I left my chair and wrapped my arms around him. He returned my embrace and began to shudder again. I held him some time as we both struggled to control our emotions. We became closer than any father and son had ever become. But in spite of the new Helorum my eyes had been opened to—the son of King Benjamin, now a patriarch of the church—I still had to know why I was so important to his life.

He answered me in a reverent tone. "Because I have had the chance to point you on a very important path you probably would not have found on your own."

140

"If this path is so important, why can't you take it instead of me? You are certainly more worthy."

"Because I could never fulfill it completely. You see, I am going to die on this journey."

"No!" I gasped.

He held up a quieting hand and smiled. "I am a very old man, Gideon. Even though my mind is still fairly sharp, my body is rickety and feeble. I have known for some time that I must join my fathers to rest in the earth, and I am not afraid. I fear for Aiya, but know she will be provided for. The Lord has assured me of that. But my one wish has always been to play a part in preserving the Nephite people for their divine calling in preparing the world for the restoration of all things before the Lord's second coming. The Nephites are a beautiful and blessed people, but they will fall from the grace of God because of prosperity, greed, and lusts of the flesh. It has always been so, and their chosen status will not protect them from wandering down that worldly path. They will be wiped out by the Lamanites a few hundred years after the Savior visits this land. It has been prophesied by our forefathers, and I have also seen it. But a few Nephites must survive to fulfill the greater prophecy, the one concerning their part in the second coming. And, like it or not, Gideon, you are one of those who must survive. You and Elsha."

And I thought my mind was whirling before! This was more than I could absorb, let alone comprehend. My offspring were to be responsible for the preparation of the Lord's return? What kind of unrequested responsibility did that place on me and how I reared my children? I would need to teach them history, economics, horticulture, animal husbandry, medicine, art, and more importantly, the gospel of our Lord. I knew the scriptures, but didn't have them memorized by any means. More to the point, I didn't even have any children yet, let alone a wife. How was I to fulfill these great expectations?

Once again, I felt as if I would have been better off not knowing these important things. Ignorance can be blissful after all.

I didn't know what to say to my patriarch and my friend, Helorum. I sat numbly, staring at nothing, trying to make sense of my chaotic thoughts. There was so much to yet learn, so much to discover and profit by, but I had no more time. Elsha and I were to leave in a matter of minutes.

All that was left was to say good-bye. I tried desperately to find the best way to express myself, but came up mute. I loved this man as my own father, and the thought that he would soon die burdened my heart with a heaviness I had never known before. I felt hot tears trace down my cheeks as I looked at the friend I was just beginning to know. I wondered if he would ever understand how much he meant to me, and how much I would miss him. He slowly nodded, as if reading my thoughts, and said without words that he indeed understood, and that he loved me too.

I choked down a sob in my throat and said, "Helorum, I . . . I want you to know . . ."

He reached over and gripped my arm. "It is all right, Gideon. You need say nothing, my son. I understand. I have never been good at farewells either."

We embraced again, and this time it was he who consoled me.

Elsha entered the room and said she was ready to leave. She hugged Helorum and Aiya, and wiped back painful tears. We stood in humbled silence for a moment as we shook hands and shared hugs again.

"I won't say good-bye," Helorum said gruffly, "I don't know how to. But I can admonish you one last time to counsel with the Lord in all your doings and He will direct you for good. Now, go with God, my children."

"Go with God," I said hoarsely.

"Thank you," Elsha said with emotion, and hugged Aiya again.

We left the house and donned the two packs that Aiya and Elsha had prepared. We walked away in silence, not knowing exactly where we were going, or how we were going to accomplish the seemingly impossible tasks before us. The only comfort I felt at the moment was that Elsha was by my side, and she was depending on me. That alone kept me going as I silently struggled with the powerful emotions that beset my heart and mind.

"Elsha, there's something I must ask you before we get much further," I said timidly.

She looked at me—almost through me—with those beautiful eyes of hers, and arched her eyebrows in a way that bade me to continue.

"This might sound a bit confusing, but I want you to understand something . . . before it's too late."

"All right," she said.

I cleared my throat and took a deep breath. "I want you to know I'm helping you out because I truly want to. As I said before, my father taught me to always do what I can to help those in need, and the fact that I consider you a friend makes it that much more important to me. But I'm also doing it because I feel it's partly my fault your father is being held in prison."

Elsha stopped in her tracks and stared at me. "How can it be your fault?" she asked, openly confused.

"Because I insulted, and sort of threatened, that rude bald guy at the marketplace, and I fear he has taken it out on your family. I'm sorry for what I have done, Elsha. I truly am."

We continued down the trail toward Nephihah in silence for a time. I had chosen this trail because it was one not frequently traveled, yet it ran almost exactly parallel with the main road to that city. A drizzle of rain moistened the ground and slowed our progress, but it also helped to mask our presence, and stealth was something we wanted to maintain. What were we going to do when we got to Nephihah? I did not know, but I felt assured we would be given a clue. I had mentioned my concerns to Elsha because I wasn't all that confident in my ability to rescue her father from the clutches of the Gadianton Robbers, in their own stronghold no less. That she had not given an immediate response created a huge knot in my stomach, as I thought she was angry with me again.

Finally, Elsha broke the silence by saying, "I appreciate your honesty, Gideon, but I don't think you had anything to do with my father's imprisonment. The Gadiantons put an impossible tax on the merchants in and around Bountiful, and my father finally had enough. When he refused to pay, they took him away. There was nothing I could do to stop them. That's why I went to Helorum's for help, and he asked you to help me, which you graciously accepted. You were at the wrong place at the wrong time, so it is I who should be apologizing to you."

143

At first I thought Elsha was mocking me, but the sincerity on her lovely face told me otherwise. Fortunately, I had enough presence of mind to simply thank her.

That evening I found a small cave in which to camp for the night. We both wanted to keep moving, to get to Nephihah before anything unspeakable happened to Ashod, but fatigue was exacting a brutal toll on our bodies and minds, and we both agreed it was best to get some rest so our minds would be clear the following day.

To my absolute delight, Elsha and Aiya had filled our packs with plenty of food, light cooking utensils, and other supplies necessary for living on the trail. I offered to do some hunting to supplement our stores, but Elsha thought it best to stay low and remain undetected, as other people—good and bad—might be traveling along the same path. For the same reason, I suggested we not light a fire, but simply eat from the dried goods in our packs.

After a light meal of seasoned meat and dried fruit, we laid down on separate blankets and listened to the soft patter of rain on the ferns at the cave's entrance. It was dark, but not impossible to see vague shapes of gray and black. I laid on my back and laced my fingers behind my head as a makeshift pillow. I was about to drift off, letting my body succumb to the emotional and physical fatigue built up over the past few weeks when Elsha spoke.

"Gideon?" she said softly. Her voice had such a lyrical quality to it that I smiled broadly in the darkness.

"Yes."

"I'm sorry for misjudging you earlier."

"Oh, it's all right. You had every reason to do so."

She chuckled lightly, playfully. "Yes, I did. But I shouldn't have."

"I forgive you."

I heard her move, then felt a gentle kiss on my cheek. "Thank you," she said sincerely.

"You're welcome," I said, utterly surprised to find my tongue working.

I heard her turn away and adjust her blanket. Soon I heard the deep breathing that accompanied a person's sleep. I was glad Elsha was able to drop off so easily. She desperately needed the rest. Tomorrow was going to be an interesting and potentially disheartening day, to say the least.

As for me, sleep seemed to ignore me, in spite of my fatigue. I lay there in the darkness and touched the place on my cheek where she had kissed me. I sighed, certain I had that silly grin on my face again.

PART TWO

RESCUE & REUNION

FOURTEEN

Nephihah was a large city but not as well organized as Bountiful. That was to our advantage. We were able to mingle among the citizens like typical commoners, looking every bit the part of carefree youth or vacationers seeking excitement. I had suggested to Elsha that we not skulk around, but rather walk right down main street and enjoy the scenery. I doubted very much that we would be recognized, as neither one of us had ever been there before, and assured her of my confidence in remaining unnoticed. She agreed to trust my instincts, which made my heart swell with pride.

"Hey Gideon!" someone shouted from the crowd in front of us.

My pride immediately wilted as panic made my heart skip a beat. Elsha grabbed my arm tightly as a large man made his way through the crowd, coming directly toward us. I tried to look casual and pulled Elsha to one side to look at some silk scarves and shawls being offered by a merchant. A middle-aged woman began holding up some of the finery, letting Elsha examine the ultra smooth texture and delightful colors of each piece.

We were both hoping the stranger would pass us by, that he had been calling after another Gideon, or that he would lose us as we mingled with the other patrons at the merchant's stand.

It didn't work.

A heavy hand gripped my shoulder. "I never expected to see you here, Gideon," the man said from behind me.

I clenched my fist, making ready to spin around and smash the stranger in the jaw, but then decided that would attract more attention than we wanted. I whispered to Elsha to keep looking at the shawls as I slowly turned around.

"Do I know you?" I asked as I rotated my head to look into the stranger's face.

He turned out to be no stranger. It was Corianton.

"Of course you know me," he said with a slight chuckle. "And I know exactly who you are, Gideon, son of Hezikiah, shipbuilder from Mulek."

I took his arm and led him away from Elsha and the rest of the crowd to a bench a few paces away. As I did so, I eased the Nubian dagger from a pocket inside my tunic and held it against my forearm so that he could not see it.

"Look, Corianton," I began rather forcefully, "If you're here to arrest me you're going to have a little problem."

Still gripping his arm firmly, I pressed the point of the dagger against his ribs in a way that no one else could see it. He flinched and looked down at the weapon poised to pierce his lungs.

"Do you understand?" I asked with more than a little hate in my voice.

To my surprise, Corianton smiled broadly and clasped a hand on my shoulder. "You are definitely the son of Hezikiah."

I pressed the point a bit harder into his side but didn't say anything.

"Ouch, hey, all right," he said, lifting his hand from my shoulder. "Calm down, Gideon. I am not here to arrest you, I swear."

Still holding the dagger to his ribs, I indicated the bench, and we sat down slowly.

"Then what do you want with me?" I asked cautiously.

"Nothing, Gideon. I was simply surprised to see you in this city, that's all. Nephihah is not what you'd call the most attractive city for a faithful member of the church. Or the safest. What are you doing here anyway?"

"Just act casual and let me ask the questions for now," I said, applying more pressure to the dagger at his ribs.

"Sure, fine," he said, looking at the passing people instead of at me. "But let me reiterate that I'm not here to arrest you. I know you didn't kill that judge in Moroni. I've done a lot of searching over the past few weeks and found out a lot of things that point to your innocence. In fact, I'm no longer Chief Law Officer of the Coastal Cities area. I was fired because I wouldn't conform to the ways of the Gadiantons."

I stared at him in disbelief. "Then what are you doing here?"

"I'm on an errand for my cousin Hagoth, trying to gather as many faithful members of the church as I can. He sails in just a few days, you know."

His story matched what Helorum had told me, and I felt I could believe him. I put my dagger away as I said, "I am sorry about not trusting you, Corianton. I wasn't sure if you were still a King Man, or a Gadianton."

He winced. "I never was a King Man! What gave you that melon-headed idea?"

"Well, you did come with Kumran to arrest me that one night," I reasoned.

"No, I didn't. I came to ask you some questions, remember?"

I reviewed that evening in my mind, and decided he was right. He had asked that I not leave the city, but he hadn't actually put me under arrest.

I shrugged. "But why were you working for the King Men then?"

"I wasn't. Kumran claimed to be a witness to your crime. I was just doing my job and following all the leads I got. As it turns out, the more I looked into the matter, the more convinced I was of your innocence. It was the King Men who wanted you silenced." He scratched the stubble on his jaw. "I'm not so sure that they weren't the ones who did the deed in the first place."

"That's what I tried to tell you before."

He nodded. "I know. But enough of that. I am here gathering what's left of the saints who want to escape the influence of the Gadiantons and go to a new land. But I'm afraid I'm not having much success. Most of the members of the church here have come to tolerate the Gadiantons, and seem to enjoy the worldly things they provide."

"Then you better get back to Bountiful. Hagoth is leaving tomorrow."

"I know that, too. I'm going to meet them on the road to the west coast. It'll save me a full day's travel at least."

We sat in silence for a moment before he turned to me and said, "What I can't figure out is what *you* are doing here. Even though I am no longer looking for you, I'm sure the Gadiantons are."

"I am helping a young woman find her father. I doubt anyone here will recognize me, and besides, I thought the Gadianton fortress was in Limhi."

Corianton gave a low whistle. "You've been doing your homework. The main fortress is in Limhi, and it's a place I would not want to enter. Bad things happen in there—secret combinations and occult rituals, sacrifices and unspeakable evils. You'd best stay away if you can. But make no mistake about Nephihah either, Kishkumen basically owns this city."

"All the more reason I need to help my friend quickly find her father."

"Is the young beauty with the auburn hair whom you were with a moment ago your friend?"

I nodded. "Her father was taken by the Gadiantons, and we think he's somewhere here in Nephihah. His name is Ashod."

Corianton scratched his jaw again and looked around thoughtfully. "I don't know the name, but I can tell you where the prison is, and when it is the least guarded. After that you'll be one your own."

"I understand," I said.

Just as Corianton finished his descriptions of the prison architecture and the guards' shifts, Elsha came up to us wearing a new light green scarf with lambent tracings of rust-red weaving a curious, random pattern across its shimmering surface. It accentuated her hypnotic green eyes and chestnut hair beautifully. I introduced her to Corianton, then went over the information with him once more. He then gave me his law officer's identification card.

"It's no good to me anymore because it has been revoked, but no one ever checks that closely. It might help you out in a pinch."

Corianton stood and offered his hand. "I better be going. The less you're seen with me the better. Because I'm faithful to the church I'm somewhat of an outcast here. I will be leaving just before sunup tomorrow. If you need further help, I'll be just outside the west gate, but I cannot wait too long. Good luck, Gideon, Elsha."

"Go with God," I said, taking his hand warmly.

We sat for a while in light conversation so as not to draw attention to our meeting with Corianton. I asked Elsha how she had found money to purchase the scarf. She held out a small pouch filled with her father's jewelry.

"I traded it for a piece of this," she said. "I brought it thinking some type of barter might come in handy in case we had to buy anything."

I smiled at her. This young woman had more common sense and intuition than many of the men I'd worked with throughout my years. I gave her a hug and commented on her insight. To my delight she returned my hug and thanked me.

We spent the day wandering around the city, blending in anonymously. Nephihah was indeed a city of worldly pleasures and evil. There seemed to be a tavern on every corner, and we saw numerous gambling centers and places to satisfy the lusts of the flesh. Some scantily clad women openly advertised their lascivious services as if it were as common as selling carpets or clothing. It was disheartening to see how the citizens of the city seemed to accept it as perfectly normal and commonplace.

Several times during our wanderings a merchant or restaurateur referred to us as husband and wife, which made sense, considering the fact we were both new to the city and of approximately the same age. I never shied from the notion, but neither did I encouraged it. Elsha pretty much did the same. However, she did blush wonderfully whenever we were referred to as newlyweds.

We waited until nightfall before approaching the prison. It was an impressive structure on the crest of a knoll near the edge of the city. Both front and rear entrances were guarded by armed men, but a small door in an unlit side wall seemed unprotected. We discussed how best to enter without attracting too much attention. To my surprise, Elsha suggested something that made my heart ache with worry. I said no, but she insisted it was the best way, and after a time I reluctantly agreed.

I went to the side door and waited ten minutes. Elsha walked directly into the front entrance to the front desk. She had brushed her hair back and applied some light makeup that highlighted her wonderful eyes and overall beauty. Not surprisingly, the guard at the door followed her inside like a wolf sniffing out a fresh kill. She told the guards inside that she had just run away from an abusive ex-husband and, now that she was single and all alone, wanted to know how she could get some protection from the local law offices. I was certain that within ten minutes, the entire prison staff would be at her beck and call, and I would be free to roam the cell blocks unnoticed. I eased through the side door without a hitch.

The hallways were dark and moldering. It was clear that the prison workers did not consider sanitation and cleanliness to be high priorities. It suddenly occurred to me that I didn't even know what Ashod looked like, having never seen him before. I prayed the Spirit would provide a way for me to find Elsha's father quickly.

Making my way to an antechamber, I discovered a desk covered with papers and writing instruments. A ledger lay open on one corner of the desk. It contained a manifest of each prisoner. Ashod of Bountiful was in cell number twenty-nine.

When I reached the cell, I found, to my surprise, that the cell door was not locked. I opened it, and found Ashod on his knees in prayer. I waited until he looked up before I entered.

"Thank you for letting me finish," he said, rather astonished at my show of courtesy. "You are new to this prison?"

"Yes and no," I said quietly. "I am not supposed to be here, and neither are you."

He tipped his head to one side and frowned, appraising me with a skeptical glare. I smiled at his open confusion.

"I am here to rescue you. Elsha is with me."

Ashod's eyes immediately shown with delight, then were suddenly masked with worry. Still on his knees he asked, "You brought her here? To this place?"

"Yes, but she is all right. Nobody knows who we are, and we haven't been asking a lot of questions about you, so I doubt anyone expects ill of us. We weren't even sure where to look for you, so it's lucky I found you as quickly as I did."

I stuck my head out the door to look up and down the hall. "Let's go before somebody comes."

Ashod nodded and picked up two canes. He strapped them to his forearms using bands of leather and struggled to his feet. I went to help him, but he waved me away.

"I can move all right if given enough room. Let's go."

I closed the door and we made our way toward the side door through which I had entered from. I heard voices coming from the front of the prison, and they were moving our way. Ashod was hobbling at a good pace, but it was much too slow for my liking. The voices were getting louder. Just as we neared the side door, I saw a guard turn the corner at the far end of the hallway. He paused, facing the opposite direction to say something to another guard on the other side of the corner. I shoved Ashod into a darkened archway a few feet from the door. The guard finished his conversation and walked toward us. I whispered to Ashod to hold perfectly still. My Nubian dagger was in hand and poised for a thrust. The guard paused at the side door and fumbled with some keys, locking it from the inside. He then walked past us, whistling off-key. I told Ashod to stay put while I checked out the door. The dead bolt was firmly secured. The door would not open.

I went to the opposite end of the hall and peered around the corner. A guard sat at a desk at the far end of this corridor. There were several doorways along the corridor, one of which had to be another hallway. The guard was busy writing something on a sheaf of foolscap. I went back and collected Ashod. He looked pale and weak. The strain and anxiety of the situation was taking its toll. He didn't have much energy left.

We neared the corner and I again peered around. The guard was still busy with his writing. We eased silently along the wall, moving like so many shadows, without substance or sound. The first three openings were doorways to other cells. The fourth was a passageway into darkness. We slipped into the passage just as the guard leaned back to stretch his powerful arms. I prayed he hadn't seen us, but didn't take the time to double-check. Time was a commodity we had precious little of. We walked blindly into the darkness.

Suddenly, a wall loomed before us. It was too dark to see if there was another door or hallway or other means of escape. I began feeling the walls for any openings that might lead out of the dead end. I worked my way back up the passage about twenty feet before finding a small door, more of a hatchway really, that stood waist-high. Tugging on it, I felt it move a fraction, so I put my feet on either side of the opening and heaved back on the latch. The hinges groaned open. A breath of fresh air blew past my sweaty face. The guard must have heard the hatchway open, so I whispered urgently to Ashod to follow.

"I can't," he whispered back.

"Why not?"

"They broke both my ankles. Without my crutches my legs don't work, and I haven't the strength in my arms to drag myself along. That's why they never lock my cell."

The sound of footfalls echoed down the passageway accompanied by the flicker of torches.

"Give me your hands," I whispered.

"But my crutches . . . they're the only way I can walk."

"Leave them," I almost shouted. "I'll carry you. We'll get new crutches later."

"But these were made especially for me."

Two guards paused at the junction of the passageway and stared into the blackness, in our direction.

"It came from down here," one of them said.

"Who's down there?" the other one shouted.

I reached out for Ashod and grabbed his wrist.

"Come on," I breathed.

He laid the crutches to one side and gripped my wrist with his free hand. I leaned back and dragged him through the hatchway. I went to shut it, then thought better of it. The noise would only confirm our location. I leaned back through the hatchway to retrieve the crutches, but one of the guards was already making his way down the passage with a torch. He would see me for sure.

I returned to Ashod and hefted him onto my back. It was pitch black, but I didn't care. We had to get out fast. Ashod clung to my shoulders as

I followed the breath of fresh, cool air. I paused frequently to determine the direction the draft was coming from. At one point I came to an abrupt halt, sensing a cold hardness inches from my face. I slid my foot forward. It bumped against a moist stone wall. I turned and tried to feel the breeze again. Nothing. There seemed no visible means of escape. Panic began setting in as I tried to figure out what to do next.

Then Helorum's words filled my mind: "Taste the flavor of the wind, smell the clouds on the horizon." I opened my mouth and breathed deeply with my tongue extended. To my right I tasted a moldering humidity, and smelled a fetid dampness. To my left I tasted a clean, cool emptiness with no particular smell. I moved to my left. The further along the passageway I moved, the less closed in it felt, though I could still see nothing. We had to be nearing an exit.

Time passed, and my legs began to burn from the added weight of Elsha's father. Each raspy breath I gulped seared my lungs. Yet, I could find no opening. I paused and let Ashod to the ground to rest my arms and legs. I was panting, trying to fill my burning chest as quietly as possible.

We moved on when my breathing slowed.

Finally, I came to a point where a breeze seeped through a crack. It was barely perceptible, but definitely fresh. Putting my face against the wall, I thought I could see a faint glow of subdued light outlining what appeared to be a doorway. I again set Ashod down and pressed against the door. It scraped open with a bit of effort, and I fell out onto an overgrowth of vines and sour grass. Rolling to my back, I sucked in the night air with huge gasping breaths. The smell, the taste, the very feeling of the cool air against my skin was like a sip of water to a man lost in the desert. The comforting twinkle of stars could be seen here and there through the thick canopy of trees that lined the wall I had come through. I could not tell if the wall was part of the prison itself, but at that point I really didn't care. It was enough to be free again.

Ashod called softly from within the doorway. "Gideon, what is out there?"

"Nothing," I responded in hushed tones. "A whole lot of beautiful nothing."

FIFTEEN

shod rested in a safe hiding place where few would think to look. Actually, I was more concerned about Elsha. It took a lot of guts to go boldly into the prison and fabricate a story with enough credibility to lure all the guards to her side. How had she had fared?

It took some time and the night was mostly spent before I found Elsha. She was on a bench not far from the prison in a torch-lit plaza. A large guard sat with her holding her hand. She seemed to be unaware of his presence, even tough he kept trying to initiate a conversation with her. I scanned the area carefully, but could see no other guards. A few people, couples mostly, wandered the plaza, stopping to admire the tranquil fountain in its center, or glance into the windows of the shops there.

My blood boiled seeing the guard's big hands holding my Elsha's hand.

My Elsha?

Why not? The idea was not a new one, and I was even beginning to think she felt the same way about me. Still, I didn't want to be too presumptuous and forcefully blunder into a relationship that might be entirely one-sided.

The guard placed an arm around Elsha's delicate shoulder, but she gently shrugged it off. I unsheathed my dagger and approached them in shadows. A battle with this guard would not be an easy one, but I could not think of any other way to rescue Elsha. I paused when the guard spoke.

"But, Sara, you said you wanted to be protected," the big guard argued. "If you're with me, no one will ever come near you."

"I'm not so sure I want that much protection," Elsha/Sara countered.

She had given them a false name! Of course she had, I reasoned. Her real name might link her to Ashod. I wondered what other kind of stories she might have come up with.

I suddenly had an idea. Silently I retreated to the far side of the plaza. After straightening my tunic and hair, I wandered casually into the plaza. I began calling out her name and looking around as if I had no idea where she was.

"Sara! Sara, time to come home," I called out, randomly looking about the plaza as I made my way slowly toward them.

From the corner of my eye I saw her head come up. The guard's did too.

"Sara! Come on, my sister. Father will be angry if you don't come home and talk with the doctor right now," I continued calling, moving ever closer.

Elsha stood and took a step toward me. I paused at the fountain and stood on its raised rim for a better look around. Then my gaze fell on her and I hopped off and walked over, shaking my head.

"Sara, where have you been? Mother and Father are both very worried about you. Come on, we have to get home."

The guard stepped forward and stayed me with a meaty hand. "Hold on, you. She's with me. Step back or you'll be sorry."

I gawked at the guard with a look of amazement. "Do you even know who this girl is?" I asked in feigned amazement.

The guard looked at Elsha with wariness. "She is Sara . . . just new in town from Zarahemla."

I looked at Elsha and put my hands on my hips. "Sara, what lies have you been concocting this time?" I questioned her sharply. "I'm sure this fine guard has better things to do than listen to your mindless babblings."

Elsha flashed me a glare before changing to a look of pure innocence. "What babblings are you talking about, my brother?"

I folded my arms, totally ignoring the confused guard next to us. "What is it this time? You're running away from your destitute father because he wants you to marry the balding, wart-covered son of a wealthy merchant? Or are you the kidnapped daughter of a rich king with more land and gold than Gadianton himself?"

The guard stiffened when I mentioned the name of his leader, but said nothing. He looked blankly at Elsha then back to me, trying to make sense of the act unfolding before him.

When Elsha didn't answer, he stammered, "She . . . she said she is a divorced woman . . . seeking protection from an abusive ex-husband."

I rolled my eyes and shook my head. "Not that one again!"

Elsha stepped forward and poked me in the chest. "And why not? It's my best one yet. I have men eating out of my hand each time I use it."

The guard turned on Elsha. "Hey, what is this? What's going on?"

She dropped to her knee and began weeping, "Oh please, kind sir, help me. This young man has been sent to take me away, and I fear for my life."

The guard whipped around, his sword in hand so quickly that I didn't even see it happen. Amazingly, I didn't flinch at his threat. I shook my head again and chuckled lightly, ignoring the guard.

"Oh really?" I asked. "Why don't you tell this brave guard just who sent me and exactly where I am to take you."

"You were sent by the evil Frog King who lives in the river Sidon, and you're going to take me to Croakmore Castle to be his wife and bear him hundreds of tadpoles for sons." She wept even more then cried out hysterically, "I don't want to go! Don't make me marry a frog! I don't want to go!"

The poor guard had such a confused look on his face that I almost pitied him. I leaned close to him and whispered out of the corner of my mouth, "She's been this way ever since she took that fall on her head a few years ago. Her mind is completely gone, and the doctors say she'll never be the same again."

The guard frowned at me then turned and frowned at Elsha.

"You are not Sara . . . from Zarahemla?" he asked her stupidly.

Elsha instantly stopped weeping and stood up abruptly, squaring up to the guard. "How dare you talk to a princess like that! I shall have you put in irons for your insolence."

The guard turned back to me. "Princess?"

I tapped my finger knowingly against my temple. "She sometimes thinks she is Princess Dogbark, from Ammonihah. It's another story . . . a long story."

I reached into my tunic and retrieved a silver coin.

"Here." I said, handing the coin to the guard. "This is a small token of appreciation for your troubles, and for watching over my sister. She got away from me in the market place and I've been searching for her all day. I am very sorry for any difficulty she may have caused. She is a sadly demented girl with more problems than I care to mention."

Elsha flashed me another glare, then began humming a nonsensical tune while twirling around carelessly. The guard looked at the coin in his hand, then shook his head.

"You should watch your sister more carefully," he snapped. "I could have gotten in trouble taking the time to watch over her while you wandered aimlessly through the streets looking for her."

Elsha took my arm in hers. "Come Prince Dogbark, let us retire to the kennel at the palace for a nice brushing and flea bath."

I rolled my eyes at the guard, then winked and patted him on his shoulder. "Thanks again," I sighed heavily.

His hand shot out and gripped my arm. I almost panicked and reached for my dagger, but willed myself to stay calm. He quickly looked around, then leaned close and whispered, "No, thank *you*, my friend."

He then stepped back and laughed openly. "I must admit, I thought her story sounded a bit strange. Now I know why."

Elsha and I walked calmly away, as I chastised her and she continued to hum her silly tune. The guard did not follow us.

As we turned a corner I chanced a look back. The guard had gone. Elsha threw her arms around my neck and hugged me tightly. She was trembling and wouldn't let go for the longest time. I wrapped my arms around her and held her until she settled down. Pale with fright, she was softly crying.

"Hush now," I soothed. "It's over. I am so proud of you, Elsha. You are the bravest woman I know."

She let go and wiped her eyes. "I'm sorry, Gideon. I was so scared you wouldn't come back in time. He was so insistent . . . I didn't know how much longer I could—"

"Shh, it's over now. Don't think on it any more."

I put my arm around her shoulder and led her down some random streets toward a large stable filled with horses and llamas. It was only an hour or so before dawn when we arrived. I made sure the place was vacant before going to a mucking stall filled with animal droppings. Ashod was lying behind a large pile of muck on a borrowed horse blanket. He sat up painfully and smiled. Elsha was on her knees, hugging him tightly and sobbing. I stood off to one side and kept watch for guards or stable workers. Elsha looked at her father's swollen and scarred ankles and drew a sharp breath.

"Father, what have they done?" she cried.

"I'm all right, my angel," he said, stroking her hair. "They tried to get me to tell them where I hid all our jewels, but I would not. I'm sure in time my ankles will heal."

Having seen injuries of his sort before, I knew Ashod was only trying to make Elsha feel better. In reality, I doubted he would ever walk on his own again.

He hugged his daughter warmly. "I am so glad you are safe."

They held each other and talked softly about the events of the past few weeks. I heard my named mentioned several times but thought little of it. I waited patiently until I felt we had better be moving on. Guards would be looking for their escaped prisoner, and it would be near sunup before we reached the west gate. I was praying Corianton would still be there.

I threw a blanket over a llama and lifted Ashod on its back. I chose the llama over a horse because its soft foot pads would not create as much noise as a horse's hooves on the cobbled streets of the city. In the moonlight of the street, I saw how pale and sickly Ashod had grown. I hadn't noticed his decrepit state in the prison before because of how dark it had been, and the rest of the time I was carrying him on my back. The poor old man was not long for this earth, and having the added injury of broken bones only compounded his misery. Yet he never complained. My heart was filled with pity and admiration for him. What a horrible life the Gadiantons had forced upon him.

Elsha and I led the llama toward the west gate of Nephihah. We encountered no one on the streets, but we were careful to take as many back alleys and side roads as possible, just to be safe.

When we reached the gate, there was a guard sitting nearby. While Elsha and Ashod waited in a dark corner, while I crept up to the guard. He was slumped in his chair and fast asleep. An empty bottle of wine was at his feet. I returned to Elsha and her father, and led them through the gate. Once outside, I was stopped by the look on Elsha's face. She was pale and withdrawn, unresponsive. Tears glistened in her eyes and trickled down her smooth cheeks.

I led them to a stand of trees and whispered, "What's wrong?"

She looked at me blankly then fell against my chest and sobbed. "I'm so sorry," she said in a tremulous voice.

I held her close and stroked her hair tenderly. "Don't worry, Elsha. We're almost free. Once we meet Corianton everything will be all right."

"I'm so sorry," she kept repeating.

"Sorry for what?" I asked softly.

She looked up at me, her eyes red with emotion and fatigue. "I'm sorry for ever thinking ill of you; for doubting your intentions. I treated you so badly before and I shouldn't have. You are truly the most wonderful man I've ever met. You've risked everything to help me."

I didn't know what to say. Her outpouring of emotion had me speechless and her display of affection had me floating on air. Yet I knew better than to think of it as a romantic overture. Elsha was expressing something much deeper. And my feelings toward her were the same.

Finally, I said, "Hush, now. Let's get moving before that guard wakes up."

I went to Ashod. He was slumped over the llama's neck, unconscious. I led the llama through the darkness with Elsha right behind. Down the trail, a few hundred yards from the city wall, Corianton appeared out of nowhere. He had with him three other people, two older women and one young boy. They each carried light packs, and looked nervous and frightfully anxious.

I explained the events of the night to Corianton and gave him the lead to the llama. He said they had some horses farther up the trail and should make good time for his rendezvous with Hagoth. I asked if he had an extra horse for Elsha, or if she could ride with the young boy.

"Aren't you coming with us?" Corianton asked.

"I still have to find my parents," I told him. "I think they're in Limhi."

He looked at me curiously. "You mean you don't know?"

"Don't know what?"

"Your mother and brother are in Tonalai helping load Hagoth's ship."

"What?"

He nodded. "Joshua took her there a couple of days after your house was burned. Because he was allied with the King Men, they thought nothing of letting them go, but I believe he and your mother plan on leaving with Hagoth when he escapes. I believe he had second thoughts about joining their forces, God be praised. I thought you knew all that."

"Corianton, I've been on the run ever since the night you came looking for me," I explained. "The only clue I've had since then was from Ham. He thought my family was being held in Limhi."

Corianton rubbed his dark whiskers and frowned at me. "I don't know where your father is, but if he really is in Limhi, you'd best forget it and come with me."

I flinched. "You can't be serious. Just leave him there in the hands of the Gadiantons?"

Corianton placed a consoling hand on my shoulder. "Gideon, you don't know what these Gadianton Robbers are like. They are ruthless men who delight in the shedding of blood and torturing innocents. If your father is still alive, I'm sure he would not want you to try to help him. Your life would be in jeopardy if you did."

"But I can't simply leave him."

"Your mother needs you more now. I think it wise to come with me and help her all you can."

I slumped onto a log and rubbed my temples. My head was suddenly pounding and my legs were weak. Once again I had to decide between which parent to help. My stomach knotted painfully. If Corianton was right, and my father was dead, then I would not hesitate to go with him. But he wasn't certain about my father's condition. I shook my head and tried to hold back the queasy feeling rising in my throat. What was I to do? I couldn't simply turn around after coming this far. But would it do any good to keep going, just to learn that my father had been murdered, and risk landing myself in a Gadianton dungeon?

I tried silently calling on God for help. I needed a clear mind and guidance regarding which path to take. Corianton and the others were leaving with Ashod and his daughter. Should I stay with them, after all Elsha and I had been though? Would she need continued assistance with her injured, possibly dying father? I was so torn, so emotionally spent, so filled with confusion and anguish, I had no idea what I should do. I prayed desperately for an answer, a sign of some kind.

I heard Ashod call to his daughter. When had he regained consciousness? A moment later, however, Elsha was at my side, a caring arm draped around my shoulder.

"Let's go find your father, Gideon," she said resolutely.

I searched her face as if to better understand just what she was saying.

She smiled softly. "You helped me rescue my father. Now I want to help you rescue yours."

I was on my feet in an instant. "No. Absolutely not."

She stood, frustrated. "Listen, don't try to be a hero here. I know what I'm getting into. I know Limhi is dangerous. But I also know I want to help you. I feel . . ." She paused to organize her thoughts. "I believe I'm *supposed* to help you, Gideon. Even my father thinks so."

I turned to Ashod, who sat on the llama, smiling at us. He nodded solemnly. "Go," was all he said.

Corianton shook his head and returned to the others he was helping. I knew he didn't approve, but then, it wasn't his decision.

Elsha touched my sleeve and moved closer. "Gideon, please let me help you. My father will be fine with Corianton, he told me so. He feels I should be with you. He is very impressed with you, and . . . and so am I." She blushed slightly but never took her eyes from mine. "I . . . I want to be with you."

Even though my head was spinning with confusion, my heart soared at her confession. She did feel for me what I felt for her? Could I love her and still willingly lead her into unquestionable danger in Limhi?

The look in her eyes gave me my answer. The endless depths of those beautiful green eyes, the slight crinkle of a smile at the corners of her mouth, the very spirit that radiated from her face told me what I had longed in my heart to have confirmed. I wanted to always be with her . . . and she wanted to be with me.

I held her in my arms and whispered, "Are you sure about this?"

"More sure than anything I've ever known before," she whispered back.

"It could be dangerous."

"We'll be all right."

I held her at arms length and looked deeply into her eyes. "How can you be so sure?"

She smiled. "Because I have a blessing from Helorum, as do you, that says we're to take the same path, and we have my father's blessing too. So let's just go and see where this tide takes us."

I drew my breath in sharply when she unknowingly quoted my father's favorite saying. I then felt a curious warmth enter my soul.

I looked at Ashod. He nodded again and repeated, "Go."

I called to Corianton, "Tell my mother we'll be coming along soon. If we don't make Hagoth's ship we'll find some other way to catch up to her."

He waved an acknowledgment and straddled his horse.

I held Elsha tightly and whispered, "I love you."

She whispered back, "I love you too."

SIXTEEN

There was a surprising amount of traffic on the road to and from Limhi. We stayed on side trails and causeways, but several times the road bore straight through a narrows forcing us to mingle with the other travelers. Each time I prayed that Kumran, or anyone else who might recognize me, would not be among them. Thankfully, the Lord answered my prayers.

The jungle grew thick and menacing in this region. It was lush with tropical plants and flowers, which drew the eye from one beautiful scene to another. But it also exuded a disturbing wrongness; a tangible emanation of death, decay, and danger that both attracted and repelled the onlooker. Eyes were watching us, but I did not know if they belonged to friend or foe or wild animal.

Limhi turned out to be a fairly good-sized city right on the Lamanite border. To my astonishment, we saw numerous Lamanites wandering about as commonly as Nephites. There were also Amalekites and Zoramites, and a few Mulekites. The city was a melting pot of nationalities which on the surface appeared very harmonious, but later proved otherwise. I was initially impressed that so many former enemies could cohabitate with so little outward conflict and discord. Elsha commented that we might be able to blend in rather comfortably with this mix of humanity. Such was the case, only we never felt truly comfortable.

As we strolled through the streets, we felt a palpable, nervousness among the many citizens. Everyone looked at each passerby with mistrust and fear, glancing at them with an appraising look, then averting their eyes when challenged. Neither authority nor seniority seemed to have importance here; might and brawn were the ruling officiators.

Taking the cue from my surroundings, I adopted a menacing scowl and darting eyes. I rolled up my sleeves to expose my arms which, from my years of working in the boatyard, had more than a little muscle on them. In all, I thought I looked quite the imposing character. Elsha looked at me and giggled, covering her mouth so as not to burst into open laughter. I looked at myself in a reflecting glass and conceded that I probably did look more foolish than fierce.

Limhi was an easy city to figure out. Everything radiated from a central point in a semi-circle whose diameter was delineated by a large river. At the center was the fortress Moroni had started and Gadianton had finished.

We found a small eatery on the river front near the fortress and sat for a quick bite. Even though we had ample food in our packs, I thought it prudent to save that for our journey to Tonalai. Besides, we were hungry and something fresh sounded pretty good. The proprietor, a man of medium build and closely shorn hair, brought us each a glass of wine. We were never much for alcohol in my family, and Elsha said her parents never touched the stuff, so I asked for two glasses of water instead. The man blinked in surprise and then squinted his eyes in leery appraisal of us. I told him I was on an important mission and needed to keep my head clear, which really wasn't a lie. He seemed to accept that and brought us the water. We ordered the house special, onion-fried monkey and sweet potatoes. It was actually quite good, much better than it sounded anyway.

The eatery and a few other shops were located on a small peninsula that extended into the river thirty yards or so, giving it a pleasing ambiance. As we ate, I studied the layout and dimensions of the fortress. The vantage point was exceptional and no one seemed the least concerned that my attention was focused on the fortress instead of the beautiful girl across from me. I did notice a number of men, both young and old, who were blatantly ogling Elsha, and that stirred up a painful stab of jealousy. And the looks the women of Limhi gave her were anything but charitable.

After lunch, we strolled near the fortress but kept our eyes on the river. Across the river was Lamanite territory. I could see buildings and piers on the other side, but nothing of the magnitude of that in Limhi.

The fortress was buttressed in front and well guarded. The back was a sheer rock wall facing the river with towers on each point and crenelations running in between. It looked as if it had been built to defend an attack from the river, and I wondered what kind of sailing craft the Lamanites had developed. Turreted, the towers would allow several men at once to fire down upon the river and surrounding land with perfect accuracy and complete protection. There were no large windows or entrances on the side facing the river. That meant the only way in was through the front door. Not a welcome thought, considering what I was up against.

Elsha and I sat on a grassy knoll that overlooked the river and talked of pleasant things until evening. It was actually a very pleasing time. A cool breeze drifted from the river and helped to evaporate the sweat on our faces. It was another hot and humid day, though there was a hint of rain in the air. I wasn't sure if a thunderstorm would help or hinder us, but one was on its way.

I had learned long ago how to read the signs in the sky—the pressure changes in the air and smell the charge of lightening building in the clouds. At sea, where a storm could come up in a matter of seconds and reek havoc on an unfurled sail or a cat-napping sailor, it was especially important to be aware of changing weather patterns.

It turned out that Elsha and I had quite a lot in common. She loved to read and learn new things as much as I did, and she had an incredibly retentive memory for details and facts. Her knowledge of the scriptures was remarkable, and as we quoted our favorite passages, she would often stop me to correct a word or two I had memorized incorrectly. I began to wonder if she didn't have a perfect memory, one that allowed a person to recall with flawless accuracy every word seen on a page. Elsha remarked on my ability to quote passages and facts, and on the number of volumes I had read. Apparently, she was as impressed with me as I was of her.

"I assumed you were simply a good-looking shipwright, with little schooling in matters other than boats and the sea. Boy, was I wrong," she admitted.

"That's interesting," I mused aloud. "I assumed you were perfect from the first time I saw you. And I was right."

She punched me playfully, then gave me a warm hug. Finally, I had said something right! The hug was a wonderful feeling, one that I didn't want to end. But as we broke from our embrace, a shout came from the fortress, causing us to turn in that direction. A guard was calling down to another one from the massive wall.

She sighed and shuddered. "What are you going to do?" she asked, nodding toward the fortress.

"The only thing I can do. I'm going to walk in there and ask for my father."

It took some time to locate what I was looking for. The bathhouse was at the end of a crooked alley. Though its entrance was well lit with torches and a brazen sign displaying both men and women bathing, the path to it was as dark as midnight. Elsha stayed behind at a good-sized bazaar, trying to inconspicuously mingle with the evening shoppers.

I entered the house and asked for a hot bath. The owner led me to a dressing room and told me the bath was through the far door. I scanned the room quickly and found what I needed—the uniform of an officer was hanging from one of the wall pegs. Luckily, it belonged to someone about my size.

I left the bath house quickly, tossing a gold coin on the desk. The owner scrambled for the coin and didn't watch me leave. As I marched through the streets toward the fortress, Elsha joined me, and we discussed the options that lay before us. Unfortunately, they weren't many. We decided to meet at a cattle pen we had seen at north end of the city. Hopefully, we would meet safely again in only a few hours.

Near the entrance to the fortress we paused and said a quick prayer. I asked that my efforts would not be in vain, and I would find my father alive, and that Elsha would be protected and safe in my absence.

The guards at the entrance looked as if they had never smiled once in their lives. I needed a distraction to get by them. Elsha nodded and went to an open-air tavern in plain view of the entrance. She singled out a rich-looking man who had plainly had too much to drink. She jumped up on his table and stood before him.

"All right, I'll dance for you," she announced boldly, her intended audience being the guards and those around the man, not the man himself. "I'll dance, but only if you buy me another drink."

Almost instantly a dozen men were offering to buy her drinks, but she ignored them in favor of the wealthy drunk in front of her. He readily agreed, and Elsha began clapping her hands rhythmically while dancing on the table top. I must admit I paused for a moment to watch her just like every other man within eyesight of the open-air tavern, including the guards at the entrance of the fortress.

As I passed through the door, the guards only half saluted me, their attention riveted on Elsha. I kept my helmet low to darken my face and hide my youth. I returned a bored salute and continued on inside. The inner court was stockpiled with all sorts of provisions, both of war and general commerce. Horses, llamas, cattle, chickens, and sheep also had their place inside. It was clear that the prison keepers were well stocked in case of attack.

The entrance to the keep was more than fifty yards across the compound. I marched directly toward it as if I had an important assignment to accomplish, which I did. At the door, another guard saluted me and asked for identification.

In a husky voice I replied, "Just open the door. I've got orders to deliver important information immediately."

The guard hesitated then said, "I'm sorry sir, but I have my orders too. No one enters without identification."

The guard was a younger man, probably near my own age, and strongly built. I was sure I could bluff my way in with threats, but decided that that would raise too much attention. Instead, I reached inside my uniform and removed the law officer's pass Corianton had given me. I flashed it at the young guard.

"I'm not in the habit of pandering to upstarts," I growled, "but I suppose you have your job to do too."

I pocketed the card and pushed my way past before the guard could say anything further. When the door closed behind me I began to breathe a sigh of relief, but it caught in my throat as a large man, a guard of obvious authority and remarkable size, approached me with a drawn sword.

I marched toward him, meeting him halfway in the antechamber.

"I'm here to see the prisoner Hezikiah," I snapped.

The guard stopped and looked me over in angry appraisal. "Who are you?" he growled.

I stepped up to him, my face inches away from his. The only way to sound convincing was not to cow to his fierceness, and try to act fierce myself.

"I'll make the demands here, you dog." I grabbed the front of his uniform and hissed, "I'm a captain in the Gadianton Secret Service, and I am here to gather information from Hezikiah of Mulek."

Shoving him back, I added, "Now, where is he?"

The guard didn't back off as I had hoped he would. He jabbed my chest with one of his thick fingers. "I've never heard of a 'Secret Service' before."

I rolled my eyes. "Of course not, you moron, that's why it's secret."

He stood his ground, eyeballing me with suspicion. I stepped up to him again and looked around quickly, as if justifiably suspicious of everyone else in the fortress, then leaned toward his ear.

"Listen," I whispered, "we have reason to believe Hezikiah knows of secret plans regarding the Nephite's preparations for attaching the coastal waterways. He is a shipbuilder, you know."

"Yes, I knew that," the guard said, also in a hushed voice. "He's supposedly working on a ship design for us."

Was this man implying my father had defected from his government and church and joined the Gadianton Robbers? I played along, but refused to believe my father was freely offering them his help.

"It seems you are more informed than I gave you credit for, my friend," I said softly. "But we must be careful. There are always ears which hear things not meant for them. This is top secret information."

The guard seemed to soften with my confidence. I told him I needed to confer with Hezikiah about some design information I had recently memorized at the headquarters in Nephihah.

"We just had another man arrive from Nephihah," the guard said, leading me to a desk to one side of the antechamber. He picked up a scrap of parchment. "He brought this."

It read: *Two men just escaped from Nephihah prison. One man, Ashod the jeweler, is a traitor to Gadianton. The other man is unknown. Be on the alert for any suspicious men in your area.*

I looked at the guard and smiled. "Good work, soldier. It's this kind of information that keeps us one step ahead of their ever-controlling church." I leaned closer. "Let me tell you something else . . ." I paused and looked around slowly. "We have reason to believe the Lamanites are building their own armored boats, and plan on attacking soon."

The guard blinked. "But the Lamanites are allies with the Gadiantons."

I scoffed. "That's what they want us to think. Have you ever met a Lamanite you felt you could trust? Really trust—with your life?"

The guard's brow knotted in anger. "No. I have always thought it a mistake to let them join our forces."

"There is strength in numbers, and I'm sure that's what Kishkumen had in mind when he covenanted with them. But we have reason to believe they plan to double-cross us."

The guard punched a fist into his open palm. "I knew it!"

"Hush, be silent," I cautioned, and looked around again. "No one can know of this. That is why I must see Hezikiah, to ready our forces for their attack."

The guard slapped my shoulder and told me to follow him. We ascended several flights of stairs, passing guards all along the way. We were stopped and questioned a number of times, but the man I was with explained his way through, and within minutes we stood in front of a bolted door. Another guard sitting on a stool outside the door, questioned our presence.

"This captain has important information to discuss with the prisoner Hezikiah."

The door guard appraised me carefully. "Please show me the sign, sir."

Inside, I panicked. Which sign could he want? I recalled the few signs and codes Ham had shared with me, but wasn't sure which one was for which occasion.

"Would I be here if I didn't know the signs?" I hissed, trying to sound as perturbed as I was scared. I'm not sure which showed through.

The guard rose to his feet and placed a hand on the hilt of his sword. "I need to see the sign, sir," he said in a measured tone.

I sighed heavily in exasperation and placed my right hand over my heart with the middle and ring fingers crossed. I quickly dropped my hand and said, "And the secret password is: 'Amulek sucks eggs'."

The door guard's eyes lit up as he burst out laughing and slapped the other guard on the shoulder. When my guard questioned him, he replied, "There is no secret password." He regained some composure, then added, "But if there was, that's what it should be!"

I shrugged my shoulders. "Sometimes I get fed up with all these secret signs and combinations. Half the time I end up with a cramped hand and a finger up my nose."

Both guards burst out laughing again. "It's about time we got an officer with a sense of humor," my guard said.

The guard unlocked the door and let me pass. The door was then closed and locked behind me. I didn't know why they had locked it, but I assumed it was standard practice.

The room was dark, with only one small candle burning in a embrasure on the wall. It was a fairly spacious room, circular in design, with a small slit of a window on the far side, and nothing in the way of furniture that I could see. I assumed we were near the top of one of the towers. The smell of rain wafted gently through the window.

I heard a rustling in the far corner. "What is it now?" my father asked.

My heart fairly leapt at the sound of his voice. It was a firm voice, deep and sure, which could simultaneously comfort and reprimand, and I suddenly realized how much I had missed it. I tried to speak, but ended up standing mutely, like a confused orator lost for words. I took a step forward, then stopped as my foot touched what felt like a rug of some sort. I could not see well, as my eyes were still not accustomed to the darkness of the room. My father's were. As I listened intently to get my bearings, his voice suddenly sounded from off to one side.

"You have a lot of nerve coming in here unarmed," he commented without emotion. "Are you so brave . . . or foolish?"

I removed my helmet and let it fall to the ground. I then slipped off the captain's coat, revealing my simple tunic beneath. I heard him draw a quick breath.

I turned toward his voice. "Father," was all I was able to say.

Suddenly I was in his embrace, feeling his tears against my neck and struggling to keep from sobbing. I felt more than heard him whisper my name. We held each other for a time in silence, neither of us sure of where to begin or what to say.

Finally, he held me at arm's length and asked, "What are you doing here?"

"I am here to rescue you," I replied softly.

He stepped back and looked at the clothing on the floor. "You're not one of . . ."

"No, Father, I'm not." Pointing at the clothes, I added, "That was the only way I could think of getting in."

He nodded. "Put them back on and take me out of here."

I quickly donned the coat and helmet, and pounded on the door. "Open up," I called to the guard outside.

The flash from a crack of lightening ricocheted through the room, and thunder grumbled in complaint. I looked at my father, who nodded toward the door. Perhaps the guard hadn't heard me over the approaching storm. I repeated my knocking.

"Open this door right now," I yelled.

"Why?" the guard asked.

Why? What would he ask that question for? I swallowed hard and tried to sound annoyed. "Because it stinks in here."

When the guard didn't respond, I shouted, "Why do you think, you imbecile? I'm taking the prisoner out."

"You'll have to wait one minute, sir," the guard finally called back through the heavy door.

"What for?" I demanded.

"I'm just checking out your story with my commander."

"What?" I shouted. "How dare you question my authority. I'll slit your throat myself when I get out of here."

"I'm sorry, sir, but I have no choice."

I looked at my father, who simply shrugged his shoulders.

"I command you to tell me why," I told the guard sharply.

"Because you gave me the wrong sign."

SEVENTEEN

"Will your story hold water?" my father asked.

"No. I bluffed my way in, and was hoping to do the same on the way out."

He nodded. "Then we'll have to take my way."

I looked at him curiously, but he simply patted my shoulder and bade me follow him. Toward the far side of the room was a pile of materials—various cloths, writing instruments, sewing things, paper, rope, a table, and two chairs. Now that my eyes had adjusted to the darkness, I could see what I had felt on the floor was actually a large piece of what appeared to be light sail cloth.

"What is all this stuff for?"

"Delay tactics," my father answered. "The Gadiantons are forcing me to help them design and build a fleet of fast boats, large military versions of the catamarans we used to build. They bring me almost any material I need for the design and construction, but won't allow me into their shipyard for fear I might try and escape. Some of their suggestions have actually be very impressive—like using a heavy silk for sailcloth."

I scanned a drawing of a rather bulky-looking catamaran rimmed with shields. There was also a curious weapon on the bow of each hull. Other than that, the design looked like any other catamaran we had built.

"What are these weapons?" I asked, tapping the drawing. The paper felt very dry and brittle, which also struck me as curious.

"I call it a swivel bow. Here's a closer look at one," he said, pulling a drawing from another pile. "It's pretty much like a regular bow and arrow rig, except that this one is mounted horizontally on a rotating armature, and the arrow sits in this channeled guide. I think it'll prove to be very accurate, but I haven't tested one yet."

"If it's mounted on an armature like this, then you wouldn't have to worry about projectile size," I said, thinking out loud. "You could even make the bow much bigger and fire large arrows, lances almost, because weight wouldn't be an issue."

My father smiled at me. It was so good to look at his face again, strong and lean, with deep-set blue eyes that instilled confidence and trust. And love. But this time I also saw the hollow look of desperation, of worry and fatigue. I was certain his imprisonment had been anything but pleasant. I could see no overt signs of torture, but I knew my father would not freely give the Gadiantons what they wanted.

"It is a shame we couldn't be discussing these design ideas under better circumstances," he said with a sigh.

I agreed and ran my finger across the drawings again. "Why is the paper so brittle?"

He smiled again. "A last minute option, if needed."

I gave him a confused look, but he said no more.

"So how are we to escape?" I asked, looking out the window, which was too small for any man to slip through, not that anyone would want to. The drop to the river below was much too high for someone to jump.

I looked out across the river. An intense storm was indeed building, and would soon dump more than the sprinkle of rain we were now receiving. I heard some commotion coming from out of my line of sight, and knew word of my deception was spreading quickly. We were in grave danger. Instead of helping my father, I had placed myself in his same predicament.

"We don't have much time," I said, turning to meet his eyes.

"Agreed." He pointed up. "There is a trapdoor in the ceiling. I assume it is used to access the turret atop this tower. I have no ladder, but if you stack one of the chairs on the table, you can get out."

"Is there a way down from there?" I asked, not remembering any external walkways to the towers.

"Yes, but probably not what you're thinking."

He gathered up the cloth from the floor and then removed several thin lengths of cord from a chest. I helped him move the table under the trapdoor and position a chair on top of it. My father climbed up and pushed the trapdoor open. Cool night air, scattered raindrops, and the ambient light entered through the opening. I handed him the cloth and cord, and he tossed them through the door. He then climbed down and made a pile of everything else—his drawings and other materials that might be of use to the Gadiantons—and slid them all under the table.

A noise at the door indicated that the guards had returned.

"Quickly! You go up first," my father whispered.

I climbed up and pulled myself through the opening. Just as I did so, I heard the rattle of keys opening the lock on the prison door. My father grabbed the lone candle from its place on the wall and lit the pile under the table. He then climbed onto the table and chair and reached for the opening. The papers caught fire quickly, and I saw flames licking around the edge of the table as I reached down and helped my father up through the trapdoor. Swinging down through the opening, I kicked the chair from the table, then hoisted myself back outside. By then, the flames had consumed most of my father's things. The door to the tower cell opened as I closed the trapdoor.

"Why did you burn everything?" I asked.

"The Gadiantons are smart enough to know whether or not I was working on serious designs. I drew them so everything would actually work, but I kept the paper very dry so it would burn easily because I never wanted them to have the final product."

I could hear quite a lot of shouting from several guards in the chamber below. Unless they knew about the trapdoor, we would have appeared to have vanished. But I doubted we would have such good fortune. The smoke in the room would give us a few precious minutes before they discovered we were gone.

My father was already busy with something. He had the sail cloth laid out in a huge rectangle and was tying the ends of the cord to each corner. As I bent to help, I found that the silk was milled incredibly strong. We then folded the silk by bringing the four corners to the center of one edge, then folded the new corners to the same central spot, and repeated this until we had a neat compact bundle.

The rain had increased, and the lightning and thunder sounded much closer. A horn sounded from within the fortress—a signal that we had gotten loose. As far as I could tell, we were still very much prisoners of the fortress, for I still envisioned no apparent way out. To illuminate the night and lessen the ease of our escape, several torches were lit on the grounds around the tall tower. I then saw a few guards moving along the connecting wall in our direction. We would be at a military advantage if we had bows, arrows and slings. But we had none of those things, not even a good sword. I still had my Nubian dagger, but that was the extent of our weaponry. I looked around for stones to throw, but I only found a few. I asked my father for a strip of the silk with which to make a sling for hurling the stones, but he waved me away, concentrating instead on fashioning some curious knots at the loose ends of the cords. I had no idea what he was doing, but I was sure I could trust him.

A jagged flash of lightning lit up the sky just as an arrow sailed overhead and landed a few feet from us. I moved to toss it over the side, but my father stopped me.

"Wait, Gideon. There are steel loops on either side of the trapdoor. Break the tip off the arrow and slid the shaft through them. That'll buy us a few more seconds. I'm almost finished with this."

"And just what is that?" I asked as I slid the arrow into place.

Suddenly, a grappling hook flew over a crenelation and scraped to an edge where it dug in. I peered over the edge and saw several guards, their faces distorted by flickering torchlight and flashing lightning, climbing the rope. Periodically, their dark forms stood out in stark relief when sheet lightning brightened the sky, though their eyes remained black sockets, devoid of life. They were steadfastly making their way up the tower wall.

The rope and stone were slick with rain, but they continued to inch their way up. I threw a stone at the lead guard, who took it squarely on the forehead. His grip slackened, causing him to slide into the man directly below him. There was some vile cursing directed at us, followed by more angry yells. They warned me not to try that again. I picked up another stone and leaned over the edge.

Fierce banging sounded from the trapdoor as a few Gadiantons tried to break through. The arrow was holding well, but it was an old door, and the hinges looked as if they would not withstand much more of the abusive pounding.

Another grappling hook flew over the opposite edge and scraped to a hold. Before moving to that one, I hurled another stone, missing the climbing guards, but hitting an unsuspecting soldier standing below. He collapsed without a sound.

Almost simultaneously, a terrific bolt of lightning hit a large tree next to the fortress, sending a shower of sparks in all directions, and an ear-shattering crack of thunder directly over us. My heart skipped a beat, and I prayed that my father and I, standing on perhaps the highest point around, would not be the target for the next life-rending bolt from the heavens. In answer to my prayer, the bolts of lightening turned to sheet lightning, the kind that lights up the black, roiling clouds with an amazing display of sporadic, intense energy.

I ran to the other grappling hook and tried to wrench it free, but it was well secured with several hundred pounds of angry guard on the trailing rope. I cast my last stone at the ascending guards and ran back to the first rope.

"Use your dagger," my father yelled over the deafening thunder as he made his way with the bundle toward the side of the tower that overlooked the river.

My dagger! Why hadn't I thought of that? I unsheathed my dagger, leaned over the edge, and commenced to cut through the rope.

"Back away, you dog," the lead guard yelled from a few feet away. The speed at which they had ascended the rope was astounding. I flinched, but continued sawing through the rope.

I turned my head to warn my father when a large hand reached through the crenelations, and grabbed the edge of the stone. Before I could react, another hand grasped the collar of my uniform. I struck at the hand on the wall with my dagger. The man screamed and let go, but he still had an unbelievably strong grasp on my collar. As the guard fell backwards, he pulled me with him. I stopped my fall by spreading my arms and locking them around the battlements. I found myself staring straight down the wall of the 400-foot drop with a weakening grip on the wet stone, and a 250-pound guard hanging from my collar. Had I not had any strength in my arms, the guard would now be plummeting to his death—with me in tow.

Lightning flashed again, revealing the guard's contorted face. To my surprise, I didn't see a man afraid of falling to his death, but a demonic personage glaring vengefully at me, bent on my utter destruction. I let go of one battlement to retrieve my dagger, but in doing so inched farther over the edge. Wide-eyed, I stared into the evil face of my attacker as he dangled from my collar. My other hand started to slip on the wet stone as the rain intensified.

By now I was sure the guards on the grappling rope opposite me had breached the tower wall and were sneaking up from behind.

I yelled to the dangling guard to let go of my collar.

"Not likely! You'll die with me, Nephite, and I'll be a hero," he hissed at me.

Then I felt the stitching in my collar begin to give way. I leaned even farther over the edge to increase the pull on my uniform. The collar began to separate from the rest of the uniform as the threads popped.

"You won't be a hero," I said during a pause in the rumbling of thunder. "You'll just be dead."

I shucked my shoulders and felt the last threads from the stitching in my collar break. Another flash of sheet lightning illuminated the guard as he tumbled end-over-end toward the ground. I turned before he hit the stone pavement, not wanting to see the gruesome demise of another human being, not even an enemy.

My father was standing on the top of a battlement, testing the pull of the wind. I ran to him, while keeping an eye on the second grappling rope.

"What are you doing?" I called out.

"Getting ready to jump," he said, sliding a loop in the cord over his head and securing it under his arms. "I think we can easily make the river with this wind."

"Are you insane?" I yelled. "Even if we do reach the water, the fall will kill us. It's much too high. We can't jump."

"And if we don't jump, the Gadiantons will kill us for trying to escape. Which do you prefer?"

A bolt of lightning flashed, simultaneously accompanied by a bone-rattling clap of thunder. It was so close I could feel the hairs on my arms stand on end from the energy. Another burst of lightning followed almost immediately, and by its light, I saw a smile on my father's rain-soaked face. How could he be happy at a time like this?

I clambered onto the battlement as he handed me a length of looped cord.

"Put this around your shoulders—under your arms like I have," he instructed.

"Why?"

I knew I shouldn't have questioned him, but we were talking about my life. He looked into my eyes, and for the first time, I saw a look of concern in his.

"Son, you'll simply have to trust me," he said, helping me loop the cord around my shoulders. "I've been working on this idea for some time. When we jump, we'll toss the silk out at the same time. The wind should catch it, like it does in a sail, and slow our descent."

Like the wind catching a sail . . . only used to slow us instead of propel us. I had to admit it made sense.

"Have you tested it?" I asked.

"Only on small models."

"Then how can you be sure it will work?"

"I can't."

Just then, a guard breached the wall on the far side of us, and began advancing with his sword drawn. He paused to remove the arrow bolting the trapdoor shut, and guards began pouring out like angry ants from damaged nest. Sheet lightning illuminated the sky and I counted at least a dozen guards within fifteen feet of us.

My father handed me half of the silk and motioned to hold it over our heads.

"On three toss it out and jump," he yelled over the thunder.

I nodded, but wondered if this was how I was to leave the earth to begin my voyage in the heavens. What if the rain had soaked the silk to the point that it would not open?

"One," he called.

The guards yelled at us to climb down. I doubt they had any idea what we were up to.

"Two!"

I bent my trembling knees in readiness. I had to trust my father.

"Stay where you are!" a guard commanded, as he reached for my ankle.

"Three!"

We leapt into the air and threw the silk out at an angle in front and above us. I felt my body plummet toward the rocky shore as the rumpled silk began to spread open. My stomach was in my throat. My heart had ceased to beat.

I closed my eyes, sure that in moments my legs would be shattered as they hit the ground with unchecked velocity. I prayed that perhaps we had leapt far enough to make the water. But even if we did, it would be much too shallow to break our fall without serious injury.

Next to me, my father cried out with a whoop of glee. I opened my eyes and saw him staring heavenward.

Suddenly, our fall was halted with a popping sound above us, and the cords under my arms jerked tight. My chin slammed into my chest and the air was forced from my lungs. My father and I collided.

I forced myself to look down. The ground was no longer racing toward us. Instead, we were drifting at a more acceptable rate, though still descending too fast for a delicate landing.

I glanced up and saw the silk, now looking very much like a sail filled with wind, wide open above us, the corners where the cords attached bent toward our weight. My father was still whooping with excitement. I was still too scared to even breathe.

Just then a gust of wind blew from behind us and caught the silk. It carried us farther over the river. Another flash of lightning revealed that the river's surface was a dozen yards away. We were still falling at a rate that made my stomach turn, but at least now I felt we would not be killed.

I could no longer hear the angry calls from the fortress behind us. With the heavy rain and it being so dark between the bursts of lightning, I doubted they could see us anymore.

The wind shifted, this time coming from upriver, which slowed us even more. My armpits burned from the abrasive tension of the cords, but I wasn't complaining. I knew my father's invention had, for the moment, saved our lives. Once we landed, we still had to escape from Limhi itself.

Another gust felt as if it lifted us upward, but it probably just slowed our fall a little. *What if we were blown to the Lamanite side of the river?* I looked at my father, who was still cheering like a small child who had just received a new toy.

Suddenly, the wind ceased, and our rate of descent increased dramatically. Perhaps only eighteen feet from the river's surface, we hurtled toward it like a falcon diving for an unsuspecting pigeon, with our imminent fate being that of the pigeon's.

Then a gust of wind struck us from the side, blowing the silk to an extreme angle and spilling the air out from its hollow. We plummeted the last few feet with nothing to slow us. I clapped my arms together directly over my head and entered the water like an arrow.

I sank deep into the river before buoyancy began pulling me toward the surface. The impact had knocked most of the air out of my lungs. I was an excellent swimmer and knew I could reach the shore, but I was concerned about coming up under the rumpled silk, or becoming tangled in the wet cords, and not being able to catch a breath. It felt as though I had not breathed since jumping from the fortress.

I blindly clawed my way toward the surface. Then a blanket of sheet lightning lit the surface, like a candle lights a windowpane from behind, and I could see that there was nothing blocking my way. Breaking through, I sucked in a huge gulp of air, filling my lungs. I coughed up some river water and took several more deep breaths as I treaded water.

To my right, my father was removing the cords from his arms.

"That was great!" he called out over the sound of the rain striking the slow flowing water.

"Yeah, great," I said, with only a fraction of his enthusiasm.

"We've got to try that again sometime," he said.

"Yeah, great," I repeated with even less enthusiasm than the first time.

EIGHTEEN

"Let's swim to the far side," my father suggested. "I know it's Lamanite territory, but we should be able to hide, then get a boat and make it back over in a week or two, when things have cooled down."

"We've got to go back now," I told him as I shucked the cords from my shoulders, letting the silk drift into the darkness downstream. "There's a girl waiting for me."

My father ducked his head under the surface, then came up shaking his head back and forth, as if to clear the water from his ears.

"I'm sorry, son. For a moment there I thought you said you had a girl waiting for you."

I knew he was goading me. "I do, Father. Her name is Elsha. She's from Bountiful. I helped her father escape from the Gadiantons in Nephihah, and now she's helping me rescue you."

"And how is she doing that?" he asked skeptically.

"She provides quite a distraction."

"How?"

I smiled at the thought of seeing Elsha again. "You'll see."

We swam downstream with the current until we were about a mile from the fortress. The commotion created by our escape was concentrated around the main compound itself. A few canoes were launched, but they returned to the fortress after only a few minutes of searching. The thunder clouds darkened the night to pitch black, and the rain, which had

Gregg R. Luke

become a deluge worthy of Noah and his ark, created such a disturbance on the river's surface, that the Gadianton's attempts to search for us proved futile.

Climbing ashore, we made our way into the dark streets of Limhi. I led my father to the cattle pens where Elsha and I had agreed to meet. The streets were devoid of people because of the intensity of the storm. Arriving at the designated meeting place, I discovered that Elsha had not made it. My father and I waited in a deep shadow for a time before I lost patience, and I ventured out to look for her. I searched for almost twenty minutes with no luck; she was nowhere to be found.

I returned to my father, who had fallen asleep on a pile of dry straw. I couldn't blame him. He probably had not had a decent night's rest since his capture. I studied him as he slept, and my heart sank. My father, a man I had always known as having an eternally youthful mind and infinite strength seemed much older and considerably weaker. He was still strong, but it did not come without concerted effort. I could remember swimming with him for hours without him showing the slightest hint of fatigue, yet he had been totally worn out by floating a mile downstream. And as we had worked our way back into Limhi, I noticed that he walked with a pronounced limp. I hadn't asked him about it, or about anything else for that matter. I figured there would be time enough later for catching up. Now, we had to find Elsha and get out of Limhi, but since she was not at the rendezvous point, I didn't know where to begin looking.

I considered going back to the fortress where we had parted to see if her dancing had gotten her into a situation like her play-acting had in Nephihah. The thought of her fending off another enamored Gadianton did not set well with me. What if she were not so lucky this time? What if she had been forced to do something . . . unspeakable? I shook my head, not wanting to dwell on such a vile, degrading thought.

By now the brunt of the thunderstorm had passed us by, and a gentle, misty rain fell softly on the soggy ground. I had found a tattered, musty cloak in one of the stalls to cover myself with, and left the pens looking every bit like an old drunk wandering the streets in search of his next bottle. I headed for the fortress, trying not to be seen but also trying not to conspicuously avoid all contact. Still, at this time of night there was

190

little activity in the streets to worry about. I paused to get my bearings in a large courtyard surrounded by shops.

The sound of hoofbeats echoing down a narrow street kept me still. The horse stopped in the shadows before entering the courtyard. Since I was in the open, I decided to weave my way to a lit tavern at the opposite end of the courtyard. The horse and rider left the security of the shadows and cautiously made their way forward just as a break in the clouds allowed the moonlight to illuminate their movement. The rider was coming straight for me.

I staggered to a stone bench next to a fountain, thinking I could lay down and pretend to have fallen sleep if the rider approached and began asking questions. Then I realized that the horse was actually hors-*es*, two of them, one with the hooded rider who was leading a riderless horse behind him. The rider must have been a dignitary or official of some kind, and not a guard, because he was small of frame, yet rode a muscular stallion adorned with an ornate saddle and bridle. The second horse was also a magnificent creature, one sturdy enough to carry a man hundreds of miles without tiring.

The rider studied me as he urged his horse forward. The rest of the courtyard was empty. Judging from the glimpses of sky I had caught through the breaks in the clouds, dawn was at least a couple more hours away. I figured that I could easily overpower this small man, take the horses from him, and use them to aid our escape once I found Elsha.

Feigning a drunken slur I said, "Who'sth there?"

When he didn't answer I added, "Go away, you pomposth pig."

I attempted to stand, but collapsed back onto the bench as I slid the Nubian dagger from under my cloak. The rider approached slowly, his mount's hooves clopped with a hollow sound on the cobbled courtyard.

"Leave me be," I said, turning my back as I crouched on the bench, ready to spring on him. I didn't want him to see how young I really was.

The rider came on and stopped right beside me, exactly between the fountain and the bench I was on. He was so close, in fact, that I could feel the horse's breath on my back. This was too easy, way too easy. Something wasn't right. I could be on this man and slit his throat in one fell move. Why hadn't he said anything yet?

"I said leave me be," I whined, adjusting my stance to better my attack. "Pleeeease, sir," I continued, "I don't want no trouble."

"Then let's get out of here before any shows up," the stranger said in a low tone.

I sprang up, angling for the rider, my dagger poised and ready. My muscles exploded like a tightly wound spring suddenly loosed, but my mind had registered something that told me to stop. It was something in the rider's voice. Not so much *what* was said, but *how* it was said. The tone of his voice told me I had nothing to fear from him. No. *Her.*

I moved my dagger just in time to miss the rider's neck. Instead, I wrapped my arms around the rider, and both of us plunged into the fountain behind. I came up with the rider's collar in my hands and dragged the unknown horseman to her knees.

"Gideon, wait!" she said, spitting out a mouthful of water.

I let go long enough to rip the hood from her head and look into eyes that were scared and confused and angry all at the same time; beautifully translucent green eyes.

"Elsha? What—"

"Thanks a lot," she grumbled as she pushed me back and stood up. "As if I wasn't wet and miserable enough before."

I rose quickly and wrapped my arms around her. "Elsha, I was so worried."

She was rigid at first, but when I refused to let go, she softened to my embrace. I felt her arms go around my back to hold me close. Words fail me when I try to describe the wonderful feeling, the sheer, sweet energy and emotion, the inexplicable rightness that passes between two bodies in such an embrace. I could have stood there, shin-deep in a cold public fountain for eternity just holding her in my arms.

"Gideon, I'm all right, really," Elsha said softly. "Let's get out of this fountain and get going."

I squeezed her even tighter. "Not until you tell me you love me," I said with a surprising amount of emotion in my voice.

She eased from my embrace and looked deeply into my eyes. "I love you. But I'll love you a lot less if we get caught standing here like fools when we should be getting out of this city."

"That's why I love you, Elsha. You have brains as well as beauty."

She scoffed, "I'd say that getting out of Limhi was more common sense than anything brainy."

I chuckled, "See what I mean?"

She proceeded to ring as much water out of her clothes as she could, and asked, "Did you find your father? Is he all right?"

"Yes, he's fine, though a little weak. I left him at the pens, where we had agreed to meet."

"Good. I was just on my way there when I ran into you here."

Climbing on a horse I asked, "How did you know it was me?"

"Gideon, you make a lousy drunk, which actually is a good thing. A true drunk wouldn't have avoided puddles and animal droppings the way you did. I figured you were faking inebriation, but I really wasn't sure it was you at first. That's why I approached so cautiously. You could have been a decoy or spy of sorts."

I gave a low whistle and turned my horse toward the cattle pens. We found my father still asleep on the straw. I awakened him and gave him his own mount. Elsha joined me on mine.

We reached the edge of the city in a minutes. A few souls could already be seen moving about in preparation for another day, and some light traffic had already sliced new markings in the mud. We had been concerned about the wet ground allowing for easy tracking, but the commerce in and out of the city would make it nearly impossible for us to be followed.

We were well along the road to Bountiful when my father suddenly suggested we head down a narrow animal trail to one side. When I asked why, he responded, "We're being followed."

"Can you tell by who?"

He shook his head. "But I don't doubt the Gadiantons will be sending a search party very quickly, and this might be them."

We worked our way through dense jungle choked with underbrush. The trail faded in and out, but my father seemed to know exactly where he was going at all times. Our progress was slow but steady. Even with the imminent threat of danger we were in, I didn't mind our slow pace. It felt good to have Elsha behind me with her arms around my waist.

"So what happened back there?" I asked her softly.

"Nothing much, Gideon. The wealthy official I danced for took me into the tavern for a drink and whatever good time he thought he might have with me, but it never happened. As soon as I found out where he lived and that he had several fine horses there, I convinced him that the public scene made me nervous. I told him I had a large, abusive, over-protective father who might catch me there, and that we should go to his place. The guy was already pretty liquored up, and swallowed my story hook, line, and sinker."

I patted her hand. "But how did you end up with his horses and not him?"

"After we got to his house, I got him to drink so much alcohol that he passed out," she answered matter-of-factly.

"Just like that?"

She sighed a bit. "Well, not as fast as I would have liked. While I kept calling for servants to come in and refill his cup, and he kept trying to kiss me and put his hands all over me. I didn't like it, but I had to pretend to be interested in him for a while."

"Interested?"

"Yeah . . . you know."

"No, I don't," I said sharply.

"Interested, like I wanted to be his girl. I pretended that I . . . liked him."

"And how long did that take?" I asked in a voice that sounded more perturbed than I wanted it to.

I felt her arms slacken from my waist. "Why are you grilling me like this?"

"Because I want to know exactly what you did to convince him to give you these horses and simply ride away."

"I told you, I got him drunk and he passed out. He didn't simply *give* me the horses," she snapped.

"So did you kiss him?"

Suddenly, a hand smacked the back of my head and a fist punched me in the kidney "I don't like the way you're questioning me, Gideon, like I intentionally did something wrong. What is it with you anyway?"

What was wrong was that I was jealous, incredibly jealous. The thought of any man making lustful overtures toward Elsha made me bitter with anger. And the fact that she had willingly encouraged it made my blood boil. It sounded as if she had liked being the object this man's lust. Had she actually enjoyed doing these things? Had she led this man on because she found sport in it? Because she got a thrill out of playing the brazen vixen?

The answers were obvious, and it suddenly occurred to me that I was acting like a fool. I knew Elsha better than that—or should have. She was right. She hadn't done anything wrong. On the contrary, she had done everything right. Exactly right. If she had tried to overpower or tie this man up, he would have sounded an alarm that would have ended in her immediate capture. If she had killed him, his servants would have found him and sought her life. To encourage him into a drunken stupor was undoubtedly something everyone in his household was used to, and she could easily have made up a story about being allowed to borrow the two horses. It would be hours before he woke up and could confirm or deny the loan.

I sighed heavily at my own stupidity. "I'm sorry, Elsha."

She smacked me again on the back of the head. "You should be."

"I don't know what got into me. I guess I was a little jealous."

"A little? You practically accused me of wanting to bear his children," she said bitterly.

"All right, I was insanely jealous. Absolutely blinded by it, and I am sorry. But just the thought of another man looking at you, ogling you up and down, makes me angry."

She snickered softly. "It doesn't matter where I am, Gideon. Men have always looked at me that way, including you."

"I have not," I protested.

"Oh, yes you did. Only it wasn't in a lustful way, the way I'm used to being looked at. That's part of the reason why I liked you from the start."

"I thought you hated me."

She chuckled again. "That's because I had such high hopes at first. Then when you deceived me—"

"I did not," I protested again.

"All right. When I *thought* you were deceiving me, I was a bit angry. But when I realized I was wrong, I liked you even more."

I placed my hand on her knee and squeezed it gently. "And I should trust you more. I am truly sorry for doubting you, Elsha."

She slid her arms around me and said, "Well, I guess I would be concerned if you weren't at least a little bit jealous."

"I love you," I sighed, my voice constricting with sincerity.

"I love you, Gideon."

An arrow slammed into a tree exactly on my left. My father turned at the sound of it as another arrow whizzed past my ear and glanced off his shoulder.

"Go!" my father yelled as he moved his horse between us and our attackers.

I started to protest, but he added, "I'll be right behind you. Now go!"

I spurred my horse into a gallop. Elsha clung tightly to me as we crashed through the foliage encroaching on the narrow trail. I glanced back to see my father directly behind us, ducking to miss the branches that whipped back as we passed through them. I could not see who was following us, but it had to be guards from the fortress. How had they had followed us through the dense jungle? It didn't matter. They were there now, and they were close.

The trail appeared to widen ahead, so I drove my horse even harder. We rounded an outcropping of boulders and found ourselves in a small clearing surrounded by trees. On the far side of the clearing, not fifteen yards away, stood a battle-dressed stallion with a fierce-looking guard sitting atop him, with a lance cocked and ready. My horse skidded to a halt, stopping only a few feet from him. My father rode up beside me and stopped. An instant later two riders entered the clearing behind us. All three had their weapons trained on us. None of them were smiling. Neither were we.

NINETEEN

The large man in front of us lowered his lance and laid it carelessly across his lap. The two behind us kept their bows drawn. No one spoke as we cautiously appraised each other. Finally, the big guy cleared his throat and spat on the ground.

"Personally, I can't see what all the fuss is over you people," he said with an annoyed impatience sharpening his voice. "I think we'd be better off if you were dead. You are a respected man, Hezikiah, and many would bend to our wishes if they knew you were beaten. Besides, there are other ship designers around, ones who are more willing to help our cause . . . with less persuasion."

My father gently rubbed his wounded shoulder. The blood was already soaking through the cloth of his tunic. "I agree. I'd be much less trouble to you Gadiantons if I were dead. But think of how persuasive I could be if I actually aided your cause."

The guard nodded. "Yes, that's true. But you and I both know that will never happen." He sighed and shook his head. "No, I think it'd be best if we killed you right here. The news of your death while trying to escape would carry some weight, I should think. We could still return with your son and this girl and consider our efforts successful."

The two behind us chuckled knowingly. I hoped that my father's relaxed manner made them think they could lower their guard, if only slightly. But I didn't dared to turn around and find out.

"So what are we to do?" the big guard asked rhetorically, while examining his lance with an appreciative eye.

"You could let us go and simply claim you killed us," my father suggested.

The guard snorted. "Yes, I suppose that's true too, but it certainly would not be much fun."

"What if we promised to head north and never return?" Elsha said from behind me.

The guard's eyes twinkled as he leered at her. I wanted to wipe that grin from his face with my fists. One did not have to be a mind reader to know exactly what he was thinking.

"Oh, you won't be involved in anything we do to them, my sweet thing," he said. "You're much too fine a possession to kill or imprison without having first rendered some satisfaction."

"She's not a possession, you filthy pig," I hissed. "And you'd best not try and touch her or you'll be sorry."

The guard raised an eyebrow at my remark and leaned forward in his saddle. "You're Hezikiah's younger son, am I right?" He shook his head slowly without taking his eyes from mine. "The young are always so cocky. It's too bad your father hasn't taught you better manners. I'm not accustomed to tolerating insults from belligerent whelps like you. So if you do not wish to die right here, right now, I suggest you keep your mouth shut from here on out."

He had a confident manner about him, and was well-spoke. He was obviously a man of importance to know so much about me and my father. But I knew this carefree banter could not go on forever. Eventually we'd either be killed or taken back to Limhi. I didn't fancy either option. It was time for a distraction, something that would give us some kind of an advantage.

"You seem very articulate for a lazy, inane Gadianton-want-to-be," I said while removing Elsha's arms from around my waist. I whipped a leg over my saddle horn and dropped to the ground. "Let's see if the rest of you works as well as your mouth."

The guard urged his horse forward a few steps and he lowered his lance to my chest. "There's a distinct difference between bravery and foolishness," he said, anger punctuating his words. "Apparently your father hasn't taught you that lesson either."

"My father has taught me many things," I said, grabbing his lance and holding it firmly. "In fact, I have probably forgotten more than you could ever hope to absorb with that pea-sized brain of yours."

One of the guards behind me snickered. Anger glowed in the eyes of the guard whose lance I was holding. As he tried to jerk the weapon free, he was surprised by the strength in my arm. His lance didn't move.

"Go on, Argob," one of the guards said from behind me, chiding his leader into action. "Show him who's the teacher and who's the student."

He moved his horse into me, causing me to move off-balance, then yanked the lance from my grasp. He then slid gracefully form his horse and squared up to me. Again I detected a glint of surprise in his eyes when he discovered I was the same height as he.

"Gideon, I don't think this is wise," my father said in a measured tone.

"Shut up, you," one of the guards said as he clubbed my father from behind, knocking him unconscious and causing him to fall from his horse.

Argob nodded toward my father. "He's got more smarts than you'll ever have. You'd best do as he says or I'll teach you the last lesson you'll ever learn: how to die."

Argob retreated a step to bring his lance up to my belly. Suddenly, there was a rustling sound behind me. A couple of quick grunts, muffled cries of pain, and the distinct thud of heavy objects hitting the ground. I kept my eyes riveted on my adversary's.

"Come on," I said, ignoring the sounds behind me and bringing my feet and fists to a combative stance. "Let's see if you can fight as well as you blabber. Or are you only a well-oiled mouth in a fat, bulky frame?"

Argob's eyes suddenly went large with fright, only he wasn't looking at me anymore, but slightly behind me. I doubt if he even heard my last insult. I waited for him to make the next move, and when he did it was a nervous, fumbling step backwards. Had I been that intimidating? No, something else was happening. Then I felt a presence directly behind me and I heard Elsha gasp in shock. I was about to turn when Argob cried out in fear, and sprinted into the jungle. I turned quickly and found myself staring at an enormous chest. It was Noah.

I reached up and punched his large shoulder playfully. "It's good to see you again, Noah. Thank you for your help."

"You're welcome," the giant replied in a voice so deep it felt like the ground shook when he spoke.

I stepped back in shock. "You can speak?"

He nodded. "But I get more out of listening."

"But . . . Helorum said you were mute."

"No, he said I chose not to speak."

"All right, you got me there," I said. "Now—not that I mind—but why are you here?"

"Aiya sent me. She thought you might need some help. And I needed to deliver a message."

"Well, I'm glad you came," I said, staring at the two unconscious guards on the ground behind him.

My father began to stir, moving to rub the back of the bruised head, but instantly collapsed again. I knelt to help him as Elsha handed me a moistened cloth.

"How did you know where to find us?" I asked Noah.

"I listened," he said, without further explanation.

Elsha could not take her eyes from the huge man beside her. He smiled, looking directly into her eyes, she still sitting atop a horse and he standing on his feet beside her. Elsha suddenly realized she was staring and quickly averted her gaze. But it was only a moment before she was gawking at the giant again.

Noah smiled again and nodded.

Elsha shook her head to break her gaze. "I'm terribly sorry. My name is Elsha," she said, extending her hand.

Instead of shaking it, Noah gently took her hand in both of his and kissed it tenderly. Elsha blushed deeply and thanked him.

"This trail leads to an old hunting path about six miles north of here," Noah said, turning to me. "You can follow that path to the western coast without much trouble."

"Aren't you coming with us?" Elsha asked.

He shook his head. "I must return. Corianton is anxious to start the journey to the land northward. Your father, Ashod, is there too, and sends his love. He is doing well. He must ride a lot because of his injuries, but he says he is in no pain. He asks that you not worry about him, as he is among friends."

"Thank you," Elsha said softly.

"Now I must return to Aiya. I promised Helorum just before he—"

Noah abruptly stopped mid-sentence as a tightness choked off his words. Tears glistened as they pooled in his eyes and coursed down his cheeks. He did not wipe them away in shame, but rather, let them fall as he stared off into the distance, trying to gain control over his emotions. My heart sank as I gleaned the message of his unspoken words. I refused to accept the painful information that passed between us. It simply couldn't be. It wasn't right; it wasn't fair. That sweet old shepherd, a beloved patriarch, my dear friend . . .

Hot tears sprang to my eyes as I forced myself to form the words I didn't want to say. "Is Helorum . . .?" was all I managed to get out.

Elsha placed a gentle hand on Noah's shoulder, her own eyes over-flowing. "Has the Patriarch passed on?" she asked reverently.

Noah nodded solemnly. "He is with God now. But he did leave a message for you, Gideon. He said to tell you, 'Thank you'."

I remembered all that the old shepherd had done for me, and how much he had taught me. And yet I felt so empty, like the life had just been sucked out of me. Ever since meeting Helorum, I had prayed for a chance to repay him, but now I would never get that chance. I wished I had told him how much he meant to me, how much I owed him, how much I cared for him. Helorum had said I was a fulfillment of his life's work, but I still did not see how that could be. To this point I had done nothing for him, nothing worthy of his admiration and love, and yet he had given to me freely. Why was I not to be allowed a chance to repay him? Why was I robbed of his wonderful company, never again to be blessed by his comforting presence? I had deserved so little, yet he had given me so much. I sank to my knees with my face in my hands.

Then Elsha was beside me with her arms around me. She held me as I openly sobbed. I cried to God for understanding. I pled with Him for help in my helpless state. Why would He take my dear friend when right now I needed him the most? Why was all this happening to my life? It simply was not fair.

I tried to picture Helorum's face, tried to remember his words and ponder their meaning, and as I did so, I felt a comforting warmth surround me and fill my soul. A calming peace enveloped my heart, and a crystalline clarity cleansed my mind. At that moment, I knew everything was as it should be. All was right in my world.

I don't know how long I sat there, but when I finally wiped the tears from my eyes I saw that the two guards were gagged and tied to a tree, and my father was slumped on one of their horses, still very groggy but conscious enough to hold on. Elsha helped me up, and we mounted our horses. Noah was nowhere in sight.

I don't recall how long the journey took, but we reached the hunting path Noah had mentioned just before nightfall. The peace and clarity I had felt in the clearing had continued to grow until I felt illuminated with the Spirit of understanding. I knew precisely what I had to do. And I swore in my heart, to God and to the memory of my dear friend, that I would fulfill Helorum's prophecy about me, or would die trying.

I paused as my father and Elsha joined me at the intersection. Elsha was leading the two extra horses behind her. My father was fully awake now and nursing a large bump on his head.

"What happened back there?" he asked, grimacing with every word.

"We escaped," I said, not wanting to dwell on the past anymore. I needed to concentrate on the tasks of the future. But my father needed more of an explanation.

"The last thing I remember," he pondered out loud, "you were challenging that Argob fellow to a fight. Then I said something . . . and then all went black. When I woke up, Argob was gone and the other two guards were unconscious and tied to a tree." He stared at me in disbelief. "Did you do that, my son?"

"No. We had some help," I said, looking down the hunting path, anxious to get moving but wary of potential danger.

My father turned to Elsha, who simply smiled at him and said, "You have an amazing son, Hezikiah."

My father gingerly touched his lump again as he drew in a hiss of breath. "Yes, but defeating three armed guards without a weapon of his own?"

Neither of us responded, Elsha was enjoying my father's confusion, and I was concentrating on what lay ahead.

When neither of us offered any more information my father said, "All right, you two can have your little mystery for now. But when I'm feeling better I want the full story."

Elsha chuckled and reined her horse next to mine. She placed a hand on mine and asked if I was ready. I nodded, then leaned over and kissed her. My father stared at the two of us as our horses moved down the path.

My father called out to Elsha, "And I especially want to know how my dog-faced son could make a girl as pretty as you fall in love with him."

Noah had been right. We had no further trouble as we rode the 200 odd miles to the western coastline. We stopped several times to camp or simply to rest, but maintained a good pace. We met only a few hunters and merchants of various nationalities who gave us no trouble. We occasionally traded supplies and information with them, and always parted company in friendship.

As we traveled, my father and I swapped stories, catching up on what had happened the past few months. He was especially happy to hear of my mother's safety, and that Joshua had helped her to escape. He thought it wise to flee this land with Hagoth as soon as possible, and start afresh in a new land.

The closer we got to the western sea, the more familiar my father was with the area. This was where he had been raised, and he regaled us with numerous—often embellished—stories of his childhood as we passed familiar landmarks. He soon took the lead and our pace increased. As we neared the crest of yet another hill, I detected the definitive tang of salt in the air. After days of traveling through the mountainous jungle, where glimpses of the sky or long, open distances were the exception more than the rule, the sharp scent of the ocean was about the sweetest thing I could remember smelling.

"The shoreline is just over this hill," my father announced. "When we get there, we'll head north. We should reach Tonalai in another day."

"All right, but we're not going to go with Hagoth," I said gently.

He reigned in his horse and turned in his saddle. "Why not?"

"I need to finish your open-ocean catamaran and sail in another direction."

"Why?" he asked, deeply concerned.

I reached into the pack which Elsha had been carrying and handed him the scroll Helorum had given me. He read it, then read it again and nodded. His eyes were wet as he handed the scroll back to me.

"I'm so proud of you, my son." It came out in a hoarse whisper.

Knowing what he had difficulty saying openly, I said, "I love you too, Father."

TWENTY

After pointing out the location of his secret project, my father led us in a northwesterly direction, following the contour of the coastline, toward the village of Tonalai. There, he said we could purchase supplies and other provisions needed for our voyage. It would take a lot of food-stuff to supply a ship even half the size my father had planned on build-ing. In discussing the details of the catamaran during our journey west, we had both agreed that a ship the dimensions his drawings called for would be impossible to build in the time we had. Since I was only planning for Elsha and myself, I figured on making the boat much smaller. In the end, it would probably be more of a bizarre, twin-hulled raft than a true cata-maran.

The reunion we had with my mother was wonderful. She looked worn and tired, but healthy. Her strong will and indomitable testimony of what was right had kept her going. Elsha and I stood back with hearts full and emotions unchecked as we watched my father and my mother hold each other silently for several minutes. Then I hugged her and we shared our concerns for each other. When I introduced Elsha to my mother, she immediately threw her arms around her and hugged her too.

"You are more beautiful than I had pictured," my mother said to Elsha as she held her close.

We were both surprised at her comment. "You already knew about me?" Elsha asked.

My mother nodded, stroking Elsha's lustrous hair.

"But . . . how?"

Smiling, my mother said, "I had a vision of sorts shortly after I arrived here in Tonalai. One night, as I was pleading with Heavenly Father to keep Gideon safe from harm, I suddenly felt a comforting peace in my soul, and I was given a profound assurance that he was being watched over. Then I saw in my mind Gideon kneeling with a very pretty, auburn-haired girl at a marriage altar."

"Mother!" I cried as Elsha ducked her head and blushed deeply.

My mother held out open hands in mock innocence. "What? I was simply answering her question."

My father chuckled and put his arm around my mother. "Come on, Tayani. Don't rush things. Let's let this tide drift at its own pace and see where it takes them."

"Where is Joshua?" I asked, trying to divert the conversation to less awkward terrain.

Mother's head hung in sorrow as she answered softly. "He went back to Bountiful."

"Is he still convinced the ways of the Gadianton's are right?" my father asked in weary exasperation.

"No, I don't think so," my mother said. "But I'm not sure he believes in the ways of the church either. I keep praying that in time he'll come to know the truth."

"Then why did he return to Bountiful?" I asked.

"Revenge," she said, her voice strained.

My father and I looked at each other, the same question in our minds, but no answer. My mother saw our confusion and filled in the blanks.

"He was very angry that the King Men had double-crossed him that terrible night when this all began. He kept saying how he had been promised that we would only be talked to, not taken captive and our home destroyed. He swore he was told we would never be in any danger."

She paused and breathed a deep sigh in an effort to control her emotions. "I think he went back to kill Kumran, or perhaps others. I told him we were safe and did not need to seek revenge. That if we simply kept the commandments, we had nothing to fear from the King Men or

Gadiantons, and that God would see to their punishment. I tried to convince him that our lives were too important to risk on something like getting even or seeking revenge. But he wouldn't have it. He said he needed his own satisfaction."

"He's always been such a stubborn man," my father commented, shaking his head. "He's more concerned about his silly reputation than his own life."

My mother smiled softly. "He's acting just like you, Hezikiah."

My father shrugged. "I suppose. But I was never so bull-headed that common sense ruled over pride."

We stood in silence, mulling over all that my mother had shared with us, and wondering what to do. Then Elsha spoke up.

"Do you want us to go get him?" she asked.

My father blinked in surprise and Mother reached out and hugged her again. "No, my dear," my mother said. "I've been praying about that too, and feel everything will turn out as it's supposed to. We must not only claim that we have faith, but we must demonstrate our faith by following the promptings of the Lord."

"Gideon was right," Elsha told her. "You have an amazing amount of trust in the Lord. I wish I had your faith."

"Oh, but you do," my mother argued. "I know you have a tremendous amount of faith. I only hope Gideon follows his own promptings concerning you before someone else comes along and asks you to marry them."

"Mother!" I cried a second time.

My father put an arm around Mother and turned her away. "Come, my meddling wife, let's go see if we can help Hagoth and the other saints with their preparations for the future. Gideon can take care of his own."

Elsha and I wandered amongst the saints who had gathered for Hagoth's voyage. His ship, floating just off a rock peninsula, was moored to it by a balsa wood pier. It was a huge vessel, bigger than I had imagined. How he had found the time and means to build such a craft boggled my mind. But then, he told me he had spent an inordinate number of seasons in Tonalai preparing for this journey.

Toward evening we had had enough of the confusion and crowds, but I didn't want to leave the security of strangers to face the inevitable task I had before me. It wasn't the building of a ship I was concerned with. All that morning and afternoon I had been trying to figure out how to go about something I had wanted to do long ago, but never hadn't the nerve. The things my mother had said had confirmed what was weighing heavily on my mind, and caused my heart to beat at twice its normal pace. When I finally recognized there was no stopping this tide, I asked Elsha to walk with me along the shore, away from everyone else.

Taking her hand, I led her to a secluded area overlooking the ocean. The evening was clear, and a mild, sweet breeze from the sea stirred the wonderful fragrance of jungle flowers around us. The cloudless day had been warm but not oppressive, and the angle of the setting sun made Elsha's skin glow with a smooth bronze tone that accentuated the highlights in her mahogany hair and the opalescence of her limpid eyes. She was simply beautiful, and I found myself growing mute again in her presence.

After a brief moment, I mustered the courage to press forward. "Elsha, there are certain things we need to do before we build our raft," I said, staring at my feet, lacking the nerve to look into her eyes.

"All right, where should we start?" she asked, a willingness to work hard firming her voice. "Should we gather building materials first or provisions for the voyage?"

I smiled at her fearless gumption.

"I've never built a boat before," she added, "so you'll have to teach me everything along the way."

I cupped her face in my hands and smiled. "No, there are things that need to be done even before we do that," I said tenderly.

She looked quizzically at me. When I didn't elaborate, she asked, "Remember how I commented on your eyes once?"

I thought for a moment, then answered, "You said they were very blue."

"No, I said they were an *honest* blue. Honest, as in truthful, sincere, trustworthy. I knew from the start that I could trust you. I guess that's why I was so upset when I thought you were deceiving me. Anyway, even though you have honest eyes, sometimes they are impossible to read."

I continued to smile at her but didn't say anything in response.

"What I'm trying to say, Gideon, is that sometimes—like right now—I have no idea what you're talking about."

"Perhaps this will help," I said as I reached into my pocket and pulled out a small, polished ring made of some multicolored metal I was not familiar with, but which was stunningly beautiful. There were no special settings or precious stones on it. It was just a simple band with what looked like grape leaves and vines winding an elegant, green and red-colored pattern around a gold circumference. I took Elsha's hand and slid the ring onto her finger. She gasped softly and blushed through her copper-toned skin.

"My mother was right. What needs to happen before anything else is me asking you to be my wife," I said, holding her trembling hand with my own shaky hands.

She looked up, tears glistening in her eyes. She mouthed the word "yes" but no sound passed her lips, then threw her arms around me and sobbed happily. After a moment—one that I wished would never end—she broke our embrace and wiped her cheeks.

"I was beginning to wonder if you were ever going to ask," she said with a nervous chuckle.

"To be honest, I never really thought about it until we were on the road from Limhi. You probably noticed I was very withdrawn after learning about Helorum's death, but I was actually doing a lot of pondering and praying. In answer to my prayers, the words of my patriarchal blessing, and yours, kept coming to mind. It was only then that I noticed that the two were actually the same blessing. Then the Spirit told me we were supposed to—"

"The Spirit told me the same thing that very night we received the blessings," she interrupted me with an twinkling eyes. "That's why I so readily agreed to go with you."

Her response answered a question I had been pondering for a long time. I smiled and put an arm around her shoulders, my heart too full at the moment to speak.

She toyed with the ring, lost in thought, then looked up suddenly with a confused expression on her face. "But where did you get this?" she asked, indicating the ring.

"I bought it from one of the merchants we passed on the trail."

"With what? Surely you didn't have that much money with you."

I opened my knife sheath and drew out a simple yet efficient hunting knife. Elsha put a hand to her mouth and drew a quick breath.

"You traded your father's Nubian dagger?"

I nodded. "Don't worry. I asked him first and he said it was a great idea."

She hugged me again, then asked, "But who's going to marry us?"

"I'm not really sure. Hopefully there's a priest here in Tonalai."

She looked at me with a slight amusement in her eyes. "Wait a minute. Don't sea captains have the some authority over these matters?" she asked, already knowing the answer to her question. "Why don't we ask your friend Hagoth to marry us?"

As it turned out, Hagoth was insanely busy getting things ready for the voyage, but welcomed a brief respite, especially for something as delightful as performing a marriage.

Several of the saints offered to help with the hasty wedding preparations. One woman offered the use of a white wedding gown, while a few others threw together some simple decorations in a cozy bamboo-and-thatch hut that doubled for a church. Everything would be humble at best, but that's the way we wanted it. My mother coordinated all the comings and goings in an efficient but typically over-zealous, motherly fashion. My father wisely stood off to one side and jumped in only help was requested. He counseled me not to voice any suggestions. As this was wholly a female extravaganza, even the most logical male opinion would only soil the blessed event.

"Just nod you head and say 'I do' at the right time," he admonished. "Anything else will only get you into trouble."

Two days later, on a gorgeous pastel-blue morning laced with gentle pink clouds, Elsha and I knelt across a coral alter in the humble makeshift church. We knew only a few of the people there, but that didn't seem to matter. The intimacy found among the saints made it feel as if everyone present were family.

"The closest temple is back in Zarahemla," Hagoth said, "so you'll just have to accept my stumblings and mistakes without complaint."

At that moment, seeing Elsha in a white dress with her hair braided and adorned with plumerea and other fragrant, delicate flowers, I had absolutely nothing to complain about.

Parting with my father and mother was not as painful as it was the last time, mostly because their lives were no longer in danger. We held each other tightly and patted each other's backs, but few tears were shed and no empty promises were made. My mother held me tightly and kissed my cheek, and then did the same to Elsha. To separate the family was not a thing any of us wanted, yet we all knew what had to be, and accepted it as the Lord's will. I would dearly miss my parents and the future we might have enjoyed together, but Elsha and I had each other now, and that more than filled the emptiness of our hearts. Besides, we had our own futures to fulfill. I expressed these thoughts to my father, who said that families that grow together spiritually will never grow apart emotionally. Even if they drifted apart physically, they will always be together. A true family lasts forever.

"I will miss you, Gideon," my father said with a firm hand on my shoulder. "It's not easy knowing I'll never see you again, but I will not be sad. I know that you will do what is right and that the Lord will always be with you. You have been given a tremendous mission to fulfill, and I am very proud of you, my son."

I was too choked with emotion to respond. We embraced again and said our good-byes.

I was my own man now and willing to accept the responsibilities that accompanied that station. But there was another responsibility, a greater one which I had not yet fully come to appreciate. Even though I was not with my childhood family anymore, I had the makings of a new family, my own family, standing next to me.

Elsha looked at me and smiled. I smiled back, realizing that, despite what I may have thought in the past, the Lord had never once turned his back on me. He was simply guiding me. Granted, it had been over a bumpy road, but He had been leading me by the hand to a better life. I thanked Him from the very depths of my soul, for I felt that I was the luckiest man, the most truly blessed man, in the whole world.

TWENTY-ONE

I was expecting a nearly completed sailing vessel at my father's secret boatyard. What I found was a pile of lumber, a few felled trees, and a random assortment of other materials overgrown with weeds and vines. To create a ship from these, especially one that would take us thousands of miles to who knows where, would require more than skill and craftsmanship. It would take a miracle.

Two other couples had come with us. At first I had protested, believing Elsha and I could handle the task alone. After all, our blessings from Helorum hadn't said anything about anyone else going with us. Then Elsha pointed out that they didn't necessarily say we'd be alone either. Just the opposite, in fact.

"You are to be the leader of a nation," Elsha said. "Do you think we'll simply slide up on some shore somewhere and have a throng of people awaiting your inauguration?"

"I don't really know what to think," I said, staring at my feet in frustration.

"Then listen to me, Gideon. These people have callings similar to ours, and they are good people, each of them, and are willing to let you be in charge because they trust you." She chuckled lightly as she added, "if only because they don't know anything about sailing and navigation, let alone boat building."

"But I don't really want to be in charge," I admitted. "I don't think I have it in me to be the leader of a nation."

"That's a bunch of mule feathers, and you know it," she said with a tinge of sharpness in her voice. "These folks have already accepted you as their captain. They want you to lead them because they have faith in you. Helorum himself said you would be blessed if you followed the course in your patriarchal blessing. So, if that's the case, and I believe it is, then you need to have faith in yourself, accept their belief in you, and be their leader."

"Well, I'll try . . . but I'm not sure how good I'll be, or if they'll even like me."

"You'll do fine. Just be yourself, Gideon. Everybody likes you that way. Don't try to be someone you're not. Remember what Alma said to his son Shiblon? 'Use boldness, but not overbearance . . . see that ye do not boast of your own wisdom or of your much strength.' That's the way good leaders do it."

After meeting the others and spending some time with them, I did not feel so apprehensive. They were good people, like Elsha had said. Zelph and Naomi were a young couple with a newborn son named Nephi. Zelph was a solidly built man about ten years my senior who carried himself like a warrior, and yet was as gentle as an ocean breeze when he was with his wife and son. He had with him a wonderful supply of gardening and woodworking tools with which he was very skilled, which surprised me. I thought a man of his stature would have an armament of lethal weapons. Then a phrase came to mind: 'They shall beat their swords into plowshares.' I knew in my soul he was a true disciple of the church. He had willingly replaced his sword and cimeter with a plow and adz, and was happier than ever. He took my hand in both of his and, with tears misting his eyes, warmly thanked me for allowing his young family to go with us.

"I am not afraid of challenges, danger, or hard work," he said with a firm voice. "Just tell me what to do and it will be done."

I thanked him, then said, "I appreciate your confidence, Zelph. I know I am good with boats because I have spent my life on the sea, but I am admittedly young, and you don't even know me. May I ask why you trust me and what I say I am able to do?"

"There is a confidence in your eyes that I rarely see in men twice your age, Gideon. I respect that."

"And when we were making this decision," his wife joined in, "we had a marvelous spirit come over us telling us this was right."

At once I had an overwhelming confirmation of the Spirit myself, and felt very fortunate that they were coming along.

The second couple were older, perhaps in their late-fifties, and had no visible means of support except for the clothes on their backs. They had no offspring to care for them and no one else seemed to want to lend them aid. His name was Jonah, and upon hearing that name, I wondered if it weren't a bad omen, considering the voyage we were about to undertake. He was a small-framed, gentle man with kind eyes and balding head. He smiled at my awkward pause after hearing his name and assured me that even if Nineveh was our destination, he would still go without hesitation, and we would not have to suffer the Lord's retribution. His wife, a large, hard-eyed woman named Libbiantiomnihah was his exact opposite, and I wondered how the two ever got together in the first place. She proved to be as formidable as her name. Fortunately, she allowed us to call her Libbi, but that was the extent of her graciousness. She was dominate and dictatorial, and she voiced her opinions without any concern as to how they might be received. It was easy to see who governed their marriage. As coarse and abrasive as pumice stone, Libbi greeted me with a scowl and a sharp string of epithets, announcing that this was her husband's idea and she wanted none of the blame when it failed miserably. She made sure to point out that most of his ventures had, in fact, brought her nothing but grief and misery.

We began by establishing some order to our project. Zelph, Elsha and I worked side by side, clearing the overgrowth from around the materials my father had gathered. I got just what I expected from Zelph, and more. He was a powerful man with sinewy muscles and tireless stamina. The more I watched him, the more pleased I was that he was coming with us. Elsha also proved to have a staying power that surprised me. She worked without complaint on whatever was needed, whether it required sweat and muscle or a gentle touch and finesse. Some days it was all I could do to keep up with her.

Naomi and Jonah worked together on the sail and braided hemp ropes. I was impressed with the skill they showed for something they had never done before. When I questioned their expertise, Jonah explained that he had been a full-time teacher and part-time cloth merchant before coming to Tonalai. From childhood until the time she was married, Naomi had assisted her mother, a seamstress. The quality of their work and the strength of the ropes they crafted was beyond anything I could have done. When I praised their efforts, Libbi jumped in with a litany of complaints about the lack of good material to work with, and the less-than-satisfactory environment they were forced to labor in. Naomi and Jonah simply thanked me for the compliment. Libbi was certain the ropes would not be strong enough because her useless husband never seemed to do anything right, or so she stated.

The more I worked with Naomi, Zelph, and Jonah, the more impressed I was with their character and will. But why the Lord was tax-ing me with the abrasive Libbi, especially on such a hazardous voyage, I thought I'd never understand. If I could have had a few more Zelphs and Naomis instead, I would have slept much better at night.

Libbi spent the time she was not complaining gathering food and caulking water casks with pine pitch, then filling them from a crystal clear spring a half mile into the jungle. She proved to be a very good cook, and provided us with excellent meals and snacks throughout the day. But she was never to be questioned or shown even the slightest con-descension. I made the mistake of offering to carry a cask full of water for her, and launched her into a tirade of expletives and insinuations regard-ing my insolent, male chauvinistic attitude toward her. I made that mis-take only once. She made it clear she wanted no help from anyone in our company at anytime for anything. She also made it a point to openly crit-icize just about everything I did, from the initial design of the raft to the way in which it was assembled. I would simply smile and continue with my original plans, but I was seething inside. Zelph and Naomi were not as patient when she began to needle them about all the things they were doing wrong in caring for their new son. Poor Naomi was so intimidated by Libbi's unending assaults she could not respond, and often broke into tears. One time, Libbi brusquely said she'd pray for little Nephi's welfare, because the way Naomi constantly coddled him guaranteed nothing more than the creation of the most spoiled brat the world had ever seen. When

I asked her to kindly keep those kind of opinions to herself, she retorted rather loudly that it was her duty as a matriarch in Zion to correct the ineptitude's of ignorant young mothers in the church.

Finally, when he could take no more, Zelph dropped what he was doing, squared up to Libbi, and pointed a rigid finger at her face.

"Listen to me, old woman," he said in a surprisingly calm but resolute voice. "If I choose to feed my son worm guts for breakfast and clothe him in banana peels, it is of no concern of yours. If I choose to hold him and kiss him when he's crying, I will do so without ever worrying if you approve or not. And know this: He is *my* son and he will never, ever want for love and kindness or a gentle hand. Nor will he ever want for protection from a meddling old battle-ax like you."

Zelph paused to take a deep breath and regain some composure. Libbi stood, with her mouth agape and eyes bulging from her wrinkled face.

"Now, while I appreciate and respect the wisdom of your years," Zelph continued softly, "I would also appreciate you letting my wife and I make our own mistakes and learn our own lessons along the way. I know we're not perfect, but if we were, then life would not be worth living. So, let us raise our son the way we deem best, and when we want your advice, we'll ask for it. Agreed?"

Libbi's mouth clamped shut as she turned every shade of red I've ever seen, then stormed off, calling for her husband to follow. I pitied Jonah and wondered if he might be in need of a little protection himself. But Jonah simply winked at us and continued on with his work, indicating that, 'she's all bark and no bite.' Luckily, Zelph smiled and returned the wink. The endless babbling which spewed from Libbi's mouth did not bother him . . . much.

Their silent communication only slightly calmed my apprehension. In spite of Zelph's impressive strength and size, Libbi's indomitable nature was wearing down his restraint. I prayed it would never come to a physical battle between them, but I couldn't help but wonder who would win.

Work on the raft progressed quickly, mostly because the construction site was perfect. My father had chosen a location that allowed for ease in assembling a large vessel, as well as launching it when completed. An abundant supply of available raw materials, and the fact that few people if any were ever seen, lent to a project that ran smoothly, without delay.

The site was comprised of a narrow but deep inlet that worked its way some 200 yards into the shoreline. A small, slow-moving stream fed into the inlet from the clear flowing spring a half mile or so into the jungle. The thick vegetation in that area consisted of all manner of deciduous and evergreen trees, and countless varieties of bamboo, hemp, and other plants necessary to construct a boat. More importantly, there were large balsa trees which grew almost to the water's edge. This allowed for ease of felling and positioning the main logs that would provide buoyancy for the craft.

Using a long pine trunk, my father had built a check dam that bridged the narrow inlet only inches above the waterline, allowing the stream to flow freely underneath yet holding back any large items floating on the surface. There was always debris of one sort or another carried to the sea by the stream, but most of it made its way under the check dam without any problem. Since the site had been left unattended for nearly a year, however, a few larger pieces of flotsam had caused a pile up of rotted vegetation and muck. After establishing the camp and construction site, Zelph and I spent an entire day clearing the dam.

We began building the raft by felling ten huge balsa trees, each about fifty feet long, then trimming them of their limbs and bark. This proved to be more of a challenge than I had planned because our axes simply bounced off the fresh cambium layer of each tree, which had a spongy quality to it. We had to first saw through the outer and inner bark before we could hack through the rest of the trunk. Crafting hollow twin hulls would take more time and man power than we had, so I opted for making stacked-log hulls. We let the large trunks float freely in the stream by tying a rope to spikes driven into the center of the end of each log, then securing the other end of rope to the check dam. After only one day in the water, the huge logs had oriented themselves to their natural floating position. We then lashed them together in two groups of five, three on top, then two side-by-side, with one on the bottom in an inverted triangle, and floated them again. When these achieved balance, we cut a 45 degree angle at one end from the waterline to the bottom log, creating a streamlined prow of sorts. Another set of smaller balsa logs were then laid in the channels created by the main logs and secured with rope. These two "hulls" proved to be so buoyant that we could stand all three men on one without sinking it more than an inch into the water. Balsa cross members were then secured perpendicular across the twin hulls, forming the base of our living area.

I was concerned at first that the cross members might pivot too freely on each hull instead of creating a ridged superstructure between them. But after observing a drifting piece of seaweed effortlessly matching the contour of each passing swell, I concluded that a flexible craft would be more likely to survive the precipitous voyage before us than one that would strain and resist every valley and crest the ocean waves threw at us.

My biggest concern was whether or not the water-logged hemp ropes would wear through with continual motion and abrasion. I made a mental note to stockpile plenty of extra hemp for the voyage.

True to my father's design, we constructed keels that extended through large chinks between the logs, two to each hull. While none dropped plumb into the water, they were each exactly parallel to the length of the hulls and would prevent the craft from slipping sideways in the water. We erected a lattice bamboo deck on the cross members, and attached to it a keel, or centerboard, of much larger size. This centerboard ran almost eight feet in length and extended some nine feet into the water. Zelph and I then positioned a large chunk of balsa with a hole bored through it on the deck above the end of the centerboard. A stout pole made of mangrove, also known as ironwood, slipped through this thick block and extended into the water with a narrow, flat rudder of the same material secured to it. This would allow excellent steerage, as the water would be guided along the centerboard and across the rudder. In the middle of the raft, we inserted a tall mast through the deck into the centerboard, fastening it with guy ropes stretched from its peak to each corner of the deck. Zelph and I then constructed a bamboo and thatch cabin on the deck and covered it with palm fronds. The cabin had two rooms divided by a thatched wall. The smaller back room was to be used for storage and miscellaneous materials. The larger, main room, had a retractable cloth covering in front that could be pulled aside and secured to the side walls, allowing the sea air to circulate in and out freely. In this main room, two cots and two hammocks provided surprisingly comfortable sleeping accommodations.

On a front corner of the deck we built a large box which we lined with two alternating layers of leather and stone. We then lined the interior of the box with thin slabs of shale which were held in place with a mud that hardened to stone when it dried. Over the top of this box we fashioned a work of metal rods to hold our cookware. This fixture allowed for a hearty cook fire on board without the fear of burning the raft out from under our feet.

As work progressed, we decided to move our camp onto the raft to give it a "dry run." Fortunately, everything proved to be acceptable. The only drawback to the cabin was its low ceiling of about six feet. When Zelph and I lost track of where we were, it was not uncommon to be rewarded with a painful crack on the skull.

With four extra pairs of helping hands, the catamaran-raft was completed many times faster than I could have done on my own. Within five weeks, we had a curious-looking but reasonably sound vessel. We named it the *Hezikiah*, after my father. Looking at the craft with an aesthetically discriminating eye, I'm not sure he would have appreciated the accolade. It looked more like the aftermath of a hurricane, a ramshackle chaos of lumber, bamboo, and rope miraculously floating as a single unit.

We spent the next few days stocking the raft with all manner of food. Water was a high priority, since we didn't know how many days we would be at sea before we sighted land. We lashed nearly fifty two-gallon water casks around the outer edge of the cabin.

The evening when the work was finally completed we lit a small campfire on the beach and huddled around it. Not many words were spoken as we stared silently into the flames, each of us wondering if we were sailing toward our destiny or our doom.

I was immensely proud of my friends and the work they had put in on our vessel. With a full heart, I looked from one to the other. Some returned my gaze with a wistful smile, others were lost in their own thoughts. Then my gaze rested on Elsha. A knot formed in my throat as my eyes watered uncontrollably. How could I be so lucky to have such an incredibly wonderful wife? What had I ever done to deserve such a spiritual, intelligent, caring helpmate? How was I ever going to prove myself worthy of her eternal companionship?

She looked up at me and smiled. The fire danced in her entrancing green eyes and caused her mahogany hair to shimmer. She put her arms around my waist and hugged me tightly.

"You're too wonderful for me," she said softly.

"I was thinking the same thing about you," I croaked through the burning in my throat.

"I know," she whispered.

The moon crested the eastern mountain range and began its incessant journey west.

"We sail with the tide then?" Jonah asked with a detectable anxiety in his tone.

I nodded. "It'll take us further out to sea, away from the currents flowing northward. If we're blessed with an offshore breeze we'll make it a good forty miles by nightfall."

"And why aren't we sailing north, in the same direction as Hagoth?" Libbi asked in an unpleasant tone.

"Because we're not supposed to," I answered matter-of-factly.

"Oh, and just how do you know that?" Libbi snipped. "I haven't seen a Liahona on board, or are you planning on making one out of a coconut?"

Zelph sighed heavily. He and Naomi took Nephi and left the campfire for a final walk along the shore.

Jonah also sighed. "Libbi, please. Not now—"

"Then when?" she snapped. "When we're lost at sea with no way of getting home?"

To my surprise, Elsha went over knelt in front of Libbi. "My husband has been sailing the oceans since he could walk," she said calmly. "He knows the currents, the stars, and the compass. He can read the wind like you or I read a book. We will be safe, of that you can be assured."

"Is that so?" she growled at Elsha. Then, turning to me, she spat, "Well, I'll have you know, Captain Knowledge, I'm not as easily convinced as your little wife."

"That I can see," I said flatly.

"It'll take more than a fancy raft and some pretty words to make me believe I'm going to survive this ordeal. As far as I'm concerned, you can sail off into the sunset without me. I don't trust any of this."

"Libbiantiomnihah, do you trust me?" Jonah asked.

She was poised to make what looked like a scathing retort, but then dropped her eyes and softly said yes.

"Why?" he asked.

She looked out over the ocean and was silent for a time, her lower lip quivering. "Because you love me . . . even though I'm a mean old woman."

"I love you for being you," he corrected her. Then with a determination firming his words to an intensity that astounded me, he added, "We are going with Gideon and Elsha because we have God's promise we will survive. I need no other confirmation than that. And neither do you."

She nodded and looked off to the horizon again. Elsha came back to my side and put a hand on my knee. Her touch was as soothing as a cool ocean breeze on a hot, muggy day.

When Zelph and Naomi returned, the fire had reduced itself to a few glowing coals. Zelph knelt down by the embers, his sleeping son in his arms. Naomi joined him to one side.

"We all need to follow my son's example if we're to sail with the tide at dawn," he softly said. "But before we retire, I wonder if our patriarch would offer a prayer for us."

Jonah beamed as if he had just been given the highest complement in the world. "I would be honored," he said humbly.

We all joined Zelph and his family, kneeling around the glowing coals. Jonah offered a prayer that was humble and yet profound. When he finished, I thanked him, then stood and gave everyone a warm embrace, even Libbi.

Without a doubt, everyone knew the Lord was with us.

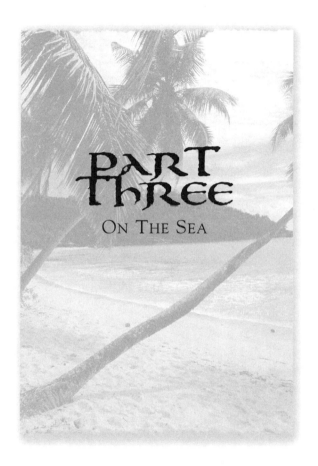

PART THREE

ON THE SEA

Twenty-Two

The sky was just beginning to gray when the tide showed signs of receding. It was time to cast off. I had been up for an hour already, kept from sleep by a nervous tension in my gut, mixed liberally with a boyish excitement in my heart.

With all hands awake, we said a quick prayer and manned our designated posts. I at the rudder, Zelph stood by at the sail, Naomi and Elsha sat at the bow of each hull to watch for obstructions in our path, and Libbi and Jonah walked the main deck, rechecking the security of everything else.

Because I was not familiar with the temperament of west coast weather, a bank of dark clouds on the horizon almost convinced me to delay our launch. But I felt confident in my ship and crew, and decided to put to sea, knowing the Lord would be with us.

"There's a fair wind off the mountains and a beckoning from the deep blue," I sang boldly so that everyone could hear. "Let's cast off and see where this tide takes us."

I cut the rope that anchored us to the check dam and the raft immediately moved with the current into the widening inlet. Because the tide was receding, there were several large breakers we had to crash through, but with the deck situated astride the hulls, little if any water splashed higher than our shins. The women on the prows, however, were not so fortunate. Each comber we plowed through completely covered Naomi and Elsha in shower of white foam. Within minutes they were drenched, and we weren't even past the coastal shelf. Yet despite their miserable station, both young women whooped and cheered with each successive wave as if they were riding giant surf boards for the thrill of it.

After a moment, Elsha stopped her cheering and sat up straight. Pointing dead ahead, she yelled, "Reef! There's a reef ahead!"

"We're going to hit it!" Naomi added.

Elsha's call reflexively knotted the muscles in my entire body. I scanned the area and saw the churning of water on rock stretching from the northern point of land to the southern point. I had suspected there would be some reef structures off the shore but did not think they would create a solid wall like this one. There were no charts of this shoreline that I knew of, but I had heard many sailors claim the continental shelf dropped dramatically from the western coast, and that reefs similar to those on the east coast were uncommon. Obviously they were wrong.

Because of *Hezikiah's* deep keels, I was beginning to think Hagoth was right in his criticism of my father's design. The raft might clear the reefs but the keels would certainly be ripped apart, rendering the vessel unnavigable.

I called to Zelph to raise the centerboard, which he did. He then dropped to the hulls to raise the keels, but they would not budge. The time in the water had swollen the balsa logs to the point where the chinks between them were almost completely sealed shut, and the keels were wedged in firmer than a skilled carpenter's mortise and tenon joint. They were now permanent fixtures. With the fresh offshore breeze swiftly moving us out to sea, there was little time to react to what lay in our path. The centerboard was my main concern and fortunately Zelph had reacted quickly there. But the keels were also important to our maneuverability and we would certainly lose them if we went straight across the reef.

"Coming about," I hollered as I leaned on the rudder, veering the raft to run parallel to the reef. Our progress instantly slowed as the wind spilled from the sail. Zelph hauled in one of the side ropes to bend the sail to the wind, but our angle was too sharp to allow for efficient tacking. From the perch on which the rudder was situated, I strained to see an opening, a place where the waves did not run as high or crest into whitecaps, indicating a deep, passable channel. In the vague light of early morning, there were none to be seen. And with the tide ebbing ever faster, and our forward momentum slowing by the second, we were loosing time quickly. Soon we would be trapped behind the stony reef and would have to wait several days for a high enough tide. I cursed myself for not checking out this possibility before hand, being so caught up in the building of the Hezikiah.

I called to Zelph to man the rudder, then climbed the main mast supporting the sail. A small platform—or, nest, as I called it—had been constructed atop to allow for better long-distance sighting of land. I never imagined I would be using it to look for water to free us *from* the land.

From the high vantage point of the nest, I could see the ebbing tide churning against the swells breaking on the protective reef. The resulting mounds of water formed by this collision washed over the reef with enough volume that would enable our raft to clear the rocks without difficulty . . . I hoped. The problem was timing. The swells were nearly impossible to predict. I watched in earnest, knowing our chance of escape was reduced by every second that passed.

Then it came to me; something my father had taught about waves and breakers. Ocean swells often came in sets of seven, the seventh being the largest of the sequence. I looked out to the sea and began counting the swells after a particularly large wave washed over the reef. I then estimated the spot where we needed to be when the seventh crossed the reef. To my dismay, the reef abruptly angled toward the coast at the same place, dramatically lessening our chances of clearing it successfully. If we swung around and headed north, paralleling the reef again, the wind would prove even more inhibiting, and we would undoubtedly end up grounded on the beach or dashed against the rock reef. Our escape had to be here, and it had to be right now.

I yelled down to Zelph to turn toward the shore on my signal, and had him move everyone else to the rear of the raft in an attempt to raise the bow slightly, my idea being to create more surface area for the wave to strike the hulls and launch us over the reef. I yelled the command and Zelph steered the raft toward the shore without question. Keeping my eye on the breakers building on the shelf, I estimated the timing as best I could, then hollered at Zelph to turn Hezikiah toward the sea. He tried valiantly, but with the centerboard raised, the catamaran did not respond as quickly as she should have.

"Put your weight into the rudder and point us directly at the reef!" I screamed.

We had to catch the full force of the wind to hurl us into the seventh wave just as it crossed the reef. Our speed increased dramatically as the wind finally popped the sail taut to full capacity. At the same moment, the sun crested the mountain, and a mass of cooler air careened down the mountainside and slammed into our sail, bending the mast I was perched on and almost sending me flying out over the bow of the raft. With the sudden force of added wind, we fairly skidded across the surface of the lagoon toward the reef. At first it looked as if we would beat the seventh wave to the rocks, but it actually timed out perfectly. The Lord was certainly with us. The *Hezikiah* struck the large wave with a reverberating *whumph!* and, with more than half of the length of each hull leaving the water, we literally flew over the reef. We landed with a tremendous splash that drenched everyone on deck except me, as I was still in the nest, high above all the action.

The swells were much easier to negotiate after we passed the reef. Having cleared the continental shelf, the frequency of waves died down quickly. The swells were still there, but spaced much further apart.

With the centerboard back in place, the *Hezikiah* handled very well, and Naomi and Elsha each took a turn at the rudder from time to time to get a feel for her temperament. Jonah had earlier fashioned a compass for us out of a half coconut shell filled with water and a sliver of metal stuck in a bit of cork that spun freely on a wooden dowel. The metal had been magnetized by rubbing it vigorously with a remnant of silk before pushing it through the cork. It worked remarkably well, and I was able to get a bearing on our position without difficulty by correlating our current direction with known landmarks on the mainland behind us.

With the sun high above us, and estimating the amount of time we'd been at sea, I judged it to be about noon. I decided to keep a log of our progress and information that might prove useful later on. The first thing

I noted was the temperature of the water. It was unusually warm. I guessed that, owing to its northern flow, it must have originated at the equator. The current was strong but not so much as to alter our westward course. There were faint wispy clouds way up high, long thin ones pointing to the horizon, and thick bulbous ones with black bottoms rising from the horizon. It was the last of these that gave me the most worry. I had been keeping my eye on them, hoping they would thin and lift before we reached them, but they only seemed to thicken as the day passed on. It did not bode well for a peaceful night.

After traveling a few hours in relatively comfortable sailing, a sharpness in the wind brought with it a rough chop to the water. The others did not seem to mind, being absorbed in the adventure. I decided not to deflate their high hopes and present joy with portents of danger. They would find out soon enough.

Jonah came up to me at the rudder and stood by my side for a time in silence, staring straight ahead. He then cleared his throat.

"I have tried not to question your skills at shipbuilding, Captain Gideon (they had all taken to calling me 'Captain' after Libbi's comment a few nights before), but I wonder if I might ask a technical question or two about the Hezikiah?" the old man asked with a pronounced uneasiness.

"Yes, of course," I answered, feeling quite the authority at the moment.

"I am not familiar with the long-term characteristics of the wood used to build these hulls," he began. "I know balsa is very buoyant when dry, but these logs have been in the water since they were felled. Aren't you worried about them becoming waterlogged and losing their buoyancy?"

I smiled at his understandable concern. "Not really. If the logs had had time to cure and dry I would actually be more worried about saturation. But fresh cut balsa has a peculiar sap underneath the cambium that acts as a repellent of sorts. I know the logs feel spongy to the touch, but if you were to cut into one of them you would find it relatively dry only inches below the surface. This is also because most of the logs are never completely underwater for more than a few seconds. As long as a portion of each is exposed to the sun and wind, the water will wick away and evaporate, keeping the logs dry enough to retain their buoyancy."

Jonah knotted his brow in concentration, taking in what I had just explained. Finally he nodded and took in a resolute breath.

"And what of the ropes?" he asked. "I have noticed a constant chaffing and pinching of the ropes between the logs. Won't they be worn through in a matter of days?"

I had noticed the same thing and did not have as confident an answer. "The fact that they are also soaked gives them a softness and elasticity. You know the old saying that the tree that stands stiff against the wind will break before the one that bends with the wind? It's the same kind of idea."

He nodded again and thanked me, then made his way forward. But his last question plagued my thoughts for a time. How long would the ropes last? My father and I had always used pins and bolts in our boats and rafts, making for a much more rigid vessel. The *Hezikiah* had few pins, and was mostly held together with hemp ropes of varying thickness. This allowed for a curious, incessant flexing of the raft. Instead of riding up each swell and flopping down on the far side as in a traditional boat, we actually melded with and mimicked the contour of the water, much like the piece of seaweed I had observed when we were first building the vessel.

That night a gentle rain began to fall. We soon realized that we would never be totally dry again until we reached land. Even inside the bamboo cabin, one often found it necessary to shift from side to side to avoid being dripped on. Libbi launched into another tirade of complaints about the wetness, but since her only other choice was to swim back to the mainland, which was no longer visible, she quickly reduced her expletives to barely audible but still annoying grumblings.

The following day the rain continued. Our spirits were still high with the newness of the voyage, but few cheers were voiced. Perpetual rain has a way of tainting even the happiest individual with melancholy. We took turns at the tiller and with the many sundry jobs around the Hezikiah. Even though our meals had to be served cold, Libbi and Elsha performed culinary magic, and threw together plate-fulls of breadfruit mash and seasoned beef that tasted like something the finest restaurant in Zarahemla would serve.

The rain increased as we sailed into our second night on the open sea. The horizon still loomed as a black abyss, and I continued to pray that the portentous clouds would disperse before we reached them. To divert our minds from the impending storm, we took the opportunity to catch some of the fresh water in empty casks. In spite of the rain, my throat was parched. As I lifted a goblet to my mouth to quench my thirst, I saw a small fish in the cup. I wondered how it got there, but didn't know who to ask. I removed the fish and took a drink, then set the goblet in the open to catch more rain. A moment later I lifted it again for another sip, and found another fish inside.

Elsha came up to me and said, pointing to the roof of the cabin, "Look at all the fish up there."

She was right. I hadn't noticed before because the wet thatched roof had a glossy texture that hid them, but there were indeed several dozen small fish the size of large minnows laying on the rooftop.

Just as Elsha was about to ask where they were coming from, a slightly larger fish landed directly on her head and flopped to the deck. It was raining fish!

"What's happening?" she asked over the rising wind.

I pointed ahead. "Do you see the exceedingly dark clouds on the horizon?"

She nodded.

"That's a big ugly storm, just waiting for us. I've been watching it since yesterday hoping it would blow out, but it hasn't."

"How big?"

"Could be a hurricane. But even if it isn't, a severe tropical storm like that one on the horizon can form waterspouts that suck salt water into the clouds and rain it down miles away. Sometimes schools of small fish get sucked up into the spout, and are dropped a long ways away."

Elsha giggled merrily. "That's really amazing."

I sighed heavily. "Yes, but it means we could suffer the same fate as the fish if we get too close to one of those waterspouts."

"Oh," she said suddenly humbled. "What should we do?"

"We need to make doubly sure everything is tightly secured. The thickest clouds appear to be moving northeast, so I'll try and steer south, but it'll be slow going. We're fighting a north current and we don't have much of a following wind."

I looked up at the dark, bloated thunderclouds. "We're not far enough out to catch the trade winds. That would help," I added wistfully.

Elsha got all hands to help lash every loose item to the deck or cabin. I suggested Libbi make some ginger tea for everyone to drink. The waves were going to get very big very quickly, and I didn't want anyone leaning over the edge to throw up, and getting washed over in the process. A warm wind kept the rain's chill away, but I felt the downpour's temperature steadily dropping. Zelph furled the sail and stood by my side. Everyone else entered the cabin and began to pray. I figured that would help more than anything else.

"Here it comes," I said, squinting against the rising wind and sting of the rain. At that moment the wind shifted and the rain poured down in huge cascading sheets of water. We were in for a storm of ferocious magnitude.

Within seconds the sea turned from a high but navigable swell to a foreboding, undulating nightmare that was impossible to predict. As the wind whipped up a veil of froth and spray, the horizon vanished. Massive, black clouds hung low and seemed to merge with the froth, allowing for only a few yards of visibility. It was probably a good thing anyway. The less we saw of the mammoth waves looming over us, the better we'd feel. Or so I thought. Several times we balanced on the crest of a mountain of water, only to be hurled down the liquid slope on the other side at a horrific speed and slammed into the next wave. The fact that we did not know how long this terrifying ride would continue did not help matters.

To my tremendous relief, the raft's design proved brilliant. As we entered the deep trough between each swell, the front portions of the hulls dug into the oncoming wave and disappeared. But as the wall of water raced toward the platform, the buoyancy of the hulls lifted the raft in time for most of the swell to wash underneath, and only a small volume of seawater cascaded over the deck.

We climbed and fell like this for what seemed an eternity, each wave promising to bring our demise, yet each time it passed under us with nothing more than an angry roar. A few times we were hit the side by a rogue wave, but the nimbleness of the raft never fought against the onslaught of ocean. Instead, the Hezikiah simply worked its way over the frothy crest and down into the next valley. I no longer worried about whether or not we would be able to ride out the storm, but whether the ropes would hold the flexible raft together was another story. Perhaps Jonah was correct in his fears. Each time we bounded up a new swell the ropes would groan and strain. It was obvious they were taking the brunt of the abuse. For hours I listened to their chaffing and squeaking, sure that each complaining groan would be their last. It was like one loud, ill-tuned chorus; a cacophony of demon voices wailing like banshees over the screeching of the wind, each rope having its own strained note according to its thickness and tautness.

"Captain!" someone called from the doorway of the cabin. It was Jonah.

I yelled for him to stay inside, but the wind threw my words back at me, and Jonah never heard what I said. Instead, he called out again and began making his way toward Zelph and me. The two of us had secured ropes to our waists for safety, just in case we lost our balance or footing, or were struck by an unexpected wave. Jonah had no such security measure, and the minute he came alongside the cabin, the raft pitched violently to one side, and he plunged headlong into the boiling water. I heard Libbi cry out as she watched her husband rapidly drift away from the raft. Without thinking, I placed Zelph's hands on the rudder and dove into the churning sea. I swam as hard as I could but never seemed to be gaining on the old man, whose head was only intermittently visible between the mountainous swells. It occurred to me to let the ocean do the work, so as not to tire too quickly. I crawled up the crest of one wave, then pointed my hands in front of myself and belly-surfed down the near vertical face on the other side. Within moments I was at Jonah's side and wrapped an arm around his torso.

I then tried to claw my way back to the Hezikiah but the wind was pushing her in the opposite direction. Then I felt the rope around my waist go taut as we were literally dragged back to the raft by Zelph's powerful arms. As we neared the raft, I saw Elsha at the rudder and Libbi clinging to the cabin with a look of horror blanching her face. Zelph hauled us onto the deck with little effort, and I thanked the Lord again for his presence on this voyage. We collected ourselves quickly and sent everyone back to the cabin for safety. Jonah was completely sapped of strength, and I realized had I hesitated, I would not have reached him in time. Libbi helped him lay on one of the cots, but paused briefly to smile and nod in my direction before ducking back into the cabin. Zelph remained at my side. I wanted to hug him and thank him for saving me, but we concentrated on guiding our vessel through the ferocity of this maelstrom.

To my astonishment, Zelph showed no sign of fear as he looked straight ahead at each oncoming mountain of water with jaw set and eyes narrowed. With a vise-like grip, he held on tenaciously to the tholepins, two vertical poles secured to the deck, which prevented the rudder from swinging too far to one side or the other.

"Captain!" he suddenly called over the bellowing of the wind. "What is that?"

I followed the direction of his pointing finger. At first I saw nothing more than a wall of water because we were deep in the trough of a swell. Upon cresting the swell, I gazed forward into the stinging rain. There was a blackness some hundred yards off, directly in our path; not the blackness of the night or of the storm, but the blackness of something solid, massive, and impassable. We dropped into another trough before I could get a true look at what was causing the black void before us, but as we crested the next swell it had covered half the distance and was now clearly identifiable.

"God in Heaven," Zelph breathed, his eyes bulging from a heretofore fearless face.

Hurtling toward us was a wall of water at least 200 feet tall. I yelled at Zelph to hang onto something as I crouched and hugged the tholepins around the rudder, praying like never before that the *Hezikiah* would hold together.

TWENTY-THREE

We were ascending vertically, or so it seemed. I literally dangled from the tholepins at the rudder, and stared down into the frothing abyss from which the behemoth wave grew. I half expected to either tip over or slide back into the trough to be swallowed up in the boiling green waters. But neither happened. Instead, we glided forever up the wall of water, then fell over the crest like a dead tree toppling into a river during a violent windstorm.

On the leeward side of the gigantic wave we slid down into a black valley, skipping and careening over the surface of the water at breakneck speed. The only thing that kept us in control were the deep keels on each hull and our centerboard. Earlier that morning I had cursed their existence. Now I thanked the Lord for them. I threw all my weight against the rudder to keep us pointing into the trough, hoping our bow would rise above the swell of the next wave. When we reached the bottom, it was as if the water formed a ninety-degree angle, with no curve melding into the next churning mass of liquid. I instinctively held my breath as the twin prows stabbed into the molten wall like knives into raw flesh. Huge plumes of seawater blossomed from each bow and obliterated the cabin and deck from my view. The heavy spray brought with it an empty water cask that had become dislodged. I tried to duck but was not quick enough. The oak cask smashed into my forehead and shattered into pieces, littering the ocean with shards of wood. Everything went hazy. I collapsed to my knees, fighting to stay conscious. I lost my natural orientation and balance, but I would not let go of the rudder. I could not. If I did, all would be lost. A murky blackness filled my head.

I don't remember a thing after that.

A gentle rocking motion and a tender caress stirred me from my slumber. The muffled sounds of the ocean and the creaking of ropes against wood made me realize I was still on the *Hezikiah*, and I was alive. I had been dreaming, but an excruciating pain in my head made it impossible to remember about what. I vaguely recalled it wasn't a very pleasant dream.

I cracked my eyes open for a glimpse of where I was, only to be greeted with a bright glare of sunlight so intense, it seemed to burn a hole through the back of my head. I flinched and screwed my eyes shut, but the harsh movement almost made me pass out again. Then a cool touch gently pressed against my throbbing brow and swollen eyelids.

"Shhh, you just relax now, Captain Gideon," a serene but happy voice instructed. The pounding in my skull made it difficult to determine who was speaking to me, but I guessed it had to be Elsha. The gentleness of her touch and the comforting manner in which she nursed my forehead were very familiar.

"Is—everyone—all right?" I croaked through a parched throat.

"Yes, we're all fine, thanks to you. You saved our lives, you know. Even with a blow to the head that would have killed any other man, you still brought us through the storm."

With my eyes still shut against the torment of the sun, I took the hand that was washing my wounds and tenderly held it against my cheek. I wanted to ask how I had saved lives, to find out what had happened after we rode over the monstrous wave, but couldn't bring the words to my lips without an unbearable amount of pain.

I held her hand to my cheek as her other one continued to gently wipe my brow and face. It felt wonderful. There is a certain perceptible healing in a simple touch, and I felt myself grow stronger each time Elsha daubed the cool moist cloth against my forehead. That she was at my side, helping me recover from . . . what? Oh, yeah, the projectile bucket knocking me out. That Elsha was with me now, comforting me and helping soothe my wounds with her gentle touch meant more to me than anything in the world. Only, the constant exposure to the sea must have been hard on her, because her hands were not as smooth as I remembered. I turned my head and kissed the back of her hand, wanting to express my gratitude and love for her.

"Shhh, now, Captain," she whispered. "You just rest and get your strength back."

Why was she calling me captain? She was, after all, my wife.

I cracked my eyes open again, longing to look at her—and saw Libbi leaning over me with a broad smile splitting her wrinkled face in two. I flinched again and the resulting pain shot through my head like a thousand drums pounding inside my skull. Libbi laughed gently, a sound I don't think I had ever heard before from her, as she continued daubing my head. She gently pulled her hand from my cheek and reached for some fresh water.

"Here, sip this," she said while tipping a gourd to my lips.

The water seared my parched throat, but it was delicious. When I began to drink deeply, she pulled the gourd from my mouth.

"Not so fast, Captain. A little at a time, or you'll get sicker than a yellow dog with a belly-full of worms." I already felt that way knowing I had kissed her hand, but wasn't going to say so.

After napping again, I crawled from the cabin and pulled myself to my feet. A large bandage was wrapped around my head in turban fashion. I was certain it made me look like Lehi from Jerusalem, but I wasn't concerned about appearances right now. I turned to look at the person manning the rudder. It was Elsha, and she never looked more beautiful.

"I see you're feeling better," she beamed cheerfully. It was the most wonderful sound I could have heard. I tried to answer, but the words burned my throat as they came. So I nodded instead, and was instantly rewarded with a skull-cleaving stab of pain that blurred my vision and destroyed my equilibrium. I gripped the edge of the cabin to steady my wobbling knees.

"Don't push yourself too hard, Gideon," Elsha warned. "That bucket cracked your head clean open. I'm surprised it didn't take it right off your shoulders."

The forensic coolness with which she spoke made me wonder if I had offended her again in some way. Then she smiled her perfect smile and blew me a kiss. I tried to smile back, but it probably looked more like a grimace.

"Quite so. We were all worried you might not recover from it," a voice said from behind me. I think it was Naomi.

"And I didn't want to have to sail this thing all the way to our new home by myself," Zelph said, moving next to me and placing a hand gently on my shoulder.

"Thanks a lot," Elsha said, gripping the rudder with more determination than ever.

Then Libbi was next to me, handing me a cup of coconut milk. The sweet liquid coated my throat and landed with a delightful swishing in my stomach that made me feel much better. I thanked everyone as best I could, then returned to the cabin and fell into a fitful slumber.

When I awoke again it was night. A cool breeze filled the cabin with the sweet smell of the open ocean. When the sea meets the shore it is mixed with all sorts of detritus: dead plants, seaweed, and whatever else washes into it from rivers and estuaries. The resulting odor is often not very pleasant. But out on the open ocean there is little in the way of decaying matter, and the sweet-salty tang of even the slightest breeze is delightfully refreshing. I inhaled deeply and reveled in the tranquillity it brought.

Sitting up slowly, I surveyed my surroundings. The ferocious pounding in my head had diminished to a dull thud. The dressing on my head had been changed and I wore a clean tunic. I didn't want to know who had dressed me. The dark cabin held four others, all fast asleep. Jonah and Libbi were on the cots toward the back, Naomi and Nephi were in the hammocks. All was blissfully serene.

Zelph was at the rudder, his eyes glued on the horizon. He acknowledged me with a nod and checked the compass. I was grateful we had mounted the compass firmly to a post in the deck and quite relieved that it still worked.

"What course are we following?" I asked after drinking from a water cask.

"Southwest, following the current and the trades," he answered with confidence.

I checked the compass against the bow of the Hezikiah and the position of the north star. He was right on the mark as far as our direction was concerned. But it seemed more logical that we'd been going *against* the current, given our present position. He must have been mistaken.

The moon was full and lit the ocean's gentle swells almost as well as the sun. I surveyed the raft carefully. Everything looked to be in good repair. If the storm had been meant to destroy us, it had failed.

A soft glow flashed sporadically from the twin bows as the raft broke through the occasional small wave. I watched this for a while, basking in the rush of childhood memories it brought. In many parts of the sea there are countless small creatures with the ability to generate their own light. These animals float freely on the surface in huge colonies and glow brightly when agitated. The phosphorescent green hue is warm and entrancing, and always bodes well for a calm voyage. I remembered the first time I saw it as a child. My father explained that it was a curiosity of nature and nothing more, but I always held that it had to have mysterious origins to be so breathtakingly magical. Just then a wave hit the bows and flicked a few of the glowing creatures at my feet. Upon inspecting them, I found that these were very tiny shrimp-like animals with large eyes. I tossed them back into the water.

"Where is Elsha?" I asked Zelph.

"I'm up here," a voice called from above, like a ministering angel from on high.

I looked up to see Elsha perched happily in the nest at the top of the mast.

"Get down from there," I said too forcefully, eliciting a painful throb between my temples. "It's too dangerous," I added a lot quieter.

"Don't be silly, Gideon," she called. "I've been climbing trees since I was able to walk. This little mast is nothing. Besides, the view is marvelous from up here."

I couldn't argue with that. I asked Zelph how long he'd been at the rudder. He looked haggard and worn out. In the full light of the moon, I thought I also detected an unusually heavy blackness around one eye.

"Not long," he answered softly; but there was an unmistakable weariness in his voice that belied his words. I thought maybe some conversation would enliven him.

"Why do you think we're sailing with the current? My understanding is that the west coast has a fairly wide northbound flow from the equator."

"We're not near the coast anymore," he said with a heavy sigh and forced smile that again showed he was nearing the end of his endurance.

I looked at the compass again. "We couldn't have made it beyond the coastal current in just one day."

He rubbed one eye, intentionally avoiding the puffy dark one. "We've been sailing for more than one day, Captain."

I gingerly fingered my swollen forehead. It occurred to me this latest wound was in the exact spot were I had been clubbed the night our house had been burned to the ground. If my skull wasn't damaged, I was certain the brains just behind it were.

"How long have I been asleep?" I asked, trying hard to concentrate on everything he said.

He looked at me and smiled. "Eight days."

"What?" I asked, thinking I had misunderstood him.

"That's right, Gideon," Elsha said, sliding down from the mast with ease. "You only awoke once, two days after the storm, then lapsed into a coma until now." She moved next to me, easing her arms around me and looking deeply into my eyes. "Are you feeling any better?"

"Well, I'd be lying if I said it doesn't hurt, but I think I'll live."

"Good," she said, hugging me tightly.

Turning to Zelph I said, "How did you know which direction to head?"

He shrugged. "I figured west was about our only option, so we've headed west-by-southwest ever since the storm."

His simple faith and boundless courage touched me. "You look about done in, my friend. Why don't I take the rudder this watch?"

"Hey, it's my turn next," Elsha argued. "You can be Captain again in the morning. For now we have a calm sea and a good breeze. Besides, I love sailing this thing."

"You like fighting the rudder all night long?" I asked skeptically, remembering how I had battled with it ever since we set sail.

"She's actually very good at it," Zelph admitted. "Better than I am, anyway. She has a certain feel for the way the current hits the center-board and the amount of pressure on the sail. She steers this raft like she was a part of it, with hardly any effort at all. I tell you what, your wife's a natural born sailor if ever I saw one."

I looked down at Elsha, who was beaming at Zelph's praise. She too looked drawn and tired, but there was a definite spark of excitement in her eyes that told me she was having the time of her life.

"Zelph has been very good too," Elsha said, returning the comple-ment. "He's really been a blessing to have along. I can't imagine what this voyage would be like without him."

"Well . . . I do all right," Zelph said, yawning broadly, "but, no offense Gideon, give me a horse any day over a boat. Life on the sea is not all romance and glory, I've come to find out." He touched his bruised eye and grimaced.

I chuckled lightly. "No offense taken, my friend."

"Go to bed, Zelph," Elsha said, also snickering at his last comment. "I'll take over for the rest of the night."

From behind me a solid voice called out, "Oh no you won't, young lady." It was Libbi. "Your husband just returned to us from the grave's edge and needs to be pampered generously. I'll take your watch and you take care of our Captain."

"Are you sure?" Elsha asked, a true disappointment saddening her tone. I couldn't believe she was actually wanting to sail the raft over being with me. But a squeeze from her arms around my waist let me know she meant otherwise.

"I insist," Libbi said. "It's a calm night and I've had plenty of rest."

Zelph relinquished the rudder to Libbi and made his way wearily to the cabin. Elsha and I moved to the front of the deck and hung our legs over the edge. She still had her arms around me and seemed to never want to let go. The cool ocean spray on my feet felt refreshing.

"I noticed a couple of baskets filled with fish by the cabin," I commented lightly. "Someone must be spending all day behind a pole and line."

"Not at all," she responded. "Those are flying fish. They start skimming over the surface of the water just before sunrise and invariably several always land on the deck or crash into the cabin. All we have to do is pick them up the next morning."

"Flying fish?"

"Yes. Their front belly fins are very long and flare out like a bird's wings. They glide more than fly, but I watched one sail along for almost one hundred yards once. And they're fast too. If one hits you, it'll knock the wind out of you. In fact, that's how Zelph got his black eye."

"From a fish?"

"Yes," she said stifling a laugh. "But he won't talk about it. He was laying with his head out of the cabin one night and turned to one side to get comfortable and *wham!* a flying fish nailed him right in the eye." She snickered and shook her head. "I think that was the first time I ever heard him curse," she added playfully.

"Then perhaps we'd better not be sitting here just dangling our feet dangling," I said with equal mirth.

"Oh, the flying fish won't be along for a while, but they always come. We've been eating fresh fish every day, good tasting fish too, and we don't even have to work for it. I think we should be more afraid of the sharks."

"Sharks?"

"Yes, they always come around too, but mostly during the day. There is a curious pattern to the life in the ocean, a kind of cycle that repeats itself each day. I assume this raft presents something out of the ordinary, so lots of fish and other creatures come to investigate, including sharks."

"Other creatures?"

"Oh yes, bizarre-looking things that I can't even begin to describe, some as big as Hagoth's ship, that glide underwater at amazing speeds.

Sometimes they stop and stare at us with enormous glowing eyes as big as serving plates. Yesterday we even saw a group of whales, but these other things weren't whales because they never came up to breathe."

I was fascinated and impressed with Elsha's calm acceptance of things that would scare the daylights out of most other persons not accustomed to sea life.

"You're amazing," I said lovingly.

Elsha hugged me tightly, trembling, and whispered, "Gideon, I love you so much. I was afraid you weren't going to recover from your accident. Everyone on board knows that what you did saved our lives. And everyone respects you and honors you, and cares for you deeply, even Libbi. They all say they owe their lives to you. They will always love you for the sacrifices you have made for them. But I love you even more because you're my husband. I am so very proud of you."

I felt awkward and somewhat embarrassed by the praise she shared from the others. I didn't have the heart to tell her that I hadn't only been thinking of the others during the storm. I had also been very concerned about saving my own skin. Everyone else had just happened to benefit from my efforts. No, wait. That wasn't quite true. There was another person I thought about constantly.

I turned to Elsha and held her face gently in my hands. "I'm glad everyone is well and happy. But I'll be honest with you. I was being very selfish that night during the storm."

"Selfish? How?"

"I fought to keep this raft afloat because the thought of you drowning tore me apart. I did it for you, Elsha. No one else. I would do anything for you," I said, struggling to stave off the emotion straining my voice. "Even give my life for you."

The words surprised me as they flowed from my mouth, but I meant each one from deep within my heart. I suddenly recalled the recurring dream from my coma: I remembered hanging onto the rudder, battling the sea and wind, salt and blood stinging my eyes, and watching a beautiful young woman with translucent green eyes who had trusted me with her life, sink into the black depths of the sea. She was within my reach, but I was unable to grab her, paralized by some unseen force. I shook the thought from my head.

Elsha hugged me again and I felt the warmth of her tears against my neck. She mumbled something, but her emotion made it unintelligible. It didn't matter. I understood her perfectly.

TWENTY-FOUR

The following morning confirmed Elsha's fish story. A bright lantern hung on the mast, all night, and come morning we found the deck littered with flying fish, bonito, tuna, and a number of other fish I didn't recognize. The light attracted the fish in hordes and many of the hapless adventurers ended up in Libbi's frying pan.

My head healed quickly in the fresh air of the open ocean. I took my turn at the rudder more than required because I felt obligated to catch up for the time I was unconscious. Everyone took a watch except Naomi and Jonah. The former tried valiantly once or twice but never got the hang of following the undulating current while still maintaining a westward course, and the latter was simply not strong enough to last more than a few minutes at the helm. A watch of alternating two-hour shifts was established for Elsha and Libbi, and four-hour shifts for myself and Zelph. That allowed for a rest period of eight hours in which one could sleep, swim, eat, or otherwise occupy themselves with any of a hundred chores needing completion.

Over the next few weeks, there were a number of things I noted in my logbook. The most important of which was a slow settling of the raft in the water. It was not drastic, and I doubted if anyone else had noticed, but the waterline had risen half a dozen inches on the twin hulls, and the person manning the helm found it more and more common to have his/her feet drenched by the current pushing the raft along. I figured the rate at which the balsa logs were loosing their buoyancy was slow enough to allow us about 100 to 150 days of worry-free sailing. After that, we'd all have to become very proficient swimmers.

My concerns about the hemp ropes proved needless. The chaffing between the balsa logs had lasted only a few days. By then, the outer layer of the balsa had become so waterlogged that the ropes became embedded in it and never again rubbed against adjacent logs or bamboo. The rope itself, however, also became saturated, and we found it necessary to constantly re-stretch and re-secure them. In fact, before long Zelph and I made it one of our daily chores to check the lines, and every once in a while a rope was stretched beyond its limits and snapped, necessitating its replacement with a new length.

Another thing I noted was the characteristics of the ocean itself. Instead of a greenish color dulling the water, the ocean now almost glowed with the most intense crystalline blue I'd ever seen. The water was amazingly clear, and only occasionally was it obscured by whitecaps and foam, whipped up by the incessant wind. It was easy to see the many animals that frequented our little home on the waves, down to forty feet or so beneath the surface. On especially dark nights, the phosphorescent glow of certain creatures could be seen down to sixty feet or more.

The absence of seabirds told me we were far from land, and the number of new creatures I did not recognize either by sight or by legend told me we were in a part of the deep few, if any, adventurers had ever traveled—and returned to talk about.

One particular creature that visited us almost defied the imagination. After a full week of blissful monotony had passed without incident, I was awakened one morning by Naomi screaming hysterically from the rear of the raft. Libbi was next to her at the helm and was pale with fright. Zelph and I literally flew from the cabin with spears in hand, but we both set aside the obviously insignificant weapons when we gazed into the huge face of the creature that was swimming only a few feet from our stern. It was the head of a veritable sea monster, so enormous and so hideous that it would have made one of Satan's own nightmares pale by comparison. The head was broad and somewhat flattened like a frog, with two beady eyes on either side, and a toad-like jaw that created a cavern some eight feet across when opened. Thick whisker-like appendages hung from either side of the tremendous mouth that fluttered as the great fish swan lazily behind us. I say fish because I was certain it was not a whale. The creature never released air from any blowhole that I could see, and its tail, some seventy feet at its other end, swished back and forth instead of up and down. Its huge body looked brownish-blue under the water, and from head to tail was covered with dull white spots centered in a perfectly straight grid-work of pale yellow-white lines. A large, rounded dorsal fin consistently projected from the water, so that if any birds had been present, they would have found it an excellent perch to rest on. In spite of its frightening, hideousness, and behemoth proportions, the creature didn't exhibit any signs of hostility toward us, only a healthy curiosity. It was only a matter of minutes before we realized we had little to fear from this gargantuan visitor, unless it accidentally bumped us with a swipe of its powerful tail. We must have stared at the beast for the better part of a half an hour before Elsha awoke and joined us. She had been dead tired, having just finished the watch before Libbi's.

"What's going on back here," she asked, poking her head out of the cabin, "A secret meeting?"

I waved her over. "You have got to see this!"

She made her way to the stern and gasped loudly, then started laughing. "That has got to be the ugliest face I have ever seen," she chuckled nervously. "It's so ugly, it's kind of cute."

"Cute" was not the word that came to my mind, but it wasn't far off. The giant fish's face was so incredibly grotesque, repugnant, and stupid-looking that when viewed head-on, we could not help but double over with laughter. At the same time, we silently prayed our visitor did not have the intelligence to take offense at our outbursts, for we realized it had enough power to smash our little raft to splinters.

After a time, the huge fish sank lower in the water and swam directly under the raft. If it had chosen to surface midway, we would have been capsized for sure. Luckily, it swam ahead of us, then circled around and underneath the *Hezikiah* again at a perpendicular angle, so that the head and tail could be seen on either side of the raft at the same time. Then, as suddenly as it appeared, the monstrous creature dove below the surface and out of sight, never to be seen again. I don't know what the fish was, but we referred to it from then on as a shark the size of a whale, or a whale-shark.

A few days later, Elsha called out, saying that there was something floating off to one side of the raft. Zelph was at the rudder, so I climbed up the mast for a better look. From this vantage point, I recognized the back of a rather large green sea turtle. Its head was just above the surface of the gently swelling ocean, and it appeared to be asleep. I motioned for all to be quiet and had Zelph direct the *Hezikiah* toward the napping animal. If we could manage to capture the thing, it would provide a delicious change to our diet of fish, dried meat, sweet potatoes, and old breadfruit. I began preparing a lasso as the raft drew closer to our target. When we were right next to the turtle, it raised its head lazily and stared at us with half-interested eyes. When it saw us moving about on the raft, it must have sensed we were a threat, because it immediately began swimming away with surprising speed.

My lasso wasn't ready and if I didn't act fast, we'd loose our quarry. I ran to the edge of the deck and dove head-first toward the turtle. I barley managed to grab hold of a rear flipper as the animal surged forward with tremendous thrusts of its large front flippers. I reached desperately for a better hold and eventually found purchase on the front edge of its carapace. I could not believe something so bulky and lumbering could swim with such speed, but I found myself gasping for breath as the turtle thrashed the water into a violent spray while trying to flee from my clutches. Then it dove and I barely had time for a quick gulp of air. We must have sank thirty feet, but the animal showed no signs of slowing. Finally, my air supply was exhausted and I regretfully let go. When I reached the surface, I found that I had been towed nearly a half mile from the *Hezikiah*. Zelph had furled the sail to make it easier for me to reach the raft. When I was about halfway there everyone on board began shouting and pointing at me, or at something behind me. Then I heard Libbi's strong voice above all the others. A shark!

I continued to swim with slow graceful strokes because I knew that clawing through the water in an attempt for greater speed would bring my certain demise. A shark has very poor eyesight but an incredible sense of smell and movement. As dying or wounded fish thrash about, sharks sense their harried vibrations through the water, and know there is an easy target ahead. I didn't turn around to locate the shark and continued to head for the safety of the raft. I knew it was close because of the fervent screams from everyone on board telling me to hurry. Then I felt the shark. It nudged my feet before passing by me, slowly rubbing its gritty head against my legs, then gliding in close to stare at me with a dull, lifeless eye. The predator was a big one, probably fifteen feet long with a slack jaw that revealed a mouth full of triangular, razor-sharp teeth. The shark passed by me, then circled about a time or two before coming straight for me. It rolled to one side, exposing its white belly as it scraped by me without biting. It was testing my response to its aggressiveness, seeing if I would panic and try to swim away. Instead, I swam slower, wanting to resemble nothing more than some floating debris, but continued my casual progress toward the raft. Then the shark was at my feet again, nudging them with his snout as if deciding which tender morsel to bite off first. I curled into a ball and bobbed on the surface with little or no movement at all. Then I heard a violent splashing ahead of me. Jonah had taken an oar and was striking the water with all his might. Zelph caught on and did the same. The shark nudged me once more, then went to investigate the noise at the raft. As its blue-gray body slipped past me, I reached out and grabbed onto its dorsal fin. The fish was large enough that I don't think it even noticed it had a passenger. My enemy and would-be executioner towed me quickly to the raft's edge. Libbi had cut up a large tuna and was tossing the pieces over the far side of the raft. The shark gave a quick lash with its powerful tail and darted under the *Hezikiah* for its free meal on the other side. At the same time, Zelph hauled me out of the water and literally threw me onto the deck.

"What kind of a crazy fool are you?" he said without any mirth in his voice.

I caught my breath, then explained, "I thought I could catch the turtle and steer it back to the raft."

He slumped down beside me and handed me a cloth to dry myself with. "I don't mean that, Gideon. I mean what kind of fool would catch a ride on a man-eating shark?"

This time there was a good deal of laughter in his tone, and I knew he was expressing incredulity as well as anger and concern, along with a high degree of machismo admiration.

Another two weeks passed without us seeing so much as an inkling of evidence to indicate we weren't the only human beings on the planet. No storm or inclement weather harassed us, and no monster from the deep bothered us with more than just a curious glance. The whole of the ocean was ours. With nothing more than indolent day-to-day living to occupy our thoughts, I half expected us to be stark raving mad in no time. However, just the opposite occurred. We found ourselves enlivened both in body and in spirit. It was as though the fresh salt tang in the air and all the blue purity that surrounded us had washed and cleansed our souls. To us on the raft, the seemingly endless conflicts between the Nephites and the Lamanites, or the political infirmities brought about by the secret workings of the Gadiantons, or even the fate of Hagoth and his ship of adventurers had no bearing on our existence. All the troubles of the past now seemed like a bad dream that had all but vanished upon awakening. I still prayed for the safety of my parents and my brother, but I knew the Lord had different plans for me—for all of us on the little raft—and no matter what concerns filled my mind, the only things that mattered were the elements around us. And for the moment, the elements were being very kind, even generous. The wind blew constantly to the west and the waves, though they occasionally pounded us and gave us minor challenges, allowed us to follow the flow of the current, which drew us inexorably toward the setting sun in the west.

Rain was infrequent on this part of the ocean, so we had to rely mainly on our supply of fresh water from the casks and gourds we had lashed to the deck. On particularly hot days with little wind, we found it very refreshing to take a quick plunge in the sea, then lie down in the shade of the cabin to dry. But as we often had sharks milling around, looking for something they could sink their teeth in to, we frequently drank more of our stored water than we had allotted at the beginning of the voyage.

When pondering this problem one lazy, scorching afternoon, a passage I had read in Jahrim's book on healing came to mind. He had mentioned that satisfying excessive thirst rarely has much to do with the amount of liquid one consumes. Rather, it was the content of the liquid that mattered. When we sweat, the body looses copious amounts of salt and other minerals through the skin. We often replenish the water but think nothing of the minerals. On remembering this, I decided to try an experiment. I took one cask of water and mixed it with about twenty percent seawater. The brackish concoction was none too pleasant tasting, but it took only a few gulps to be totally quenched of thirst. And as far as I could tell, the body suffered no ill effects from the mixture. We decided to reduce the formula to a ten percent mix, if only to make it more palatable, and this was what we drank from then on. Our thirst rarely got to the point of being intolerable.

What did prove intolerable were the tiny crabs that infested our stores. Most were no bigger than a thumbnail. No one knew how they got on board, but they were there in hordes, and when one was tossed to the mercies of the deep, two others seemed to take its place. Our fresh fruit lasted for only the first two weeks before it was either rotten or totally devoured by the crabs. It wasn't until Libbi thought of capturing them in a tightly woven wicker basket, using a flying fish as bait, that we actually enjoyed their presence. If we set out the basket at night with a freshly sliced fish or two, by morning the basket would be teaming with crustaceans. Libbi would cap off the basket and dump it into a pot of boiling water, and then she'd make the most wonderful paste that tasted like the fine shrimp and crab dishes offered in expensive restaurants.

The crabs served another helpful function. They provided garbage detail. There were evenings when so many fish landed on board that we found it necessary to dump many of them over the edge. Invariably, we would miss one or two that had wriggled their way into inaccessible crevasses and chinks. If they were not removed, they would rot in the hot tropical sun and produce a noxious scent that made one wish for a storm to wash it away. With the aid of our stowaway crabs, few of these marooned fish were ever left to the point of decomposition. Where the crabs came from remained a mystery until one afternoon when Zelph decided to take a dip to cool off.

Zelph was an excellent swimmer and would often paddle circles around the slow-moving raft on a windless day. One day when the seas were particularly clear, he swam under the raft to inspect the ropes and condition of the balsa logs, and discovered a small forest growing from the hulls. What had started as a film of algae grew into small lengths of sea-weed. Barnacles, mussels, and various other forms of plant and animal life had attached themselves to the hulls, combining to form a veritable jun-gle dangling from our raft. Within this jungle, Zelph was found hundreds of crabs and shrimp, and fish of every kind. What really surprised him was a large grouper that had staked a claim on the area directly under the deck between the twin hulls. A grouper is a fat, lumbering fish with nothing better to do than swim idly along waiting for a hapless fish to drift by its enormous mouth. Then, with a sucking sound that is audible from the surface of the water, the grouper will draw the scaly meal into its mouth in the blink of an eye. Some of the deepwater groupers reached weights of 400 pounds or more, but this guy was only about 150 pounds. Fortunately for him, groupers were only so-so eating, and as the big guy didn't present any threat to our voyage, we decided to let him journey with us. Naomi found him cute and promptly named the grouper "Big Al," in honor of a fat merchant named "Alma" who had befriended her when she was little. She said there was an actual physical resemblance, but she didn't mean it as an insult, to either party.

When we crossed the equator, there was a perceptible change in the water temperature and current. We moved along at a good clip, not as fast as a real sailing vessel, but more than one would expect from a balsa cata-maran. I calculated that we were averaging about 45 miles per day. At that rate we should cross the ocean in . . . I didn't know. As far as I could remember, no one had ever charted the entire western ocean. But I knew the world was a sphere and that eventually we would have to run into land again. Either that, or die of boredom. As long as we stayed in the equatorial current, we had more than enough food to eat. Fresh water had been a concern, but within a week's time, we had drifted into a tropical area that produced rain every other night.

My main concern now was our general health. Nephi was doing well nursing from Naomi, but Naomi herself was showing signs of wear and fatigue. Jonah, feeling his age and the effects of his plunge from the raft, was spending most of his time sleeping in the shade of the cabin. Libbi was indomitable, and I didn't dare ask how she felt for fear of damaging her pride. Zelph was well and had finally adapted to life on the open ocean, though he did say he craved fresh fruits, especially bananas, from time to time. We did have a good supply of coconuts, which we hung from the top of the cabin to keep them out of the salt water. Many had sprouted, providing us with a delightful spray of green foliage along our roof top.

Elsha said she was fine, but often looked pale and drawn, especially in the morning. When I tried to offer aid she would wave me off and go about her duties with firm resolution. But there were many times I caught her with her head over the deck, throwing up her breakfast into the sea. I assigned her lighter tasks from then on, and she accepted these without resistance, but meager gratitude. She refused to say what was wrong, but assured me she loved me very much and was having the time of her life. Her happiness was my main concern, and when she looked at me with those sparkling green eyes and told me she was happier than she'd ever been in her entire life, I simply had to believe her.

TWENTY-FIVE

A week after crossing the equator, I noticed a perceptible change in the temperature of the water and the direction of the trade winds. The water, while still quite warm, took on a coolness which I assumed came from the current rising from the southern pole. And the trade winds, which faithfully had been blowing us due west, began directing us in a more southerly direction. To our great relief, the sea never again struck us with such violence as it did the first week of our voyage. This did a lot to lift the spirits and boost the confidence of the crew of the *Hezikiah*. There were the occasional high seas in which our raft would be lost for an instant between two large waves only to be elevated to the crest of a following wave for a momentary view of the churning mass surrounding us. The waves, however, were rarely large enough to break over the deck or put us in risk of floundering, though there were still frequent rogues that would sneak up and soak the unprepared sailor to the bone. Still, when the seas were high it was simply accepted that when we ventured outside the cabin, we would be constantly wet from the spray, rain, and wind.

About this time, the weather took on a consistency that was both refreshing and monotonous. During a calm, the temperament of the wind and sea became so reliable that we could lash the rudder to the tholepins and finish our watches fishing or sunning or even taking a swim—when there were no sharks present, of course. At night, the same held true, and the person at the helm could while their time away observing the mysterious, glowing wonders, some of which were disturbingly large, that swam beneath the raft, or watching the numberless stars run their course across the immense canvas of the sky.

One does not realize how big the sky looks until they are in a place where the horizon all around contains nothing higher than the surface on which they stand. There are no mountains or trees to give reference to distance, and even the clouds seemed to rise from the seamless horizon, though most simply formed over us out of clear air. Quite often, the sky took on a tone that exactly matched the color of the ocean making it difficult to see any horizon at all. This gave us the illusion of traveling forward at a steady pace but never gaining any ground. I took the opportunity to teach the others about some subtle differences to look for which indicated we were actually progressing, but it was often easier to simply toss a chip of wood over the side and watch it slowly fall behind.

A few readily noticeable changes were the temperature variance in ocean, and the very color of the water itself. Also, the temperature of the air around us and the direction of the wind, though this last detail was harder to recognize because the *Hezikiah* always ran best when the wind was at her back, pushing against the cabin as well as the sail. And as I had no idea precisely which direction we were *supposed* to be going, we followed the current and the breeze like a river follows the earthen banks which holds it captive.

The thing that confirmed our forward progress more than anything else was the changing night sky. The north star soon dropped below the northern horizon and we no longer were comforted by the familiar shape of the big dipper. But I knew the other stars, and I had a parchment chart, copied from one of my father's, showing various constellations in this part of the world. I never learned how he had obtained these charts, but I knew there had been sailors from the beginning of time who had navigated using only the stars as their map. It really was not that difficult to do. All I needed was a compass and a clear night, and we often had both. The trick was to align the rise of a constellation to an aft portion of the raft, then note the direction of the compass. Next, compare the alignment of the same constellation to the front of the raft and make sure the compass was still on the same heading. Following this technique, we knew fairly accurately where we were in the ocean at all times. What we didn't know was what lay ahead of us, or when we'd find it.

Another indicator of our progress was the change in indigenous marine life. While we always had our regulars—the self-sacrificing flying fish, shoals of striped pilot fish, the all-too-frequent shark, and our reclusive companion, Big Al, the grouper—there were fascinating new creatures that debuted almost daily as we continued south of the equator. One type of fish in particular became so numerous that we sometimes found them more of a bother than a free meal. It was the dolphin. Not the air breathing mammal that chattered and chirped while dancing around the raft and performing acrobatics with powerful leaps in the air, but the dolphin fish, a sleek, shiny, blue animal that resembled a war club more than a fish. It had a large, solid, blunt head that tapered back along its flat, one- to five-foot body to a spiked, bony tail. Its body was an astoundingly, bright, almost iridescent, blue-green color, with glittering golden-yellow fins. The dolphin was a predatory fish whose main meal appeared to be the ubiquitous flying fish. They would slice through the water with astonishing speed and latch onto its prey with tiny, sharp teeth and powerful jaws. They would also leap into the air like flying fish, but instead of gliding along like its graceful prey did, it would flop with a resounding splash shortly after breaking the surface. The dolphin was good eating, and rivaled the bonito and tuna as our favorite fresh catch of the day. Dolphins traveled in schools from a dozen to three dozen individuals, and always lit up the seas with their brilliantly-scaled bodies and whimsical play. But they were formidable beasts of prey that would snap at anything splashing on the surface.

One day, Libbi sat down on one of the hulls to wash some clothing. She would dip the cloth in the sea and pound it on the side of the hull, then dip it again. Upon her third submersing, she pulled up the cloth only to find a two and a half foot dolphin latched onto the end. She tried to pull the creature free but it resolutely would not let go. Finally she put aside the garment until the fish died, and even then she had to pry the jaws open to free her clothing. We joked about her being the most clever fisherman in the world, but she failed to acknowledge the humor in our quips.

One more week passed before we noticed how rancid our water stores were tasting. We did our best to conserve the fresh water we had sealed in the oak casks, but the stuff in the gourds and bamboo flasks was no longer potable. We used this for cooking and washing, as it hadn't fouled so much as to become totally useless, but to drink it was beyond anyone's capacity. Jonah thought to pray for rain to replenish our supply, and I agreed. We all made it a matter of earnest communication with the Lord, and within two days He answered us—an hundred fold.

The storm was a devilish one, which made me wonder who the others had been praying to. The wind whipped at us from several directions and we found it necessary to furl the sail. This did little to slow our progress, however, because the gale struck the cabin instead, eliciting the same results as if filling the sail. The thing that kept us heading true was the centerboard and keels. We spent a miserable ten days taking turns standing in the rain at the rudder or dodging drips in the cabin ceiling, never achieving total dryness or complete sleep.

Everyone took it in stride, but Elsha seemed to fare the worst. Her sea sickness—which is what I assumed it was—became worse during the storms, and she spent many nights huddled under a blanket, doubled up with a sour stomach and convulsing with dry heaves. A gauntness hollowed her cheeks and dulled the glow of her skin, but her eyes still shown with an inner happiness I could not understand. Naomi spent a lot of time with her, and in spite of her constant sickness, the two of them would spend hours whispering and giggling like shy yet mischievous school girls at a social function filled hoards of the opposite sex.

Jonah kept asking gallantly to take Elsha's place at the helm, but I did not want another episode like the last one. An unscheduled swim in these rough seas would not be a delightful thing to be forced into . . . again. Instead, Zelph and I and Libbi took more turns at the rudder to compensate for Elsha's absence. It didn't matter much anyway. The constant undulating of the balsa hulls riding the chop and churn of the ocean, and the unpredictable gales striking the cabin made it difficult at best to control the course of the *Hezikiah*. So it was inconsequential if Elsha took her turn or not.

The truly frustrating part was that everyone on board seemed to know what was wrong with my wife except me, yet no one would share their information. It was like having a miniature Gadianton sect sharing their secret combinations, plotting against me in the middle of the ocean.

Nothing I did seemed to help Elsha feel better either. I gave her some ginger tea and light soups to drink, but that did little to quell her nausea.

The abundant fresh water falling from the sky gave some relief, and we took the opportunity to empty our casks and other stores and refill them with fresh supplies. By the end of the ten days, the sea had calmed somewhat. It was still running high, but was much more tolerable. A new breeze freshened and blew in a constant southwestern direction with a following sea, and everyone took turns catching up on lost sleep.

A few days later, my frustration with Elsha's mysterious ailment peaked. I decided that if I could not help her feel better physically, I would try to help her feel better emotionally. I had noticed a while back during one of my swims under the raft that there were a few abalone growing on the inside face of one of the hulls. These probably started out as smaller, free-swimming larvae that had attached themselves to the balsa logs, thinking the constant movement of water across its surface indicated it was in a tidal zone. They were still in a juvenile state, but were big enough to have begun the formation of their characteristic hard, oval shells. I pried the largest one I could find from the hull and slipped it into a pouch before surfacing. Big Al approached me and watched with placid, uncaring eyes, and I knew he was waiting for any morsel that might slip from my hands. I removed the abalone and carved the meat from the shell. Normally this was very good eating, and I sighed, knowing I was missing out on a delicious meal for the sake of secrecy. But I could not let anyone know I had the shell because it would ruin the surprise I was working on for Elsha.

Having dislodged the abalone meat, I held it out, teasing Big Al with the succulent white flesh. I have always found it amazing how fast a big, bulky fish can move underwater. Before I could blink, Big Al's mouth had engulfed the abalone, my hand, and my arm, clear up to the elbow. I knew better than to jerk my arm free because it would be severely scraped by his nubby teeth, so I waited patiently for Al to decide he wasn't going anywhere with me hanging from his greedy jaws, and that it would just not be feasible to try and swallow the rest of me along with the abalone. After two or three minutes of tugging on my arm, the big grouper let go and resumed his post under the deck of the Hezikiah, with the abalone meat comfortably in his stomach.

I spent the next few days scraping the rough exterior of the abalone shell down to its opalescent, mother-of-pearl interior. I found I was very lucky, for the translucent multiplicity of colors which waved throughout the remaining shell were the most beautiful I had ever seen. With some careful carving and excruciatingly detailed work with a awl I borrowed from Zelph, I shaped the shell into the silhouette of a seagull flying, then drilled a fine hole near the top of the bird and looped a delicate strip of shark leather through it. The resulting pendant was about three inches wide from wing-tip to wing-tip, and about one and a half inches tall, and if I do say so myself, was stunningly beautiful, especially in the sunlight.

That evening I asked Elsha to join me at the helm during my turn at the rudder. The clouds from the afternoon's rain had vanished, leaving a crystal clear night in which the stars in the firmament twinkled like a million fireflies. The others were in the cabin, listening to Naomi play a flute she had carved from a length of bamboo.

"Are you feeling better today?" I asked my wife tenderly.

She smiled and looked up at me with those hypnotic eyes I had fallen for the first time I had seen her. "I am fine, Gideon," she chuckled. "How many times do I have to tell you that?"

"I haven't seen you paying homage to the gods of the sea today," I commented.

"What?"

I smiled. "You haven't had to throw up today, have you?"

"No, I haven't," she laughed. "In fact, I haven't had to do that for a few days now. I think I'm over that stage."

What stage? I wondered, but didn't ask. Instead I said, "I wish there were something more I could do to make you feel better."

She hugged me tightly. "Don't worry, Gideon. I'm feeling much better. There's nothing more you need to do for me."

That wasn't the answer I really needed. I pressed on. "Still, I'm sorry this voyage has been so hard on you," I said, trying to segue into my presenting the abalone pendant to her.

"I'm adjusting to it like all the others," she sighed. "I have no other choice."

"Just the same, I hope the seas stay calm for the rest of the voyage."
She sighed again. "And how long will that be?"

I shrugged my shoulders. "I wish I knew. I've been praying for some guidance or an answer of some kind, but haven't received anything yet."

Elsha hugged me again and said, "Oh Gideon, I love you very much, but you really can be rather obtuse at times."

"Rather what?"

"Obtuse: insensitive or slow to understand or see things the way they really are. Just look at what we've been through the past twelve weeks: We've survived storms that would have sunk any other ship; we could have starved out here, but the Lord has provided a never-ending supply of fish that land right at our feet; and when we needed fresh water, we prayed for rain and we got all we could drink and then some."

"But all has not been perfect," I argued. "You've been sick most of the time, and I've haven't been able to do much for you."

The reflection of the Pleiades constellation sparkled in her beautiful eyes. "Well, it's not totally your fault I'm sick . . . and then again . . . it is."

I stared at her, not knowing how to respond to her inconsistent logic. "It's no wonder I'm slow to understand when you make statements like that."

She smiled, but added nothing more to her comment. I shook my head and reached into my pocket for the pendant. I turned her so that her back was to me and draped the seagull pendant over her head and secured it behind her neck. She gasped lightly, and lovingly inspected the home-made jewelry. The fullness of the moon made it glow with a whole new set of colors just as alluring as those made by sunlight.

"Tell me you haven't been hiding this since we set sail," she breathed softly.

"No, I made it just last week."

She leaned into me and I slipped one arm around her waist, which seemed slightly bigger than it had before. "Oh, Gideon, it's beautiful. But you didn't have to—"

"I wanted to give you something that would make you feel good inside," I said, interrupting her.

She turned her head and looked up at me with so much love in her eyes I chided myself for not making her something sooner. "But Gideon, you already have given me a gift I will cherish forever."

For the life of me I did not know what she was talking about. I thought perhaps she was referring to her wedding ring, but somehow realized it wasn't that. Elsha, understanding my confusion, reached behind my head to direct me toward a tender kiss.

"You have given me the gift of life," she said warmly.

I tilted my head to one side and said, "But . . . if you mean saving your life during that first storm, I gave that gift to everyone on board."

She smiled and closed her eyes in mock exasperation. "Not that," she said as she moved my hand to cover her belly. "This. There is a new life, in here, that you have given me. That's why I've been so sick . . . and *so* happy lately."

It finally dawned on me. If the mast of the *Hezikiah* had broken free and landed right on top of my head I could not have been more dumbfounded. A warmth coursed through me I had not felt since the day she accepted my proposal of marriage. I felt my entire frame swell with pride, not only of myself but for the amazing young woman in my arms who called herself my wife.

"What are you saying?" I asked, knowing full well the answer, but wanting to hear it from her lips.

She smiled demurely, blushing wonderfully in the moonlight. Then she turned and draped her arms around my neck and raised to her tip toes to give me another kiss.

"You know," was all she said.

"Elsha, I'm not sure I'm ready for this," I said honestly.

"Don't you worry, Gideon," she said lovingly. "You're going to be a wonderful father. I just know it."

TWENTY-SIX

As if it were a talisman foretelling good fortune, Elsha's pendant heralded the most significant event of our voyage thus far. I had unwittingly given my wife her gift on the eve of our 100th day at sea, and for all I knew it would be another 100 days before we saw a real seagull. The very next morning, however, as I was gazing at the nebulous, white, billowy formations of cumulous clouds overhead, I spied what looked like several dark specks within the cloud. I watched those specks move about within the cloud and glide from cloud to cloud for some time before I realized the specks were actually birds! Terns, I guessed from their streamlined shape and effortless flight. And while terns were tremendous ocean navigators capable of traveling vast distances over water, they also were creatures that had to roost occasionally, and that meant land. Solid ground.

I watched the birds in earnest as they moved along. Occasionally, a pair would perform some random acrobatic dance in the air, then continue with their flight westward. *Westward!* They were heading in the same direction as the *Hezikiah*, which meant we were heading in the right direction.

The terns had dissolved into the clouds marking the horizon before I thought to point them out to anyone else on board. It didn't matter. The very next day we woke to the sounds of cackling and squawking coming from the nest on the mast. As I left the cabin I saw two large pelicans sitting atop the nest playfully jousting with their huge beaks. Zelph was at the rudder, smiling up at them.

"Do you know what this means?" I asked him, pointing to the birds with a boyish grin on my face.

He nodded. "I believe this little adventure is about to come to an end."

"Yes, but how soon is the real question," I added, almost to myself.

The others joined us on the deck and we all stared gleefully at the large brown birds with sagging lower jaws and puffy round bellies. A passerby would have thought we were worshipping the two seabirds as we danced beneath them, singing stupid little ditties and acting in every way like imbeciles or drunken sailors. The birds stopped their clattering as they in turn watched the creatures on the bamboo deck below them whooping and howling as if we had red ants in our breeches.

Just then a big flying fish landed with a thud on one of the hulls. The larger of the pelicans immediately left its perch and swooped down on its six foot wingspan to gobble up the fish whole.

"Did you see the size of that thing?" Elsha asked no one in particular.

"Yes, but that's quite a normal size for a pelican," I offered in what came across as a know-it-all attitude.

"Not the bird," she said, "the fish. It was huge."

"Yes, I've been noticing that, too," Naomi joined in. "The last few mornings, as Libbi and I gather them for breakfast, we both commented on how much larger the flying fish are becoming."

The pelicans stayed for an hour or so, occasionally leaping from their perch to plunge head first into the water and come up with a flopping snack in their pouch-like bill. Then they squawked one last time and took to flight, circling overhead a couple times before heading off in a westerly direction.

"Follow them," I called to Zelph as I climbed the mast to the nest.

We were already heading in that general direction, and with a slight push on the rudder, Zelph had us shadowing our recently departed visitors. From the mast perch I strained to see any stationary mass on the horizon which would indicate an island, but I saw nothing except the ever present clouds. Throughout the rest of the day we saw other birds winging along overhead following the same course we were now taking.

It was nearly impossible to conceal our excitement. Even Elsha, who had been sick again from her pregnancy, beamed with new vitality at the prospect of our long voyage coming to an end.

I decided to take a quick swim to check the ropes and condition of the balsa logs again. It was never wise to assume everything was shipshape on a voyage such as ours. Those who do often sink within sight of their destination, and with the constant companionship of sharks and other dangerous sea creatures, a last minute ordeal of that magnitude would not be a welcome ending to our adventure.

I had scouted for sharks from the nest but saw none, so I stood up and did a graceful swan dive from the masthead. Just before entering the water I thought I heard Elsha call out my name, but in a moment, I was eight feet under and figured I'd find out what she wanted soon enough. The hemp ropes appeared to be all right, though a little loose in spots. Some were worn half way through, but still held together as if they were made of steel, and I gained a new-found respect for the strength of that fibrous material. The balsa logs were another story. They were pliable and spongy, and many of the tag-along marine plants and animals that had made our raft their home had done considerable damage by burrowing deep into the wood and boring trenches along their lengths. If we were forced to spend more than another month or two at sea, we would be sailing on faith instead of balsa hulls.

I surfaced for a deep breath then dropped under and swam to the other hull. Expecting to see Big Al, I paused under the deck to pay my respects, but the grouper was not there. I didn't know when he had abandoned our vessel, but I was curiously saddened by his absence. I surfaced on the other side of the Hezikiah to catch another breath, and came face to face with the most dangerous jellyfish known, the Man-of-War. I did my best to scramble onto the hull but in thrashing about, my left leg kicked one of the long tentacles festooned with hundreds of poisonous stingers. A jolt of pain shocked me, rendering my ankle hopelessly numb. The searing pain and paralysis radiated quickly up my leg and within seconds it was completely useless. I had only gotten a partial grip on the top of the hull and felt myself slipping back into the water, directly on top of the dangerous jellyfish. I tried to kick the bulbous blue sail that sat atop its gelatinous body, but only managed to make it wobble with a hollow plopping sound. If I fell back into those tentacles I would be completely paralyzed and unable to swim or even breathe. As it was, I knew I was going to lose the use of my leg for several days.

The wind-driven animal rode silently alongside the *Hezikiah*, unaware of the menace it threatened. I did not blame the jellyfish outright, for I knew it had no conscious intelligence of its own. Rather, it was at the mercy of wind and tide just as we were. Yet I hated its presence at the moment because I was about to be trapped in its lethal tentacles and stung to death without the Man-of-War even knowing who it was annihilating. I was much too large for it to eat, but that did not stop the hair-triggered barbs from piercing my flesh and automatically injecting their toxin.

I kicked the rubbery balloon-like sail again as I slid deeper into the sea, which was constantly rewetting the slick balsa logs. Then a hand grabbed my wrist and hauled me out of the water. A long tentacle was still wrapped around my ankle, though my leg was too numb to feel it. Still, I knew poison was being pumped into my blood with every passing second it was attached to me. A knife cut the tentacle a fraction of an inch from my ankle.

I was about to chastise Zelph for getting so close to my skin when I realized it was not Zelph's hunting knife but Libbi's cooking knife. I turned to watch as Libbi removed a cloth soaked with boiling water with her bare hands and apply it to my wounds.

Then Elsha was at my side asking me if I was all right. Though she asked several times, I found myself unable to answer. Instead, I noticed I was gasping for breath as I grimaced at the throbbing pain in my groin and lower back.

"Yes—I—think—so," I stammered between huge lungfulls of air. Needless to say, I was more than a little perturbed with myself for being so careless during my swim.

"No, you're not all right," Libbi said daubing more hot water onto the swollen red welts forming on my leg. "We've got to neutralize this poison before in gets into your nerves and shuts down your heart."

Elsha gasped, then asked what she could do to help. Libbi had Elsha wipe my sweating brow with a cloth soaked with cool water as she took her knife and scraped the hair-thin tentacle from my ankle. She then broke a stem from an aloe plant we had brought and daubed it generously over my leg.

"Alcohol will help dry it out," she said to Naomi, instructing the younger woman to fetch the flask of wine from the storeroom. She poured this onto another cloth and held it to my swollen leg.

My breathing slowly became easier and the pain receded to an area just below my thigh. When the numbness turned to a throbbing ache I knew I was getting better. Sometimes pain is the best indicator of how the body is healing.

I spent the rest of the day in the shade of the cabin. When I began to thank Elsha for trying to warn me about the Man-of-War, she ducked her head and looked away.

"What's the matter?" I asked.

She thought for a while before answering. "I wasn't trying to warn you, Gideon. I didn't even see the thing until it had stung you."

"Then why did you call out to me?" I wondered.

She smiled coquettishly. "I just wanted to tell you, 'Nice dive'."

The next morning I woke to find that my leg was wobbly but functional. The sound of excited voices brought me from the cabin into the morning breeze. There were perhaps a hundred birds flying overhead, calling out to one another and chirping noisily. I asked Zelph, who was still at the rudder, to follow their flight.

"No need," he replied simply.

"Why not?" I asked, clearly befuddled.

"Look," he said pointing with his chin toward the front of our raft.

On the horizon lay a bundle of curious-looking clouds—not really thunderheads and not the usual cottony formations that lifted from the horizon—they were thick and solid and rose from the sea like a column of smoke from a very green fire. The tops of the clouds were continually whisked away by the higher trade winds, but the base of the clouds didn't appear to move at all.

"What do you make of it?" I asked Zelph.

"I've been watching them all night, and they haven't moved an inch from our compass heading."

"You mean you haven't been to sleep in all that time?"

He smiled. "Oh, I've had plenty of sleep. Ever since I noticed the birds heading toward the cloud, and that the cloud never moved, I figured I'd just lash the rudder to the tholepins to maintain this heading and grab a few winks."

I scratched my head. "So are you thinking what I'm thinking?"

"If you're thinking there's an island there, then, yes. I'm sure of it."

I had to agree.

That evening no one seemed able to sleep. The excitement on board was palpable and for the first time since we first discussed this voyage, everyone was smiling from ear to ear. Even Libbi went about her tasks with a spring in her step. Jonah spent hours at a time gazing at the mysterious cloud bank ahead of us.

"Are you sure it's an island?" Jonah asked me when I joined him.

"Yes, definitely. When you see columnar clouds like those, they always indicate land. You see, when the sun bakes the sand and island plantlife, a mass of moist air rises and condenses in the cooler air higher up, thus forming a cloud."

The old man nodded. We stood in silence for a time, both wrapped up in the excitement. He then turned to me and with tear-filled eyes asked, "Gideon, why did you allow Libbi and I to come with you on this voyage?"

His question caught me off gaurd, but I answered as honestly as I coud.

"Some of the church leaders back in Tonalai asked me to take you," I said, surprised at his show of emotion.

"So you really didn't *want* us to come then, did you?"

"No, it's not that," I said, shaking my head. "I just wasn't *expecting* you, or anyone else, to come, that's all."

He nodded and lowered his eyes. "Would you be surprised if I told you the Lord wanted us to come?" he stated humbly.

I thought for a moment, then said, "No, not really. There are lots of saints trying to escape the influences of the Gadiantons and Lamanites."

He looked up with a concerned ache worrying his eyes. "But why with you? Why not with Hagoth or some of the saints who traveled northward by land? Why were we supposed to sail on this raft for four months in this direction?"

I shrugged my shoulders. "I can't answer that, Jonah. Maybe it was so I could save your life. Maybe it was so that Libbi could save mine. To be honest, I'm not even sure why I'm doing this, other than I know I'm supposed to."

A slight smile creased the corners of his mouth. "What do you mean?"

I leaned against the mast and drew in a long breath of air. "Both Elsha and I received blessings from Helorum, a patriarch in Bountiful, before we came to Tonalai. The blessing stated something about our seed—and I assume by that it means us as Nephites—being the ones responsible for helping to restore the church of Christ to the earth before His second coming. The gist of it was that we were supposed to sail off to an island and perpetuate a nation to help fulfill this responsibility. Both Elsha and I feel that it is our mission, it's what the Lord wants us to do. But to be honest, I've never quite felt worthy of it. It's rather humbling in a way."

The tears were now running freely from Jonah's eyes. His scraggly growth of beard quivered as he fought his emotions. He wiped his eyes and cleared his throat.

"Did you know before this adventure I was a teacher?" he asked softly.

"Yes, you'd mentioned that once. What did you teach?"

"Religion. The scriptures. The very word of God, and I thought I knew everything. But you have just taught me a great truth to which I have been blinded. And I too am humbled by the responsibility to which you have just opened my eyes."

I looked at him earnestly but did not say anything. Too many thoughts were whirling through my mind to be able to latch on to and utter a particular one.

"Gideon, I know of the prophecies of which you have spoken. They are true and must come to pass or we will be judged for not fulfilling our part in them."

I sighed heavily. "I will do what I can, Jonah. I only wish I had the faith to get definite answers now and then. I feel like I'm sailing around blindly."

He placed a weathered hand on my shoulder and stood straighter than normal. "You have a tremendous amount of faith, Gideon. You just don't know it. When I followed the advice of the church leaders to come, I didn't know why either. And as we progressed on this journey I assumed my part in teaching in the Lord's kingdom was pretty much over, even though I knew from personal revelation that my work was nowhere near completion.

"Gideon, I have received the ministering of angels. I have no doubt what my calling in life is. Yet, when we undertook this expedition, I was actually beginning to doubt what God himself had told me. Now I know better."

"I am happy for you, Jonah. Truly, I am."

He grabbed my other shoulder with his other hand and turned me squarely to him. "Gideon, this is not simply an exploration of the great unknown. It is not just a voyage to escape from the evils growing in our government and in our church. We are not wandering aimlessly on the great deep in order to land on some island by happenstance. You are like Lehi of old. You are taking your family, and a few others, to a place designated by God himself for your posterity."

"That's what Elsha says, too. It's mostly because of her I'm leading this strange voyage."

"No, Gideon," Jonah said with a tinge of reproach in his voice. "This is not a strange voyage; it is a sacred voyage."

TWENTY-SEVEN

The cries of countless seabirds was more refreshing than annoying. The noise had an earthy quality that seemed to breathe new life into the crew of the *Hezikiah* We had listened to the lifeless groaning of ropes stretching against soggy wood, and the droning monotony of the sea for too long. In spite of its brashness, the bird cries were a comforting sound that helped lull me to sleep after a long night's watch.

I had been asleep for about three hours when Jonah came and gently shook my shoulder. "Captain Gideon?"

I knuckled the sleep from my eyes and asked, "What's the matter?"

"Nothing. I just thought you'd like to come out and take a look at your island."

I almost knocked the poor old man over as I flew out of the cabin and looked around. Elsha was in the nest on the masthead, Libbi was at the helm, and Zelph and Naomi were still asleep in the cabin. There were hundreds of birds circling in a violet-blue sky highlighted with orange and pink whispy clouds. The vast canvas of sky stretched unbroken from one horizon to the other; but to the northwest a darker blue-green shape rose slightly from the ocean like a capsized boat whose keel was just catching the first rays of a new sun.

"There's an answer to a prayer if I've ever seen one," Jonah said at my side.

I was elated, yet apprehensive. We devoured the sight greedily. Jonah stood silently for a time before going back to the cabin to wake the others. The birds formed a bridge across the sky to the island, which stood out sharper against the horizon as the sun rose above the mists of the ocean and spotlighted the verdant mass ahead of us.

"Is that our new home, Gideon?" Elsha called from high above.

"Maybe," I said, taking a look at the compass and feeling the wind.

"It's the most beautiful thing I've ever seen," she sighed, mostly to herself.

Looking around I could tell that everyone else on board felt the same. There was a tactile sensation of anticipation, a longing to have this last part of our voyage over and done with. I couldn't blame them. While I loved everything about the environs of the sea, I also wanted to feel sand between my toes and taste cool coconut milk and fresh vegetables.

I rechecked the compass and measured the current. This might prove more difficult than it first appeared. We had a calm sea and a steady wind, and all seemed perfect for a straight shot to the greenery which grew steadily before us. The trouble was that the island was to the northwest, and the current and wind were easing us to the southwest. I directed Libbi to point the *Hezikiah* to a point a few degrees north of the island. Without command Zelph trimmed the sail to maximize its capture of the breeze to hurry us along. He was becoming a true sailor, whether he wanted to admit it or not.

Our course changed accordingly, but only enough to point us at the island. Unfortunately, we were still heading more west than northwest. Soon it became clear we were going to overshoot the island by no more than one mile. I can't describe the pall of disappointment that blanketed our little raft. We watched as the shoreline passed slowly by, a tropical paradise of trees and underbrush packed tightly together behind the narrow strip of a white sand beach. No one spoke, but no words were necessary to express our sadness as we watched the first possibility of closure to our voyage pass just beyond our reach. We laid on the rudder with all our might and even tried paddling with the long oars, but to no avail. It was as if we finally had proof that we had really been moving all these months; we had not just been tumbling about in the center of the same eternal circular horizon. Curiously, it almost seemed as if the island were the mobile entity which had suddenly traveled into our realm of existence; as if the island were drifting slowly across our domain, heading for the eastern horizon in a course exactly opposite from ours.

"Can't we do anything?" Naomi asked, the pain clearly evident in her tone.

"I'm afraid the wind and tide have other plans for us," I said, trying to act unconcerned, as if this sort of thing happened all the time.

Then Jonah spoke up, and his voice took on a timbre that reminded me of my old friend Helorum. "Where there is one island, there will be others. Be comforted in knowing that this bit of land is not the one the Lord had reserved for us."

Amazingly, I had never thought of it in that way. I admitted that I was part of a greater plan, that God had something specific in mind for Elsha and me, but that He had prepared and reserved an island just for us had never crossed my mind. Suddenly the loss of our first opportunity to land did not bother me as much. I could tell that the others felt the same way, though admittedly, to differing degrees.

Naomi could not hold back her tears of disappointment, and Zelph did his best to comfort her. Little Nephi, who spent most of his time sleeping, might have been equally distraught, but I don't think he understood the importance of the island falling behind us. Elsha was still in the nest but was no longer looking at the lost paradise. She had her attention focused directly ahead, wanting to be the first to see our new home, wherever it may lie. Libbi and Jonah were saddened but resolute in bearing this latest let-down with stoic perseverance.

As we passed to the leeward side of the island, a new sensation played havoc with our emotions. The fragrance of landlife wafted with the breezes and tickled our salt-numbed noses. Scents of wood, wet vegetation, and flowers filled our minds with memories of places where such scents had been taken for granted. I even detected the musty, rich odor of dirt which smelled at that moment like the most intoxicating fragrance in the world.

By evening, the smells were gone, and the island was nothing more than a faint blue streak lying beneath a billowing mass of amber clouds.

The birds had also disappeared. When asked why, I explained that sea fowl often fish on the windward side of the island so that when they return with bellies full of food, the flight will be much easier. The dolphins had also vanished, indicating we were now in shallower seas than before.

To help boost our spirits, Libbi had Naomi fashion a fine net from bamboo thatch, which Libbi used to troll behind the raft. After about an hour, she retrieved the net and found it overflowing with countless large shrimp. Naomi trolled for more as Libbi steamed the first catch, turning them a bright reddish hue. She then prepared a thick sauce from dried tomatoes and spices. That night, we ate like kings.

The next morning we detected two new clouds rising up from the horizon. The first cloud, larger in size than the other, was again positioned to our northwest but the second, smaller cloud was directly in our path. I was at the helm and set our course slightly to the north of the smaller cloud bank, judging that the currents would shift to the south near its shores. For two days and nights we sailed along this point of the compass. It was a lonely, drawn-out two days in which even the simplest of tasks became unbearable drudgery. Tempers grew short, but usually cooled quickly when we talked of the wonderful things that awaited us on our island.

Our island!

An island of our own. It seemed almost too good to be true. That was exactly what we were expecting, and it filled our dreams both day and night with images of swaying coconut palms, crystalline lagoons, and abundant wild game and edible plants. No internal strife or conflicts from neighboring tribes of people. No Gadianton influences to lead us astray or prevent us from worshipping our God as we had been taught. It was shaping up to be a Utopia limited only by the depth of our imagination and dreams. But those dreams were shattered during dinner the second night when Jonah posed a few questions to us.

"You are all familiar with the scriptures that mention of the isles of the seas, are you not? Those same scriptures also mention that the islands have existed for some time. My guess would be since the days of Peleg, when the earth was divided."

"Yes. That's probably true," Elsha said, she being very familiar with the scriptures herself.

"Is it not also true that the scriptures state that the Lord leads away choice people from time to time for His own purposes, according to His will and pleasure?"

We all nodded in agreement before he went on.

"Then what are the chances of 'our' island already being inhabited? After Lehi made it to *his* promised land, his offspring found that other people had already been there. Mulekites and Jaredites to name a couple. I think that we should not assume our island will be ours alone."

No one spoke the rest of the evening. We wrestled with Jonah's comments all that night, wondering exactly what the Lord had in mind for us, and who else might be involved.

On the third morning Libbi's boisterous lungs belted out, "Land Ho!"

We all scrambled out onto the deck and stood staring at a green mound rising high above the surface of the ocean. It was still a good ten miles away, but a cloudless sky and a steady breeze kept the vapors from the sea to a minimum, and we could clearly see the verdant land which lay directly in our path. A curious, glimmering reflection of green and brown lit the sky between our raft and the island, creating an image of the lagoons and shores that awaited us. It was a phenomenon similar to the one in the desert where the heat creates the illusion of an oasis by refracting the image from actual trees and water miles away. I had heard it told by sailors that some low atolls and lagoons throw up their images hundreds of feet in the air, so that they belie their position many days before they are actually sighted on the horizon.

By early afternoon we could distinguish individual treetops, and could make out rows of tan coconut palms from lush, shadowy green backgrounds. Ahead there was bound to be a reef, an insidious boat-eating structure made from the sharp, calcareous bodies of millions of coral polyps, probably similar to the rock reef we encountered at the beginning of our voyage, only far more dangerous. If we were caught unawares, the reef would not only break our raft into splinters, but we would very likely be cut, sliced, and chewed like a piece of meat in the maw of a voracious predator.

We followed the push of the waves and influence of the wind, looking carefully for the dangerous reef. But we saw only the gentle, rolling backs of the waves guiding us to the island. I climbed the mast to the nest and surveyed the lay of the land before us. It was only then that I could distinguish the stretch of lagoon that ran from north to south, and out from the white, sandy shore about 100 yards to the churning, frothing cauldron that indicated a treacherous reef. The waves pounded the structure relentlessly, but in doing so, only added to its size and strength by bringing deep-sea nutrients to the millions of hungry polyps forming the reef. I tried to locate a passage, a deeper channel in the reef through which we could enter, but could see none. The thought of having to pass this island as well sickened me, for the island itself looked ideal. There were plenty of tall hardwood trees, coconut palms laden with delicious fruit, a stream (I assumed of fresh water) cascading over an escarpment back in the jungled mountains, and birds of every sort flying overhead. The island was large enough to support numerous indigenous animals we could eat: wild fowl, feral goats and sheep, as well as plentiful shoals of fish and crustaceans in the lagoon. From the nest, the island looked perfect. This had to be our home, I resolved, and I prayed that we would find some way to safely breach the protective reef that surrounded it.

By late afternoon we were skirting the now visible reef by about 200 feet, searching desperately for the opening that would allow us passage. We were at the direct lee point of the reef where the waves hit with such force that huge plumes of spray burst into the air in brilliant displays of raw power. The thunderous noise that resulted matched the pounding of our hearts. We knew that if we were caught in the roiling mass, we would most certainly become fish food for the denizens of the reef. Yet I did not dare cruise farther out to sea because we might lose our chance to gain a break in the reef should one reveal itself at a moment's notice, or unknowingly pass one by before we could alter our course.

The current was directing us to the south side of the island but the breeze blew directly west, so I opted to take a northern route, hoping the diminished current would allow us more time to survey the lagoon. I began to slowly tack in and out, just missing the reef's menacing grasp. Every time we got close to the undertow, I saw the other crew members tighten their grip on whatever they were holding, then noticeably relax as I veered off at the last moment and headed oceanward.

From our position, the lagoon appeared to be deep enough from our catamaran to navigate. The tallest mountain rose to an impressive height but not so high that the vegetation thinned or was ever dusted with snow. From my study of the shore, I could see no indication that other people had ever inhabited the land.

After two hours of sailing along at half speed, the jungle forest opened to reveal a wide inlet with a stunningly blue pool fed by a small waterfall and surrounded by so many different colored flowers it almost hurt the eye to look at it. We were all so engaged by the gorgeous vignette that I almost did not see the smooth water coursing between two gnarled coral formations that were totally obscured when the rhythmic waves slammed against it.

"Furl the sail!" I yelled to Zelph as I leaned my body against the rudder.

He responded with lightning speed and we turned in at a severe angle to the reef. The nose of the *Hezikiah* poked into the narrow channel but a receding wave washed against us at this moment, and we felt ourselves being carried backwards. If the current grabbed the centerboard we could be nudged off center, and with the following surge of wave action, be rammed right into the rust-red coral which, at that moment, seemed to be glaring at us with malformed eyes and thousands of jagged teeth.

"Raise the centerboard!" I yelled, but Zelph was temporarily tangled in the sail cloth and could not move. Before I could call out again, Libbi and Elsha were at the centerboard hauling on it with all their strength.

Then a large surge of water picked up the rear end of the *Hezikiah* and forcefully slid us toward the passage. One of the hulls, however, was not in true alignment and the short keels underneath scraped against the rough coral like skin against rock. The raft pivoted on the stranded hull and the water pushing us now washed over the hull and inundated the deck. Both Elsha and Libbi were washed over the side, but fortunately they were thrown well clear of the jagged coral. The centerboard dropped back into place and caught on a deeper chunk of coral, preventing us from being completely washed onto the reef structure when the waves receded back through the opening.

"Everyone to the other hull, quickly," I called out, and all hands still on board leapt to the inshore hull. This created an imbalance that allowed the next incoming wave to lift the captured hull from the reef and wash us into the lagoon.

Once inside, I had Jonah and Naomi raise the sail again as Zelph helped Libbi and my wife from the water. A fresh breeze caught the sail, making it flap and sway like the many palms along the shore. As soon as it was trimmed, the breeze popped it into full efficiency, and we headed away from the deafening struggle between reef and wave at the lagoon's edge.

Instead of heading directly for the shore, I thought it would be prudent to circle the entire lagoon to look for signs of life or human visitation. The water depth varied from a foot or two near the shore to a generous thirty-plus feet in the center, then shallowed to about ten feet by the coral reef, with plenty of room to tack as needed. The others, while aching to get on solid, unmoving ground for the first time in 130 days, agreed to make this last leg of the voyage to check out the place.

Returning around the southern side of the island, the opposing wind picked up a bit and made our progress painfully slow, but we managed to travel the length in a few hours without incident. The island was approximately seven miles long and four miles wide at its thickest point. There were no overt signs of human presence, but I did notice a few logs that had been laid out in a fashion that was anything but random, indicating that someone had once been here, perhaps form the island to our north, or from any of the other islands that seemed to dot this area of the ocean.

Rounding the eastern shore, the breeze took us quickly back to the inlet with the clear water and beautiful surroundings. I angled the raft to a shallow bank just inside the inlet. The *Hezikiah* ground to a stop and bobbed slightly with the gentle ripples created by the small waterfall at the head of the inlet.

We all went to the deck's edge and stared at the solid ground before us. To my amusement, we were all holding on to something and weaving back and forth like drunken party-goers. The raft had ceased its incessant rolling and our equilibrium had over compensated for the pitch and yaw of life on the waves. Now that the raft was stationary, we continued to weave back and forth as if we were trying to adjust to the lack of movement.

We had grown accustom to endless blue vistas and perpetually undulating surroundings. Before us now was a palette of so many shades of green it was incomprehensible at first. Scattered against the backdrop of green were flowers of all colors: pinks, yellows, reds, purples, and all colors in-between. The intensity of the colors fairly glowed from the hundreds of flowers before us. And the fragrances were overwhelming. To pinpoint a single scent would have proved a task confusing enough to turn a sane man into a babbling imbecile. We were cast into a state of numb euphoria, and we stood there with tears streaming down our cheeks and wonderfully bright smiles adorning our faces.

We looked at each other, but didn't say a word. What could one say at this moment? A profound love radiated from each person as we quietly thanked one another for all they had done to make this voyage possible. Zelph took Nephi in one arm and held Naomi's hand with his free hand. He stepped forward to help his family onto the shore, when Libbi stopped him.

"Wait a minute, please. We are here because of our Captain. I think we would all agree to that," she said with a humility I had not heard from her before. "I think we should let Gideon be the first to set foot on our new home."

For the first time on this voyage, no one had the slightest argument with Libbi. I was flattered, humbled, and honored to have been part of this venture, and to be given this recognition and opportunity. I nodded to Libbi and the rest, and made my way to the edge of the hull. I eased myself down onto the sand and let the marvelous sensation of the loose sand crystals tickle between my toes as I wiggled them about. The feeling radiated throughout my entire being and caused goose-bumps to rise from my flesh.

I then turned and held my hand out to Elsha. "Princess Dogbark, your kingdom awaits."

TWENTY-EIGHT

Paradise! The island proved to be everything we had hoped for. There was an abundance of food, both animal and vegetable, plenty of fresh water, and limitless supply bananas and coconuts for dessert. Building materials abounded with hardwoods like teak, ebony, mangrove and such, in addition to the bamboo and hemp. Beyond the heavily wooded hills at the base of the mountain, a massive slide had formed a grassy plateau on which grew wild sweet potatoes, taro, breadfruit, and even some sugarcane. The Lord had truly blessed us with everything we needed on this small dot in the middle of the ocean. When I considered the chances of our ever sailing from Tonalai again and landing precisely here on this small island, my mind was overwhelmed by the odds. Jonah was right, our landing here was not mere happenstance; it was providence.

The first few days were spent getting a feel for the terrain around us. There was much to do in the way of food gathering, shelter making, and the like, but we had been confined to the dimensions of the raft for so long that to stay in one spot was more than we could stand. The week after we landed, Zelph and I decided to climb to the top of the highest peak to get an idea of the lay of the island, its position in the ocean, and the placement of the surrounding isles. Elsha had wanted to come, but she found herself growing tired very quickly, so she opted to stay with Naomi and help with little Nephi. The two young women had grown closer than twin sisters, and I couldn't have asked for a better brother-in-law than Zelph. With Elsha's belly swelling more each day, I grew more anxious to have everything secured and organized. Elsha felt comfortable with the things we had presently—she was too easy to please—but our temporary shelter and food stores simply weren't good enough.

It took us nearly half the day to reach the summit of the mountain. We followed an old goat trail to the top and saw many interesting things along the way, including an old goat. A ram with gnarled, dull horns that curled behind his ears, he reminded me of Riplikish, Helorum's old pet. The ancient ram regarded us with passive interest, then slowly ambled in the opposite direction. Apparently, he had never been harassed by humans before and was unaware that we considered him a potentially fine meal. His presence also suggested the existence of ewes, which meant fresh milk and cheese.

The day had cleared considerably from the morning's overcast and Zelph and I could see for miles in every direction. The first thing that caught our attention was the ability to see many details of the larger island to our north that we had not been able to see from sea level. Also, the question as to whether we were alone in the vastness of this ocean was immediately answered.

A thin column of smoke rose from the west shore of the larger island. It was not a forest fire or the smoldering remnant of the volcanoes which formed these islands, but a deliberate, man-made fire rising from a village. It took us both by surprise, for throughout the preceding week we had seen no indication of life on the other island.

"Who do you suppose they are?" Zelph asked, the warrior in him adding a defensive edge to his voice.

"I have no idea, but I think Jonah might not be far off the mark in guessing there are other Nephites out here."

"Nephites, eh?"

I shrugged. "Well, whoever they are, they will be just as curious and leery of us as we are of them when they realize we're here."

The rest of the ocean around us was dotted with small atolls and palm-covered isles. A few, including ours, had interconnecting reefs which could allow a person, at low tide, to cross from one to the other. The panorama was breathtaking, and I could not wait for Elsha to get the chance to come up for an eyeful of God's majesty.

I located the inlet where we had landed. The lagoon looked especially placid and blue, and was outlined with a fluorescent-green. I was reminded again of my wife's captivating eyes. From our height, we could see clear to the bottom of the deepest parts of the lagoon, and even into the seas beyond the reef.

"Someday I'll have to build a boat with a draft shallow enough to cross the reef without scraping," I said out loud to myself.

"All right," was Zelph's noncommittal response.

The small clearing where we had set up our first camp was also visible from this vantage point, though it was only a speck along the verdant shoreline inside the lagoon. A small trickle of smoke rose from the center of the clearing as Libbi was undoubtedly cooking up something for our evening meal. The sun had crested long ago and it was time to start heading back.

"Well, my friend, what do you think our first task should be this week. Building houses or exploring more of our new home?" I asked Zelph whimsically, knowing which answer I preferred.

"We'll first need to become good hosts," he answered flatly.

When I questioned his remark with raised eyebrows, he pointed toward the big island and said, "It looks like we're going to have visitors."

I did not have Zelph's remarkable vision, but I could tell that two large canoes were headed our way. Zelph and I flew down the mountain at a breakneck speed, hoping to reach camp before the strangers from across the channel did.

Halfway down the mountain we met the old ram again, this time with three ewes at his side. They regarded us curiously as we sailed past them, stumbling over rocks and crashing through the underbrush. We reached our little camp in a quarter of the time it had taken to climb the mountain, and collapsed in some hammocks to catch our breath.

Our harried entrance put the camp in a state of anxiety. Elsha and Naomi ran up to us with confused, worried looks an their faces. Libbi and Jonah were not far behind.

"Is something wrong?" Jonah asked.

"Were you being chased by a wild beast?" Elsha wondered.

"I'll get your spear," Naomi said to Zelph.

Just then, the old ram and one ewe came traipsing through the jungle into our camp. They stopped and stared at each of us, then buckled their knees and flopped on their bellies, and commenced to lazily chew their cud.

Everyone burst out laughing at Zelph and me and the two goats, who had obviously followed us from the meadow plateau. I admit, without knowing the whole story, it must have looked a ridiculous site: two strong men running from two dried-up old goats. But there was a much more serious reason for our flight.

"There—are—pe—people—coming," I managed to gasp out.

Zelph nodded agreement and pointed in the direction of the big island. From the shore, the canoes were not visible over the swell of the ocean. In fact, little of the big island could be seen except for its lofty mountain peaks, which were usually shrouded with clouds. But we knew they were coming nonetheless.

"Where?" Elsha asked, standing on her tiptoes, searching the horizon.

"We saw them—launch—in canoes—about an hour ago," Zelph said, swallowing hard between words.

Once Zelph and I had regained our breath, we made hurried preparations for the strangers arrival. We had no idea if they were friend or foe, but we needed to be ready for either contingency. Jonah came forward and offered a suggestion which I did not care for, but the others readily agreed on it. And so it was decided.

The visitors arrived in about three hours' time. They knew of the small channel in the reef and glided through without incident. There were two canoes with three men in one and two men and a woman in the other. We stood in plain view, lined up in two rows with Jonah, Naomi (who had Nephi in a pouch on her back), and Elsha in the front row, Zelph, Libbi, and myself in the back. Zelph said he would have preferred a more defensive line-up to indicate our strength, but I felt a show of friendship would make a better first impression. Elsha and Naomi had with them several wreaths made from plumerea and other fragrant flowers near camp. Zelph had his spear, I had a club.

When the canoes ground to a stop on the sand, the riders disembarked, and I saw that they were all well-built, good-looking people with fair but very tanned skin, and light-brown to black hair. Zelph whispered that only one of the men appeared to be armed with a weapon. He admitted it was a good sign.

As they approached us there was a certain directness about them, as if they were expecting us to be here. They stopped ten feet from us and smiled. The woman was of medium height with long, shiny black hair. She was a bit older then Zelph, and had a very nice smile of perfectly straight, brilliantly white teeth. As a group they bowed slightly to us. We looked at each other, then returned the bow.

Jonah stepped forward and brought a hand to his chest. "I am Jonah of Zarahemla. We are Nephites from the land across the ocean," he said, pointing to the east. "We have come as friends in search of a new home by commandment from the Lord our God."

Elsha then stepped forward and placed a wreath around the neck of the man who appeared to be in charge. Naomi did the same for the woman, who smiled even brighter at the gesture. The other men received wreaths and bowed thanks in return. The tension seemed to diminish a bit with Elsha's overtures. To my astonishment and relief, the men did not ogle Elsha as other men had done when they first saw her. Instead, they seemed to notice her pregnant belly first, and lowered their eyes in humble respect.

The lead man bowed again and said something in a strange language that sounded slightly familiar, like something I had heard on the docks as a lad. It was very close to . . . what? I couldn't put my finger on it, but the tone of his words was very friendly.

Jonah pointed to his ear and shook his head. "I'm sorry, my friend, I do not understand you."

"But I understand you," the woman said, smiling brightly. She stepped forward and continued, "I am Kiale'e. I am daughter of our chief, Rarotiki. We have been expecting you."

"You've been expecting us?" I asked, setting aside my club and stepping forward. "I don't understand. Why us?"

Kiale'e laughed. "Not *you* in particular. Travelers, like you. Our fathers have handed down legends from the time they landed on these islands that a great and important people would someday come to live with us. There have already been many other visitors. Some have stayed, some have sailed on. It doesn't matter. We were never told specifically who to look for, except that they would look like us, with fair skin and light eyes, and they would be kind and God-fearing. And we were told to honor them and give them help in whatever way we could."

"But, how do you know our language?" I asked.

She bowed her head humbly. "I have a gift for tongues," she said without the least amount of pretense. "I have learned the languages from many people who have come to our islands. That is why I am among those who greet newcomers."

"Aren't you worried that some might not be friendly?" Elsha asked.

"Yes. Some have been hostile, and we were forced to . . . persuade them to leave."

A very diplomatic way of putting it, I thought.

"Are you Nephites?" Zelph asked, somewhat forcefully from behind us. He still had his spear in hand.

"No," I answered before Kiale'e could. "They are descendants of Jared from Babylon," I stated, staring straight at the leader. "You are Jaredites, aren't you?"

As if in unison, the men all turned to look at me, astonished. Kiale'e bowed again, and the men followed suit. She then conversed with them in their strange tongue, which I assumed was a dialect of Jaredite, and they all beamed with gladness.

"You are a wise man," Kiale'e said to me, "but you are only partly correct. Jaredite was the name of one of our first ancestors. Though there are some among us who call their forefathers Nephite, we use the Jaredite language as our native tongue. Do you understand our speech?"

"Only a few words and phrases," I said. "But I too have a love of languages and would appreciate you teaching me yours."

She bowed again and said she would be honored. "You are a good people; we can tell that right away. If we can help you, we will."

Jonah returned the bow and said, "Before we accept your offer, I must ask a question. I believe your God is our God, but I could be mistaken. Tell me, whom do you worship?"

"We pray to the Father above," she answered. "Unfortunately, many of our scriptures have been lost or destroyed over the years, so now only legend and tradition teach us of Him."

Jonah smiled brightly. "I am a teacher of religion, and Gideon and I both have scriptures with us. My companions are all faithful followers of the Lord and they know much about religion themselves. We would be honored if you would allow us to teach you, as you teach us."

Kiale'e translated Jonah's words and an animated conversation ensued between the strangers. I caught some of the words and was certain that, with time, I could speak their dialect of Jaredite fluently. I even heard a few words of Nephite, and suspected that their language was an amalgamation of several tongues, as Kiale'e had indicated. The leader then stepped up to Jonah and took him by the shoulders. He smiled as he stumbled over the words, "It—is—good."

Jonah held the man by his shoulders and repeated his words. The other men let out a cheer and any remaining tension between our two parties instantly vanished. We chatted with Kiale'e for well over an hour, explaining our voyage and the events surrounding it. Kiale'e translated for the men with her, who reacted to our story with excitement and awe.

The sun was riding the horizon when our new friends climbed back into their canoes to head for their home. Before leaving, however, Kiale'e asked Elsha about her pregnancy.

"I feel fine; the voyage was hard but not unbearable," she told her. "My husband, Gideon, knows a little of medicine, and has helped me greatly."

"How much time before you deliver?"

"About four months, I should think," Elsha answered, a slight blush coloring her cheeks.

"We have an excellent midwife on the big island," Kiale'e said. Then added, "You are a fortunate woman to have a husband such as Gideon. I sense he is a leader among men. I too have a good man. We must get together often and share our stories."

Elsha hugged her and said, "I would like that very much."

"So would I," I said. "I have a feeling your legends will sound very familiar to us."

"I would like to learn what has become of my people to the east," Kiale'e said.

I didn't have the heart to answer her right then, guessing that the knowledge of the Jaredite's total destruction would be anything but pleasant news.

That evening Elsha and I laid out on the warm sand under the stars. She was quiet and meditative, and I notced tears on her cheeks.

"Is something wrong?" I asked gently.

"No, Gideon," she answered, taking my hand and holding it tight. "Everything is just perfect. I have been pondering over all we've been through and feel so very blessed. I feel the Lord is with us. No, I don't feel it. I *know* it."

A warmth tingled through me and enveloped my heart. Elsha was right. As I thought about past events, the answers to all my questions and doubts became wonderfully clear. The Lord had never turned His back on me, even though I had often felt that was the case. When the journey got rough, it was I who had let go of His hand, not the other way around. Helorum had said that I was to be the leader of a nation. My lack of faith caused me to wonder how that could come to pass. I wondered if I was prepared for such a calling. I wondered if I would be able to keep my posterity from falling into spiritual darkness. I wondered if my children's children would read Helorum's scroll and see the significance of it in their lives. Questions such as these haunted my soul and humbled me. Was I upto fulfilling such a great mission, such a marvelous prophecy? The answers lay in sincere pondering and humble pray. But I did know one thing for sure. The voyage we had just completed was only a part of the sacred voyage Helorum had mentioned. The biggest part of the journey was just beginning.

The Spirit burned within me as I realized each of us has our own sacred voyage to complete; that every life has purpose and meaning, and it is up to each individual to keep their voyages true and heading in the right direction, that is, back to our Heavenly Father. We all have this sacred goal to complete, regardless of where the tide may take us.

I made a new resolution to do God's will and accept His guidance from then on. With a wonderful companion such as Elsha, I knew I could do whatever was asked. I doubted it would be easy, but I knew it would be worth it.

"So, my wife, do you feel this is going to be a pretty good life for us?" I asked softly, my throat constricting with emotion.

"No," Elsha said as she leaned over and tenderly kissed me. "I feel it's going to be a *wonderful* life."

The End.